Also by Mia Sheridan

AVAILABLE FROM BLOOM BOOKS

Travis

Kyland

Stinger

Grayson's Vow

Becoming Calder

Finding Eden

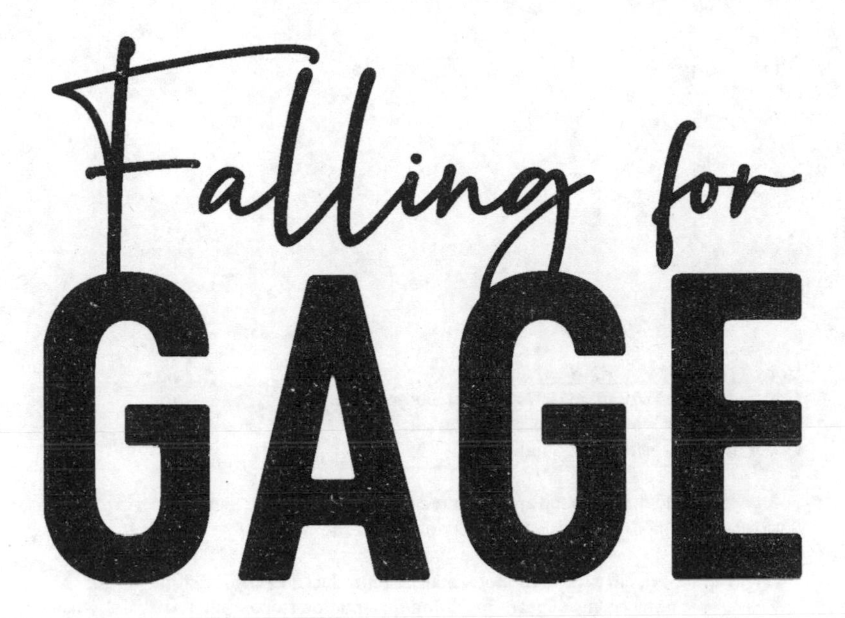

MIA SHERIDAN

Bloom books

Published by Bloom Books, an imprint of Sourcebooks
P.O. Box 4410, Naperville, Illinois 60567-4410
(630) 961-3900
sourcebooks.com

Cataloging-in-Publication data is on file with the Library of Congress.

Printed and bound in the United States of America.
LSC 10 9 8 7 6 5 4 3 2 1

To those who feel an unceasing pull.
Follow it. Wonderful things await.

CHAPTER ONE
Gage

"Gage? Earth to Gage."

I snapped out of the semi-trance I'd been in as I stared mostly unseeing at the baristas behind the counter, who were expediently whipping up frothy drinks for the waiting customers. I turned to see Haven Hale peering curiously at me, a smudge of dirt on her cheek and a leaf dangling from the braid trailing over her shoulder.

"Haven," I said, giving my head a small shake. "Sorry. I didn't see you there."

She smiled, cocking her head to the side. "You must have something important on your mind."

"Uh." The truth was, I hadn't been thinking about anything. I'd been completely checked out. "Work," I finally said before clearing my throat. "Busy day at work." I inclined my head toward her, noting her baggy jeans with grass stains on the knees and the bright yellow crewneck she was wearing with the *Haven's Gate* logo over the pocket. "You must have started early today."

Her grin widened the way it always did right before she was about to talk about annuals or perennials or tubers or seedlings or whatever. I didn't know much about gardening, but it always struck me that Haven was doing just the thing she was obviously meant to be doing. *One's true purpose.* The phrase that popped into my mind caused an odd pinch in the center of my chest that I had no explanation for because Haven was a little quirky, but she was a nice girl who deserved every bit of happiness that had come her way since she'd moved to Pelion. I didn't know all the details of her background, but I knew life hadn't been easy for her or her brother, Easton, before they'd moved here. "We're installing a water feature at the Fillmore Estate. They have this big hill behind the house that's always been a challenge landscape design-wise. I suggested a water feature that starts at the top and winds down to the base with large rocks and plantings along the way and they went for it! It'll be the first one we design and install and so it has to be right. It has to be perfect. And then, who knows, maybe we'll hire a bigger crew and expand the business." She pulled in a breath, winded from the long string of words that had emerged in an excited rush. "So I was up early measuring and planning and well—" She waved her hand around and let out a small laugh as though she'd just realized she'd gotten a little carried away.

"It's going to be spectacular. I have no doubt," I said with a smile.

"Thanks, Gage. That's really kind of you." She moved aside as the woman next to her stepped forward to grab her drink.

"How's Travis doing?" I asked. "I haven't seen him in a while."

Her face went sort of soft and slack the way I imagined might happen right before a person was about to faint. But she remained upright and conscious as she said, "He's good." And for whatever reason, the word *good* sounded sort of salacious and made me want to glance around to make sure no one saw us dirty-talking. "He's off today but he's out hunting a cat." She rolled her eyes, but even that managed to come off as adoring.

"I'm sorry. Hunting a *cat*?"

"Mm." Someone else stepped around her and picked up two cupholders, turning carefully as he balanced eight coffees all topped with whipped cream and caramel drizzles. But then the customer turned back to the counter. "Excuse me, two of these are supposed to have chocolate sprinkles." Good grief. No wonder there was a wait. When I looked back at Haven, her lips thinned as she watched the man hand his drinks over for an additional dose of morning sugar, certainly some sort of cardinal sin to a woman as health-conscious as Haven. "Clawdia just had kittens," she said as her gaze moved back to me. "We assumed she was spayed but she obviously wasn't. Well. You can imagine Travis's outrage when it became clear his beloved cat was pregnant."

I could absolutely not imagine any such outrage.

"Anyway," she went on, "the kittens were born yesterday and they're all orange. Each one!"

I stared. I had no idea what she was talking about or how I was supposed to respond.

She stared back. "Clawdia's *gray*," she finally explained.

"Ah. I see. So, the guilty party clearly passed on his telltale orange genes. Travis is out hunting a lustful tomcat because he outrageously knocked up his cat without first being granted permission."

She bobbed her head as I worked not to laugh.

Oh, Travis Hale. Once Pelion's Most Eligible Bachelor and all-around player.

My how the mighty had fallen.

The last time I'd seen Travis, he'd been helping dig holes for new trees Haven's business was planting at the revitalized park entrance.

I'd only been passing by but by the radiant expression on his sweat-streaked face, it appeared he believed himself to be doing the Lord's work.

The laughter that had threatened now disappeared completely, leaving an uncomfortable void.

If Travis had fallen, why did I feel like he'd surpassed me?

I cleared my throat, forcing my thoughts back to the mating habits of cats. "What's he going to do when he finds the bastard?" I asked.

Haven's brows sort of went in two different directions as though she hadn't quite considered that part. "Well, he just wants to speak to him."

"He wants to speak to the cat?"

Haven laughed. "His owner."

"If he has one."

"Right, if he has one." Someone bumped into her, and she took a small step toward me and I caught her clean scent: lavender, lilies, and grass. It was pleasant and so very *her*.

I'd gone out on one date with Haven a couple of years back before I'd found out she had it bad for Travis Hale and vice versa. I'd happily—and easily, truth be told—stepped aside and I was glad they'd ended up together. Nothing permanent would have come from dating Haven, not to mention, Haven and Travis were clearly madly in love, had formed a little family, and seemed to have found everything they didn't even know they wanted out of life.

Good for them.

Meanwhile, even though I'd determined years ago that it was time to settle down, I still hadn't met the right woman.

Maybe she didn't exist.

Except I didn't want to consider that. Not only for myself, but because my parents expected me to pass on the Buchanan name. If I didn't, our family legacy would be no more. That responsibility fell to me and me alone.

"Hey," Haven said, drawing me back to the present, "do you want a kitten in about eight weeks?"

"My condo doesn't allow pets."

Her shoulders dropped. "Oh. Well, spread the word for us. Otherwise, we'll have several more barn cats, I guess."

"Also, I'm moving to London in a couple months."

Her eyes widened. "London! For work?"

I nodded. "We're opening a hotel in Westminster."

She frowned. "Oh. I see. Well, I know you already travel a fair bit, but Calliope won't be the same without you. However..." She reached out and patted my shoulder. "I get needing a change of scenery." She tilted her head, studying me, her expression slightly troubled as though she knew something about me I didn't. But then she smiled. "I wish you all the luck in finding just what you're looking for." She paused, chewing at the side of her lip for a brief moment. "Sometimes, it's closer than you think."

"Gabe," the barista called, a young blond kid who was obviously a seasonal employee.

"Gage," the owner, Peggy, corrected over her shoulder with a wink and a smile in my direction. That was the thing that made my hometown of Calliope different than

Pelion, which was right across Pelion Lake. Whereas they were almost exclusively small-town, we were a mix between small-town and tourist mecca—at least during spring break and throughout the summer season. And there were undeniably more upscale areas of Calliope, including the gated community where my parents lived, in which I'd grown up. I found Pelion charming and appreciated that they'd made the choice to preserve the quaint nature of their town, but I'd always preferred the variety of traditional and modern offered in Calliope and the fact that there was a little bit of everything.

I picked up the drink as the kid muttered, "Sorry."

"Don't worry about it." I turned back to Haven. "It was great to see you. Tell Trav I said hi and good luck with the hunt. If he's looking to form a posse, I might be able to make myself available on Monday after I get back from the weekend golf trip I'm going on with some college buddies."

Haven laughed. "That's very kind of you, Gage. Have a fun weekend."

I lifted my cup in a toast and moved past her toward the door, exiting the crowded coffee shop and heading to my car.

I turned the ignition, cranked up the AC and sat there drinking my coffee for a minute, staring out the windshield again and bouncing my knee. I caught myself and stilled my leg, giving my head a small shake as I attempted to move my mind toward the work I had on my agenda that day. God, why did I feel so damn restless? I'd thought taking the next step on my career path and moving to London would help dispel the feeling of general agitation I'd been experiencing for the last year or so, but it'd really only increased the sensation. I had to figure that was due to a mild case of nerves at such a momentous impending change, but it was still distracting as hell and the only thing that helped was making a conscious effort to ignore it. Surely it'd get better once I was settled in my new home.

In my rearview mirror I saw Haven exit the coffee shop with her drink in hand and turn in the other direction toward the old-fashioned, turquoise blue pickup she drove with the *Haven's Gate* logo emblazoned on the side. You couldn't miss that thing, that was for sure. I pressed slightly on the gas just to hear the purr of my Audi, but rather than bringing me the satisfaction it always had, emptiness loomed inside.

I'd built my life around luxury cars, tailored suits, exclusive memberships, and the like. Those things spoke of who I was and the life I wanted. I was about to leave this small, lakeside town behind for the sophistication of London. In recent years, I'd only grown more established in my career, and I was about to make a move that would increase my success, and my wealth. I stood on the precipice of everything I'd ever worked for and all my father had dreamed for me and all I felt was...stuck. It made no sense.

Haven's truck bumped past me and she grinned and waved out the window. I tipped my chin, watching as the bed, filled with cheery flats of flowers, moved away. I brought my fingers to my lower lip, realizing that instead of smiling back at Haven, my mouth had tipped into a frown.

I sighed and, once again, emptied my mind as best as possible, pulling away from the curb and heading to the office where I had back-to-back meetings.

I was glad I had a packed schedule today and tomorrow, but a short break from the rigmarole would help me get my head back in the game. The upcoming guys' weekend would be good. No—the guys' weekend would be great.

CHAPTER TWO
Rory

The bevy of starstruck women let out a collective squeal as my uncle tossed the ice from the glass in his right hand and caught it in the empty one he was holding in his left, that slow, one-sided smile causing his dimple to appear. The squeals melted into delighted sighs. I pressed my lips together, working to keep my expression neutral. I had plenty of practice resisting the eye roll that still naturally threatened such blatant reverence. *Such a simple bartender move and still they swoon like lovesick puppies.*

I wiped down the table that had just been vacated and picked up the tray of empty glasses as another chorus of "oohs" came from the bar. I gave my head a small shake. Easy tricks aside though, I could see why my uncle received so much female attention and adoration. He did bear a striking resemblance to Elvis Presley in his heyday.

"That man is truly God's gift to Mud Gulch," Karla, one of three servers, including me, working the floor, said, her eyes glued to my uncle as she waited for a check to print.

"Not a difficult feat considering the competition," I said breezily as I passed by. The man didn't need anyone else, especially his niece, fawning over him. And his name was Romeo to boot. My grandmother must have had some foresight where he was concerned because that would have been a difficult name to manage had he been anyone other than himself. But Granny had had an affinity for Shakespeare and, apparently, believed her second-born son would bear the name of a famous fictional lothario well.

Another burst of squeals went up, confirming that thought.

I wove through the crowded tables with the full tray balanced in one hand, shouldered the door to the kitchen open and deposited the dirty glasses near the dishwasher. "Order up, Rory," our cook called from where he stood at the grill.

"Thanks, Eli," I said as I picked up the two plates of food sitting under the warmer. Eli nodded but didn't look at me, a spatula held in his hand and his gaze focused on the TV mounted to the wall in the corner of the kitchen. "You have one job! Hit the damn ball, you dipshit!" he yelled as I pushed the swinging doors open.

The smack of a bat hitting a ball met my ears as I walked back into the bar. Apparently, the dipshit had indeed managed to do his job.

"A burger, medium, no onion, no tomato, with a side of onion rings, Larry," I said as I set the food in front of one of our regulars.

"Thanks, Rory."

I gave him a nod. "And for Kip, fish and chips with extra slaw," I said, reaching across and handing the other man the loaded plate.

I stopped by my other tables quickly and then made my way to the computer to print up the bills. "You have got to be shittin' me," Sherry, the third server, said, her gaze trained somewhere behind me. I turned, my mouth falling open. "No, don't look," Sherry said, grabbing my arm and forcibly turning me back to the computer. But it was too late. I'd already seen.

My ex-boyfriend and his new girlfriend were sitting at table six. The ex-boyfriend who'd broken up with me to start dating the new chick he was currently sitting with. At my family's bar. Where I worked.

"What a *dick*," Sherry hissed as she started picking up the beer bottles at the end of the bar and setting them on her tray. "How dare he come here?" She turned her head and looked at me. "Do you want me to have him removed?"

The way she said *removed* made me think she meant from the planet, not just from this establishment. I almost answered in the affirmative, but decided I wasn't quite angry enough to risk Sherry's freedom.

"I'll do it," she threatened as she turned to go deliver the drinks on her tray.

I managed a tight laugh. "That's sweet, Sher," I said to her retreating back. "But he's not worth it. And an orange state-issued jumpsuit will clash with your hair."

She made a sound in the back of her throat that either meant she concurred or that she didn't actually need my permission to *remove* said ex-boyfriend and risk a lifetime of being orange from head to toe.

The ex—Thaddeus Willoughby III—leaned around Karla who was taking their order and met my eyes. I glanced quickly away but not before I saw that he at least had the grace to look uncomfortable.

What the hell was he doing here anyway? He lived in Claremont Landing, the town over, an upscale locale that featured a well-known golf and country club and had a wealth per capita on the opposite end of the spectrum to Mud Gulch. I'd met him when he'd made a trip to the docks with his buddies for a bachelor party and turned the charm in my direction. I inwardly cringed as I remembered the past. God, he probably hadn't even extended much effort before I'd practically fallen at his feet. Dating rich pricks with starched collars had only ever ended in disaster for me, and I renewed my vow never to fall victim to a megawatt smile paid for by expensive dental work again.

I delivered the checks, making a concerted effort not to look in the direction of table six again. As I grabbed a couple drinks from the bar, Romeo mouthed, "You okay?" Clearly he'd also seen Thaddeus and the stunning woman he was sitting with.

I nodded, flashing him a smile as if I couldn't have cared any less that the man I'd been dating less than three weeks before had the absolute gall to bring a date to my workplace. Romeo's eyes narrowed slightly but he tipped his chin, focusing back on his fan club.

From the corner of my eye, I saw that Thaddeus was no longer sitting at the table and when I turned my head a little more, noted that his date had her face resting on her hand and was gazing dreamily at Romeo across the room. I felt a brief buzz of satisfaction that was immediately swallowed by alarm when someone pulled my arm from around the corner that led to the restrooms and yanked me into the dim hall.

"Rory."

"*Thaddeus*." I pulled my arm loose and took a step back. "What the hell?"

"I'm sorry. I know being here is a low blow. She wanted to come to the docks. I tried to suggest places other than your bar, but she was insistent. She practically dragged me in here. She said she'd always wanted to..."

"Slum it?"

"That's not how she put it."

"I'm sure she didn't." But that was the gist. And by the color that had started creeping up his neck, I could see he knew it. Country club girl wanted to get up close and personal with the rough-and-tumble crowd down on the docks. And then she'd hightail it right back to greener pastures, all the more worldly for it.

"This is her summer of *experiences*," he went on.

I resisted the flinch that threatened to reveal itself. "We aren't experiences, Thaddeus. We're people." I put my hands on my hips. "I suppose that's what I was to you as well?" I asked. *An experience.* I held a hand up. *Remember your vow, Rory.* "No, don't answer that. I don't care."

"Aw, Rory, don't be like that." He leaned back slightly, turning his head and risking a quick glance into the bar. When he turned back, he reached out, tucking a piece of hair behind my ear. I leaned away, giving his suspended hand a death glare. "Listen...Rory. There's no reason we can't continue to see each other."

"Under the cover of darkness? Should I wear a disguise?"

"Geez, Rory. Don't be dramatic. A disguise isn't necessary. We could just stay inside."

"Behind locked doors and closed blinds?"

"Of course—"

"Not interested. And if I were you, I'd quickly come down with a stomach bug because Sherry is *itching* to cause you bodily harm and I'm certainly not going to stop her."

His eyes widened, and he opened his mouth to say something, but I turned and dashed back around the corner and out onto the bar floor.

A moment later, I saw Thaddeus and his date headed for the door, Thaddeus clutching his stomach dramatically, his face twisted in mock-agony as she trotted next to him, wide-eyed and appropriately worried. But I didn't miss the glance she threw Romeo over her shoulder, obviously wanting one last look at the raven-haired, blue-eyed Dionysus serving libations from behind the bar. And I didn't miss the fact that Romeo threw her a wink and his famous half-grin, causing her to trip and fall against Thaddeus, both of them lurching over the threshold.

The door fell shut behind them just as Romeo flipped a bottle behind his back, caught it with his other hand and was rewarded with a robust round of applause that would have fed the ego of the most jaded Hollywood star.

I quickly checked on my tables and then walked toward the front door. "I'm going to get some air," I called over to Romeo. He tipped his chin at me as he filled a line of shot glasses in front of him. Once outside, I took a moment to look up and down the docks but when I saw no sign of Thaddeus and the woman, I let out a sigh of relief and walked across the street where there was a railing that looked out to the sea.

I leaned my elbows on the sun-bleached wood, clasping my hands and staring out at the moonlit water, feeling that same pull I always did when I stood here just like this. What was that hollow longing that rose up whenever I stared over the horizon to places beyond? Generations of my people had felt drawn to the water itself, their sea legs strong and sturdy. The sea had provided them peace and purpose, and also a way to feed their family. For a long time, I wondered if that was the same pull I felt, and I kept waiting for the desire to be out on the water more often than on land. Unlike Romeo, my uncle Cassius had felt the call of the ocean and now captained a boat. I liked being on the water, but I was always eager to put my feet back on good ol' terra firma. I much preferred to look out over the sea than to brave its choppy waters on any regular basis.

So no, that wasn't it. And yet the nameless pull remained. It made me confused and frustrated and I had no way to respond, nothing to act on, because I didn't know what it was specifically asking of me.

A nudge at my thigh scattered my thoughts and I looked down to see soulful eyes staring back up at me. "Loki," I greeted the black and brown mutt, squatting down so I was at his level. "What are you doing here this early in the evening?" He stepped toward me and I took his head in my hands, leaning in and bumping my nose with his before leaning back to look him in the eye so I could gauge his mood and make sure nothing was wrong. "It's not dinner-time yet. Come to the back door later and I'll have your usual." He let out a soft moan and nuzzled his wet nose against mine. I smiled. "Oh, I see, it's just some affection you're after. Well. We all need some now and again, even a tough guy like you." He stared at me, his gaze so tender that I wondered if it was me who needed affection, and this gentle soul had known it.

I scratched behind his ears, dragging my fingernails over his head and then down his back. "Thank you for the love. I needed it. I tend to look for it in all the wrong places."

Loki let out another soft whine, tipping his head so I could scratch his chin. "You could come home with me you know. The offer's always open…regular meals…regular baths." Loki let out a short growl, stepping back. I laughed. "Fine, then. You're not ready to live by the rules, then you remain a free agent."

I heard the door of the bar open and close and moments later, footsteps sounded behind me. I glanced over to see Romeo approaching and stood as Loki went trotting off, away from the threat of a bath. "Let me guess, table eight wants another round."

He turned and placed his elbows on the ledge and leaned forward. "Yeah. I sent Sherry to take care of them." He squinted at me. "Figured you needed another minute or two out here."

I sighed, resting my hands on the railing as I again, stared out over the water, rolling and shifting under the moonglow. "Thanks."

I felt Romeo's considering gaze on me but didn't look his way. "What are you looking for, Rory?"

What are you looking for? I glanced over at him. I knew he meant it as a general question. He was asking why I was always searching and never finding. He wanted to know where that pull I talked about might be coming from. He was suggesting that I was never satisfied because I was blindly reaching for something I couldn't define. And he was right. "I don't know," I admitted. *Myself, maybe.*

Romeo turned and raised his chin as he gazed out at the sky, the stars milky and faded in the midst of the streetlamps. He let out a sigh. "Well, can we agree, at least, that it's probably not in Claremont Landing?"

I let out a quiet laugh. "It doesn't seem to be, does it?"

He flashed me that staggeringly beautiful smile of his. "No, it doesn't seem to be."

“Come on,” I said, pushing off the wooden rail and yanking on his shirt. “Your groupies are likely suffering from withdrawal as we speak. Last time they rushed me on this dock, I got a splinter in my ass.”

He laughed. “Storyteller,” he said, turning and walking with me across the street.

“Is that a nice way to call me a liar?”

He winked, and I grinned before I filled my lungs with a deep inhale of the briny air I’d been breathing all my life and then pulled open the door to the bar. My customers would all be banging their tables for another round soon enough, and at least that was one call that I knew how to answer.

CHAPTER THREE
Gage

The guys' weekend was already a complete catastrophe. The four of us, completely drenched, stood in front of a sign that read: *Mud Gulch, Population three thousand, seven hundred.*

It'd taken us twenty miserable minutes to walk here after Trent's car had blown a tire on the dark back road we'd found ourselves on after taking the wrong exit.

No spare.

No cell service.

Not a single car had driven by since we'd stopped.

In unison, our heads pivoted in the direction of the arrow pointing toward the coast. "I've heard of Mud Gulch," I said. "It's a fishing town."

"I just hope someone there has a phone," Trent said.

"What fishing town doesn't have a phone?" Grant asked. "Of course they'll have a phone. They're situated *on* the water, not under it."

God, despite his genius-level IQ, Trent could be a dope.

A dope who had used his spare tire weeks ago and hadn't replaced it before a road trip.

I heaved a deep breath and turned toward the road that disappeared through thick trees. At least the rain had let up slightly. Not that it mattered—all four of us were soaked to the bone.

It took us about forty-five minutes to make it down the road that wound through the trees, finally emerging on a cliff that overlooked the shore. There was a lighthouse on a small island to our right, the top of which disappeared into the fog, its pale light cutting through the mist and guiding the fishing boats home. There were residences scattered here and there, but from where we stood, the only lights of public establishments that I could see were far down by the docks.

"That's a ways down," Aidan noted, obviously looking in the same direction as me.

I stretched my stiff neck from side to side. I wasn't necessarily up for more walking in the rain either, even if the lights down below likely had food. I was starving. "Let's save ourselves the walk. There are some houses over there." I pointed at a road to my left where porch lights glowed. "We can ask to use their phone and call a—"

My feet were sucked down and the ground fell out from under me.

I clawed at empty air, flying downward in a torrent of slick mud, grabbing at roots that slipped through my fingers, completely at the mercy of nature.

"Shitttt," someone yelled from behind me—we were all being flung down the hill in a massive mudslide.

We were all going to die. *This is it.*

I was turned sideways and backward, bumping over rocks and plants and who knew what else as I grunted and swore and finally landed hard on my ass in a puddle that engulfed me up to my shoulders. "Holy fuck!" I barely had time to register the fact that three grown men were hurtling my way but moved just in the nick of time not to be buried beneath them before they hit the water in three loud smacks.

We sat there, stupefied, breathing hard, looking around in shock at what had just happened and the fact that we were still living. "Is everyone okay?" I asked, testing my own extremities to make sure nothing had broken. They all mumbled in the affirmative and we pulled ourselves up and stepped out of the deep ass puddle onto the road. Directly in front of us was a sign that pointed to the docks where the lights were that we'd seen from above.

"That was one way to get down here," Grant said, flinging a glop of mud off his cheek.

"Worst guys' trip ever," Aidan murmured.

I barked out a laugh, and then so did they, all of us doubling over, our howls seeming to stem as much from hysteria as from hilarity. "What the fuck was that?" Grant asked.

"And how did we not die?" Trent added.

After a few minutes, we all caught our breath, shaking ourselves off as best we could and heading in the direction of those lights.

We made our way through the rain-drenched streets of the business district, such as it was. The docks were old and somewhat rickety and groaned under our feet when we stepped onto them. But this area of the town appeared to have the most nightlife. The lights were brighter, and I could hear the low hum of voices coming from somewhere just up ahead.

A quaint-looking tavern materialized out of the mist,

and I almost ran toward it in joyful relief. Though we couldn't see all of it through the rain and fog, the portion that was visible glowed with light and invited us in with the faints sound of laughter and conversation. "Looks promising," Aidan said.

God, did it ever.

I pulled the door open and we all stepped inside, the scent of beer, savory food, various cleaning products and the bare hint of mildew met my nose.

There was an ornate hand-carved, mahogany bar to our left with lighted shelves of liquor on the back wall and a row of lanterns hanging above. Customers occupied all six barstools and they swiveled their heads in unison, taking us in as the woman behind the bar with orange hair paused, a silver shaker held immobile in the air.

We stood there, dripping on the floor as every head in the place rose, gazes aimed in our direction. "Hey," Trent said with a wave and a smile.

No one greeted him back.

"I'm not sure this place is as promising as it seemed," Aidan mumbled.

"What do you expect? It's a dive bar on the docks," I blurted just as the song on the jukebox switched over to another one, my statement ringing out in the interim silence. The faces still turned in our direction simultaneously morphed into scowls. *Shit.* That sentence hadn't come out exactly as I'd meant it, and I certainly hadn't meant it to be overheard.

"The bathroom's that way," a female voice said tightly. "If you'd like to clean yourselves up and stop dripping on my floor."

I turned my head to see who'd spoken just as a flash of

lightning made the lights flicker slightly. The server who'd spoken was standing with her hands on her hips, lips pressed together as she stared at our feet. I followed her gaze to where the puddle beneath us was spreading. My friends started moving next to me, the rustle of clothing letting me know they were removing the matching nylon windbreakers Trent had brought us and that we'd all pulled on when the tire had blown, in an attempt to stay partially dry. But for whatever reason, I felt glued to the spot as I raised my head to look back at the young woman.

Jet-black hair pulled up in a ponytail with tendrils falling around her face. Light blue eyes framed by dark lashes and two perfectly peaked brows. Her full breasts pushed against the white cotton, long-sleeved henley she was wearing, cleavage peeking between two undone buttons.

My God. She was stunning.

I felt momentarily woozy as if I'd just stepped into some strange dream rather than a grungy bar in a small harbor town on the northern coast of Maine. Aidan bumped into me, and from my peripheral vision, I saw that the windbreaker was stuck over his head, his arms raised as he hopped around, struggling to remove it. The woman met my eyes, clearly waiting for me, as the only one currently not losing the battle with a wet item of clothing, to say something. "Food," I managed, the word emerging on a croak. Was I suffering from hypothermia? All my systems seemed to be misfiring at once.

She tilted her head, measuring me, those pale eyes moving down my body and then rising slowly. Her lips were pressed tightly together as though she'd observed something about me that displeased her deeply. I wasn't used to that reaction. I had come to expect that when a woman's gaze traveled my body, the response would at least be appreciation.

Not...disdain.

I peered down at myself as though maybe something had changed since I'd last looked. Nope. Still me, but in a sopping, mud-streaked pair of khakis, Polo shirt, and windbreaker bearing the Harvard logo.

"Food?" she repeated. "Do we serve food? Is that what you're asking, Ivy League?"

Ivy League. Okay, I deserved that after my insulting outburst that I hadn't meant to be insulting or an outburst. Next to me, Trent had managed to get the windbreaker off and shook his head like a dog, water flying out around him and bringing me out of the odd dream-like space I'd been occupying since we walked in the door. Likely the sudden change in weather had caused my body to have to recalibrate in some way I didn't know how to describe. I gave the woman a pleasant smile. "Yes. Are you still serving food?"

She sighed. "The kitchen's open until ten." She waved her hand in the general direction of the tables where people had gone back to their conversations, the ring of chatter and laughter filling the space.

"Great..." I moved my eyes to the name tag she had pinned to her shirt. "Cakes."

She appeared confused for a moment, but then glanced down at her name tag. "The name of the *bar* is Cakes and Ale," she clarified. I looked back at the name tag, noticing that the line above—likely her name—had been rubbed off, and apparently the words *and Ale* had worn off too. "The people here know me," she said, presumably explaining why her name tag that featured no name was immaterial. She turned and headed away.

"Guys, let's go get cleaned up in the restroom and then order some food. We can call for a tow and eat while we wait." I turned back to the woman who had grabbed a roll of paper towels from somewhere, obviously to wipe up the small flood we'd caused in her entryway as the other guys walked toward the back to find the restrooms. "Can we take any table?" I asked.

She gave a succinct nod. "Jim Moseley might get out of bed to give you a tow," the woman said as she bent to sop up the water. My gaze held on her cleavage, made even more visible from this vantage point. The tops of her breasts looked smooth and soft and I could even see the lacy edge of her bra. My body stirred, the waterlogged pants making the reaction less than comfortable. I cleared my throat, forcing myself to look away as she went on. "But the garage doesn't open until the morning."

"Oh. Well we don't require a local garage. We'd need a tow to Claremont Landing."

"I figured." The woman stood and tossed the wet paper towels into a trash can sitting next to the bar and put the roll under her arm. She shook her head. "Jim doesn't tow that far."

"Okay. Then I guess we could get a tow from a company in Claremont Landing."

She shrugged. "Good luck finding one that's still open. Be right there, Ted." And with that she went sauntering over to a table where three men were sitting.

I schlepped to the bathroom and joined the guys who were using napkins to wipe the mud that still remained and dry off enough that they were no longer dripping. The windbreakers had actually done a decent job of keeping our shirts dry despite sliding down a hill and then being submerged in a giant puddle so that was something anyway. "Damn, I didn't know condom machines were actually a thing," Grant said, pulling a few wet dollar bills from his wallet and inserting them in the machine. A few individually wrapped condoms fell into the tray and he plucked them out, tossing one to each of us in turn. "You never know," he said with a wink. I rolled my eyes and stuck the red condom into my pocket and then continued drying my shoes the best I could as the other guys did the same. Luckily we were in a warm bar where we could order a shot of something that would also warm our insides. Not that it was chilly. In fact, we were all sort of…steaming.

Great.

"Hey guys, this is already funny. It'll be a great story, right?" Trent said, clearly trying to redeem himself from the situation at hand. When the three of us only glared at him, he let out a weak chuckle. "Too soon, I guess," he murmured.

We exited the restroom and walked to a table situated at the back of the room in front of a pool table and sat down.

"Damn it," Grant said, wiping his phone down his shirt. "My phone won't even turn on."

I pulled mine from my pocket and attempted to turn it on. "Fuck." I'd tried to protect my phone from the downpour, but the mudslide and subsequent submersion had obviously done it in. Trent had dropped his in the mud before we even went shooting over the rain-softened cliff, so we already knew his was a lost cause.

Next to me Aidan was holding his phone up with a similarly bleak expression. "Dead as a doorknob," he said, dropping it on the table. "Maybe they have a bowl of rice here." I rolled my eyes. These phones were far beyond a bowl of rice. I doubted they'd ever work again.

"What can I get for you?" the woman with the dark hair and incredible blue eyes asked as she came up to our table. A wave of mild dizziness overcame me again. She was beautiful, and those eyes…I'd never seen any eyes that shade of blue before. But I'd seen *lots* of beautiful women in my time. I'd dated many of them. And yet, I'd never become woozy in their presence.

"Gage? Gage, come back to us."

I snapped to, realizing the other guys had ordered and everyone was waiting for me to speak. What were we doing again? Right. Ordering…"Food."

That dark brow arched again. "Is there a particular type of food you'd like, or should I just guess?"

I let out a thin laugh. "Sorry. It's been a long night. Ah. A burger would be great. Medium rare. And a shot of your best bourbon."

She stuck her pad back in the apron tied around her waist and looked at Aidan. "By the way, it's dead as a doornail."

"Huh?" Aidan said.

"You said your phone was dead as a doorknob. But the saying is dead as a doornail. I've never had the chance to correct a Harvard grad and it sort of just fell into my lap, so I had to take the opportunity."

Aidan shook his head and pulled his phone up again as if to google it and then dropped it to the table when memory dawned. She turned on her heel and walked away. I watched her hips sway as she walked away. *My God.*

"She's misinformed, of course," Aidan said. "But she sure is one gorgeous piece of—"

"Applesauce." At the one word that released on a growl, I felt three pairs of eyes turn my way.

Aidan laughed. "Oh shit, Gage has got a thing for the hot bar wench." He raised his hands as if in surrender and then flashed his wedding band. "Well, lucky for you, I'm already taken, and these two losers couldn't compete with you on their best day."

Bar wench. Why did the slight make me want to punch Aidan in the face? Grant and Trent did some mild grumbling in response to Aidan's comment but neither challenged it. I took a deep breath. I hadn't even meant to spit out that word, the one we'd agreed to use in college if we were calling dibs on a woman. The one I'd never used even once...until now. It'd just sort of...made its way up my throat of its own accord. Which was completely stupid for a couple of reasons, one being that she didn't seem to have any interest in me whatsoever. "Listen, we're eating a meal here and leaving," I told them. "There's no competition for anything." Speaking of which...I caught the woman's eye as she turned away from the bar with a tray full of drinks and gave her a short wave.

If she thought her eye roll had been discreet, she wasn't very good at discreet. "Yes?" she asked with contrived sweetness when she arrived back at our table and began setting the cocktails in front of each of us in turn.

"Apparently none of our phones are in working order," I said. "Do you have one we can use to call this Jim you mentioned who has a tow company?"

"Oh, Jim doesn't have a tow company, just a personal truck with a hitch on the back."

I stared. "Okay, well, can I use your phone to call Jim with the truck?"

She shook her head. "Jim's sleeping by now." She set the tray down and put her palms on the table, leaning toward me. I caught a whiff of her and without even meaning to, I drew in more of her scent, my gaze drooping as the fragrances separated and drew back together. Orchid. Jasmine. Saltwater. And beneath all that, a delicate understated musk that I couldn't put my finger on but was the thing that made me woozy. I inched forward, trying to inhale more of it while also maintaining some form of public decorum. "But I'll tell you what, Ivy League," she said, breaking me from my fragrance trance, "if you buy the bar a round, I'll call his wife, Patrice, who's almost certainly up watching one of her Netflix shows right now, and she'll rouse him for me."

Patrice? Who is Patrice? My brain scrambled, quickly putting together what she'd said. Jim. Truck. Patrice. *Right.* So she was playing games with me. An odd thrill whirled through my blood. I leaned closer until our faces were only inches apart. I narrowed my eyes and in response, she narrowed hers and we engaged in a short stare down, invisible sparks igniting my blood, that delicious smell washing over me, through me. "Are you blackmailing me, Cakes?"

She raised her eyes and put her tongue on her top teeth as though considering my word choice. I almost groaned at the sight of the pink tip of her tongue so close to me but swallowed it down. She pushed up off the table and crossed her arms. "That's a big word, Ivy League. I demand nothing. The choice is yours." She sighed as she raised her hands to study her nails. "I just hope Patrice didn't decide to turn in early on this one. Particular. Night."

I chuckled. What an act. "Fine. I'll buy a round for the bar." I held eye contact as I took my credit card from my damp wallet and handed it to her. "If you could kindly have Patrice rouse Jim with the hitch on his truck, we would greatly appreciate it."

She flashed me a smile, plucking the card from my hand and turning away. *Little schemer.*

"I don't think she likes you," Trent noted before tipping his beer back and taking a long swallow.

"Everyone likes me," I murmured. It was true. I never gave anyone reason to dislike me. Sure, there'd been a few people over the years who'd misinterpreted my drive as dismissal, but those people were few and far between. I strived for peace over strife and I didn't enjoy hurting people's feelings.

And I hadn't been rude to the beautiful server. I'd made sure to only allow my gaze to wander down her shirt when she was looking the other way, and she hadn't been able to see me checking out her ass, unless she had eyes in the back of her head.

So the only possible reason for her disdainful reaction was that she'd misjudged me due to some personal bias.

Ivy League.

The nickname made me suspect she thought I was a stuck-up rich boy who considered himself better than the working-class people in this bar. Calling this place a dive bar by the docks upon entering had probably not helped.

"How about a game of pool?" Aidan asked.

"Sure. Why not?" Grant answered. I sighed and then threw back the shot of bourbon. I'd expected it to burn, but the smooth flavor glided down my throat, the nutty, vanilla aftertaste a welcome surprise. My false assumptions took another hit and I was happy to be proven an ass. This bar knew good liquor.

"I play winner," Trent said.

I turned slightly in my chair and watched Aidan rack the balls. Thirty minutes later, the woman came out of a hallway on the other side of the room and headed in our direction. *Took you long enough.* "You're in luck," she said. "Patrice was up, and she's woken Jim."

Imagine that. "Thank you," I said as kindly as possible. "We really appreciate your help."

She gave me a small smirk. "Where's the car?"

"Mile marker fourteen," Grant said from beside the pool table. He raised a hand and circled his finger behind him. "On that dark as hell road that turns into town."

Her gaze moved to him. "Make and model?"

"Lexus LS."

She let out a short grunt. "Keys?"

"We can give Jim the keys when he comes by," I said.

She looked up. "Oh, um…well, Jim's not coming by. Because see…his truck is too wide for the narrow streets down here. But," she smiled, "another round of drinks will buy you key delivery service out to Jim and Patrice's house."

"Who will deliver the keys?"

"Who?"

"Yes, who runs this key delivery service?"

"Hmm, well, Ernest…next door is about to close up his shop and he lives up the road from them."

"Ernest?"

"Mm-hmm."

"What's his last name?"

She paused a beat, her eyes sliding to the side. "Ernest… Buffalobeam."

"Ernest Buffalobeam?" I looked off behind me at the bourbon barrel tops decorating the walls, sporting logos such as Buffalo Trace and Jim Beam.

"And what business does this Ernest Buffalobeam run next door, exactly?"

"He sells…" Her eyes slid behind us again, darting to the ceiling and then back to me. "Lights."

"Lights. Really? Ernest Buffalobeam sells lights next door?"

"Everyone needs lights," she said, pressing her lips together. "They help us see in the dark."

"Brilliant." We held eye contact for a beat, then two, both our eyes narrowing slightly as we tried not to smile. I would have bet anything that Jim's truck fit just fine down these streets and she was just trying to milk me for another round of drinks. "Trent, hand the keys over to the lady," I said.

"What if this Ernest Buffalobeam never comes back?" Trent asked skeptically.

"Where's he gonna go with a car with only three working tires?" Aidan asked.

"He might steal our stuff," Trent said. He leaned toward Aidan and "whispered," "We left all our bags in it."

"Listen, Ernest is full up on Polo shirts and Calvin Klein boxer briefs, and he's no thief."

I let out a low whistle. "That's pretty judgmental, Cakes," I said.

"How'd she know what I packed?" Trent "whispered" again to which Aidan shoved him in the arm. "Ouch," Trent murmured before taking his keys from his pocket and handing them to the server.

She turned away and shouted to the bar at large, "Who wants another round?" to which a loud cheer went up.

We played a game of pool and drank the drinks that had been delivered to us as part of the round I'd paid for and then she came back with our food. "Jim just called and said he's got your car and is delivering it to the repair shop. I'm sure they'll fit you in in the morning. Another round?"

"Why not?" Aidan said. "We're not driving!"

The waitress turned away with smile and a wink and it suddenly occurred to me that our car was here, which meant that even if we had a working cell—which we currently did not—taking an Uber to Claremont Landing would mean having to take one back in the morning. Whether one of our phones turned on or not, an hour round trip seemed impractical, especially being that our luggage would be unavailable to us until morning. Perhaps I should have inquired as to whether this Jim person with the truck hitch could retrieve and deliver our bags, but that ship had sailed.

I saw the woman come out of the kitchen and put my pool cue down as I made my way over to where she was now spraying a table and wiping it down.

"I'm almost afraid to ask," I said to her when she looked up, her brows raising, "but since our car is here in your town, we'll need a place to stay."

She tossed the towel over her shoulder, stuck the spray bottle in the large pocket on the side of her apron and smiled prettily. "Mimi Jenkins rents a room over her garage to out-of-towners. I could see if it's available."

A room over a garage? I almost scoffed, but I refused to play into her obvious assumption that we were snooty Ivy League types. Also, it was only for one measly night. I could cope. "How many rounds will it cost me?"

"Not more than two."

I laughed. "You're a shyster."

She laughed too, shooting me another wink over her shoulder as she walked away. I returned to my table, catching sight of myself in the glass of a framed photograph on the wall and realizing I was still smiling. Apparently, I liked being bamboozled.

By her. You like that saucy little smile and those crystal-blue eyes. And you like it when she turns them in your direction, even if it means another swipe of your credit card.

Pitiful. And I'd rarely been pitiful. I was always tempered, always even-keeled. And yet…

"What are you smiling like a loon about?" Aidan asked.

"I'm happy because I'm about to kick your ass in pool," I said, picking up the cue and chalking it. "Move aside."

Another couple rounds of shots showed up and I decided to forgo both so that one of us remained sober. I mopped the table with Grant, both because I was better than him and he was beginning to slur his words and when I sunk the eight ball, I looked up to see the little shyster herself delivering yet another round. "Mimi is leaving the key under the mat," she said, as she set the last shot on the table. "There's a dryer in the garage and your room is up the stairs to the left. Throw your clothes in the dryer before you go to bed. Don't mind the dog. He's…mostly friendly. I vouched for you, so don't make me look bad."

"Why'd you vouch for us?" Despite having no problem charging me for rounds for the locals, she didn't seem to like us all that much.

She tapped her tray against her thigh. "You don't look like the types to stiff an old lady on a bill, Ivy League."

I leaned closer. "Assumptions can be dangerous, Cakes."

Her smile was slow and knowing and made me feel like she'd taken a sledgehammer to my chest and knocked the air from my lungs. "Don't I know it," she returned smoothly.

I smiled back, even if mine felt both sort of wobbly and a little dazed. Something went flying past my cheek, pulling me from the fog I'd been in just as it lodged in the wall next to where I stood. *What the hell?*

I whipped my head over my shoulder to see Grant squinting at the dartboard, another dart poised in his hand to throw. The dartboard wasn't anywhere near my head, but that hadn't stopped him from nearly impaling me. "Whoa, sharpshooter. Put the weapon down." God, my friends were sloshed. Grant lowered the dart, leaning on the wall next to him for support.

"I should settle out my tab," I said to the woman.

Her lip quirked as she watched Trent slump into a chair. "I'll say. Hold on and I'll print up your bill."

When she came back, I scrawled my signature on the line, wincing when I saw the total. I should've passed Trent what-are-the-odds-of-getting-two-flats-in-a-week Howell the bill, but I wouldn't. I was the one who'd willingly allowed the little scammer to play her game with me. And truth be told, I wasn't even annoyed about it.

"These are on the house," she said as she handed me a white paper bag.

I looked at it dubiously.

"Cakes," she said.

I took the bag. "Ah, Cakes and Ale."

She gave me a quirk of her lip. "It's a Shakespeare thing. Anyway, we make them in-house. Enjoy."

Grant leaned on me a little too heavily and almost caused us both to topple over. "Whoa, buddy," I said as I worked to manage his weight.

"Whasha navado," Grant slurred. But he pulled himself straight and allowed me to lead him to the door. Behind me, Trent and Aidan had their arms around each other and were singing some song that was completely unrecognizable to me.

We all stumbled to the door and I pushed them through it, the three of them tripping out into the rainswept night. At least the storm had passed. "That moon!" Aidan exclaimed, raising his hands to the sky. "It's bootyful." The other guys cracked up, echoing, "Booty, booty," like twelve-year-olds, and doubling over as the door swung shut behind them. I turned, wanting to catch one more glimpse of the girl whose acquaintance, for some reason I couldn't explain, felt fated, even if our paths were only meant to cross briefly.

Or maybe it was the alcohol. I'd only had two shots, but perhaps they were extra strong.

"Does Harvard give refunds?" she asked, her lip quirking.

I laughed and ran a hand through my hair. "Despite some evidence to the contrary, they're wicked smart." I glanced back. "Maybe not always in the common sense arena. But otherwise, trust me, IQs off the charts."

"Hmm. Well," she sighed. "It takes all kinds."

I smiled and our gazes clashed, something moving between us that I'd never once experienced in all my thirty-three years. It confused and intrigued me.

She cleared her throat. "So, ah, turn left at the end of this block, go up the hill four blocks, and Mimi's house is the second on the right. You can't miss it. It has a bright red door."

"Thanks," I said, and for some reason, I couldn't get my damn hand to push the door back open. It was like my arm muscles had ceased to follow my brain's orders. Our gazes lingered and it seemed like she wanted to say something, her mouth opening very slightly before falling shut again.

"Thank you," she said, waving her arm in the direction of the last of the lingering customers. We didn't break eye contact though, our gazes holding. "For taking such good care of my patrons."

I didn't want to say goodnight. Which was ridiculous. I didn't even know her. I was only here for the night…in fact, if we got up early, I was only here for a few more hours.

But, ah, the things that could happen in a handful of hours…

I hadn't had a one-night stand in years. I wasn't interested in that anymore.

Still, I opened my mouth to speak…to say what? To ask what? The words hadn't exactly formed when I heard a loud sound from outside that either meant someone was experiencing bodily injury or vomiting violently.

"You better put them to bed before someone falls over the railing and drowns."

I huffed out a laugh. "Yeah. Well, goodnight, Cakes. And…it was a pleasure being bamboozled." The crazy thing? I actually meant it.

She laughed. "It was nice meeting you, Ivy League. Be well." Then she pulled the door open for me and I walked out into the night, the smells of sea and salt and old wood filling my nose. I glanced back at the bar and for just a moment, our eyes met again, before she turned away.

CHAPTER FOUR
Rory

"Are you sure you don't want me to stay and help with the rest of the cleanup?" Sherry asked, stifling a yawn.

"The cleanup's virtually done, Sher," I said. "And you've already worked over time. Go home to Bud."

"Bud's been passed out in his recliner for hours." But the affection in her voice told me she was still looking forward to seeing him, snoring or not.

"Go home and help him up to bed. You know how his back gets if he stays in that chair too long."

She gave me a weary smile but didn't argue. "I hope you're not planning on staying too much longer," she said as she removed the elastic band from her orange-blond—but mostly orange—hair and shook it loose.

"Not too much longer. I just need to count the register and bake a quick batch of cakes. We're out."

Sherry's dark brows rose, her expression morphing into concern. "Shouldn't you leave the baking to Eli?" she asked. "Last time you used the oven—"

"The fire department helped us out in a jiffy," I said. "Plus, I just got distracted. I won't do that again."

"Well, okay," Sherry said dubiously as she removed the apron tied around her waist. "Just…have the fire extinguisher at the ready."

I let out a laugh as I gave her a small push. "See you tomorrow. Lock the door behind you."

"Will do. See you tomorrow," she said as she turned for the front door.

I did a few more minutes of pickup and then ran the vacuum, feeling unusually blue for the end of a shift. Our part-time dishwasher had run the machine after the kitchen closed so I gathered the last of the glasses and set them on trays on the kitchen counter to be loaded in the morning, going about the work slowly and distractedly.

I wandered over to the pool table and racked the balls, and then hung the sticks back up on the wall. My head tilted as I recalled the way Ivy League's eyes had tracked my movements, watching my expression closely with each interaction. He was obviously a man used to being in control of every aspect of his life and so it'd been particularly satisfying to throw him off a few times. At the thought of the man who'd arrived in the bar doorway earlier that evening, soaked and steaming, my ribs tightened, and I felt a minor version of that pull I felt when I stared out to sea.

Why?

Why did that man inspire that same bewildering twinge? Maybe it was that just like the horizon, he too exhibited the concept of *away*.

I huffed out a breath, dropping the darts in the basket holder on the wall next to the board. There was no need to dwell on Ivy League because I'd never see him again and knowing my track record with men of society's upper crust—of which he was definitely a member—that was a good thing.

I headed back into the kitchen and mixed up a quick batch of batter and then slid the tray of mini cake pans into the oven.

The office in the far back of the bar across from the restrooms was small and cramped but it worked for our needs. Romeo spent the most time here as he usually did the books, but he was off tonight and so it fell to me.

I spent twenty minutes counting the take from the register and separating it into petty cash and tomorrow's bank deposit. There was a stack of bills that Romeo had left off to the side and I rifled through them quickly, one of them catching my eye. I picked it up and read through the quote for a new roof. *Shit.* I stuffed it back in the envelope. Every time the wind blew hard and rattled the shingles, I worried that we needed to undergo some restaurant renovations. Romeo obviously did too and had reached out to a company. God, just when we got a little bit ahead, something like this came up. I dropped the quote onto the desk and set the pile of bills back in place.

Cakes and Ale was a profitable business and it paid our salaries, but after the bills and the taxes and the constant fixes that the weather at the docks made necessary, there was little left over. As long as the fish kept jumping and the Mud Gulch fishermen kept reeling them in, we would continue serving them beer and clam chowder, but there would never be money for fancy things. Which…for me, was fine. I'd make do without fancy. So far, all *fancy* had done was bite me in the ass. But…for Romeo…

My gaze slid to the bottom right desk drawer and I

reached down and used my index finger to pull it open. There they were, all the way at the back. I reached in and grabbed the stack of brochures and set them on the desk in front of me, my heart rate increasing as though I was handling stolen goods. They weren't ill-acquired documents though. They were Romeo's unfulfilled plans and dreams.

I fanned them across the desk, my gaze moving from the bright lights of New York City to the canals of Venice to the cliffs of Ireland. This was where Romeo's pull came from. He'd identified his. The *world* called to him, just as it always had.

Before.

Before his personal world had turned upside down.

Before me.

My gaze lit on one I hadn't seen before and I picked it up, unfolding the colorful ad. It was new. Romeo had added to the collection as recently as the last couple of weeks. *Tuscany.* My eyes moved over the lush rows of vineyards, to a stone inn and a sun-dappled courtyard with a low fence draped in lacy, white flowers. I could practically smell them from here, the scent of earth and honey overtaking the dankness of this back room that had once sustained water damage and never quite aired out.

The lingering odor of mildew remained.

A sudden knock at the front door made me jolt, my arm sweeping to the side and causing several of the brochures to go flying off the desk. I jumped up, going down on my knees and hurriedly collecting the ones that had fallen, placing the one for Tuscany on the top of the pile where it'd been as the knock sounded again.

What the hell? It was after two in the morning and Mud

Gulch residents knew very well Cakes and Ale was closed for business.

I stood up and stuffed the brochures in the back of the drawer, kicked it closed and headed for the front door. I leaned in from the side and moved the short café curtain very slightly, so I could see who was out there, my heart giving a gallop when I saw it was…I moved the curtain farther aside to make sure my eyes weren't deceiving me. Nope. It was definitely Ivy League. And he'd spotted me. He gave me a small wave and pointed at the front door, obviously asking permission to enter.

I dropped the curtain back into place and stood there, my heart beating swiftly. I pulled in a deep breath and then took the step around the corner to the door and unlocked it. "Are Mimi's accommodations not adequate?"

He smiled and my heart lurched. God, something about that smile made my insides twist. *Stop getting taken in by handsome rich boys looking for an* experience. *That's all you'll ever be to them*. "Mimi's accommodations are more than adequate. We got settled in and I realized I forgot my credit card in the bill folder."

"Oh." I pulled the door open wider and he entered, following me over to the bar where I grabbed the leather bill folders off the top of the short pile and opened the first one. That one was empty, but when I opened the second one, his card was lying there. I picked it up and handed it to him. "An oversight."

He took the card and stuck it in his pocket. I noted that his clothes were dry, if very wrinkled. I didn't remember if they'd been mostly dry when he left or maybe he'd stuck them in Mimi's dryer for a few minutes before returning here. "Or maybe you were planning on buying the place a round on me into perpetuity." He raised a dark eyebrow, but his tone was clearly teasing.

I laughed. "I'm a negotiator, not a thief, Ivy League."

He grinned and so did I, our eyes lingering. I propped an elbow on the bar casually, suddenly feeling slightly unsteady and needing the support. "My name's Gage," he said.

"I know. I read the card."

"Ah. Right. What's yours?"

"Rory."

"Rory," he repeated as if trying it out on his tongue like a new, delectable flavor. My internal muscles clenched like he'd just used that tongue on me in some extremely pleasant manner.

I laughed to release the sudden tension. "Yup. That's it."

His smile suddenly turned to confusion, followed quickly by alarm. "Rory, is something burning?"

"Oh shit!" I yelled, turning on my heel and running to the kitchen. I screamed again when I flung the door open to the noxious smell of smoke and burnt sugar. "Grab the fire extinguisher!" I shouted at Gage who I heard on my heels, gesturing my arm over to the wall on our left.

I turned off the oven and pulled the oven door open, coughing and turning my face away when a cloud of smoke burst forth. I used a mitt to grab the tray and pull it out, tossing it on the counter to my right in a blaze.

"Stand aside," Gage said, and I did right before he used the fire extinguisher to put out the flaming cakes.

We both stood there, breathing heavily and waving our hands around to disperse the remaining smoke as we looked upon the charred remnants of the ruined batch of cakes I'd forgotten about. I put my face in my hands and groaned.

"Hey, all's well that ends well," Gage said from beside me. "You can make another batch."

I let my arms fall to my side. "I hate baking," I mumbled. Thank goodness I'd—or rather, Gage had—caught this in time so I didn't need to call the fire department for assistance. Again.

Gage set the fire extinguisher down, crossing his arms as he studied me. "Listen, I realize they're your namesake," he shot me a wink and I couldn't help the quirk of my lip, "but have you considered…doing away with the cakes entirely?"

"For an establishment called Cakes and Ale? That's unacceptable," I insisted. "Wait." My mouth fell open in offense and I turned his way, crossing my own arms, "Did you try my cakes and find them…disappointing, Ivy League?"

Gage laughed, his eyes dancing, and that stupid flutter took up under my rib cage again. "There's nothing disappointing about your cakes, Cakes." He squinted one eye at me as if suddenly deep in thought. "But, you know," he waved to the still-smoldering pile of black ash on the counter, "this choice might be overly literal. Perhaps it needs to be expanded."

"I'm not sure I follow."

"Have you considered crab cakes rather than dessert cakes?"

"Crab cakes?"

"Right. You could do all kinds. Parmesan crab cakes. Chipotle, lemon zest. You could also use different types of crab…king crab, blue crab. Perhaps consider salmon cakes too. There are a hundred different recipes and they can all be virtually the same except for a little twist which would change the taste pairing of earth and sea. It'd be easy for the kitchen. Or you could differentiate with types of aioli—"

"'Taste pairing of earth and sea'? That's pretty poetic, Ivy League."

He smiled. "Maybe appropriate for a tavern that pays homage to Shakespeare?" He set his hip on the counter. "A menu sets a whole mood. Food is a necessity, but it's also a great pleasure. People bond around it, deals are brokered over it, it provides comfort, and can be medicine for both the body and the spirit."

I stared at him for a moment. "Whoa. What are you, some sort of top chef?"

He laughed but looked mildly embarrassed like he hadn't meant to get quite so enthusiastic about the topic of appetizers. I'd liked watching his eyes fill with the spark that had been in them while he spoke though, as he came alive in some way, I couldn't exactly put my finger on since I'd just met the man. "Sorry. No. But I've always loved to cook, since I was young. I work with spreadsheets most of the day, but I've taught myself a thing or two in the kitchen. The real point here is that everyone loves crab cakes and they go with liquor a hell of a lot better than...carrot cake."

I laughed despite myself. "That was red velvet I gave you."

His eyes widened, and his mouth did a small twisting thing. "That was not red velvet."

"It was!"

He appeared deeply pained. "It had raisins in it."

"It makes them special."

"It definitely does do that."

I snorted. "Watch it, Ivy League."

He grinned. "How about I show you a quick recipe. I bet they'll sell better, and you'll be off the baking hook."

I sized him up. "Is this your way of making up for that dive bar comment? We don't need your pity recipe here."

"It wouldn't be a pity recipe. And I didn't mean that dive bar comment the way it sounded." He looked thoughtful for a moment. "I meant your establishment is a place where you can feel comfortable being yourself. The people in a bar like this are genuine and helpful and don't put on airs. Believe me when I tell you I've had a bellyful of *airs* and walking into this place felt like taking a deep breath. That feeling only increased as I spent more time here."

"Okay, that was a good answer," I admitted. "Still, you must be tired. There's a bed up the street waiting for you."

He shrugged, his expression enigmatic. I wanted him to stay and teach me how to make crab cakes. I wanted to watch him laugh and get that surprised look on his face when I said something he obviously hadn't expected. I knew I made bad decisions where men were concerned. I knew that I'd only ever be a one-night fling to a man like this. But he was only in town for the night. No expectations. No promises. "Yes, I do have a bed up the street," he answered. "With three snoring drunk men in the room." He smiled, but it quickly dropped. "I'd like to teach you how to make crab cakes if you'll let me. No strings. Just a thank you for helping us out of a bind."

"I could have made it easier. I sort of gave you the runaround, only without the sort of."

"I know."

I laughed, feeling slightly shy all of a sudden. When I glanced up at him from under my lashes, he was watching me with that intense look that told me if I went up on my tiptoes and kissed him, he'd kiss me back.

Crab cakes, Rory. Just crab cakes. "Fine then, teach me your crab cake ways." I raised a finger. "But only if you let me treat you to a drink this time."

He grinned. "Absolutely."

He followed me back out to the bar where I opened a bottle of red wine and poured two glasses and handed him one. We clinked. "To Ernest Buffalobeam," he said.

I laughed. "Best lights salesman in Mud Gulch."

As we entered the kitchen, scratching suddenly sounded at the back door. Gage looked up at me questioningly. I set my wine glass down and hurried to the refrigerator where I removed a pile of takeout containers I'd prepared toward the end of my shift. "Hold on," I said. "This will just take a second."

I exited the kitchen and made my way to the back door where the scratching sounds were getting louder. "Hold on, hold on," I said as I twisted the lock and pulled the heavy door open. My smile was instantaneous as I went down on my knees to greet the hungry visitors, setting the containers on the floor.

The four dogs all came toward me in a rush of wet noses and doggy kisses as I laughed. "Okay, step back, and I'll give you your dinner," I said as I reached for the containers. They danced around and whined but made room for me to open each box and set them on the ground one by one.

I stood up as they started hungrily eating, glancing at Gage who was standing a little behind me on the other side of the doorway, his lips tilted in a small smile.

"Gage, meet Loki, Alamo, Katniss, and Tahoe," I said, pointing at one after the other.

The dogs finished their food and Gage stepped forward, squatting as he let each dog sniff his hand before petting them sort of tentatively. They leaned into him, clearly smitten, and my heart gave a hard knock. "Hey, guys," he said. "This must be a regular thing." He glanced up at me. "Do they need homes?"

I shook my head. "No. I've tried to take them home several times to join the rest of the brood, but they keep running away. They prefer life down on the docks."

"The rest of the brood?" he asked as he stood.

"I have four rescues."

"And you want more?"

"I would if they showed any interest, even though the brood and I live in close quarters. I got my mom's house when she died. It has a small yard. I wish I had more space, but we make it work. And I…well, I like animals, so…" I shrugged. It wasn't only that I liked them. I'd always sort of…understood them in a way others didn't seem to. It was hard to explain except that I'd just always instinctively known how to handle different personalities and because of it, they seemed to trust me right off the bat.

His eyes moved over my face, his expression one I didn't know him well enough to discern. "My family, we work with several charities that help animals too."

"What do you know? We have something in common after all."

"Who would have guessed?" He smiled and one of the dogs butted his leg and he laughed, going down on his haunches again. After a few minutes, Alamo's ears perked up and he turned in the other direction, heading toward whatever had caught his attention. The other dogs began wandering off too and I gathered the containers and locked the door.

I turned to Gage, our eyes meeting in the dim light of the back hall. My heart picked up speed and I felt that pull once again, only like before, it was the pull only enhanced by something I couldn't put into words. It made me feel confused and slightly needy. Insecure.

"You okay, Cakes?" he asked softly.

I let out a breath, tearing my eyes from his. "Yes, yes, I'm fine. Let's go make some crab cakes, shall we?"

CHAPTER FIVE
Gage

"Here, put this in your mouth." She gave me a raise of her brow before parting her lips so I could put the bite of crab cake I'd just cut onto her tongue. Her eyes met mine as I slipped the fork between her lips and I swallowed, the moment slow and intimate and heavy with delicious possibilities that had nothing to do with food.

I watched as she chewed for a moment, her eyes widening and then rolling upward as she groaned and clutched the side of the metal table. *Jesus.* It was warm in the kitchen but I suddenly felt hot, my clothes far too tight. "Oh my God, that's good. Wait, did you really make this with ingredients from this kitchen?" She looked around. "Or did you sneak in a few magic crab cake fairies while I wasn't looking?"

I laughed. "I not only used ingredients you already had around here, but only six of them."

"Just how?" She ran her finger over her bottom lip and I followed the movement. I was simultaneously turned on and deeply pleased by her reaction to the food I'd made.

"That's all you need," I said. "You wrote down what I did. You can do it too. You just swap out that sixth ingredient to make them all different. But it's basically the same recipe. The trick is getting that outer shell perfectly golden brown and then serving them piping hot."

She nodded but still looked dubious. "I'll certainly try to recreate this magic." She took a swig of her wine and I picked up my glass and drained it. "Thank you, Gage. It was really nice of you to take the time to give me a cooking class."

A form of panic sluiced through my veins, an internal ticking that I knew was the countdown to our parting. I didn't want it to end, but I knew it had to. I was only passing through. I had a life in Calliope, and very soon, in London. And this girl was here, in a harbor town where she helped run the family bar and went home every night to a motley crew of rescue animals.

And God, I couldn't believe my mind had gone to a place where there was any chance of us seeing each other again when the truth was, I didn't even really know her. I was merely *attracted* to her, that was the overwhelming pull I felt. Because I hadn't been quite as attracted to any other woman...maybe ever. But that was physical, and in the end, a merely physical bond wasn't what I wanted. In fact, I'd sworn it off. I wanted more. I wanted it all. And I wanted it with a woman who was looking for the same.

So...a cooking class it would be. A brief foray off the beaten path to a waterside bar on the docks where a beautiful woman made me laugh and feel alive and remember what I was looking for and what I was not. "You're welcome."

Our eyes held. Her mouth opened, then closed and I had the feeling she wasn't quite ready to say goodnight either.

"Well..." she sighed, breaking eye contact and looking away as she fidgeted with the hand towel laying on the counter next to her.

"I should...let you finish closing so you can go home to your brood." I tilted my head. "Who takes care of them while you're at work anyway?"

"A teenage girl who lives next door comes over and feeds them and walks them and gets them settled for the night. They usually don't even move when I come home." Her voice was a murmur, her gaze moving from my eyes to my mouth and back again sort of dreamily as though her mind was somewhere other than on her words.

"Not the greatest attack dogs then."

Her laugh was mostly breath. "No, they'd lick you to death before anything else."

Another flush of warmth moved under my skin at the phrase *lick you to death* which I was *not* thinking about in relation to hounds, but to her, and *Christ,* but I was turned on. Part of me worried that deciding to not engage in one-night stands had caused my libido to dry up. For the past year or so, I'd been fine with taking things into my own hands. But now? Just looking at this woman, just breathing in her intoxicating fragrance and watching her take a bite of food, had me ready to combust. "I'm moving to London," I said.

She stared blankly. "Oh. Okay. Well that's...far away."

I felt my expression twist. "Yes. I just...you know, I'm not sure why I said that. I guess I'm tired."

"I bet." She drummed her finger on the counter distractedly as she turned her head away. "You should get some sleep..."

"Right..."

"Right..."

Our eyes met again and we both let out small laughs, color rising in her cheeks. I didn't feel tired at all. *Don't do it, Buchanan. You have a life plan. International business mogul and heir to Buchanan Corporation. Marriage to a woman who will complement and support you within that world. A few Buchanans to carry on the name, and eventually the family business.*

Random sex in a dive bar with a waitress you'll never see again isn't on the agenda.

Only, whatever inner voice was speaking wasn't convincing me in the least. In fact, at the moment, I didn't like that guy at all, or his "life plans," and if he materialized somehow, I might push him off the dock and watch him sink below the water.

Rory pulled in a breath, sticking her hand out and giving a small nod as though she was having an inner conversation as well, and something had been definitively decided. "Goodnight, Gage."

Ah, well, then, she'd made it easy. *Good.*

We both took off our aprons and set them on the counter, our hands brushing and causing her to startle and pull hers quickly away as though she'd been burned.

She let out another small laugh that faded quickly and turned toward the door. I followed her out into the bar, noticing that outside the window, the sky was just beginning to lighten from black to sterling. Soon the sun would be peeking over the horizon and this day would be nothing but a memory.

"Any good at darts?" I asked, and she swung around so that I came up short and we nearly collided.

"Are you kidding me? I'm the reigning local champion," she said, her voice breathy.

"Are you now?" I raised a brow.

She set her hands on her hips. "Are you challenging me to a game, Ivy League?"

I stepped closer so that our shoes were touching. "Maybe I am, Cakes."

Her grin was slow, and she did that same something where she sort of cocked her hip and raised her shoulder and God, whatever combo of slight movements she used along with that wide smile knocked me on my proverbial ass for the tenth time that night. That smile, it was a deadly weapon. "Challenge accepted," she said.

We headed over to the dart board that was on the wall next to the pool table and Rory handed me several darts. "What games do you know?" she asked.

"Cricket's the only one."

"Works for me." She shot me a wink and then tossed her dart, easily landing a triple.

I whistled. "I have a feeling I'm about to be bamboozled again."

She laughed, pulling her dart from the board. "You had fair warning this time."

"Nothing about you is fair warning, Cakes."

She smiled, and this one was sort of sweet and sort of secretive and did nothing to cool my blood.

We moved through the numbers, closing them out one by one, and though she was clearly better than me, I held my own so that when it was time to hit the bullseye, it was anyone's game.

The sky had morphed from dark to pale gray, a slip of lavender peeking from the bottom of the window pane. I leaned on the edge of the pool table, taking the opportunity to let my gaze roam slowly over Rory as she pulled the last round of darts from the board. Then she took her position and looked over at me, meeting my eyes and giving me a wink as she tossed the dart, hitting the target with perfect precision.

"Holy shit!" I laughed. "How in the hell did you do that?"

She laughed too, giving a deep curtsy before rising and taking the few steps to me. "I'll tell you the secret, but only because I know it's safe since you'll take it with you when you go."

My heart sped, then slowed, that panic scratching the underside of my skin. I swallowed. "Tell me."

She inclined her head behind me and I looked over my shoulder at a polished sign advertising some pale ale. "You can see the reflection of where you're holding the dart in that sign. If you line it up with the arrow in the artwork, and toss it just right, it hits the bullseye every time."

I grinned. "A trick."

She shrugged, a smile playing on her lips. "A trick that still takes skill. And lots of practice."

She glanced to her left, out the window to where the first golden rays of the sun were making the slip of visible water sparkle. I swallowed, that internal countdown growing louder, my blood whooshing to its beat. I couldn't have moved even if I'd wanted to. "What other tricks do you know?" I asked, my voice thick with the lust that had been building steadily since the moment I'd laid eyes on her. She was so close. I could feel her body heat, smell her earthy yet delicate scent, feel the magnetism we created simply by being near one another.

Her smile faded, her gaze sliding to my mouth. I hardened fully, pulling in a breath, feeling woozy from the mixture of pleasure and pain. I'd decided that a one-time hookup wasn't what I wanted and served no purpose other than momentary bliss. It didn't further my plan. It was a *diversion* from my plan. But it seemed that I'd been overruled by some part of my brain that had never overruled my more rational gray matter, and I didn't know how to shut it down.

"Not as many as I pretend to know," she murmured, color infusing her skin, her nipples hardening under the stretched material of her shirt. She blinked, appearing briefly baffled as if those words had slipped out without her permission. I struggled to remember what she'd been responding to. Tricks.

What other tricks do you know.

Not as many as I pretend to, she'd confessed.

It was late. Neither of us had had a moment of sleep, and we were both clearly aroused, blood rushing everywhere except our brains, latent lizard-controlled synapses taking advantage and clouding judgment. "What about you, Mr. Perfect? You must know quite a few tricks."

Mr. Perfect. Ivy League. I'd heard variations of both of those all my life, mainly delivered as compliments. But, truthfully? Each time a comment like that was uttered, it felt like a weight bearing down. It felt like a *reminder*—mostly from my family—not to stray from the lane I'd been set to walk. And sometimes, all I wanted to do was step outside those rigid lines, even if I rarely ever did. "I'm not as perfect as I seem," I said, blurting out my own confession.

Her eyes softened, and she leaned in even further, our breath mingling. "No?" she whispered.

"No. And also...I have another confession. I left my credit card here on purpose, Cakes."

She let out a small, surprised laugh that turned into a

sigh when I wrapped one arm around her waist, pulling her into my body and supporting us both with the other hand still behind me on the pool table.

She brought a hand to my cheek. "I have a confession, too, Ivy League. I knew you left it."

I chuckled with surprise. "Ah, so you *were* going to treat your customers to rounds on me forever."

She grinned but shook her head. "No. I was just hoping you'd come back for it."

Oh, Jesus. My heart expanded with something I couldn't name. All I knew was that I wanted her and I was done fighting it whether the reasons to do so were good ones or not. I groaned and brought my lips to hers, our mouths meeting as she pressed her soft breasts against my chest. I swept my tongue into her sweet mouth and she met it with her own, sliding and playing slowly.

"Goddamn, you taste good," I said, when our mouths parted. I tilted my head, bringing my lips to her throat as she arched her neck and I licked down her skin.

She moaned and climbed up on the pool table, straddling me and causing the room to spin when she pressed her core firmly into my aching erection. "If you're not perfect," she whispered into my ear, biting the lobe and causing a lightning bolt of lust to shoot from that small bit of cartilage straight between my legs, "then what are you?"

"I don't know," I said, meeting her eyes. And I suddenly knew that was true. I didn't know if I'd ponder it later—maybe there was no point—but in that moment, I'd surrendered and within that surrender, there only lived honesty.

She sat up slightly and pulled her shirt over her head and I let out a sound that was a mix between a groan and a growl, my gaze drinking in pink lace covering full, round breasts. I brought my hands up which caused me to fall back on the table and Rory laughed, coming with me. We kissed for a few more minutes, licking into each other's mouths with increasing urgency, and when I flipped her over, she laughed again. I gazed down at her, a distant stream of golden light falling over her skin and causing it to glow. "You're so beautiful."

"So are you, Ivy League," she said, her voice both soft and throaty. "Now take off your clothes."

I grinned, leaning up and pulling off my shirt and tossing it aside. Then I quickly undid her bra, her breasts spilling from the material and rendering me momentarily speechless.

I ran a finger around her nipple, her breath hitching as the berry-colored peak hardened. I stared, mesmerized, my mouth going dry and for a second, I forgot what I was supposed to do next. I had the sudden flash of the time I'd gotten lost in the woods on a Pelion Lake fishing trip. I'd been there a hundred times before and yet somehow, I got turned around, my internal overhead map blinking off and rendering me disoriented and confused. My instinct then had been to run, to go crashing through the woods as I yelled for help. But I hadn't. I'd taken a deep breath, centered myself and found my way home. Now though? I wasn't sure which direction to head in. My instinct was only to put my mouth on her. It didn't matter the order or the technique. I just wanted to taste every part of her. To feel her skin, to relish her most intimate scents. I chuckled at my disjointed thoughts and the foreign feeling of being lost on familiar territory and the choked laugh sounded as bewildered as I felt. And again, there was only honesty. "You make me forget what to do." *You make me forget who I am.* And that felt scary but somehow good too. Like being lost…and then found.

She wove her fingers through my hair as I kissed the dip between her breasts, licking the skin there and finding it both sweet and slightly salty. "Is there an agenda?"

Was there? There always had been. Wasn't an agenda good? An agenda meant skill. And skill ensured both parties were ultimately satisfied. *Right?*

No. No, suddenly that seemed so boring. So choreographed. My mind half removed as I shifted through the motions.

At my hesitation, Rory tipped my face to hers, her heated gaze meeting mine. "No agenda. No perfect. I don't want that. Just you and me. Just now. I just want you to touch me and I want to touch you. If this is any indication," she said, reaching between our bodies and cupping my throbbing erection, "I think you want that too. Very badly."

I groaned, pressing toward her hand. "Yes," I breathed.

"Let go, Gage."

Let go. I didn't know how to do that. But apparently, my body had some idea because when my pent-up breath gusted from my mouth and I leaned in, trailing my lips over and around her breast, drawing ever closer to her nipple, that feeling of being lost descended once again. I was only sensation and instinct and yearning. I heard her head fall back on the pool table and felt her core ground up into mine. We both made sounds of frustrated pleasure, hers turning into a sigh as I sucked one nipple into my mouth, testing and tasting as her sighs turned into pants and her legs came up, wrapping around my hips.

"Gage, I want you so much. Please," she moaned. But I wasn't done tasting her. I ached with the need for release, but I didn't want this to be over yet. *Because it's all you'll ever get of her.*

Only I wouldn't think of that. Not now when her nipple was in my mouth, her scent was all around me and sweet little groans of pleasure were growing louder and more persistent.

I grunted, and she let out a pained laugh at what I assumed to be the vibration against her breast. And so I did it again to the same result. No agenda. Just need and response. I felt free in a way I never had before. Free and more aroused than I even knew was possible.

We twisted together, pressing and touching and gasping, mouths and limbs tangled until I could barely breathe.

"I…God…"

"Yes, yes…"

"Now…"

"Yesssss."

Then I was standing, my feet planted on the floor as she lifted her ass and I removed her pants and underwear with shaking hands and then tossed them aside. "Condom," she said and for a second the word made no sense.

But then it dawned, and I reached in my pocket, pulling out that tiny package with the red condom inside. I blinked at it, gratitude flooding me as I held it up to Rory like it was a winning lottery ticket.

In that moment, that's what it was.

"Thank you, God," she breathed.

Thank you, Aidan.

I dropped my pants and kicked them aside as Rory sat up. "Let me," she said.

I met her eyes as I handed her the condom and stepped forward and then we both watched as she stretched it over my shaft. A shiver went through me, lust pumping so feverishly I wondered if I might spill in her hand. I almost laughed but didn't have the breath. I hadn't lost control like that since I was a teenager.

I needed to get inside her, needed to feel her tight warmth envelop me, but first, I had to taste her. I gently pushed her back on the table and she let out a squeak of surprise as I bent forward and pushed her knees apart inelegantly, so desperate I practically dove between her legs. I inhaled as she fisted my hair and then put my lips around her clit, giving it a long suck. She bucked against my mouth and I growled in response, her orgasm shuddering through her as she panted and moaned my name.

I couldn't wait another second. I stood and then used one arm to hitch under her and drag her back before climbing on top. The sun was streaming inside now as I lined myself up at her entrance, our eyes meeting as I pushed inside her. Her sated gaze widened and she reached for me, pulling me down into a kiss.

Our mouths met as I rocked into her, surrendering to the push and pull that was those few dwindling moments of this unexpected rapture I'd somehow found in this unplanned place. Time slowing, blood rushing, something crumbling, breaking apart.

I swallowed down her staggered breaths and small gasps of bliss, the feverish pitch of my own pleasure growing ever louder as I careened crazily toward climax. "Oh God, Rory, Rory, I can't—" I pumped faster, all control gone as I flew toward the edge of some internal cliff, the ground dropping out from beneath me, in the same but much different way as had happened earlier and caused me to end up here, with her. Every muscle in my body suddenly released and I could do nothing but throw my head back and let myself go, the ground rising up to meet me. And when it hit, the orgasm rushed through me so intensely it felt like I really had flown apart, my very being scattered far and wide, never to be put back together again.

I came back to reality slowly, Rory's fingers running through my hair. She was murmuring, but the words I thought she'd said were, "I've got you."

I've got you.

We lay like that for mere moments and a lifetime, our lungs filling with air, my atoms reforming into some semblance of who I was.

Gage Buchanan. Most Likely to Succeed. Ivy League. Mr. Perfect.

So why didn't any of those titles feel like they fit suddenly?

God. It was just great sex but…wow. It had turned me inside out.

She rubbed her cheek slowly against mine. "I like you with scruff," she whispered, turning slightly so her lips dragged across my chin. *Scruff, she liked my scruff.* I'd spent so much time with her, I needed a shave. And Jesus but the way she was peppering small kisses along my jaw was turning me on again.

"What'd you slip into those crab cakes, anyway?" she asked.

I laughed, leaning up, realizing that in my fervor, I'd scooted us across the table so that her head was practically in one of the pockets. "What did *you* slip into—"

Loud banging sounded at the front door and we both jumped, me slipping out of her as I practically toppled off the table, landing on my feet, but just barely. A deep voice called Rory's name from the other side of the door.

"Oh, shit!" she said, hopping down from the table too. "That's my uncle! He'll kill me! And you!" For a few seconds we just stood there, utterly naked except for my—obviously used—red condom, staring at each other in alarm before both moving at the same time, bending to pick up a piece of clothing, our heads colliding.

"Oof," we said in tandem, staggering back as we both rubbed our heads.

"He has a key," she hissed as we began picking up clothing items and pulling them on as quickly as possible.

The sounds of a key being inserted into the lock made Rory let out a small squeak, both of us bending to pull on our socks and shoes as the door banged open. "Rory!" the deep, gruff voice called.

"Uh, over here," she called back breathlessly, giving me a wide-eyed stare as I looked up at her from where I was tying my shoe. There was really nowhere to hide and if she hadn't answered him, he would see us in a few more steps anyway. She jerked her chin and I stood just as a very large man came around the corner sporting a trimmed black beard and an eyepatch.

A pirate. Her uncle was a pirate. He stopped short, his gaze flying from her to me and back to her. My God the man was huge, not just in height, but in breadth. His arms were the size of my thighs and he could probably crush me if he wanted to. Or make me scrub a deck. Or walk a plank. And by the way he was staring at me, one icy blue eye narrowed and suspicious, he was definitely considering doing all of those things, and much worse.

"What's this?" he barked.

"Why are you wearing an eye patch?" Rory asked.

He reached up and removed the patch, squinting the eye that had been covered. "I took a rope to the eye last night. I'll ask you again," he growled. "Who's this?"

"Him?" she asked, sweeping her arm in my direction as if her uncle might have been asking about some ghost or other invisible person in the room. "He's uh...he was servicing the...uh..."

"Pool table," I cut in, forcing myself not to grimace. *Nice save, Buchanan.* Apparently my brain cells were still scrambled from the sex.

Her uncle's eyes narrowed further, his hand curling into a fist. "What kind of service does a pool table need?" he asked, his voice low and measured in a way that was scarier than the way he'd first yelled.

I glanced over my shoulder at the table, my eyes widening when I saw the clear ass imprint in the felt. I shifted my body, hoping to hide the evidence. "Uh, the pockets have to be...calibrated," I said.

The giant pirate's eyes narrowed to slits. The room brightened another degree, morning asserting herself over the dawn.

"And the balls," Rory said. "He was checking the balls." She tilted her head. "Balls should have a certain feel in the palm." She raised her hand and massaged the air. "Isn't that what you were about to show me?" She gave me a wide-eyed innocent look and batted her lashes.

The pirate growled.

"Uh..." My eyes locked with Rory's. The corner of her mouth trembled though her eyes looked just a little sad. I realized what she was doing. She was saying goodbye. She was going to end this as it'd began. With barely suppressed laughter and good-natured teasing. And as far as endings went, it wasn't a bad one. So why did I feel equal parts alarmed by the giant, and regretful that I was about to walk away from this woman?

I heard shouts from the front door and the sounds of palms slapping the glass. *My friends.* They were calling my name. Had it really been hours since I'd left them sleeping? It felt like mere moments. Their calls got louder.

And yet I couldn't look away from Rory. We'd both known it was temporary. Just a chance encounter. Reality that would soon seem like nothing more than a fantasy. A fever dream.

"Those are, ah, my calibration experts and…but, I think we're done here," I told the big man who looked like he was seconds away from hanging me on the coat rack. I turned to Rory and reached for her hand. Our palms met, my fingers wrapping around hers. "Cakes…"

"Ivy League." She inclined her head toward the door. "You better go before they break it down." I paused, somehow not able to let go.

I've got you.

But then she was the one to pull her hand from mine and I released an exhale and turned away from her before I figured out a way to stay, scooting carefully past her uncle and then jogging for the door. I flung it open and my friends almost fell in, all chattering at once. "Did you stay the night here?" Aidan leaned his head in and I pushed him out, letting the door slam shut behind us. "Details later," he whispered, holding his hand next to his mouth, and then looking over his shoulder.

"The repair shop's open and they're putting on a new tire now," Grant said.

"My phone is working," Trent told me, holding his up. "Grant's and Aidan's are permanent goners. Check yours."

Check mine? Check my what?

"It's a glorious day to golf!" Aidan declared as we walked down the dock.

Golf?

Something about heading out to a day of golf seemed hilarious but I couldn't figure out why. And I loved to golf.

"We'll check in to our hotel, take showers, change, and be on the course in a couple of hours. Mud Gulch will be nothing but a bad memory by noon."

Their chatter faded away. I picked up my pace in order to keep up with the other guys, the dock squeaking beneath our feet.

I looked over my shoulder, just once, but the only one staring back was a huge, black-bearded pirate.

Mud Gulch will be nothing but a bad memory by noon.

Those blue eyes flashed in my mind, the way they'd grown hazy with lust.

Mud Gulch would never be a bad memory for me. I looked out at the gently rolling waves, watching them swell and recede. For one night, I'd been given the opportunity to shrug off all the responsibilities I carried on my shoulders. All the limits and expectations. And though that couldn't and shouldn't last, the chance to very temporarily let down my guard had been a blessed relief. Perhaps it had been exactly what I'd needed in order to move forward into this new chapter of my life.

I squinted as I turned my head, looking forward once again, facing what was in front of me, not behind.

CHAPTER SIX
Rory

The restroom door slammed closed behind me, my uncle Cassius turning from where he'd stood at the window watching Gage and his friends walk away.

I'd headed to the restroom not only to clean up and get myself together, but because I couldn't bear to watch him leave. My uncle interrupting us—or near enough, anyway—had meant that our parting was as brief and uncomplicated as it was ever going to be. No hemming and hawing, no words to search for, no promises that wouldn't be kept. Only the veiled laughter of a private joke, and the understanding that passed between us that we'd had a very enjoyable interlude that was never going to be anything other than that. And if Gage thought of me as an "experience," then I hoped it was a positive one, fashioned by the fate of a busted tire and a rainstorm. Just like the wet and the cold would be difficult to conjure someday soon, so too would the texture of my skin beneath his hand and the taste of my nipple—

I shoved those thoughts aside, shivering at the memory

of what we'd done on the pool table that I'd never look at the same again. Okay, so it would take some time—at least for me—for the specifics of that memory to fade. And even if my heart squeezed with melancholy at the fact that I wouldn't see him again, I'd known we were very temporary from the start and made the choice to be intimate with him anyway. I wasn't in the habit of having random sex with strangers just passing through town, and there would likely be emotional consequences because damn it, I'd liked him. But I was also no stranger to being disappointed when it came to men. At least this time, I'd understood the terms. I sighed as I removed my phone from my pocket to call Ashley and ask her to let the brood out and then feed them their breakfast. I'd tell her I got bogged down at the bar. Which was true in a manner of speaking.

"Who was the guy?" Cassius asked as I rounded the bar a few minutes later and headed for the coffee maker. Caffeine would help soothe the ache.

"What guy?"

He gave me a decidedly snarly look. "The pool table inspector with his shirt on backward."

I raised my head and looked at him as I filled the pot with water. "He wasn't really a pool table inspector."

Cassius grunted. "Gee, you think? You really had me fooled, Rory."

"Sarcasm doesn't flatter you," I said as I poured the water into the machine.

"You're lucky I didn't beat him to a pulp, because I sure wanted to."

I reached for the jar of coffee grounds and removed the scooper. "Nah," I said. "I propositioned him, practically forced him into that thing he did with his—"

"Rory."

I laughed. "I'm a big girl, Uncle Cash." I leaned across the bar and gave him a kiss on his grizzly cheek.

"You're still a kid to me," he muttered.

Cassius and Romeo had basically raised me after my mom died when I was eleven. They were my uncles, but also father figures, and best friends, a sometimes strange mix of roles that had leaned heavily in one direction or another and then swayed back the other way over the years.

Cassius, being the elder of my mom's brothers, leaned more toward being a father figure, whereas Romeo, as the baby of the family, was more of a protective older brother. And my confidante. I told Romeo almost everything, within reason of course.

There was also the small matter of Cassius naturally being a grumbly bear of a dude, and so he'd happily taken it upon himself to scare the bejesus out of any males who looked at me the wrong—or according to me, right—way over the years. And Romeo. Well, Romeo tended to stay mostly out of my love life, likely in part because his own was already quite the time commitment. They were both so different, even if we were all similar in that we had the same black hair and blue eyes of the Casteel clan.

The bottom line was that I loved them both and because of them, I had survived the wreckage of my mother's unexpected death. Because of them, I had family, and stability, and love.

The squeak of the door sounded, and I looked up as Romeo entered as if my thoughts had summoned him. Cassius turned his way and Romeo stared at us over a box in his arms, his expression registering surprise. "What are you two doing here?"

My mind scrambled to come up with a decent excuse for the reason I was in the bar this early, but before I could concoct a plausible story, Cassius said, "My boat got caught up in a squall from that storm last night. It's a total wreck."

I blinked, sucking in a breath. "What?" I practically dropped the mug I'd just picked up, the bang startling me even though I'd been the one to make it. "Why didn't you tell me? I've been here jabbering and *brewing coffee* and your boat wrecked? Are you okay?"

Romeo set the box of what I now saw was a case of whiskey on the bar, and then took a seat at the barstool next to Cash. "Shit, man, how much damage?"

"I'm okay," he said, rubbing at his eye. I gently moved his hand away so he wouldn't make it worse, because now that I was closer, it looked like he'd scratched his cornea pretty bad, though that was obviously the least of his problems. As for me? I felt awful. I'd been here sexing up a customer while my uncle was braving a storm at sea that might have killed him. No wonder he looked exhausted. I'd assumed he'd just had a late night, but no, he'd been battling Mother Nature. "But my boat is not okay. The damage is pretty severe."

"Fixable?" Romeo asked.

Cash grunted. "Yeah. But it'll take about eight weeks. At least we'll be back up in time to set the traps."

I nodded. The fall lobster season brought in the most money, so that was good.

Romeo put his hand on Cash's shoulder. "I'd suggest you wait tables around here, but I'm afraid you'd scare off the customers," he said, his lip quirking.

"Funny," Cash muttered.

I huffed out a laugh as I pictured Cash lumbering between the tables as he balanced trays of drinks. No, Cash had been formed to plant his feet solidly on the deck of a ship and shout orders at his crew of fishermen. I knew I could speak for Romeo when I said that neither of us would foist him on the clientele at Cakes and Ale.

I picked up the mug still sitting on the bar and poured a cup of coffee and placed it in front of Cash who wrapped his beefy hands around it so that it looked like a child's teacup. Then I poured a second cup for myself and looked at Romeo and inclined my head in question. "No, thanks," he said.

Romeo picked up the box of liquor and brought it behind the bar and began unpacking it as Cash and I sipped our coffee. My gaze caught on the photo of my mom hung on the wall behind the bar. She was standing at the edge of the docks, the sea shimmering behind her, smile as bright as the sun. I took another sip of coffee, my eyes drifting over her shoulder where the sky kissed the water. Beyond the dock my mother stood on, beyond the water behind her, somewhere under that wide-open sky, there was something *drawing* me. Even now, looking at a photograph, I felt the smallest twinge of that pull that had plagued me for as long as I could remember.

I looked up to see Romeo watching me as he unpacked the bottles and placed them on the shelf. "I know that look," he said.

"What look is that?"

"The one that makes you seem as if you're a million miles away even though you're standing right beside me." He set another bottle down. "That pull?" he asked.

I didn't deny it, conceding with a nod. I'd told Romeo about the feeling I couldn't describe. I'd asked him if he remembered my mother talking about something similar since she'd spent some time away in a small town several hours from here, before she had me. Had she felt a pull too? Toward an unknown something that she couldn't name? I sighed. Whether she'd found a form of it or not, I couldn't say. All I knew was that she'd gotten pregnant and returned to Mud Gulch to live out the remainder of her days, far too short though they had turned out to be.

My gaze moved back to the photograph of my mother's beautiful face. *If you can, send me a sign?* I asked her in my mind. Because suddenly, I had this feeling that time was slipping through some fateful hourglass. Or maybe it was just the despondence of watching Ivy League walk away, even though I'd known very well that we were only meant to experience a few brief hours.

I brought the mug to my lips and took a sip, my eyes moving away from my mother's photograph to look out the window, picturing Gage Buchanan as he'd disappeared down the docks and feeling strangely that he'd taken more with him than I knew how to explain.

CHAPTER SEVEN
Gage

I shifted restlessly in the lounge chair and then raised an arm and put it behind my head as I stared out at the shimmering pool in front of me. The water rippled under the patio lights, and my gaze moved from the turquoise of the deep end to the clear water covering the pool stairs. The varying blues were all…wrong.

They were nothing like her eyes.

I let my head fall back on the lounge chair as I stared up at the star-studded sky. *Damn it, stop thinking about her and her eyes. What is wrong with you?* I was already restless, and thinking of a woman I'd had a one-night stand with who lived in a town hours away was totally unproductive.

And completely confounding.

Yes, I'd liked her. Yes, I'd felt a connection. And yes, I'd felt…more like *myself* that night than I had in a long time. Just *me* without the pressures of all my various roles. I'd allowed myself to enjoy everything about Mud Gulch, but it was never meant to last beyond pleasant, temporary memories.

We'd both known that. I'd walked away that morning feeling invigorated and hopeful. Ready to embrace my future with open arms. And yet...those eyes kept popping into my brain every time I tried to focus on something else. *Why?*

I'd engaged in brief trysts before and had never regretted them. But I'd also quickly moved those memories aside and returned to my normal life.

This wasn't like me. All my life, I'd been cool, calm, and collected. If something was expected of me, I did what was necessary with single-minded, composed focus. I'd never waffled or become sidetracked. And because I had been given the tools—by nature and by the luck of who my parents were—I had come to expect success in all areas.

But now? I was feeling antsy and preoccupied. Instead of getting better, that random pinching that sometimes made it difficult to breathe that I'd chalked up to nerves, had gotten worse since I'd left Mud Gulch. Stronger, more insistent somehow.

The ring of laughter from my left interrupted my thoughts and I turned to see my sister, Lexi, stumbling through the gate with her best friend, Blakely, just behind her. "Well look who it is!" Lexi grinned as she teetered my way. "My favorite brother." She leaned down and gave me a quick hug, her perfume, some subtle mix of white peach and vanilla, mixed with the hints of wine still on her breath, wafting over me, and then sat down on the lounger, laying back with a sigh.

"Looks like you two had fun." I smiled as Blakely shot me a grin and a wave and then sat on the edge of the lounger on my other side. "Hey, Blakely. Good to see you."

"Good to see you too. What are you doing here?" she asked, leaning forward and patting my thigh before gathering her hair up as she began twisting it into some sort of knot at the top of her head.

Blakely had been Lexi's best friend since they were in grade school and I'd covered for them in a multitude of ways too many times to count. We'd also done our fair share of partying together when we were in our teens and early twenties, though that had phased out when Lexi moved to New York City to follow her dream of being a singer, and Blakely had gotten engaged to a guy we'd grown up with who now worked with his father at their family-owned insurance company. I lowered the arm that had been behind my head and replaced it with the other. "Just relaxing," I said.

Lexi made a small snorting sound. "That'll be the day. Since when do you relax, Go-Getter?" She yawned, her shoulders rising and falling. "If you were free, you should have come with us tonight."

"I just got off work an hour ago. Late night. I was here delivering some files to Dad that he needs in the morning. How was the party?"

"Ugh. Boring as hell," Lexi said. "I'm forever ruined by New York City nightlife. Nothing compares."

Blakely laughed. "It wasn't that bad."

Lexi made an unimpressed sound in the back of her throat. "The music was total crap. I drank too much wine to make the experience bearable and now I'm practically passing out," she said, pulling herself up. "I've gotta get to bed."

Blakely stood and they hugged. "See you tomorrow." Lexi nodded and blew her a kiss over her shoulder as she turned toward the house. "Goodnight," she sang as she walked away unsteadily. Blakely sank down on the lounger again as the patio door opened and then closed behind us.

"She's in Manhattan a few years and suddenly we're small-town hicks," Blakely said.

I laughed and turned my head toward Blakely. "How are you?" I asked. "Set a wedding date yet?"

There was a short pause. "I broke it off."

"Ah, shit. I'm sorry, Blakley." I didn't see her very often anymore since Lexi had moved, but when I did, she always seemed happy and Lexi hadn't mentioned anything about the breakup. "Are you okay?"

She sighed. "Yeah. I'm fine. It actually happened a few months ago." She played with a tendril of hair that had fallen from the twist she'd somehow secured at the top of her head. "We'd been engaged for six years, Gage. Six *years*! At first, it made sense because we were young and he was so invested in getting his career started. He was putting in crazy hours at the company and I thought it would be hard to focus on a challenging job and a new marriage too, you know?" She paused. "But then, it just seemed like the intensity of his job never lessened, not because he didn't settle into it, but because he liked it that way. It fed something in him. And I was getting older and he was still asking me to wait another year. Always another year. Finally, I had to face that he just wasn't interested in marrying me, not really, and I'd already wasted enough years sitting on his back burner."

I let out a long breath. "It sounds like you were on different pages and it was time to put yourself first." I was glad she had. If I knew anything about men, it was that if they were really in love with a woman, they'd move heaven and earth to keep her.

Blakely nodded but didn't turn toward me. I studied her profile in the dim glow of the outdoor lights. She was so familiar to me even though I hadn't seen her regularly for many years. She was like family, I supposed. I'd known her in every stage of life. I'd watched her grow from a kid to an awkward pre-teen into a beautiful woman.

She stood suddenly and reached her hand out. "Walk with me?"

I grasped it and stood too. I didn't exactly feel like taking a walk, but I didn't exactly feel like reclining either. That restlessness stirred. Maybe movement would help.

We went out the pool gate and walked across the flawless green grass for a few minutes, strolling slowly as the lights from the house grew dimmer and the moon picked up where they left off. When the gazebo came into sight, Blakely laughed softly. "Remember when we got married here?"

I chuckled. "I was ten and you were eight. You held my favorite action figure hostage until I agreed to play wedding with you."

"I'm always trying to get men to marry me against their will, apparently." She shot me a wry smile, but I saw the pain flash in her eyes.

My heart gave a knock. I bumped her shoulder with mine. "I knew where you'd hidden Iron Man. I could have retrieved him anytime and thwarted your evil plot."

She gave a surprised laugh as we stepped up into the gazebo and she took a seat on the bench. I leaned against the open doorframe and moved a tendril of honeysuckle vine out of the way. Its sweet scent filled the air, bringing with it a cascade of memories. I'd played here and later posed for prom pictures with dates I could hardly remember now. I'd kissed a few girls on this bench and gotten to second base with another. "Why didn't you then?" Blakely asked. "Rescue Iron Man and thwart my evil plan?"

I blinked, moving my mind away from the memory of

that first thrill of soft breast under my palm back to Blakely and Lexi's constant requests for me to participate in their make-believe scenarios. "Because I liked being the hero," I said with a smile.

A smile played at Blakely's mouth as she looked at me from under her lashes. I stilled, feeling suddenly confused. Were we…flirting? Where had this come from? Of course I cared for Blakely. And she was sweet and pretty. But…I'd always considered her another little sister.

She ran a finger over the edge of the bench. "Do you ever think about…what we promised at Kate and Tanner's wedding?"

I cast my mind back. That had been…what? Seven years ago when I was twenty-six? And I'd had at least a few cocktails. But it came back to me. Blakely had just broken up with someone then too. It was right before she'd started dating her—now—ex-fiancé. I was single, but happily so. And yet, despite not quite being ready to settle down, I'd been aware that others—namely my parents—were hopeful that my plans would turn in that direction sooner rather than later.

Blakely and I had sat under fairy lights on the patio off the hotel ballroom and we'd jokingly promised to marry each other if we both found ourselves single once we turned thirty. I let out a short laugh, but Blakely's expression didn't change.

My laughter dwindled. "You can't be serious," I said.

She met my eyes and gave a small shrug. "I mean, we're *past* thirty now and not getting any younger." Her lashes lowered before she looked up at me again. "And you can't tell me you didn't know I had a crush on you growing up." She licked her lips. "It's not the worst idea in the world, is it?"

I gaped at her. "You're suggesting getting married? To… each other?"

"Not tomorrow. I'm just…" She played with a ring on her right hand. "Well, I mean, we could consider it. And… see how things…progressed."

I paused, waiting for her to say, *just kidding*! But she only stared as she tilted her head, holding eye contact. "Oh God, you are serious." I took the few steps to the bench and sat next to her. Yes, we'd jokingly made a "pact," and sure, I'd known she had a crush on me when we were younger. But I'd always thought that was just teenage stuff that had fallen by the wayside as we'd matured. We turned toward each other. "Blakely, we've always been like siblings."

"We grew up together, Gage. We're not related."

"Yes, I'm aware. But…why? Why would we marry each other?"

"Because we're *ready* to be married. To start a family. Because despite our best efforts, we're nowhere close to having what we want. Because we're both available. And it doesn't hurt that our parents would be thrilled."

I opened my mouth to argue. but the truth? She wasn't wrong. I'd mentioned the fact that I was hoping to settle down to Lexi, who I guessed had said as much to Blakely at some point. It wasn't a big secret. Hell, I'd made it clear to Travis Hale when we'd both been dating Haven years ago. *Years* ago. They'd gotten married and had a baby and here I was, as available as I'd ever been—available and having one-night stands with women there was absolutely no future with and feeling confused and distracted about it. Not only did I not have what I wanted, I was actually going backward in the *settling down* department.

And yes, our parents *would* be thrilled. In fact, they'd

hinted about it on more than one occasion, which is what had inspired that long-ago promise at our mutual friends' wedding. Who would be more perfect to step into the role of half of a power couple than Blakely Wingate, who'd been part of "high society" since she was born?

I let out a whoosh of breath as I sat back. "This is crazy," I murmured. Only, was it? Maybe it made quite a bit of sense. Maybe it would give me the kick in the ass I needed to get mentally back on track.

Blakely scooted closer. "We don't have to make any promises right now, Gage. Just...live with the idea for a bit. Lexi's going back to New York, so we don't have to worry about her questioning anything until we've made a decision. And if we decide it's a horrible idea—no harm, no foul. It'll just be the silly thing we once talked about and dismissed as ridiculous."

I turned my head and looked at her. Really looked. My gaze moved over her wide brown eyes to her sloped nose, down to her mouth, her top lip fuller than her bottom. Yes, she was a beautiful woman. I'd thought it distantly, the way anyone would about someone they considered family. Perhaps I'd never seen her in a different light because I'd never attempted to. But maybe if I tried to, it would change everything.

I wish you all the luck in finding just what you're looking for. Sometimes, it's closer than you think. The words Haven had said so recently came back to me. Maybe she was right.

Maybe the person I'd been looking for—the one who would help squelch this antsy, unsettled feeling *and* ensure I met the expectation that I carry on the family name—had been right in front of me all along. It would help me set my mind on something—*someone*—tangible, and it would please my parents to no end. I could already picture the joyful excitement on their faces if we broke that kind of news.

Except…

"There's a problem, Blakely. I'm going to London. In a little over two months. I'm moving to oversee the opening of our first international hotel. My dad's put me at the helm."

"Yes," she said. "Lexi told me about that and mentioned the weekend your mother's considering throwing you a going-away party. The fact that you're opening a hotel in London is incredible. You must be so excited."

"I am. But, Blakely, it's not temporary. We're hoping to open up several more in Europe, and eventually other international locations too."

She blinked and was silent for a couple beats before her face lit up in a grin. "I'm in!" she said.

"You'd go?"

She reached out and took my hand in hers and gave it a squeeze. "In a heartbeat," she said. "And think about it, Gage. It would be perfect. We could…" She let go of my hand and laced her own in her lap as she looked down, appearing suddenly shy. "Well, we could get to know each other as a couple away from the prying eyes of Calliope and Pelion."

"What about your job?"

"I'm an online stylist, Gage. I can do that from anywhere. In fact, my clients would probably love it if I was pulling together their looks straight from London."

An online stylist. I had no real idea what that was or if she was serious about it. I guess there were some things I still didn't know about Blakely. Perhaps there was more to her than I'd ever given her credit for.

I ran a finger under my lip, considering. It would take

the pressure off to explore a relationship away from the small-town gossips who'd known us all our lives. And maybe beginning something in a new and different place would help us both see each other as new and different people—help us shrug off that familial connection we'd always had.

And then when—or if—we returned to Calliope for holidays, our foundation as a couple would be well-established.

God, those terms—even though just in my own thoughts—sounded so...businesslike.

But maybe that was only because I'd begun attempting to switch gears where Blakely was concerned about ten minutes ago.

Hadn't most of my life been planned and strategized? Of course I wanted to love my wife, but why couldn't I set my intentions on someone who would meld seamlessly into the life stretched out before me?

"You've given me a lot to think about," I told her.

"I'm going out of town for a couple of weeks in the Hamptons with my parents." Her smile was hopeful and again she reached out and took my hand in hers. "Let's get together when I'm back. And then maybe we plan to wait until your party to make our final decision?"

That seemed pretty last-minute, but it also gave us the maximum amount of time left to think about the proposal. My gaze caught on the row of blue hydrangeas behind the gazebo and I quickly looked back at Blakely, unwilling to let my mind begin obsessing on the shades of each tiny petal. "Deal," I said, reaching out and taking her hand and giving it a shake.

Blakely laughed, moving closer and throwing her arms around me. "Deal," she whispered.

CHAPTER EIGHT
Rory

The box on the upper shelf of my closet contained an undisturbed layer of dust. I lifted it carefully and then brought it to my bed where I sat down, taking a minute to give the dogs laying at my feet a few belly rubs. I sat back against the pillows before lifting the top off what to me was a treasure chest filled with my mother's most personal items.

I'm lost, Mom. I need your guidance.

I *needed* her now and this was all I had. Even though it'd been a long time since I'd held it, the diary on top with the soft leather cover still felt familiar in my hand. My heart squeezed with the echo of grief as I opened it. I missed her desperately. The pages were filled with my mother's loopy handwriting, musings I'd read enough that I could still practically recite them from memory. This particular one began when I was two weeks old, the other diaries piled in the box recounting my mother's life beginning in her teen years until a few days before she died of an aneurysm—a tragic, unexpected loss that had left us reeling. She'd been here one moment, and then gone the very next.

A wistful sigh escaped as I replaced it. There was only one gap in time missing from my mother's writings about her life: the two-and-a-half month period she'd traveled to a nearby tourist lake town where she'd gotten a seasonal job.

The spring she'd gotten pregnant with me.

That diary was present, but the middle section was missing. I picked it up, easily recognizable not only by the pink cover, but also by the fact that it was flimsy and thin. It looked as if the inner binding had come loose, the only pages still intact the first and the last.

I flipped it open, and began reading her hopeful words, missing her desperately, but finding a small amount of comfort in being able to "hear" her voice again.

When I arrived three days ago, Calliope greeted me with the most breathtaking sunset I've ever seen. And that's saying something since I've enjoyed some stunners in Mud Gulch in my nineteen years. It wasn't only the colors of the sky though, it was the way it sparkled off that glass-like water and how the blues and the greens of the lake and surrounding trees all shimmered together under the golden sun. Picturesque but also...magical somehow.

Everywhere I turn in Calliope, there's something beautiful to see. There are perfect sandy beaches with sailboats dotting the horizon. There are restaurant patios with crisp black umbrellas and pots overflowing with colorful flowers on every corner.

But there are also sleek condos with glass balconies that look out onto the water, and sprawling estates with fountains and tennis courts and who knows what else, that can be glimpsed perched on the higher ground behind the town. They call it "Calliope Hills"—and it's obviously where the bigwigs live.

Oh, and speaking of higher ground, I got a job yesterday! I'll be working as a server at the most posh club I've ever set foot in. How they keep all that silk and velvet so pristine, I can't imagine. Fairies who appear in the dark of night, maybe? I was afraid to sit down on the chair when I met with the interviewer! (Who, by the way, had absolutely zero personality.) The club is dim and quiet, and everyone speaks in whispers and honestly, it's a little spooky, but the tips have got to be good in a place like that and so I almost squealed when the woman called to tell me I'd been hired. I didn't squeal until after I hung up though. I have a feeling people like her don't appreciate reactions like that. I wonder if she appreciates any reactions at all. I picture the lady going home from work at the end of the day, climbing into a box and hitting a switch so that she just completely shuts down until it's time to travel back to work and walk stiffly through those silent halls.

Anyway, training starts tomorrow so I'd better get to bed. I'm sitting on the old porch swing of the woman Lys put me in touch with who had a room to rent. The house is right on the town limits between Calliope and Pelion where property is more affordable. Pelion is a beautiful town too, though I haven't seen as much of it. I can see the shore from where I'm sitting and it looks quieter over there, more peaceful maybe, even if I myself prefer the bustle of Calliope. Anyway, I like it here on this lake that shares two towns. And the house where I'm staying is comfortable and clean and no one has to whisper or tiptoe down halls or be afraid to sit on the furniture. It's the type of house I'd like to raise a family in someday.

Thinking about family has me feeling sort of homesick for Mud Gulch. But I'm bound and determined to have a good spring break here and earn the kind of money I can't make in Mud Gulch. That mud didn't put up any kind of fuss when I left, so I imagine I had its permission to go. And Lord it's nice to have a break from that dang bar and those creaky docks.

I have a good feeling about this place too. I see why Lys

loves Pelion so much, even though things have been difficult for her here.

As for me? I sense something wonderful just around the corner.

I closed the diary, wanting to end on that hopeful thought instead of the last page, the day she left Calliope—that had a decidedly different feel. Rufus got up and walked to where I sat, laying down next to me and putting his head on my thigh. I scratched his jaw, tilting my head as I looked him in the eye. No, things in Calliope hadn't ended as wonderfully for my mother as she thought they would, though she insisted I was the best thing that had ever happened to her. But that was because she was my mother and despite the anchor to Mud Gulch I might have represented in her life, she'd loved me, and I'd felt that love until the day she died.

I reached for the top, when I spotted the edge of my baby book at the bottom of the box. It'd been years—over a decade, actually—since I'd looked through it. There was a picture of me as a newborn stuck in the plastic picture holder on the front, and I knew that the inside was filled with recordings of each of my milestones—first smile, first tooth, first steps. My mom had filled in my growth chart, jotted down the foods I'd liked best, and written about the stitches I'd needed in my knee after falling off a swing when I was four. There was love in these pages and I gripped the cover to my chest for a moment, needing that extra dose of motherly affection in the only way I could get it. Sad. Not nearly enough, but not nothing either.

I set the book on the bed beside me, running my hand over Rufus's head as I leafed through the pages, each entry a testament to how much she'd cared for me. "I wish you were here," I murmured. I used my index finger to fan through the remaining pages before putting it away when I noticed something that made me pause. I paged backward to the blank form that would have described my father, from his hair color to his profession. The emptiness of that one page had always made my tummy squeeze uncomfortably. There was still no information there, but what I did see was a cocktail napkin that had been pressed inside. Confused, I picked it up, looking at the unfamiliar logo on the back and then turning it over. I drew in a sudden breath that caused Rufus to startle. "Sorry, boy," I said distractedly, my gaze flying over the lines of the drawing. It was a sketch of my mother, and the date beneath matched the month and year she'd left Mud Gulch. I stared at the art, wide-eyed, wolfing it down with my gaze the way a starving person might ingest a long-awaited meal.

I closed the cover and set the napkin down gently on top, my hand shaking. "Oh my God," I whispered. I'd never seen this before. My mother had to have placed this inside my baby book at some point before she'd died.

And I knew why she'd placed it in that particular spot, even if she hadn't given it to me directly at the time. Maybe she'd thought I was too young. Maybe she'd meant to share more with me later, a later that never came, and this spot seemed like the perfect place to preserve such a precious item.

A wave of emotion rolled over me, the feeling that I'd asked my mother for guidance and she'd led me here, to this napkin pressed between the pages of my history. And if that was the case, then she meant me to go further.

My gaze hung on the sketch of my mother's beautiful face, so many questions racing through my mind that I had no way to have answered. But maybe...that was because the answers weren't here in Mud Gulch. Maybe the answers were in that town my mother had visited so long ago, the one where this sketch had been created, the one where she'd met a man and made me.

My mother had never told me or my uncles whether my father knew about me or not, but even if he did and had chosen not to pursue a relationship with me at the time, perhaps he regretted that now. And even if that wasn't the case, I had a right to know who I was, didn't I? Why shouldn't I at least try to fill in the gaps of my history now that I had a lead? One my mother had left for me. I turned my head, staring mostly unseeing out the window, allowing an idea that perhaps had always been floating at the edge of my mind to form: what if...what if he was the pull? My father. His existence calling to me over time and distance.

Rufus yawned and I stroked his ear, a plan already taking shape. My mind whirred, details clarifying rapidly and a person who might help immediately coming to mind. I had an angle now in this casual sketch, this singular piece of art.

My night with Gage had rattled something inside of me. I had seized the opportunity a couple of nights before because I had wanted it—I'd wanted *him*—and I didn't regret it. And now another opportunity was right in front of me. Wouldn't I be a fool if I didn't seize this one as well while I still could?

"What do you think, boy?" I asked Rufus as I stroked his ear. "Could there be something wonderful waiting for me out there?"

Again, Gage's face flashed in my mind. But I quickly moved it away. Gage had been a temporary—albeit extremely pleasant—distraction. I was seeking something far more permanent.

I picked up my phone and FaceTimed Cash. A moment later, his rugged, bearded face filled the screen. I could see that he was sitting at the bar and I caught a glimpse of Romeo working behind him. My uncle was clearly already looking for things to do if he was hanging at Cakes and Ale at four o'clock on a weekday. I grinned. "Hi."

In answer, Cassius gave me a raise of his dark brow. "I know that grin. What are you about to ask me for?"

"Cash..." I began as Romeo leaned in from the side.

Cassius's brow dipped. "Here we go."

"Since you're home for the next couple months anyway, do you think you could watch the brood?"

For a moment, both my uncles looked completely perplexed. "Me?" Cassius finally said.

"Whoa. What's this about?" Romeo asked, knocking Cassius slightly to the side to which he received a glare from his big brother.

"I'm not the person to watch your brood. I know sea creatures, not dogs," Cash insisted, his gaze returning to me as he used his shoulder to assert his place front and center of the screen.

"Dogs are easy," I told him. "Just feed them, walk them, and scratch their bellies and they'll give you their undying devotion. They're pack animals. They'll just be happy to have you there."

"Romeo, tell this girl whatever she's thinking isn't a good idea," Cassius said.

How often had I heard that very phrase over the years, tossed from one uncle to the other? I'd been a mischievous kid, and a stubborn teen. But this wasn't about some whimsical idea I'd gotten in my head five minutes ago. I'd been carrying questions inside about who I really was my whole life. The answers I might find could be life-changing. And I'd just been presented a tangible lead. "Just a short vacation," I said.

Romeo was staring at me through the screen, a look on his face that was both sad and sort of hopeful. "I think you should go," he said softly.

My mouth dropped open and Cassius turned his head to glare at Romeo. "You do?" God, of course he did. Because he never got his own opportunity to go, and he wanted to make sure I got mine, even if it was a short jaunt away, and then back again. *I'm going to make this up to you, Romeo Casteel.* "You know I love you, right?"

"Yeah," he said, his smile soft before he elbowed Cassius. "I'll help this big lug out with the brood because, honestly? They're probably going to tuck their tails and run when they see him advancing on them. Go."

Cash made some grumbling sounds but didn't resist more than that, finally giving me a practically imperceptible tilt of his chin that I knew was his form of concession. I blew them both a kiss. Romeo took the phone from Cassius. "I'll take care of things here," he said. "Go follow that pull. Wherever it may lead."

CHAPTER NINE
Gage

"Oh hello, darling. I didn't know you were here," my mother said as she removed her gardening gloves and tossed them on the umbrella-shaded patio table.

I glanced up at my mom from where I was sitting on the pool lounger, tapping my fingertips together. "Just getting a few laps in." I paused for a minute as I watched the aquamarine water ripple. "Do you know anything about the color blue?"

She let out a small, confused laugh. "I wouldn't call myself the foremost expert on the subject, but—"

"That slip of sky right above the trees there," I said, shielding my eyes from the sun and pointing upward. "What would you call that?"

My mom gave me a semi-concerned look and then shielded her own eyes and squinted upward. "Baby blue?"

"No," I muttered. "That's not right."

She placed her hands on her hips. "Um, hmm. Sky blue?"

"Well, naturally. But…no."

"Cornflower?"

"Uh-uh."

She let out a short laugh. "Sorry, Gage. I'm out of guesses. What's this about? And why haven't you shaved?"

I ran my fingers over my chin. "It's just scruff, Mom. It's a look." I glanced back to her and gave her an apologetic head shake. "Sorry. It's…ah, an advertising campaign I'm working on. It's giving the team trouble." I picked up the glass next to me and took a sip of the whiskey I'd poured from my dad's stash in the pool house. I didn't drink very often, and definitely not before dinner, but damn it, that antsy feeling I'd been fighting had only increased in the last week and I felt like I might combust.

My mother eyed the drink. "Well, you'll figure it out. You always do. But if you want to ask a person who knows more about shades of blue than I do, I'm meeting with the perfect someone in the conservatory in about ten minutes. Do you know Faith Lorenz who owns the art gallery downtown?"

"I've met her a time or two. Why's she coming by?" I asked, my gaze lifting to that small portion of sky. The blue was mostly right, but also sort of not. I let out a sound of frustration and set the drink back on the side table and stood up. *Damn it. Why are you obsessing about naming the blue of some woman's eyes who you'll never see again? What is the point other than giving yourself a migraine?*

"She's bringing an art appraiser with her who just started at the gallery last week. Faith sent out a letter to her customers who might have some art that they'd like looked at. I pulled some pieces out of the attic. I've no idea where they came from but—" The distant sound of the front doorbell chiming from inside interrupted my mother and she looked back at the house. "That must be them now. Stop by and say hi."

"Maybe," I muttered to my mother's retreating back as she breezed toward the house. I had no intention of stopping by the conservatory. I didn't know Faith very well and I was in no mood for small talk about dusty paintings found in our attic. Exercise hadn't worked, neither had the whiskey. I'd take a quick shower, and then I'd head over to the club and smack some tennis balls around to let out some aggression. Maybe that would help.

What I *could* be occupying my mind with was what Blakely and I had discussed. But despite telling her I'd think about her proposal, my mind simply hadn't moved in that direction since a few days before. Perhaps I was going to have to be intentional about considering the idea. Because it made sense on several fronts. And I knew how many people it would please, even if it had basically come completely out of the blue.

Blue…

I groaned as I brought my hands to my temples and massaged. Yes, I *would* think about Blakely's proposal, just not this particular moment. There was no rush. The timeline we'd discussed still left plenty of time, and I thought it best to allow things to percolate naturally anyway, even if I was desperate to turn my thoughts to anything other than naming a confounding shade of blue strictly from memory.

I went inside the pool house and took off my swimsuit, the sounds of muted voices walking past the open French doors that led to the patio barely drifting to where I stood. I reached for a towel and wrapped it around my waist when I heard a laugh ring out and then fade away. My head snapped up and I dropped the towel as I whipped toward the familiar sound.

That was…

But no.

It couldn't be.

There was no way.

You're hearing things, Buchanan. That's how much that damn woman got under your skin.

And yet, even so, I'd hastily picked up the towel and wrapped it around my waist again, my feet moving toward the place where that bubbly laughter had come from before I'd even made a conscious decision to do so. I moved across the patio and entered the house, standing in the hall and listening. There it was again, that laughter. And that *fragrance.* I recognized it—it lingered in the air. My gut clenched and I rounded the corner, the chatter growing louder, and then stepped into the doorway of the sunlit conservatory.

Singular blue orbs behind a pair of eyeglasses met my shocked gaze. My heart leaped and my mouth dropped open as she began blinking rapidly. I stared, almost not able to believe my own eyes. Her hair was swept up in some sort of sleek updo and she was wearing a navy-blue pencil skirt, one slim leg crossed demurely over the other, and an off-white, silky blouse buttoned up to the base of her throat, a creamy string of pearls circling the collar. If I hadn't seen the flare of recognition in her lens-covered gaze, I would have thought this woman was the conservative twin of the spunky, blue-jean clad *bar wench* I'd met.

The one I'd had mind-blowing sex with on a pool table.

The one I'd been dreaming about almost every night since.

The one I'd been trying—mostly unsuccessfully—to get out of my head for a week and two days now.

My instinct was to rush toward her, but the way she was looking at me—with barely-suppressed panic—held my feet to the portion of floor I was currently standing on.

My bare feet.

I glanced down.

In my haste at following that laugh, I'd forgotten I was only wearing a towel.

"Oh, Gage, darling," my mother said, turning in her chair, obviously following the gazes over her shoulder of the other two women across from her. She brought her hand to her chest, her eyes widening as she took me in. "My goodness, you're not dressed." She quickly composed herself. "Well. I'm, er, glad you decided to stop by. You remember Faith Lorenz, don't you? And this is Aurora Castle. She's the art appraiser I mentioned who works for Faith's gallery. She's going to take a look at a few pieces I found in storage." She gestured toward the three or four paintings leaning against a side table near the door. "Aurora, this is my son, Gage. He was just swimming which is the reason for the, um, lack of clothing."

An *art* appraiser? I almost choked out a laugh but caught myself as she suddenly stood, walking the short distance from where she'd been sitting and holding out her hand to me.

"Gage *Buchanan*?" Her eyes flared again, and I saw her throat move as she swallowed.

"That's right," I said, watching her closely. She appeared to have paled a few shades. She knew she was caught red-handed. *Good*.

"Mr. Buchanan. So nice to meet you," she said after a stilted moment where I watched her gather herself. The words came out in a rush and I narrowed my eyes at her as she pushed the glasses up her pert nose and I took her hand, enveloping it in mine. It was ice-cold.

"*Aurora,* was it?" I asked, giving her a wry tip of my lips. "Castle, you said? A regal choice for an alias. What brings you to town, Ms. *Castle*?"

"Gage!" My mother let out a short, embarrassed-sounding laugh. "What's gotten into you?"

I ignored my mother and Rory cleared her throat as she attempted to pull her hand away, but I gripped it more tightly. What in the hell was she playing at here? Was she some kind of scam artist? Had she weaseled her way into a job that would provide her access to the attics of wealthy estate owners? And how and why had her grift brought her *here*? "No alias. And please, call me Aurora." She gave her hand a yank and I let it go, causing her to have to take a step back to keep herself from tumbling over.

I raised a brow as she shot a slightly panicked look over at Faith who was staring in confusion. "Hi, Faith," I said. "Nice to see you."

"Gage," Faith greeted, the small frown tipping into a smile. Her gaze moved down my half-naked body. "You look…very well."

"Oh, I am," I said, looking back at Rory. "Very well. And I believe we've met before."

Rory let out a tinkling laugh that faded quickly as she shook her head. "No, I'm absolutely sure we—"

"Yes, the more I look at you, the more certain I am." I took my bottom lip into my mouth momentarily, casting my eyes upward as though recalling. "Are you by chance…" I clasped my hands behind my back and circled her slowly. "Of any relation at all to the Buffalobeams?"

She let out a small snort and then covered her mouth with two fingers. I faced her again, narrowing my eyes. *Little liar. Beautiful little liar.* I wanted to shake her and kiss her and I was so damn happy to see her and pissed off at the same time. Disappointed. Angry. Confused. She dropped her hands and shook her head. "No. No relation to the... Buffalobeams."

"She looked familiar to me too," my mother said. "Aurora is from New York, so perhaps we saw her in passing at some event when we were there to visit Lexi. In any case, it's too bad Lexi just left or I'd have introduced you to her, Aurora. You never can have too many friends, am I right?"

Rory bobbed her head enthusiastically like my mother had just made the most inspirational statement ever uttered.

Faith stood. "Well, Aurora. We should go. We have that other...appointment at..." She glanced at her wrist and seemed almost surprised to see it was completely devoid of any time-telling device. "Well, soon."

"Digging around in more attics?" I practically growled.

Aurora let out another thin laugh devoid of any humor. "One never knows what treasures might be gathering dust right under one's own roof."

"Mm. And you're here to uncover those treasures for just such a person? I wonder what you get out of the deal exactly. Perhaps looking to hijack as many *family jewels* as possible?" I said, my jaw tight.

"Gage!" my mother said again. "How much have you had to drink? You're not acting like yourself." She stood and came over to me and leaned in as though to investigate the strength of the alcohol on my breath.

Faith and Rory took the opportunity to scoot past both me and my mother, Faith picking up the small stack of paintings near the door. "Thank you again, Mrs. Buchanan," Faith called. "I'll be in touch."

Rory shot me one last flustered—but also somewhat

defiant—look before practically running out the door behind Faith.

Oh no you don't.

My mother held me back by placing her palm on my forehead, her second thought after me potentially being drunk was obviously that I was feverish. She let out what sounded like a relieved breath. "Yes, you definitely feel warm," my mother was saying. "And your neck is all flushed!"

I turned, attempting to follow the two shysters out the door. Faith was obviously in on this too. Their connection wasn't yet clear. And again, why here? Was it simply the wealth of this community that had drawn her? Too bad for her that I knew her real identity. Or did I? Had that been some sort of cover too? Did she just move from town to town working when she needed to and thieving when she could? My mother's hand clamped down on my arm "I'm going to call your father and tell him you're unwell. Your manners are always perfect. I knew something was wrong. Take a sick day tomorrow. No work for you, Mister."

"Mom. I'm fine. I've gotta go." *I've gotta catch a lying little thief.*

The pit of disappointment deepened. She was a fake. A phony. A fraud. And yet, that night in Mud Gulch had felt like the realest thing I'd experienced in years. Maybe ever. What a blind fool I was.

"Absolutely not. I'll have Florence make you a bowl of soup and—"

I pulled my arm as gently as I could, her hand falling away. "Mom, I'm fine. Honestly. I'll call you later." I offered her a smile that felt strangely stretched and the way she drew her head back told me I'd missed the reassuring smile mark and instead landed somewhere in the territory of Pennywise the Clown. "Bye, Mom. I love you!"

"I love you too, darling. Aren't you going to get dressed?" she called, a note of clear confusion in her voice, as I raced through the foyer as fast as I could in a snug towel tied around my waist. I flung the front door open and ran down the steps, but Faith's car was already halfway down the long drive and moving quickly away. I thought about racing after it. I'd been a track star in high school and college and was still in great shape. Amazing shape, actually. I could definitely catch up, especially where the road narrowed near—

What the hell is wrong with you, Buchanan?

I paused, huffing out the breath I'd pulled in in preparation for takeoff. *You're seriously considering chasing down a woman in a car like some hound dog? Who are you?*

I gave my head a shake, pulling myself slowly straight and smoothing my hands down my terrycloth-clad hips. *Deep breath.* I was just acting irrationally because I'd been shocked and was still scrambling to understand the situation at hand.

But really? There was no need to run after Aurora Castle, or whatever her real name was, because I knew exactly where to find her.

CHAPTER TEN
Rory

"Wait. *Gage Buchanan* is pool table guy?" Faith asked, her mouth dropping open after I'd told her how I knew the man whose family estate we'd recently left, the one who'd made it obvious he knew me.

I groaned, and then practically threw myself on the black velvet chaise lounge which was situated at the back of Faith's gallery. I heard a crack and pulled out the fake glasses that I'd worn to look studious. Another element of "Aurora Castle, art appraiser," snapped in two. I tossed them aside. "The universe is playing a practical joke on me!"

Faith nodded, taking a seat on one of the two chairs across from where I was sprawled. "It's really the only explanation," she agreed. "You must have been a real villain in a past life. Dr. Evil or The Joker."

"Or Genghis Khan."

She laughed.

I let out another groan and covered my face. No one should look at me. I was the reincarnation of a real-life criminal. There was no other explanation. Karma had found me at last.

"You never asked where pool table guy lived?" she asked.

I shook my head miserably. "No. And when I glanced at his credit card, I only looked at his first name. His friend gave me the information for their car that broke down, and it was a Connecticut plate. I just figured it was where they were all from. Honestly, I didn't think a lot about it and I tried to avoid details." I pulled myself up so I was in a sitting position. "I didn't really want to know."

Faith blew out a breath. "Okay, well this definitely complicates the plan."

The plan. I gave her a weak smile. She'd been kind to say yes to my request for help. Faith was the daughter of a woman my mother had met during the short time she'd lived in Calliope. They'd become friends and had remained so for the duration of my mom's life. Faith's mother, Donna, had brought Faith to Mud Gulch for my mother's funeral and even though it was an obviously difficult time for me, Faith and I had hit it off and we had kept in touch over the years, mostly via email and through social media.

Donna had eventually remarried and moved away to Florida, but her daughter had stayed and opened an art gallery a few years before. When I'd proposed pretending to be an appraiser who worked for her gallery in an effort to gain access to art that might be gathering dust in specific attics, she was game. As a matter of fact, I sensed that Faith was excited about engaging in a bit of a treasure hunt, perhaps because of the artistic troves that might by lying in wait, or perhaps because the life of a gallery owner didn't provide quite the adventure she craved.

She'd reassured me that though the old money crowd

knew her well from the art-focused charity events she frequented, they preferred Sotheby's over the current artists she showcased and that her gallery wasn't dependent on their patronage, or lack thereof.

So, here I was, pretending to be an art appraiser in the town where the man I'd recently had sex with on the pool table at my family bar lived. The man who knew very well I was *not* an art appraiser from New York City or anywhere else. The man who would naturally want to know what scheme I was running.

The plan hadn't only been made more complicated. It'd been completely compromised. "It's over," I said dejectedly.

"No it's not," Faith said. "We only need to visit four more homes, and we have appointments at two. We'll just keep a low profile until we can gain access to the others."

I shook my head. "We won't be able to keep a low profile. He'll expose me." And why shouldn't he? I was obviously lying to these people who'd kindly welcomed me into their homes to dig through their personal possessions. I wasn't doing it to harm anyone or damage their property in any way. I just wanted to get a glimpse of what might be locked away somewhere, just waiting to be discovered. Not any art pieces themselves, but the name scrawled in a corner—a small hidden corner that might provide a clue. *The* clue. An identification.

But Gage wouldn't necessarily see it as an innocent investigation.

And maybe it wasn't.

Because the truth was, I was gaining people's trust through deception.

And yet the reason my heart had squeezed with both shock and deep disappointment was not because of being found out by Gage, but because of discovering who he was. Who he *might* be.

I groaned again. *Oh, God.*

"I don't think he'll expose you," she said. "He could have done that today and he didn't. Speaking of being exposed, though," she went on, "did you see his *body* in that towel? Holy hell." She paused. "Wait, of course you saw his body. You had sex with him on a pool table!"

"Yes," I said. "Yes I did." I met her eyes, waiting for the moment reality dawned for her.

Faith's brow was knitted, eyes squinted as she obviously considered the situation. "Oh, God," she said after a minute, her eyes popping wide. "Gage might be—"

"Yes!" I wailed in misery.

She clapped a hand over her mouth and kept it there for several moments before lowering it and looking at me sadly. "Definitely Genghis Khan," she whispered.

"Sorry I had to reschedule, dears," Mrs. Bellamy said. "But there was an unavoidable conflict that arose yesterday with the Ladies League." She swept her hand over the silver tea service on the coffee table between us. "Tea?"

"Yes, thank you," Faith said, and Mrs. Bellamy nodded to the housekeeper who stepped forward to pour cups of tea from the sterling silver pitcher. "I appreciate you making time for us at all, Mrs. Bellamy. I realize your schedule is quite full."

There was an awkward silence as the housekeeper finished pouring the tea and handed it to each of us in turn before giving Mrs. Bellamy a slight smile and departing. Why in the world you would want someone else to pour tea that was sitting right in front of you, I had no idea. Did it simply make these people feel catered to? And being catered to in all aspects made one feel important, I imagined.

Judgy, Rory. When these might be your *people.* My gaze slid to the painting over the fireplace of the distinguished older man next to the woman I guessed was supposed to be Mrs. Bellamy. As it turned out, very wealthy people used their own version of Instagram filters, even if they paid quite a bit more for them. Mr. Bellamy was tall and slender, his head long and his features hawkish. He appeared both wise and powerful, but if he was kind, he didn't convey it in his expression nor his eyes. I tilted my head, looking for *anything* about him that might be familiar, but didn't see so much as a similarly shaped nostril.

But I was the spitting image of my mother, from her features to her coloring, to the shape of her body. I was glad of it because to me, she'd been beautiful, but in this instance, it hardly helped.

When I looked back at Mrs. Bellamy, I saw that she was watching me as I stared at her husband's likeness. She moved her gaze away and raised her pinkie finger and took a dainty sip from the delicate, floral cup before setting it down.

I offered a placid smile and raised my own cup, my pinkie bent awkwardly as I tried my best to mimic the older woman's mannerisms, the scalding liquid causing me to slurp and sputter, the cup clattering back to the saucer as I sucked my burnt lip into my mouth. *Ouch.*

Faith's thigh bumped mine as Mrs. Bellamy looked down her nose at me. "You look familiar, Ms. Castle. Have we met?"

I shook my head. "I can't imagine where we would have, Mrs. Bellamy. I only arrived in town two days ago."

She made a distracted clicking sound. "Well, in any case, I was delighted to hear that we have an art appraiser in town. Our attic is full to the brim of furniture and art from decades past. The first Bellamys arrived on the Mayflower, you know."

Faith hummed, and I made what I hoped were the appropriate sounds of being highly interested and deeply impressed. "I'm excited to be expanding my business, Mrs. Bellamy," Faith said. "And so pleased that I can offer even more services to the fine clientele of Calliope. My mission, of course, is highlighting up-and-coming New England artists. But when Aurora contacted me looking to relocate, I loved the idea of offering appraisals, so I'm hopeful things will work out."

"Yes, excellent. Expansion and business diversification is sound business. I imagine you'll have your fair share of work considering the history of the families in this town." The older woman took another dainty sip of tea. I wondered how she wasn't burning her own mouth. There must be some special technique taught in private schools.

I tapped my foot, already bored silly by this idle chitchat. My gaze slid to the canvas bag by the door that Mrs. Bellamy had had several pieces of art packed up in for us to "appraise." I did feel sort of bad about the fact that my "appraisals" were going to be limited at best. I'd do some internet research and see what I could find on each piece, but for all I knew, I'd miss the fact that one of these paintings was a priceless masterpiece.

Not that these people needed the money.

Set your guilt aside, Rory. You deserve to know where you came from. And if one of these men chose *to abandon you…well, he owes you an explanation at the very least.*

I heard the distant ringing of the front door chime just as a little black furball in a plaid sweater came trotting into the room and I sucked in a breath, bending over and extending my hand as I called to the little fellow. He ran directly to me and I scooped him up in my arms and placed him on my lap. "Well, hello. Aren't you a cutie? What's your name?"

"Bartholomew!" Mrs. Bellamy scolded. "You bad dog. Scat now. Where's Marta?" She looked over her shoulder. "Marta!"

The front door chimed again. "Oh, it's okay," I said, scratching Bartholomew under his chin as he looked up at me. I could see by his white chin whiskers that he was an elderly dog. "You're a proper gentleman, aren't you?"

He yapped once in response.

"Oh goodness. He's been in a *mood* since his nanny went on maternity leave," Mrs. Bellamy said before she called for this Marta again. "Where is she?" Mrs. Bellamy murmured. "Bartholomew!" She snapped at him and then pointed at the floor next to her. He looked over his shoulder at her and then jumped from my lap, his head held high as he walked over to her and lay down on the carpet, crossing his paws regally. "Marta simply doesn't have the time to cater to him. I think he misses his walks," she said.

Bartholomew had a *nanny*? "If you need someone to walk him, I'd be happy to," I said.

"Oh, no. I couldn't ask that of you, dear," Mrs. Bellamy said. "You're here to work at the gallery."

"Yes, but I love animals. I left my own dogs with a family member and I miss them already. I've been walking Faith's dog, Coco, in the mornings to get some exercise—I'd be happy to include Bartholomew. I could come by tomorrow morning at seven?"

"If you'd like to, you're certainly more than welcome," Mrs. Bellamy said. "Marta has a dog too if you'd like to take her along."

"Oh, I'd love that."

"Very well. I'll have Marta have their leashes ready."

"Thank you," I said, my face breaking into a smile. I shot Bartholomew a wink and I swore that little dog rolled his eyes.

"I'm so sorry, Mrs. Bellamy. There was a situation in the kitchen," the woman who rushed into the room said, her hair in slight disarray.

"That's all right, Marta. Please answer the door and then come collect Bartholomew."

"I just answered the door but there's no one there," Marta said as she smoothed her hair quickly. "They must have left."

"Speaking of which," Faith said, standing, "we should go too and leave you to your afternoon plans."

I began standing when movement at the window made me suck in a breath. I clapped a hand over my mouth as a familiar face peered in the glass, eyes narrowing as he caught sight of me.

Mrs. Bellamy sucked in a startled breath. "Is that Gage Buchanan?" she asked as she brought a hand to her chest. "My goodness, he scared the wits out of me."

Gage knocked on the glass and pointed at me, mouthing something.

"Well, we'll go now," Faith said breathlessly, pulling on me so that I stumbled after her. But my head remained turned, eyes wide and glued to Gage. What was he going to do? Call me out here and now in front of Mrs. Bellamy? Call out *Faith*? God, this plot twist in our plan had really complicated things.

But I couldn't let this affect Faith. "Mrs. Bellamy, do you have a back door we can use?"

"A back door? Why ever—"

Gage knocked at the window again, what he was mouthing now clear. *Stay there.* He disappeared, likely heading back to the front door where Marta would let him in.

"That man at the window thinks I'm someone I'm not," I said in a rush.

"I'm worried Gage has a drinking problem," Faith said as she picked up the bag of art. "The last time we saw him, he was running around half-naked."

"Drinking problem? Gage Buchanan? Absolutely not. He's one of the most upstanding men in Calliope—"

"Mrs. Bellamy, he's in your garden knocking on your window."

She frowned. "He did look quite agitated." The doorbell started chiming. "And you do have to scale a stone wall to get into that garden." She paused for only a moment. "I'll call his mother. These things should be dealt with quickly and quietly. Turn right down the hall and there's a back door off the kitchen that circles around to the driveway."

"Thank you, Mrs. Bellamy," Faith called as we fast-walked out of the room, breaking into a run when we entered the hall, and swallowing down nervous giggles. Thank God someone was baking something sweet in the kitchen because the heavenly scent of sugar and cinnamon told us exactly where to turn.

"Just passing through," Faith called to the surprised-looking man who was taking a Bundt cake out of the oven. I noticed his hair looked like someone's fingers had recently been running through it. Apparently, there was some hanky-panky going on in the Bellamys' kitchen. I waved at the man and then we opened the back door and burst out into the summer sunshine, hurrying along the side of the house and peeking around to the driveway where Faith's car sat.

"Go!" Faith said and we both ran for the car, the sound of voices coming from behind us as Gage spoke to Mrs. Bellamy. I glanced back. Was he telling her that I was a liar? Would the police show up at Faith's gallery tonight? All I had was my word against his and absolutely zero proof of my credentials because they didn't actually exist.

I groaned, my head hitting the headrest as Faith started the car and began to drive. I looked over my shoulder to see Gage who had turned from the door at the sound of the car. He stood there, his expression unreadable in the glare of the sun, the lines of his body still somehow familiar even though I'd only known him for a few brief hours. I felt a pang in the region of my chest. What a mess I'd already made.

CHAPTER ELEVEN
Gage

She was good, I'd give her that. She'd successfully evaded me for three days now. I'd gone to Faith's gallery on four separate occasions; the night before, the lights had gone off right before I'd rung the bell.

After my mother had suggested I might have a drinking problem—as if she didn't know me better than that—apparently, Faith had parroted this after I'd climbed Mrs. Bellamy's garden wall and appeared at the window like a stalker. And…fine, I couldn't blame them for looking for an explanation for such out-of-character behavior. I'd acted like a fool. And I never acted like a fool. I ground my back teeth. Even so, I wasn't going to publicly accuse Faith of aiding and abetting Rory without proof. Perhaps she'd lied to Faith about who she was as well. Maybe Faith really did think I had a drinking problem.

Maybe I was just hoping that there was some other explanation. And that hope was making me act like a lunatic even I didn't recognize anymore.

I pulled up to the curb in front of a popular Calliope restaurant and hopped out of my car, handing the keys to the valet. There was a small crowd near the front, customers who'd obviously just left and were chatting and snapping some photos as they waited for their car. I recognized Archer and Bree Hale who owned the neighboring town of Pelion and were posing with their twin sons and younger daughter as Haven Hale, a pack on her chest holding her sleeping baby, held her phone up and made goofy faces that were making the boys, at least, laugh for the photographs. Travis Hale was standing off to the side, watching Haven with that same expression she'd had at the coffee shop a few weeks before—the one that suggested an imminent medical emergency that would require resuscitation. It might be in both their best interests to carry smelling salts as a precaution. "Gage," Travis greeted me. "How are you?"

I stopped and took his extended hand. I considered Travis a friend even though, despite that I was a grade below him, he and I had always had a competitive relationship since we were teens running in the same circles. He'd always appeared polished, but in actuality had sharp edges that he hid well until you brushed up against them and got injured. A lot had happened since those days though—then Haven had come to town and inspired Travis to take accountability for the hurtful way he'd treated others, namely his half brother with the scar on his throat currently posing with his smiling wife, giggling boys, and solemn daughter. "I'm good. Celebrating something?" I asked. The Hale family lived and worked in Pelion, though they sometimes came to Calliope for some occasion or another, as this side of the lake offered more of a variety of restaurants that would accommodate groups of people.

"Yeah. It's Bree's birthday."

"Ah." I squinted at him. "And how's the cat-chasing?"

His mouth flattened and he glanced back at his wife, now doing a funny little dance as the small girl in Bree's arms continued to look unimpressed, yawning and putting her head on her mother's shoulder. "Haven told you about that, did she?"

"She did." I couldn't help the smirk.

"Don't worry, Buchanan, someday you'll be chasing down cats too."

"I'm not sure why you feel the need to threaten me, Hale."

"Ha."

"Gage!" Haven said as she put the phone away. "So good to see you."

"Hi, Haven." I looked behind her and smiled at Bree and Archer and signed hello. "Happy birthday, Bree."

"Thanks, Gage," she said as Archer signed hello back, both of them immediately turning toward the two boys when they realized they'd taken advantage of their parents' attention being directed elsewhere to begin climbing the wrought iron trellis on the front wall of the restaurant. Archer grabbed each of them around the waist as the boys erupted in squeals of laughter when their father tickled their ribs until they let go, collapsing backward against his chest.

"How was the guys' trip?" Haven asked as the baby on her chest began to fuss.

"Unexpected," I answered.

She gave me a confused little laugh, bouncing the baby whose cries became more insistent. "Well, I hope in good ways. Oh, here's our car. We better get these kids to bed.

It's way past their bedtime and the meltdown is beginning. Wish us luck."

"Good luck. Nice to see you all," I said as their group bustled toward the car, the giggling boys still clamped under their father's arms, their laughter mingling with the cries of Travis and Haven's son, all the adults talking over each other, and the little girl sitting regally on her mother's hip observing it all.

I turned back to the restaurant, and a doorman swung the door wide, giving me a nod as I passed through. "I'm meeting my parents," I told the hostess when she greeted me.

"Yes, Mr. Buchanan. They are already seated in a booth at the back of the room on the left."

"Thank you." I headed in the direction they were sitting, loosening my tie slightly as I walked. It'd been a long day—made longer by the fact that I'd wanted to leave and try to corner "Aurora" and I hadn't had an opportunity. But a dinner with my parents would be good. I'd convince them I was fine, that my behavior over the last couple of days was solely due to my busy schedule and lack of sleep, and put them at ease.

When I rounded the corner, I saw that three people were standing next to my parents' booth, both their heads turned as they smiled up at me. *Shit.*

"Gage!" Blakely greeted, stepping away from her own parents and giving me a quick hug.

"Blakely, hi. You're back."

"I've been back since yesterday, silly. I've been calling you."

Damn. I'd seen that. I'd meant to call her back. I'd just been…stalking someone. "Sorry. Work's been…insane." I turned to her parents. "Mr. Wingate. Mrs. Wingate. Nice to see you."

Mr. Wingate shook my hand and Mrs. Wingate pulled me into a hug. "Gage," she said after she'd let go. "We were just leaving, but it's so nice to see you." She gave me a conspiratorial wink. "We do hope we'll be seeing quite a bit more of you soon."

"Mom," Blakely said, her cheeks coloring as her gaze shot to me. "Sorry, I might have mentioned—"

"Oh, Blakely," her mother said, "Gage doesn't mind that we know." She grinned at my mother who put her fingers over her lips as if to hold back a smile. "We all think it's wonderful."

Wonderful? What was wonderful? My eyes held on Blakely as it dawned on me. Oh God, they were referring to our conversation about getting married. I felt a stab of annoyance. We'd agreed to discuss it when we got back from our trips, not to share it with anyone else, especially our families.

My mother laughed and gave my arm a squeeze. "Wonderful, indeed, but we'll wait for you young people to let us know if we should pop the champagne."

I chuckled uncomfortably, and Blakely gave me an apologetic look, and then mouthed "Sorry." I held back any response that might escalate matters. The pressure of our parents knowing about a possible relationship between me and Blakely hadn't been a factor when I'd agreed to think about it. Now…now it wasn't just a decision that would affect us—our families would have a reaction to the choice we made too.

And if the hopeful looks on our parents' faces were any indication, they would be highly disappointed should we choose not to pursue a romance.

But I swallowed down my irritation and gave Blakely a small smile meant to be reassuring. Because now that I was witness to the clear approval shining from my mother and father, I was again confronted with the thought that it made some sense. I obviously had terrible taste in women. It'd been years since I'd made the decision that I wanted to settle down and I *still* hadn't met *the one.* Then the first woman who'd really caught my eye in forever was a liar. And yet I'd been obsessing over her for weeks.

I was about to make a life-changing move, a team of people across the ocean were depending on me, my father had put every bit of his faith in me, my parents very obviously wanted grandchildren, and here I was distracted by a little scammer. Obviously *I* was the problem here.

The sound of the Hale twins' laughter rang in my ears, the vision of the two families out celebrating a life milestone together front and center in my mind. Suddenly, predictable sounded good. Calm. Boring, even. The deep satisfaction of making my parents proud and fulfilling the duty they'd lovingly set before me. The tradition of joining two families together who had the money and influence to make the community a better place. It was at least something to consider and yet all I'd been doing was chasing down a woman who'd obviously played me. "I'll call you," I told her, leaning forward and grazing her cheek with my lips. I lingered for a moment as I breathed in her scent. Flowery and familiar. *Blakely.* It was exactly what I needed. Perhaps she was too.

The Wingates said their goodbyes, Mrs. Wingate telling my mother she'd see her at the club the next day and Mr. Wingate reminding my father to send over the stock tip he'd mentioned. Blakely gave me another small hug, her perfume floating in the air even after the three of them had swept off and turned the corner out of sight.

I sank down into the booth next to my mother, picked up the glass of water in front of me on the table and downed the whole thing in one gulp and then set it back down. "I need a drink," I mumbled. "Something strong."

"Now, Gage, I don't think that's a good idea," my mother said.

"Mom, I don't have a drinking problem, okay? Despite… recent behavior, everything is fine with me." I felt my jaw tense as I looked over at her. "Haven't I proven to you that I'm more stable than that?" *All my life. That's all I've done. I've never slipped, never failed, not once.*

My father frowned. "Of course you have, son. We both know how steady and competent you are. But…work has been intense lately, and the move to London, including everything that has to be accomplished before then, has got to have you feeling at least a little anxious."

I released a breath, massaging the small pinch in my chest. For a moment, just one, it felt like that pinch was somehow rising from wherever it existed, becoming sound, forming words. For a moment I wanted to say, *Yes, Dad, yes, I'm anxious and confused and though I've never slipped, I feel myself slipping now.* But I'd never done that. I didn't know how to do that. Instead, I answered, "I've got a handle on it."

My dad nodded, and my mom patted my hand. "I'm proud of you," my dad said. "I couldn't ask for a better right-hand man."

Right-hand man.

The term made pride radiate inside me, relieving the pinch, and I sat up a little straighter. All my life, I'd strived to make my parents proud of me, especially my father. I'd joined the clubs he suggested I join, I dominated in the sports he wanted me to play, I'd achieved perfect grades and been admitted to the very best colleges.

I'd been the perfect son.

And then I'd joined the company he'd built from the ground up, working hard and performing above and beyond expectations. Proving that I could be his right-hand man.

The one who would carry on his legacy someday, not only here in the U.S., but abroad in London and eventually other international locations. Because of me, my father's company would not only thrive, but grow and expand, passed on from father to son, and eventually I'd do the same with my own.

I closed my eyes briefly and attempted to bring back the scent of Blakely's perfume, but the sensory recall was strangely tinged with an earthy saltiness that belonged to another woman. *Jesus.* I picked up the menu and attempted to clear my brain completely as I stared unseeing at the list of entrée choices.

"By the way," my mother said, "speaking of your move, we were supposed to talk about your going-away party. Did you consider the two dates I texted? We'll need to get invitations out right away if we're going to give people more than a month's notice."

I worked to remember the dates she'd texted over just before I'd gone on that damn guys' trip that had resulted in an upheaval of my life. Or at least my focus. And now my peace. *So get back on track, Buchanan. You've never let anyone ruin your peace. Ever.* I hardly wanted a going-away party, but the more things to distract me right now, the better. "Remind me of the dates," I said.

"Well my first choice would be the twelfth," my mother said. "But—"

"The twelfth is fine. Book it."

My mother smiled and pulled out her phone. "Wonderful," she said as she typed into her calendar, I assumed. "And," my mother said, giving my hand another pat as she set her phone down. "How exciting that you and Blakely are considering a relationship. If it works out between you, perhaps you'll be a couple by the time the party rolls around. There will be so many things to celebrate."

A myriad of emotions swirled. The pleasant anticipation that always came with the possibility of pleasing my family, the pinch of confusion and anxiety I'd been experiencing lately, and a vague panic I couldn't identify. "We're not making any decisions before the party," I told my mother.

"Oh, well that makes sense. I know nothing's set in stone," my mom said quickly, "and we don't mean to pressure you. But…sometimes passion grows with time, darling." She glanced at my father and gave him an affectionate smile. "I didn't realize I could love your father any more than I did on our wedding day, but things have only gotten better."

I resisted making an *ick* face. I definitely didn't want to think of my parents and *passion* in the same sentence. But in actuality, the only visual the word conjured was that of an assprint in green felt. And while *that* image brought with it a minor buzz of excitement, a whirl of disappointment also spiraled through my veins.

Maybe *passion* wasn't all it was chalked up to be anyway. Maybe I'd do without passion by choice.

Because look where passion had gotten me so far.

I'd decided to wait for the weekend when Faith had a public showing at her gallery to speak to her as privately as possible and demand answers about why she was collecting art from Calliope citizens under false pretenses. But fate stepped in the next day when I was driving to work and spotted a woman walking a few blocks ahead, ebony hair glinting in the sun, her arm extended as she held several leashes in her hand attached to a trio of dogs who trotted ahead of her.

What the hell are you doing now, woman? And whose dogs are those?

My heart lurched as, without thinking, I made a sudden turn, coffee sloshing from the cup I was holding and splattering across my lap as horns blared. "Damn it," I muttered, taking my hand off the wheel momentarily as I wiped the coffee that had spilled on my gray pants with my hand, only making it worse. *Fuck.* I was due to make a presentation in thirty minutes.

Up ahead, Rory must have heard the horns because she paused and turned, our eyes meeting through the windshield as I halted at a stop sign less than a hundred feet from her. I watched as her eyes widened and she pulled in a breath, glancing at the dogs quickly and then raising her head to look around, obviously weighing her options for escape.

Some unnamed thrill took up inside me and I tried my best to tamp it down. But I couldn't help the smile that stretched across my face right before she turned and ran.

Oh, no, you don't.

I pressed on the gas, shooting through the stop sign even though it wasn't my turn and causing the car to my right to hit their brakes. "What the hell, Gage?" a man yelled out his window.

Up ahead, Rory turned right into the park, the dogs all barking in excitement at the sudden, unexpected run she was taking them on. The dogs split apart when they came upon a low bush and she easily jumped it, shooting a look over her shoulder.

I swore I saw exhilaration in her expression.

"Is this a challenge, Cakes?" I caught sight of my own face in the rearview mirror and noticed I was grinning. "Okay then, it's on."

I sped up, taking a sharp turn as I bypassed the park entrance and raced around the corner to head her off on the other side. I watched out the side window as she wove and dodged, jumping over hedges, the dogs now barking and tangled and attempting to run in three separate directions. The little black one wearing the Burberry sweater looked positively gleeful.

Morning walkers scurried out of the way, turning as she flew by them, utterly out of control.

I turned again, a pedestrian who'd just been about to step off the sidewalk jumping out of the way. I raised my hand and waved, giving old Mr. Dornbusch an apologetic smile. He raised his cane and angrily waved it in the air as I sped by.

Rory did a half turn, whirling around a mother pushing her baby, Rory lifting her arm so that her handful of leashes didn't get caught on the stroller. *Nice save.* I let out a laugh, my heart pumping with the adrenaline of a chase. And damn if I wasn't having fun even while my annoyance jumped three more levels. She was *literally* running from me now. No one ran from me. Women ran *to* me. A few of them had literally launched themselves in my direction a time or two.

And this confusing little fraud was leaping over park benches to get away from me. I pushed on the gas, turning another corner, well on my way to heading her off at the only exit that wasn't fenced in. I would park at the end of the path she was currently sprinting along with her barking bevy of pups and—"Holy shit!"

My body jerked as something punched me in the face, the sound of crunching metal ripping through my ears followed by the sound of gushing water. I blinked, attempting to figure out what the hell just happened as I batted at the balloon obscuring my vision.

No, not a balloon. My airbag. Oh shit, I'd hit something. I'd crashed. I pushed at the airbag again, now deflating and making it easier to see and then opened my car door, stepped out, and was almost instantly taken down by a forceful spray of water.

"What the fuck?" I choked, using my hands to try to shield myself from the spray I could now see was coming from the fire hydrant I'd crashed into.

I fought my way out of the spray, coming to stand next to my smoking car still hitched on the red hydrant, breathing hard and soaked to the bone.

"Gage? Are you okay?" Heath McGonigal—owner of a local lunch spot by the lake—asked, his mouth agape. A group of joggers and early birds had stopped to see what was going on, and at the back of the small crowd, I saw Rory, her eyes glued to me as she struggled to get the overexcited dogs under control.

Her mouth hung open, as she stared at me with… concern. She startled as I met her wide-eyed gaze and began to turn.

Oh, no, you don't.

Behind me, I heard a car door slam and turned to see Travis Hale exiting his police vehicle. I let out a breath, turning back to Rory who was walking hurriedly away, shooting looks back over her shoulder as though she expected me to follow. Which I absolutely would have, had the chief of police of Pelion not shown up.

"Gage? What the hell happened?" he asked as he came up beside me.

I ran a hand over my wet hair. "I hit a fire hydrant."

"Yeah. I can see that." He glanced next to us where the arc of water was hitting the ground and creating a growing puddle. "I didn't think an early morning meeting with the Calliope Police Chief would result in anything interesting, but here we are," he said, looking me over. "The fire department is on their way to shut that off. Have you been drinking?"

I turned toward him. "It's seven thirty in the morning."

He let out a short grunt, his gaze moving over my face as lines appeared between his brows. "I'm just trying to figure out how you hit a fire hydrant that's *inside* the park."

I looked back, noticing that I'd veered off the road and driven into the park as I'd tracked Rory and her out of control canine posse.

Shit. I was lucky I'd hit a fire hydrant and not a person. I let out a long sigh and ran my hand over the bare bit of scruff on my jaw. What was *happening* to me? "I got distracted. I'll pay for the fire hydrant and whatever services are necessary to fix it, of course."

Travis leaned forward and peered at me as though something was written on my face that he was trying to read. I looked away just as the roar of a large truck sounded behind us.

The fire department was here, along with a Calliope police officer. I looked to the place where Rory had just been walking away with the dogs, but they'd already turned out of sight.

CHAPTER TWELVE
Rory

The distant sound of violin music filtered into the library where Faith and I sat, waiting not so patiently for Mrs. Edna Ramsbottom.

Rory Ramsbottom, I repeated in my mind.

Hmm. That would be…somewhat unfortunate.

But regardless, if my search ended here, at the Ramsbottom Estate, I'd be grateful to have solved the mystery of my origin story.

"I'm so sorry to keep you waiting," Mrs. Ramsbottom said as she swept gracefully into the room. I'd heard it joked somewhere that women of a certain upper echelon learned to walk with books piled on their heads for poise and I was beginning to believe it was true. Each woman we'd met with so far had such stellar posture. That sort of thing had to be practiced. Certainly the spine didn't do that naturally? Speaking of which…I straightened and brought my shoulders back, and then crossed my legs at the ankles as I smiled politely at Mrs. Ramsbottom. "My grandson's violin lesson is today as you can hear, and he wanted me to listen to the piece he's been practicing." She took a seat across from us in a matching high-backed red velvet chair and smoothed her pleated skirt.

"No apology necessary," Faith said. "We've been enjoying this gorgeous room. It's a marvel." I nodded in agreement as I glanced around at the orderly shelves of books that reached to the ceiling. It really was a dream. As we'd waited, I'd taken the opportunity to look more closely at a few of the titles and saw that there was a whole section devoted to Shakespeare. The Casteels of former generations would have been in heaven. I myself didn't currently have a lot of reading time, but if I were rich and had no need to work doubles and overtime and weekends and holidays, forget the tennis club or bridge with the ladies, I'd spend all my time reading and playing with my dogs. I let out a soft wistful sigh, bringing myself back to reality where I was not a lady who lunched but rather...well, a lady who served others their lunch from a decades-old griddle in a tavern on the docks.

For now.

But I could fit in among these people, couldn't I? If my father was one of them, then I had his blue blood running through my veins as well. Sure, the country club crowd had pretty much rejected me thus far. A memory of Thaddeus in that dim hallway suggesting we rendezvous behind closed doors flashed in my mind. But that didn't have to mean anything. I was already holding my own with the families I'd met so far.

Well, with the exception of one member, but I just had to continue to steer clear of him.

"...don't you agree, Rory? Rory?" Faith's voice brought

me fully from my own inner musings and I blinked at her and nodded.

"Uh…yes. Yes, wholeheartedly."

Faith smiled, turning back to Mrs. Ramsbottom. I let out a slow exhale at obviously having answered the unknown question correctly. "I can't even imagine how much art goes unseen for decades because someone didn't know its value and stuck it away in an attic," Faith said. "Works of beauty and mastery should be appreciated. I shudder to imagine the hidden gems all over town just waiting to be uncovered."

I crossed my legs, my slacks chafing the scrape I'd received as I'd high jumped over a scratchy holly bush the morning before. I bit my lip in an effort not to grimace as Mrs. Ramsbottom began speaking about a particular relative who'd had the absolute gall to install vinyl windows in the sunroom. Against my will, my mind moved to Gage, dripping wet in a pair of suit pants and a button-down shirt and tie, standing next to his wrecked and smoking car, a geyser of water shooting into the sky as we stared at each other across a gathering crowd.

At first, being chased by him had been thrilling, honestly. But stupid too. Someone could have been hurt. When I'd heard the crash, my heart had nearly stopped beating. I'd taken the dogs and booked it to where his car had decimated a fire hydrant.

It had been at least partially my fault, as I was the one who'd run from him. I needed to get out of town, and fast. It would be in everyone's best interest if I conducted my research quickly and expediently and try my very best not to run into Gage Buchanan again.

"Are you okay?" Faith shook my arm lightly.

"What?"

"You groaned."

"What? Oh. Yes. Yes. I'm fine. Just...vinyl windows." I drew my shoulders up and shivered.

"It's positively sinful," Mrs. Ramsbottom said. "My point being that I agree with you, Faith. Not every generation of Ramsbottoms has had the same good sense. If there are valuables stuffed away in our attic, I have a good idea who put them there." She leaned forward conspiratorially. "He didn't have the Ramsbottom look," she said. "I often wondered if his mother..." She raised her brows as though some evils simply shouldn't be put into words. "Anyway, my butler is bringing down what he was able to find. That must be him now," she said as footsteps sounded outside the room and the door began to open. "Thank you, Rupert—"

I froze as Gage Buchanan entered the room, his smile hyena-like as his gaze latched on to me.

"Gage? Well this is a surprise," Mrs. Ramsbottom said as she stood.

"Edna. How are you? I'm sorry to barge in like this, but I wanted to warn you..."

"Warn me? Whatever for?"

Next to me, I heard Faith suck in a quiet breath as though bracing for confrontation. Gage glanced over at me again and narrowed his eyes, one side of his mouth tipping ever so slightly before he looked back to Mrs. Ramsbottom and said, "Blight. There's a terrible blight affecting boxwood in Calliope."

Mrs. Ramsbottom blinked rapidly for a moment. "Blight?"

"Mm," he hummed.

She cleared her throat, leaning closer as though to check if his pupils were dilated. "I'll tell my gardener straightaway.

Of course. But Gage, there was no reason for you to go out of your way and come here in person. Not that it's not lovely to see you. But, you could have called about the…blight."

"I see I'm interrupting something," he said, walking farther into the room. "I apologize. Hi, Faith." He shot her a narrow-eyed look. "And you're…Aurora, right? *Castle,* was it? No, don't get up. I believe we met a few days ago." He came to tower over me as he reached his hand out.

I lowered myself back into the chair. Trapped. When I took his hand, his face blossomed in a wolfish smile, and even though he was obviously gloating about having cornered me, it still made my heart do a small twirl in my chest. I yanked my hand out of his overly tight grasp. "Did we? I'm sorry but I don't remember."

He let out a soft chuckle and stepped away just as the butler walked in the room holding the handle of an art case. The man nodded to Mrs. Ramsbottom. "Thank you, Rupert. You may leave that on the table," she said.

Rupert walked the short distance to the library table between where we were sitting and the door and placed it carefully on top and then quickly exited the room.

"May I?" Gage asked as he walked over to the table and unzipped the case.

"Oh, I…of course. Be my guest," Mrs. Ramsbottom said, giving him another slightly confused look as though he was acting quite out of character.

He opened the case and looked down at the top painting and then lifted that one slightly to look at the one beneath it. "Nice." He spun toward me causing both me and Faith to startle. "You're an appraiser, isn't that right, Ms. Castle?"

"That's right," I said with a tight smile. I almost wanted to laugh. I knew now that he wasn't going to expose me.

At least, not publicly. If he was going to do that, he'd have done it straight off. *Blight? Really?* But I saw his game. He was going to attempt to put me in the hot seat, like I'd done to him with my uncle Cash.

"Excellent," he said. "I've always been an art lover. I'd love to hear more about your training. I didn't get nearly enough time with you at my mother's home."

I tapped my bottom lip. "Wait, I think I do remember you now. Weren't you naked the last time we met?"

Mrs. Ramsbottom sucked in a shocked breath.

"Half naked," he corrected.

"Which half was it again? Remind me."

"Anyway, back to you and your considerable talent. Who was it you studied under? It had to be a master if you've achieved so much knowledge and are obviously so young."

I smiled tightly as my heart sped. Gage clasped his hands behind his back as he watched me, and I felt Mrs. Ramsbottom's and Faith's gazes on me too. My mind went semi-blank, the way it always did when I tried to lie. My eyes slid behind him to the bookshelf. "I studied under..." My gaze flew across the titles. "Professor...Hugo...Dick... Stoker."

Gage made a choking sound at the back of his throat that he covered with a cough and I heard Faith let out a hiccup from beside me. Gage turned and walked in a slow circle, his gaze hanging on the shelf behind me, likely taking in a book by Victor Hugo and another by Bram Stoker, and the title *Moby Dick*.

"Professor Hugo Dickstoker?" he asked when he faced me again, his voice strangely high.

Admittedly, it was an unlucky combination I'd come up with on the fly.

"Mm," I hummed. "Yes. He's a legend."

"I bet he is."

"Look at the time!" Faith said. "If we're going to make our next appointment, we've got to be going." She jumped up and then grabbed my hand and gave me a hard tug. I came to my feet and then followed her as she turned toward the art in the case on the table. "Mrs. Ramsbottom, we'll have these pieces back to you just as soon as Aurora's had time to look them over thoroughly."

"Yes, thank you," Mrs. Ramsbottom said, her forehead creased as though she wasn't sure what had just happened. "Ms. Castle—"

"Aurora, please."

"Aurora, it was lovely to meet you."

"You as well," I said as Faith zipped the case closed and then picked it up by its handle. "Thank you for entrusting me with your pieces. I'll treat them with the utmost care."

Faith gave me another tug and we both scooted past Gage whose eyes were hung on me, a small smirk on his far-too-handsome face.

"You have a nice day, Gage," Faith said, and I turned my head toward him as we moved past, giving him a small wave and crossing my eyes before turning and practically running from the room.

"Gage, is there something going—" I heard Mrs. Ramsbottom say, but then footsteps sounded behind us and we picked up our speed as Gage's voice called, "I have to warn the others about the blight! It was nice to see you, Edna!"

I couldn't help the giggle that exploded from my mouth as we fast-walked to the massive door in the marble entryway, a butler stepping from the shadows and causing Faith to let out a small shriek as the expressionless man opened the door and waved us through.

"Oh, no, you don't," Gage said from behind me as we ran for Faith's car. I heard Gage's feet on the pavers as he pounded after us and whirled around just as I made it to Faith's car, no time to open it and slide inside.

He skidded to a stop as I pressed my back to the door, our breath mingling as we all but collided. "Caught," he said, the wicked smile he'd had on his face as he'd pursued me dwindling.

For a few moments, we simply stood there, our chests rising and falling together, eyes held, the expressions we'd worn evening out. He leaned in slightly as if inhaling my scent and my heart did that odd spiraling again, dipping and rising and making me slightly dizzy. I felt his heat and smelled him too. His cologne brought to mind silk sheets and the leather interior of some luxury car that I couldn't begin to name because I knew zip about expensive automobiles. It made me picture a dimly lit bar in Paris where a pianist played classical music on a sleek grand piano. It was sophisticated and divine. It spoke of polished masculinity and the finer things in life.

It was so perfectly Gage Buchanan.

And I was...a fraud. A nobody.

And even more than both of those things, there was an extremely legitimate reason why I could not and *would* not engage in this strange form of flirting or foreplay or whatever it was that we'd somehow began playing at. Running from him had started from a place of panic, but there was something undeniably electrifying about—literally—being pursued by Gage and I'd given in to the impulse. I could see anger simmering in his tense expression, but I also saw the way his pulse was pumping swiftly at his throat, and I'd noticed the glint of excitement in his eyes as he'd chased me. We'd played games with each other from the start, but again, all that needed to stop. And not only because otherwise the pedestrians of Calliope were in grave danger.

I turned my head, breaking eye contact. "Mr. Buchanan. Did I forget something?"

The window rolled down at my back and Faith called from the driver's seat, "Rory, are you—"

"Give me just a minute, Faith," I said, and whatever she heard in my voice made her roll up the window.

"Is your name really Aurora Castle?" he asked once the window closed.

I turned to him again and gave him a light push so that he took a step back. I couldn't think straight with the delicious smell of him wafting all around me. I swallowed, moving my eyes to the side.

"Don't lie," he growled. "I'll know if you do. You're shit at it."

I couldn't deny that. And anyway, he could look me up. He knew enough about me to make some calls. I let out a gusty exhale. "Yes, my name is really Aurora. But um, my last name is Casteel." I held up my hand, stopping him from saying anything. "And I'm really from Mud Gulch where I've lived all my life, and my family really owns Cakes and Ale."

"So not an art appraiser who studied under the legend known as Professor Hugo Dickstoker?"

I let out a thin laugh. "Not exactly."

He cocked his head to the side and put his hands in the pockets of his dress pants, studying me for a moment so that I felt like squirming. God, he was beautiful. Everything about him. His face. His build. Even his jawline and throat and the tiny hairs on his forearms that glinted in the sun. "And what's the scam, exactly?" he asked. "Discover expensive paintings and then swap them out for reprints?" He glanced at the car behind me. "I'm surprised Faith would go along with that. Unless you're conning her too."

He definitely looked mad, but he also appeared disappointed. I pulled in another breath and again, let it out slowly. "Faith is a friend who's only doing me a favor. I'm not running a scam, Gage." My eyes drifted to the side. "I mean, not really. I can explain," I said when I looked back at him. He deserved an explanation. And why not? Maybe he even had some information that would be helpful. He was another person who'd lived here all his life, only unlike Faith, he was a member of the Calliope aristocrats. He knew the families I was trying to gain access to.

"Then what the hell is going on?" he asked. "I admit that I've had some fun chasing you around town, despite the effect it's had on my reputation and insurance premium, but enough is enough. I want answers."

Movement behind Gage in one of the windows of the massive stone house caught my attention and I peered up, worried that Mrs. Ramsbottom was watching us from behind a curtain. "I'll answer your questions. I'll...well, I can meet you later if you want. And explain then. Just please, don't say anything to anyone until you give me a chance to tell you why I'm here."

He huffed out a breath and ran a hand through his hair as he considered me. "Okay, tonight though. Meet me at my place tonight."

My heart skipped a beat. *Tonight*. It seemed unwise to be alone with Gage Buchanan anywhere there was a bed. Or a pool table. Perhaps I was flattering myself and I'd become utterly unappealing to him ever since he'd discovered I was a con artist—at least in his mind—but I didn't think so. Our chemistry still zipped through the empty space between us, and I could see he felt it too.

He'd understand why that was so unfortunate soon enough.

"Okay. But not your place. Faith has a garden area behind her gallery. I'll be there at eight tonight."

He looked like he might argue for a moment but then apparently decided against it, giving one succinct nod and then backing away. "I'll see you then. And *Aurora*, this had better be good."

CHAPTER THIRTEEN
Gage

The night was warm but there was a cool breeze off Pelion Lake that stirred up the scent of the petunias spilling from the planters in front of Faith's gallery. I set my shoulders, glancing upward as I rang the bell for the fifth time in less than a week. This time, however, Faith answered, pulling the door open and waving me in. "Gage," she said. "The door to the garden is that way," she used her thumb to point over her shoulder.

I gave her a sideways glance, murmuring a quick thank-you as I passed by. I'd give her the benefit of the doubt for now, especially considering I was going to learn whether that was warranted or not momentarily. I had to admit to the relief that loosened my muscles as I walked down the short hall to the back door. I was worried Rory would try some other evasion tactic rather than talk to me, and the fact that she hadn't made me feel far less tense than I'd been ten minutes ago. I wanted answers. I *needed* answers if I was going to get a full night's sleep again.

The door to the outside squeaked as it opened, and I stepped out onto a small patio. Beyond that was a large, open area with a fence around the entire perimeter, completely closing it in. There was a bar to my left with several barstools in front of it, and to the right there was more seating, shaded by a fabric-covered pergola. There were plant beds along the fence and large pots of flowers and greenery placed here and there, and the space was lit by hanging lights crisscrossed over the entire area. It was comfortable and charming, and I wondered if Faith used this space for art exhibits. I pictured servers offering trays of golden champagne and hors d'oeuvres named after famous artists for a touch of fun... cranberry-brie Rembrandt rolls...

I stepped around a pillar at the edge of the patio and pulled in a breath. Rory was standing near a table to the right, a glass sitting at the place she must have just been sitting before standing when she heard me arrive.

She watched me as I approached, something on her face I couldn't read. A sort of sadness maybe, or regret.

"You made it," she said.

I approached. "Did you think I wouldn't?" I wanted to be here. I'd been chasing her around town for days. So why did I suddenly feel nervous and on edge?

"I...hoped you would. I'm sorry I've been avoiding you. I swear I had no idea you lived here in Calliope, Gage. When you walked in the room at your parents' home, I thought I might pass out from shock." There was a second seating area that was uncovered, and she waved her hand to it and then walked over and took a seat on one of the large, cushioned chairs. I followed, sitting down across from her. "I've been trying to figure out where to begin," she said.

"Well, the beginning's usually a good place."

She smiled as she brought her feet beneath her, pausing as I waited for her to gather her thoughts. "For as long as I can remember, I've wondered about my father." She released a gust of breath. "My mother died before I had a chance to get more information from her than the little she'd given me. But what I do know is that she spent time here nine months before I was born."

I tipped my head. "Your father is from Calliope?"

Her eyes met mine. "Yes."

Even if I couldn't see the entire picture, a puzzle piece snapped into place. "So, you're here trying to find out who your father might be."

"Yes," she answered again.

This I had not expected. The girl I'd met in Mud Gulch by pure happenstance might have a father who lived in Calliope of all places? I'd thought it a certain kind of fate that we'd met at all considering the unlikely way I'd ended up there. And because of it, we'd spent an amazing night together that I couldn't stop thinking about. But this took fate up a notch. What was it now? Double fate? Fate squared?

I leaned forward, resting my elbows on my knees and gripping my own hands. "Where does the art come in?"

"My father was an artist. Or at least, he was very good at drawing." She reached down and pulled a canvas bag toward her and removed what looked like a journal or a diary and opened it carefully. She removed what I thought was a cocktail napkin that had been preserved between the pages. "I found this recently among my mother's things. I believe my father drew it."

She held it toward me and I took it carefully, holding it by the edges as I studied it. There was a sketch of a woman on it, sitting on a rock, knees drawn up as she looked out over a lake. And even though the woman was only in profile, it was obvious there was a secretive smile gracing her lips. I didn't know a lot about art, but it was clear that whomever had drawn this was very good. There was no signature, only a date scrawled under the drawing—April, twenty-seven years ago. "Is this of your mother?"

Rory nodded. "Yes, it's my mother. And it seems to me…well, it seems to me there's love in that drawing. That the man who sketched it knew her and cared for her deeply. He captured her essence somehow, and how can you do that without loving that person?"

I studied it for another couple of moments, finding that I agreed with her. I wasn't exactly sure *how* the emotion I felt looking at it had been conveyed—perhaps someone with a more professional eye would be able to describe the way in which feeling had been infused into such a simple sketch, but however it'd been accomplished, it was undeniable. I looked up and caught an expression on Rory's face that she quickly turned away. Longing, I thought. For the mother no longer here? Or for this unknown artist? "You're right, it's good," I said.

"And I can't imagine someone with that level of talent didn't create other pieces of art as well."

I ran a finger under my lip as I connected the dots. "Okay. So you're looking for pieces of art similar to this in an effort to locate the artist—your father. But why in my parents' attic? Why at the Bellamy's and the Ramsbottom's?"

"Turn the napkin over."

I did so, my brows lowering when I saw the familiar logo. "This napkin is from the Metropolitan Club here in Calliope." I looked up at her. "It's one of the most prestigious social clubs in Maine. My father is a founding member."

"I know. So are Mr. Bellamy and Mr. Ramsbottom."

I slowly lowered the napkin. "You're going to have to give me a few more clues here, Rory."

She released a breath, reaching for the napkin which I handed to her and then placing it carefully back in the journal. "My mother rarely talked about my father. When she did, it was only because I begged for information. However, over the years, she only divulged four things that might help me identify him," she said. "One, my mother met him at her workplace in Calliope when she lived here over the spring break season. Two, he and his family were very important in the town, and three, he was an artist—whether recreationally or professionally, I don't know. I found that sketch a couple weeks ago, dated during the exact time my mother was in Calliope, when she became pregnant with me."

"Okay..." I felt a bleat of distant panic as my mind began traveling in a decidedly traumatic direction. I tensed my jaw, keeping the idea fuzzy, not allowing it to materialize.

She lowered her chin as she watched me for a moment. "And four, my mother worked at the Metropolitan Club, serving the group of founding members who gathered there regularly. I did some online research about the five charter members of the club," she said. "Along with your father, Mr. Bellamy, and Mr. Ramsbottom, there were two others. They still live here in Calliope as well."

The ground dropped out from under me. *No. God, no.* I felt a groan of protest moving up my throat and attempted to swallow it down, but it unfortunately got stuck halfway, causing me to begin coughing violently. I stood, holding my hand up in a halting motion when Rory began to stand, obviously intent on offering assistance in the form of a back pat or the Heimlich maneuver. She sank back down in the chair as I got control of myself and then paced for a few minutes, still coughing here and there in an effort to dislodge the lump of horror, but at least getting breath into my lungs. When I was finally able to pull in an unobstructed mouthful of air, I faced her. "Are you telling me that my father might be your father? Are you suggesting we might be half siblings?"

She grimaced as she nodded, putting her hands together and inserting them between her drawn up knees. "Unfortunately, yes."

"Unfortunately? *Unfortunately?*" I paced again, a few steps one way, and then back the other. I hissed out a breath, running my hands through my hair and then gripping my scalp as I gave my noggin a firm shake.

She sighed. "Yes, well, I don't have a better word than that."

"Nightmarish? Appalling? Unholy?"

"Those work too." She gave a one-shouldered shrug and let out a small laugh. It made her look adorably sexy and I really wanted to kiss her. I collapsed in the chair, and slunk down, utterly defeated as I considered the entirety of the situation. This could not be true. I met Rory's eyes. "I…I'm not sure what to say. Setting aside the sibling thing…" I paused. I seriously felt like I might be sick. I pulled in a deep breath as I held back the nausea. "Setting aside the sibling possibility," I repeated, "now I have to entertain the thought that my father cheated on my mother when I was just a kid." They'd always seemed so in love. I'd never once considered that either of them would be unfaithful to the other. I felt my whole childhood teeter before me, at risk of toppling over some foggy edge.

She grimaced again. "Sorry. There are several reasons I hope that's not the case."

I let out a strangled laugh as I felt another drop in my chest. "Yeah. Same."

She reached in her bag and pulled out a journal that looked to be nothing but an empty leather cover, the pages gone. "My mother kept a diary most of her life. This one was from the months that she lived here. The inner pages are gone for some reason, but the first and last entry are still there." She held it out to me and I took it from her, flipping it open and quickly reading through the first entry of a young girl obviously filled with adventure and hope. Once I'd finished reading, I skimmed it one more time, looking with the eyes of a local, for anything I might be able to offer that would provide another clue. Unfortunately, nothing struck me other than what she already knew.

"Do you know who Lys is?"

"No. My mom didn't keep in touch with anyone by that name."

"Hmm." I turned to the only other intact page, this entry shorter than the first and read through that one too.

The bus pulled away from Calliope early this morning and I watched out the window until the lake disappeared. My heart aches and I'm filled with such profound grief that I don't know how I'll bear it. My only solace is nestled safely inside of me, the precious child of the man I love but can never have. His family needs him and to stay would only bring him pain.

I handed the mostly empty journal back to her, my brow creasing as she took it. Whatever had happened between the beginning and the end had obviously changed everything. "Any idea where those pages went?"

"None. I searched every corner of her house but never did find them. Either she tore them out herself and discarded them, or they fell out at some point and were scattered to the winds. Too bad, because it sure would have made the mystery easier to solve."

I sighed. We were both silent for a few minutes as I digested the information she'd just given me, and that her mother had included in her diary. After I'd pulled myself up a bit, she asked haltingly, "Is your father…good at drawing?" It appeared that her muscles tensed as she waited for me to answer.

"Yeah," I said, the word a mix of breath and despair. I pulled myself up to a full sitting position but couldn't manage to raise my slumped shoulders. "He's really good," I told her. "He used to draw funny little pictures and put them in our lunch boxes. They were always…" I let out a deep sigh. "Very good."

"Oh," she said, her mouth tugging downward. She took in a deep breath and then tapped on the journal still sitting next to her. "Did the sketch on the napkin remind you of his sketches?" Once again, she appeared to brace.

I shrugged. Before she'd told me what it was, I honestly hadn't recognized anything about it. I certainly hadn't thought of my father. But that didn't necessarily mean it wasn't his. "It's hard to say. It's been awhile since I've seen one of his sketches. They were just done for fun. And, he always used a ballpoint pen from our kitchen drawer." I gestured to the journal. "The one you showed me is done in colored pencil. It has a different feel. But it might be due to the different mediums. Or maybe my memory isn't great on that subject. I'd love to give you a definitive no, but the truth is, I can't say for sure."

"Would you be able to find one of his old drawings?"

"I didn't keep any." My eyes met hers. I didn't want this

to be true. I wanted to *prove* beyond a shadow of a doubt that this wasn't true. And there was a way to do that. "Aurora… there's a sure way to rule my father out."

"A DNA test?" she guessed immediately. "I thought about that, but stealing someone's DNA seems…unethical, especially considering I was hoping my father would accept me right off the bat. Looking around homes I've been invited into and gaining access to art that I'm going to return in the same condition I took it is one thing. Stealing bodily fluids is another."

"Agreed. But we don't need to use my father's DNA," I said. "We can use mine."

She blinked. "Oh my God, you're right." She gave her head a minute shake. "I guess I didn't think of that because I'd already dismissed the idea of DNA completely. And of course, finding out that you're…*you*, was a…shock." She looked sort of hopeful and also sort of nauseous and I watched her throat move as she swallowed. "If you're my… brother…then a DNA test would show that. If we're not, we can rule your father out immediately."

"And if we are…" I swallowed too not knowing how to finish that thought.

"If we are," she said, "we'll get a partial lobotomy and have the surgeon remove the memory of that night in Mud Gulch from our brains."

I stared but didn't laugh as the visions of *that night* wound through my memory…the feel of her tight heat, the sweet and salty taste of her skin, the texture of her nipple on my tongue. I wanted to yell and laugh hysterically. How in the hell had I, of all people, wound up in this mess? I never rocked boats or conducted myself in a manner anyone could describe as improper. And now here I was lusting after a woman who might be my sister. I groaned and scrubbed a hand down my face.

"Too soon?" she asked.

"Much." I huffed out a breath. I appreciated her attempt to lighten the mood, but I was far from ready for that.

"Let's just take the test and go from there," she suggested.

I sighed. "Okay. I'll schedule a DNA test at the hospital." There was nothing else we could do. At least for now.

CHAPTER FOURTEEN
Rory

I met Gage at the hospital the next day, late in the afternoon, and we each had our blood drawn. The lab told us it would be a week or so before we got the results back telling us whether or not we were related. The possibility for at least one answer should make me happy. An easier angle. A move forward. Either Gage's father was also mine, or I could cross one of the men off my list of possibilities. So why did my stomach roil through the entire process like I might toss my cookies?

Please don't be my brother.

I didn't have any illusions that Gage and I might have hope of some future, casual or otherwise. But I really, really didn't want to live with the knowledge that I'd had sexual relations with my relative. *God.* Just thinking about it in those blunt terms made me want to hurl again. Wouldn't our shared DNA act like some repellent if we in fact did share the same father? Wouldn't I know deep inside that biology didn't favor our union?

Because damn if my libido didn't kick into overdrive when he rolled his sleeve up to have his blood drawn and I caught a glimpse of his forearm. His *forearm*! It was so incredibly sexy.

Well. I guess I'd know soon enough if my biology wasn't smart enough to notice I was admiring the forearm—and every other part—of a blood relation, or if Gage and I didn't, in fact, share a family tree.

When we stepped out the sliding doors of the hospital, the sun was just beginning to lower in the sky. "What are you doing for the rest of the evening?" Gage asked as we walked to his car. He'd offered to pick me up and I'd agreed. Luckily, he'd been given a rental by the insurance company while the damage to his car was being repaired.

"Nothing much," I said as I got in the passenger side. "Except I haven't looked at the art Mrs. Ramsbottom gave me yet, and I have to do some research on the pieces I still need to return so I can do the semblance of an appraisal, in case any of those pieces really are worth something."

He glanced at me as he started the engine, a hint of amusement in his expression. "You're really doing appraisals for them? Based on what? Internet searches?"

I shrugged. "It's all I have access to."

"Why bother? They'll never know."

"That feels...very dishonest." I turned toward him. "Listen, I know this whole thing is based on a fabrication, but I'm not trying to cheat these people, Gage. If I can give them some information on a few paintings they've had tucked away, and they find it mildly useful, then no damage done."

"I suppose you're right. Except if you end up turning their family upside down when you tell them their husband and father had an affair many years ago that produced you."

"I'll cross that bridge if and when I come to it," I murmured. Of course, Gage was assuming that if I belonged to one of these families, that they'd be beside themselves with horror to learn that there was a secret illegitimate family member out there floating around. But what if… what if they found it in their hearts to embrace me?

"How did Faith and her gallery get twisted up in this, by the way?" he asked after a moment.

"Her mother worked at a coffee shop my mother frequented and they struck up a friendship. That's how they met. Unfortunately, my mother had been secretive about her affair with my father, so she didn't have any information to offer on that front. Faith was my way in," I told him, "and though she assured me she's not concerned, I'm worried about potentially damaging her reputation. She didn't come from wealth. Faith used her wits and her affinity for art to pave her way in the community. She's a good friend who was up for the challenge of helping me find my father. And from what she told me, the wealthiest members of Calliope aren't her bread and butter. But I don't want to risk putting her business in jeopardy. Initially, that risk seemed very low, but once I ran into you…"

He glanced at me. "I won't say a word about this to anyone, Rory."

I leaned back against the head rest. "Thank you."

He was silent for a few minutes as I watched the scenery go by, the sparkle of the lake in the distance and the glow of the setting sun turning everything dreamy. *Golden hour.* "If you do find proof that one of these men is your father, what will you ask for?" he asked quietly.

I turned, my eyes moving over his strong profile, down to his elegant yet strong hand resting on the steering wheel.

Speaking of golden. Everything about Gage Buchanan was fine-lined and perfectly chiseled. It was like he'd been created to live among the best of the best, to blend with the finest of all things, and to reside in that stately house surrounded by beauty. Maybe, in some sense, it was what had allowed me to let Gage Buchanan go that day at Cakes and Ale. I'd known he didn't belong there. He was polish and class. He fit *here,* whereas I did not. And maybe that solely had to do with where and how we'd been raised, but I also hoped it was some genetic component that meant we were in no way related.

I moved my mind back to his question. *What will you ask for?* "Acceptance, I guess. If you're wondering whether my plan is to demand my share of the inheritance, no." I picked at one of my fingernails as he turned onto the street where Faith's gallery was. I thought about Romeo though, and all those brochures he kept hidden away in that bottom drawer. I wasn't going to turn down some retroactive child support if it was offered, and I was going to send my selfless uncle wherever he wanted to go.

Gage maneuvered into a parking space and before he asked more questions that I hadn't formed good answers to, I pulled on the door handle and then stepped from his car into the warm, early evening air. I heard Gage's footsteps behind me but didn't turn. Faith had given me the code to her security system and so after I'd unlocked the door, I typed it in and then turned to Gage.

He was standing just outside the door, looking slightly uncertain as if he wanted to come in but wasn't sure he was welcome. My heart softened to see Gage Buchanan, who had likely been welcomed with open arms everywhere he went all his life, hemming and hawing for an invitation. "Would you like to come in?" I asked.

His shoulders lowered as he released an exhale. "I could help you look at some of that art and do a few novice appraisals of my own," he suggested, as though I might require a bribe to continue to spend time with him. And honestly…a reason didn't hurt, since it truly was not a good idea, at least on my part. I couldn't seem to stop picturing him naked, an unfortunate act of my memory centers that seemed to go into overdrive when he was physically present.

No, distance from Gage Buchanan would be for the best.

"I'd appreciate that," I said. *Weak, Rory. So weak.* But I would not let things go farther than some tag-teaming novice art appraisals.

"How about you bring them to my condo and let me make you dinner? If you have a laptop you can bring, I have one too."

He appeared to be holding himself quite still as though bracing for a rejection. Again, my heart softened. When it came to Gage Buchanan, it seemed that my heart was very soft and pliable.

Among other things.

"Well…"

"A working dinner."

"Fine. Okay. Thank you. A working dinner. I appreciate the help because Faith has been very busy, and I've already asked enough of her already. If you're willing…well, I still have fifteen pieces of art I need to do fake appraisals for."

He grinned, and lots more softening happened. *Damn it.* "Stay there," I told him. "I'll go get my laptop and the case of art and be right back."

Gage Buchanan's condo was perfect. It immediately brought

to mind the ones my mother had described in her diary entry with glass balconies overlooking the lake. The inside featured a large, open floor plan with sleek, modern furniture and a calming mix of cool tones. It looked like it came straight from the pages of one of those West Elm catalogs I'd leafed through at the hair salon where I'd splurged on a cut that Faith assured me would give me the sophisticated air of an art appraiser.

The sliding glass doors that opened to the balcony revealed a glorious sunset, the sky flushed in varying shades of pink, the flood of light sparkling like jewels on the surface of the water.

And it smelled heavenly, some mixture of Gage's cologne and a piney wood polish, a heady combination that seemed so perfectly suited to the place where this man laid his head at night.

"This is beautiful," I said, setting my purse and phone on the table just inside the door. "You have a designer eye." I shot him a wink. Truthfully, I knew zilch about designer anything, but I knew good taste when I saw it. Or rather, I knew expensive when I saw it. It was the opposite of the old, slipcovered sofa at my house that had once belonged to my mother. I loved that sofa though. When you sat on it, it embraced you like an old friend.

Gage smiled as he placed the bag of art carefully on the dark wood dining table. "No, my designer has a designer eye. I can't take credit for anything except the kitchen."

I turned toward it. "Wow," I said, walking over to the large island with the black stone countertop that separated the kitchen from the living and dining areas. I ran my hand over it, surprised that rather than being smooth, it had a leathery feel. The appliances were obviously state-of-the-art, the stove practically taking up half the back wall.

There was a spice rack built into the alcove that enclosed the stove and housed the exhaust fan, and my eyes lingered on them, noting that most bottles were half full, unlike the spices at my house that I bought here and there to make one thing and then had to inevitably throw out when they expired mostly unused. I recalled the crab cake cooking lesson he'd given me, my mind straying to the activities that followed and a resulting shiver rolling down my spine.

"Cold?" he asked.

"No. A goose must have walked over my grave."

He chuckled but gave me a perplexed look.

"My mom used to say that. It's just a strange expression that means when you shiver for no reason, someone is walking over the place where you'll one day be buried."

"That's a really creepy way to explain a chill."

I smiled. "My mom sometimes had a dark sense of humor. But I think she got that one from my granny."

I dragged a finger along the counter as I took in his wood cabinets that went all the way to the ceiling, the container of kitchen utensils, the knife block, bottles of oils and small bowls of salts sitting on a marble lazy Susan to the side of his cooking space. Whereas the living room and dining spaces looked virtually unused, this kitchen felt different—lived in, personal.

When I turned toward him, I saw that he'd been watching me, a small smile on his face that held some note of what I thought might be nervousness. Was he worried I wouldn't like his place? No, certainly not. First, it was perfect, and he had to know that, and second, why would he care what some waitress from Mud Gulch thought anyway?

"I suppose I'm not surprised that you like to cook, Mr. Crab Cakes Extraordinaire," I said. "Your parents must have taught you?"

He shook his head. "No. Actually, I doubt either of my parents can do more than boil water. We had a family chef growing up who'd studied in France. Jean LaCourt. He taught me some of the basics, and then when he saw I had a knack for cooking, he showed me recipes that took greater skill." He looked contemplative for a moment, perhaps a little nostalgic. "He was amazing." He turned slightly. "My father was confused about why I wanted to spend so much time in the kitchen. I got the feeling he was displeased so I stopped going to Chef LaCourt for actual lessons, but when I could, I'd sneak in there and watch him work. I had this notebook. I'd take notes in it and then hide it in my sock drawer."

He gave me another smile, but this one appeared a little brittle. *Oh.* That struck me as sad. He'd found a passion, even at a young age, and set it aside when his father preferred he turn in a different direction. "Does Chef LaCourt still work for your family?"

Something passed over his expression that looked like fleeting grief. "No. He retired when I was in high school and moved back to France. He passed away a couple of years ago."

"I'm sorry."

"He lived a good, long life and died with his family around him. Can I, ah, offer you a glass of wine?"

I watched him as he turned toward a drawer and removed a wine opener, his shoulders relaxing. It was clear he wanted to move to a different topic. "I don't know," I said. "Last time we shared a bottle of wine..." I raised my brows but then my expression morphed into a cringe. I'd attempted to lighten the mood, but even I wasn't ready to make light of... us. "Sorry. I shouldn't have brought that up."

But Gage smiled, even if it appeared a tad pained, and walked over to a wine fridge where he removed a bottle of red. "I think we can manage to control ourselves. Just some friendly dinner and group art appraising."

Friendly.

I doubted I'd ever think of Gage Buchanan in terms described as friendly, but I could pretend, couldn't I? Because he might be able to help me in my current endeavor. He might be able to shed some light in places where I couldn't.

Gage opened the bottle and poured two glasses of wine as I took a seat in one of the backless chrome barstools that was much more comfortable than it appeared. He handed me the wine and then clinked my glass. "To Ernest—"

"Buffalobeam," I finished with a laugh.

Gage grinned, placing his glass on the counter, then picking up a towel and tossing it over his shoulder. "I hope you're not averse to carbs."

"I never met a carb I didn't love."

"Okay, good." I watched him as he collected ingredients from the refrigerator and placed them on the counter, and then opened a large drawer at the base of the cabinets and chose a pan. When he turned his back again, I glanced into the open door at the other side of his condo, the corner of a bed barely visible. That goose trampled back over my grave, causing my nipples to harden. God, what would it be like to have access to Gage Buchanan in a bed for an entire night?

Stop thinking about that, Rory.

But apparently, I didn't even listen to myself, because a small voice in my head answered, *Perfect, that's what it would be like.*

I'm not as perfect as I seem.

If you're not perfect, what are you?

I don't know.

The words Gage had said to me in the heat of passion came back to me and I paused as I brought the wine glass to my mouth. What had he meant by that? In the moment, I'd just been responding to his utterances with my own, a free flow of thoughts uninhibited by walls or rationale. Passion had burned all that to the ground.

I'm not as perfect as I seem.

Interesting. But honestly? None of my concern.

"So tell me about Mud Gulch," he said, setting a cutting board on the counter and reaching over his shoulder to pull out a knife without even looking.

"Mud Gulch. What's there to say about Mud Gulch?"

He smiled as he began chopping an onion into quarters. "I don't know. You tell me."

I gestured to where he was expertly chopping some green leafy thing I couldn't even name. "Can I help?"

He slid what he'd been chopping off the knife into a silver bowl next to the board. "Nope. I've got this. You entertain me."

"Entertain you? Ha." I took a sip of wine. "You want a story about Mud Gulch? Okay, there is this legend..."

"Ohhh," he dragged out the word, "I love a good legend."

"It's named Mud Gulch because when the early settlers first landed on our shore, the mud in the valley at the edge of town mysteriously pulled at the feet of some, and didn't with others. The Indigenous people explained that the earth there connects to human heartbeats, staking claim to some, and not to others—for mysterious reasons unknown, of course."

A smile floated around his beautifully shaped lips, his

eyes held on his working hands, now chopping garlic so fast, the knife was practically a blur. "It asks some to stay and tells others they're free to go?"

"So the legend says. Only, no one really believes it at this point. It's just a fun story that probably has to do with the shoes you're wearing as you walk through the valley of mud."

"So, your family was wearing the right shoes, I take it?" he asked as he dropped pasta into the water now boiling on the stove top.

"Or wrong, depending on your opinion of life in Mud Gulch. But yes, according to legend, the earth pulled at my ancestors and asked them to stay." I thought it was more likely the sea and the need to feed their families compelled them to make a home there, as I came from a long line of fishermen. But whatever the case, generations of Casteels had raised children in that small fishing town, enough of them feeling the pull to stay that, a hundred and fifty years later, we remained there still.

"And you?" he asked. "Has the mud staked its claim on you?" Something moved across his face, an expression that was too fleeting for me to attempt to name.

I took a long sip of wine and then shook my head as I swallowed. "No. I've always felt this pull…elsewhere." I thought about how being here had seemed to free my thoughts surrounding that incessant pull. Perhaps I'd been scared to attach it to my paternal parentage because doing so would make it seem like I wasn't appreciative of all the sacrifices my mother's family had made for my sake, and the fact that I'd been loved so well. "It's so difficult to explain because even I don't understand it completely. Maybe the pull is just from inside of me…all of my unanswered questions, my longing to know who and where the other half of me came from… Or maybe it was my father," I said, the words releasing on a breath, the admittance making me quake inside just a bit. "Calling to me in some mysterious way."

He watched me for a moment, his expression soft. "Ah. You're a romantic, Aurora Casteel."

I felt heat infuse my face. It did sound romantic. *Fanciful.* And maybe silly too, though it didn't feel that way. It felt true. And that truth simultaneously brought fear and a surge of relief. "Me? No. No, I don't have a romantic bone in my body," I insisted, waving my hand as though to scatter the notion. "It's just the wine."

He gave me a one-eyed squint, his lips tipping in a smile, but didn't respond other than that. I watched him as he drizzled oil in a pan and then tossed in the ingredients he'd just chopped, a delicious aroma of basil and garlic rising in the air. Then he grabbed something from the refrigerator and added that to the pan of aromatic ingredients. Shrimp, I thought, my mouth beginning to water with all the delicious smells floating in the air. The last thing I'd eaten was a granola bar and coffee for breakfast. I'd been too nervous about the blood test to eat anything at all for lunch.

Mesmerized, I watched him work for a minute, his muscles loose, demeanor relaxed. He very obviously had an affinity for cooking. The way he moved as he chopped and whisked…it almost struck me as a sort of graceful dance. It looked natural and effortless. And something about his languid movements when he was preparing food reminded me of the way he'd moved over me on that pool table.

With skill and passion.

I quickly moved that aside with another glug of wine. "So tell me about your hometown," I said, my voice slightly breathy. "Is your family originally from Calliope?"

He opened the oven door and looked in, peeking at a loaf of French bread I hadn't even noticed him put inside, probably too busy staring at his ass every time he turned around and daydreaming about the things he'd done to me at Cakes and Ale. I picked up my wine and drained the glass.

"No, actually. My mother's family is from here, but my father is from Boston. He grew up very poor but was smart and did well in school. He bought some rental properties with money he saved from working three jobs because he had a gut feeling about the area. That gut feeling paid off and he ended up selling them for ten times what he paid. He used that profit to buy more properties, kept listening to his gut and made his first million when he was thirty years old.

"My mother was the daughter of a business associate and he met her when he was traveling, fell in love, and moved to Calliope. He got in early on the investment properties that went up on the lakeshore which increased his net worth significantly, and then built The Buchanan when I was in college, the first in a string of luxury hotels bearing the family name. In the years since I started working at his company, we've built five more across the U.S. His ultimate dream is that someday the Buchanan name will be synonymous with Marriott or Hilton."

"Thanks," I said as Gage poured more wine in my glass. "And you're following in his footsteps? To run the hotel dynasty one day?"

Gage picked up the pot of pasta and poured it in a strainer in the sink, the steam billowing in the air. His shoulders suddenly seemed stiff whereas he'd been so relaxed until he'd begun speaking about working with his father. He shook the strainer and then added the pasta to the pan of shrimp and tomatoes and whatever other delicious-smelling ingredients were in there. "Yes," he said after a moment. "I'm following in his footsteps. But more importantly, I'm helping him expand his empire internationally when we build the first of our European hotels in London."

Right, London. It sounded like it should be exciting. So why did he seem less than overjoyed about that? "Are you... is there something else you'd rather do?"

His eyes met mine. "What? No, of course not. I've known I was going to take over my father's company my whole life. It's always been the plan, and I couldn't be more honored to be entrusted with his life's work. He sacrificed so much to live the life he's created for all of us. It took perseverance and grit and drive like I couldn't possibly understand having been born into the privilege he created." He tossed the ingredients in the pan, appearing almost...breathless after the long string of words he'd just spoken.

He turned, reaching into a cabinet and pulling out two plates that he then set down, one in front of me, and the other to my left. As he was collecting silverware from a drawer next to the stove, I said, "I understand the honor of being entrusted to keep something alive that was built with the blood, sweat, and tears of generations before you," I said. When he turned back to face me, I followed with, "And I also understand the pressure."

He held eye contact for a few beats before his gaze slid away almost guiltily as he opened his mouth to say something, obviously decided against whatever it'd been as he let out a long breath. "I guess it can be both," he finally said.

I nodded. *Why do I have the feeling it's more the latter than the former for you, Gage Buchanan?*

But before I could say anything more, he began dishing

up the steaming pasta, the cloud of fresh herbs and spices mixed with something creamy and decadent meeting my nose. I closed my eyes and inhaled, all rational thoughts fleeing. "My God, that smells good," I said.

When I opened my eyes, I saw that Gage's heated gaze was hanging on me. The moment felt heavy with the potential for physical pleasure and my blood began buzzing in my veins. I saw Gage swallow and then he moved, dishing a heaping serving of pasta onto my plate and breaking the momentary spell, his voice hoarse as he said, "Let's eat."

CHAPTER FIFTEEN
Gage

I watched her as she speared a plump shrimp coated in a simple creamy garlic parmesan sauce. She placed it between her pretty lips, letting out a low moan as her eyes slid shut. *Dear Jesus.* I was as hard as a rock just watching this woman eat pasta.

I sincerely hoped she wasn't my sister.

Not that we were going to start dating if she wasn't. After all, she lived hours away from me and it was soon going to be more than that when I moved to London. Not to mention, I barely knew her when it came down to it. But to know that I lusted after my own blood relative was just plain disturbing.

"Good?" I asked, my voice emerging all choked and desperate. *Damn it. Get it together, Buchanan.* Maybe it would be a good idea for my blood pressure to pretend it was a given that she *was* my sister. In other words, totally off limits.

The irony wasn't lost on me that I was trying to see one woman as more than a sister and wishing I could feel brotherly toward another.

Rory groaned again, wrapping fettuccini around her fork and sliding that into her mouth. She nodded as she chewed and once she'd swallowed, said, "This isn't pasta. It's ambrosia. My God. What did you do to this shrimp?"

"You'd like to know, wouldn't you, Cakes?" I shook my head. "You're going to have to pay for any other recipes you get out of me."

She laughed. "Yeah? What's your fee?"

Let me lick you somewhere. Anywhere.

Jesus Christ. I shoved that visual aside with violence.

I laughed and decided to change the topic from one that felt like it could veer dangerously into heavy flirting at any moment. Likely on *my* part, but I didn't want to tempt myself. "So, Cakes and Ale has been in your family for generations. Did you always want to work there?"

She hesitated, bringing the napkin to the side of her lips and dabbing before answering my question. "No. It just sort of…happened that way. My mom died when I was eleven and my uncles stepped in and raised me."

My brows shot up. "The pirate…"

She laughed and took another bite, a drop of butter lingering on her bottom lip. I glanced away from that dangerous sight. "Yes, the pirate. His name's Cassius. Another nod to Shakespeare. He's actually a rough-hewn grumbly old bear who's as solid as a rock in all ways." She smiled, and I saw the love for him in her expression. That love decreased my bitterness toward the man who'd put an end to our night of pool table play and practically chased me away from his niece. He'd been protecting her, just as he should have been.

"My other uncle's name is Romeo, which needs no explanation."

"And your mother?"

"Ophelia."

"Your family *really* had a thing for Shakespeare."

"Indeed."

"And yet your mom didn't give you a Shakespearean name. Unless Aurora is a lesser-known side character I don't remember."

She raised a brow. "Well acquainted with the women of Shakespearean literature, are you?"

I laughed. And God she was cute. "They don't call me Ivy League for nothing," I said, giving her a wink.

She pressed her lips together as she obviously held back a smile. "*They.* Right. No, by the time I was born, and unless she'd wanted to recycle a name, my mom was left with Hippolyta or Goneril. She made the *much-appreciated* decision that there's a time to buck tradition and go a different route."

"Ah." I grinned. "Goneril. Hmm. Yes, that would be a tough name to carry."

"Unless you're a pharmaceutical drug."

I laughed again and she smiled, taking her bottom lip between her teeth as we stared at each other. Blood rushed to the place between my legs and I adjusted myself, looking away as she dug back into her food. "So, ah, is Romeo as pirate-y as your Uncle Cassius?"

Rory made a small slurping sound as she sucked in a noodle and brought her fingers to her mouth. "No. Romeo is...the quintessential Romeo. Picture a combo of Elvis Presley and Prince Charming and you'll have a good idea of my younger uncle."

"Prince Charming isn't a real person."

"Some say the same about Romeo."

I smiled as I sat back in my chair, taking her in, my

curiosity about this mysterious Casteel family growing by the minute.

"And they both run Cakes and Ale."

She took a sip of wine and then shook her head. "No, only Romeo does. Cassius captains a fishing boat. So, you were right in one regard, he's not actually a pirate, but he does live his life on the sea."

The picture she was painting was beginning to form, her place in that small fishing town where her family owned a bar on the docks coming to life. Which in some strange way was making her feel more real to me too. Since that night in Mud Gulch, part of me had convinced myself she was a fantasy that had faded to mist as I drove out of town. I hadn't actually wanted to picture her as a flesh-and-blood woman going about the business of living her life because... *Why, Gage?*

Because then I might have considered going back.

I let out a long quiet sigh that she didn't appear to hear because she was chewing a bite of bread, using her finger to wipe the butter from the corners of her mouth and introduce new levels of torture.

"And do you help run it too? Or do you mostly just make questionable red velvet concoctions?"

"You're having a hard time getting over that, aren't you?"

"I have to imagine, Cakes, that the entirety of the clientele at your tavern is having a hard time getting over that."

She laughed but pushed at me lightly. "Stop it. It wasn't... that bad."

I squinted one eye and grimaced, feigning deep suffering, to which she grinned and pushed me again.

"To your question, I do a little bit of everything, but mostly I wait tables, and sometimes bartend on Romeo's off days."

"Do you enjoy it?"

She shrugged, twirling the last bit of pasta on her plate and bringing it to her mouth. She appeared to be pondering my question as she chewed. "It's fine."

"*Fine.* Uh-oh."

She gave a small laugh but it melted into a sigh. "Yes, it's fine. Not great, not a dream come true, but truthfully? I don't even know what my dream is. All I know is that my uncles stepped up for me when I had no one else in the world, and there's no way I'd abandon them. The only reason I'm here now is because I came upon that napkin which is the first tangible clue I've ever had to follow to find my father. And I found it right after Cash's boat was damaged and is undergoing repairs. So he's available to watch the brood, while I sneak around people's homes and dig around in their attics under false pretenses."

I gave her a wry smile. "I wondered about the brood."

"The brood is being well cared for. Or at least, well fed. My uncle Cassius sends me a proof of life picture each morning." She smiled. "Anyway, you originally asked about Mud Gulch, and the main thing to know is that when you're from Mud Gulch, you either stay or you go for good. Most of my friends from high school went away to college and then made their lives elsewhere."

"Your mother came back," I noted.

She chewed a bite of bread thoughtfully for a moment. "Yes, but I think it might have been because she had no choice. Something happened here that spring that made her run back home. Maybe it was only that she got pregnant with me, but I have this feeling there's more to the story."

"Hence the art." I glanced over to where the unopened bag sat on my dining room table.

"Yes, hence the art," she said.

"Speaking of which, how about we look through it? You said you hadn't checked out Mrs. Ramsbottom's offerings yet?"

She snorted. "It sounds like there's a dirty joke in there somewhere, but I don't think I'm clever enough to find it."

I laughed as I scooted the barstool out and started clearing our dishes. "I've known the Ramsbottoms all my life. I can let you in on all the clever Ramsbottom combos."

She laughed as she stood up. "You do realize I might *be* a Ramsbottom."

I groaned and flattened my palm over my forehead. "Rory Ramsbottom. If you are...I'm so sorry."

She laughed again, a silly giggle that made her put her hand over her mouth. I smiled in response, our gazes catching and both of us looking away quickly. "Uh, so, there are only four, I believe."

Rory stepped up to the table and unzipped the zipper that curved around the canvas bag and threw back the cover. The painting on top was a pastoral in an ornate gold frame.

"Here, I'll lay them out on the carpet and then I'll go get my computer and see what we can find out about each piece. That one has a signature in the corner which is a great starting point."

I lifted that painting off the top and placed it on the large expanse of carpet between the dining area and the living area, and then turned as she was lifting off the large piece of felt protecting the next one.

That one was an oil of an old man, sitting behind the wheel of a yacht, gazing out to sea. She picked it up and handed it to me and I looked at it more closely as I set it down next to the pastoral. It had an amateurish quality to it, though admittedly, I didn't know a lot about art. And who knew—maybe it was an early work of someone who later became famous. Rory was correct, it was the right thing to do to at least look into these pieces that the wealthy families of Calliope had temporarily entrusted to her, even if her "appraisals" were somewhat lacking.

I heard Rory pull in a breath as I stood, turning to see her holding up a smaller, framed piece that she'd pulled from the stack. I stepped up to her, my eyes moving over the watercolor, done mostly in blues and greens. It was a painting of Pelion Lake. I'd know it anywhere. I took it in, attempting to determine by the placement of mountains and trees where the artist had been when he'd painted it. "It's him," she whispered.

Him. Her father. The artist who'd created the sketch of her mother on that cocktail napkin from the Metropolitan Club. My eyes moved over the lines, the feel of the piece washing through me in whatever way art sometimes did. There was probably a name for why some art affected a particular person and some did not. Or maybe there wasn't. Maybe the varied reasons for the individual response to art was an unknowable thing. A touch of preference and a trace of magic. In any case, the watercolor creation Rory was holding up in front of me hit me in the same way the first one had and I knew for sure I was looking at a piece done by the same artist. "Yes," I agreed. "It's unmistakable actually. The style is very distinct."

Rory sighed, pulling one of my upholstered dining room chairs back and sinking down into it as she pressed the framed painting against her chest, hugging it to her as though the piece itself were her long-lost father. "I didn't truly think I'd come across one," she whispered. "It seemed like the longest of all long shots. After all this time…"

I took a few steps to the table and pulled out another chair and sat down facing her. "Is there a name on it?" I asked. "Or initials?"

As though she hadn't even thought of that in the shock of finding the painting, her brows shot up and she placed the piece face up on her knees. She leaned down and I leaned forward, our heads just touching as we gazed down at the corner. "M.S." She brought her head up, our faces mere inches apart as she stared at me, her mouth forming a small O.

"M.S." I repeated, a cascade of bubbles releasing in my chest. *Not my dad's initials.* It wasn't definitive proof, but it made me breathe easier.

"Not your father's initials," she said, verbalizing my thought. I shook my head and her eyes held onto mine for a minute and I saw the tentative hope in her gaze too before she glanced away. "Do *any* of the five men who founded the club have those initials?"

She bit her lip. "Yes," she said. "Malcolm Sherrybrook and Maynard Siggins. Neither of them have returned Faith's calls yet, which might be because neither of them currently have wives. Mr. Sherrybrook is divorced, and I couldn't find whether or not Mr. Siggins was ever married. Anyway, in all the other cases, wives have returned our calls. So perhaps these men aren't great about their correspondence, or maybe women find more interest in having art evaluated. Who knows."

"Hmm. Maybe." I thought of both those men. I'd known them all my life. Mr. Sherrybrook was a dry, stuffy bastard who didn't look to have an artistic bone in his body, much less the romantic disposition necessary to view any woman the way the artist had obviously viewed Rory's mother.

But…I supposed looks could sometimes be deceiving. And Mr. Siggins was a nice man, but a bit of a mystery. I'd done some business with him but he tended to keep to himself and didn't attend many of Calliope's social gatherings. "The odd thing is that the painting with those initials came from the Ramsbottom Estate," I noted. Which was confusing all around. "Although maybe the artist used a moniker or a… pen name, if the term applies to art." Which was why my father was still a possible suspect. I felt a few of those internal bubbles pop.

She paused as she thought about that. "Yes, but they all ran in the same circle and from what I can tell, still do, at least sometimes. If one of those men painted this"—she tapped at the painting in her lap—"then it wouldn't be surprising that he gave one of his friends a gift, right? Or they purchased it at some point? Either way, it's a step forward." The look on her face was filled with so much hopeful excitement that my breath caught in my chest and it suddenly seemed imperative that this woman find the answers she was seeking. Even if M.S. *was* my own father.

Anything else felt like an injustice of epic proportions.

After all, everyone deserved to know where they came from, didn't they? My birthright, and the responsibilities it carried, along with the rewards it naturally allowed for, had set a path before me that I'd followed all my life. I knew what it was to benefit from being certain of your place in the world. I knew the confidence it bestowed.

"Let me help," I said.

Her gaze moved over my face as though she was searching for something. "Gage, I doubt you have time to assist in a hunt for—"

"I'll make time, Rory. It's…important to me. These

people are part of the community I've grown up in. I feel a certain responsibility if one of them committed a wrong against your mother. Plus, I know them, and I have access to places you might not be able to gain entrance into. They consider me one of them. I *am* one of them."

She released a long breath, looking away momentarily as if considering it. Finally, she looked back at me and nodded. "I appreciate that. Thank you."

Relief filtered through me and I wasn't even sure exactly why. It only complicated things to spend more time with Rory, complications I didn't need and ones that served no ultimate purpose. I wasn't one for senseless dalliances. I never had been.

Well, except once with the same woman on a pool table in her hometown bar.

And why the *hell* couldn't I get the image of that perfect assprint in green felt from blooming large and in living color in my brain?

And what was it about Rory Casteel that made me act in ways I'd never acted before, engaging in activities that didn't forward my own goals in any way, shape, or form? And yet I didn't seem capable of stopping.

She was staring at the painting again, a small crease between her brows. "This is Pelion Lake, right?"

I nodded. I recognized the curve of the shore and the hills rising to the North.

"Are you able to tell exactly where this might have been painted from?"

"You mean where was the artist sitting?"

"Mmhmm."

I took it from her and turned it toward me. "If I had to guess, and assuming the artist was painting the lake as he was looking at it and not from memory, I'd say it was done from right about where the Metropolitan Club is situated at the top of a hill."

"That's what I was thinking, especially since it's obvious the lake was painted from higher ground." She paused. "Do you think it's too late to call Mrs. Ramsbottom?"

I glanced at the clock glowing from my stove. It was just after eight. "No. But what will you say?"

She chewed at her lip for a moment. "I guess I could say I'm having trouble assessing the painting and was wondering if she could give me some more information."

I nodded, beginning to hand it back when I noticed a corner of white paper sticking out from beneath the backing of the frame. I pulled at it and a little more came out, indicating there was a larger piece of something within.

"What is that?" she asked.

"I don't know. Hold on." I set the painting on the table and stood up and went to the kitchen to retrieve a butter knife and one with a sharper edge. I returned and used the tools to gently pry off the inner wooden piece. It appeared that the back of the frame had been constructed by hand and was well secured, but when I exerted a little pressure, the middle section came loose. I picked it up and set it aside and Rory gasped when it revealed a note folded inside.

She picked it up and I saw that her hand was shaking very slightly. "It's a page of my mom's diary," she said. "I recognize the paper."

"Open it."

She did, unfolding it carefully and then laying it on top of the opened back of the picture. We both leaned forward in tandem and began reading the entry in the same recognizable loopy print that I now knew belonged to Rory's mother.

The men who founded the club where I work gather every Tuesday and Thursday night. It was made quite clear to us servers that we were never, ever, to discuss the things we might overhear when performing our duties. They even made us sign a contract.

Last week I was asked to take over for one of the other girls who was out sick, and I guess I did a decent job, because I was requested to serve the group of five men again. It's not like the job is that hard, so I can't imagine they specifically asked for me because I put forth such a bang-up effort delivering their port and clipping their cigars. No, I think one of them has a crush on me. Is that the right word for when an older, much-more powerful man tracks you with his eyes and goes out of his way to use your name constantly? I don't know because he makes me feel both flattered and just a bit scared. Not that he's not attractive. He definitely is. And he's the picture of decorum. But I almost get this feeling that it doesn't matter whether I find him attractive and respectful or not. That man is someone used to getting what he wants regardless of any other details.

Or maybe I'm giving myself too much credit and imagining his interest when he's really just being polite. It's hard to know because the men of Mud Gulch don't leave anything to the imagination. If they're interested, they let you know plain as day and you can take it or leave it but you sure know what you're dealing with. These men, though, they're all smoky looks, and slight pinky grazes over your knuckle as you're taking their glass from their hand. Like, what do you want, dude? Or did your finger just have a tiny muscle spasm? How these rich women ever get laid is a mystery to me because their men are downright confusing as hell.

They're also pretty boring. Considering the non-disclosure agreement, I was looking forward to overhearing all sorts of shocking secrets about where the bodies of their enemies are buried, but nope. All the bigwigs talk about are business contracts and tax laws. Like, just cut out all the paperwork and ridiculously expensive club fees and send an email like the rest of the world.

Anyway, I have started going out after work with a couple of the other servers and it's nice to have a few friends who I can vent with about the clientele (within reason, of course, I'm not about to get sued for breach of contract). They're all locals and so they've also let me in on some Pelion and Calliope gossip, and showed me the best places to eat, where I can find a private slip of shore, and so on.

Tomorrow I'm going over to Lys's house for dinner. That should be interesting. Anyway, gotta go. It's almost seven thirty and I have to be at work to serve the Mysterious Five. I'd better start practicing my removed, stoic look now.

CHAPTER SIXTEEN
Gage

"Mrs. Ramsbottom, thank you so much for calling me back," Rory said, her gaze shooting to me as she put the phone on speaker and held it in front of her.

I moved in close to hear what the woman was saying, Rory's shower-fresh scent washing over me and making me want to lean closer. I resisted, even though every instinct was compelling me to plant my nose in the side of her neck and inhale a bigger breath of her.

Not brotherly, Buchanan. Not in the least.

No, and neither was the buzz of arousal I felt in the region of my groin.

Even if the initials M.S. had given me at least a breath of hope that I wasn't in fact deeply sexually attracted to my sister.

I turned my head so I wouldn't be tempted to break down the way she smelled like I did when eating something delicious, my brain automatically separating out the rosemary and the white wine as I rolled the flavors around on my tongue…

"You're welcome, Ms. Castle," Mrs. Ramsbottom said, the old woman's pompous tone snapping me from my thoughts. "Did you find something interesting about the art?"

Rory had called the Ramsbottom Estate the night before and been told that Mrs. Ramsbottom was out at an event and the woman was finally calling back now. It was good timing, however, as I'd just arrived at Faith's house a few minutes before as Rory and I had made plans to go to breakfast and strategize. *After* she'd returned from her dog walking duties, of course, which apparently both consisted of walking her new local fur friends, and FaceTiming with the brood.

"Well, I'm not sure if I've discovered something or not," Rory answered. "I'd like a little more information on one of the pieces you gave me. It was the smallest of the four, a painting of what looks to be Pelion Lake."

"Oh yes," Mrs. Ramsbottom said with a small sigh. "I know the one you're talking about. I almost didn't include it as it was something my old housekeeper left behind. An insufferable twat who couldn't manage to follow the most simple of instructions, including leaving a forwarding address."

Rory blinked, her gaze meeting mine once more. "Oh, I see. So it wasn't done by someone in your family?"

"Absolutely not. We Ramsbottoms don't waste our time coloring pictures of lakes and grass and whatnot."

Coloring.

Whatnot.

"Of course not," Rory said, giving me a small eye roll. My lip twitched as I resisted the urge to laugh out loud. Mrs. Ramsbottom had always been a snooty old snob who I hoped Rory wasn't related to, for her sake. And though the initials at the bottom of the painting didn't match the Ramsbottom name, just as I'd thought about my own father, we couldn't rule anyone out yet as it was possible the artist used a moniker. "Do you, by chance have any idea where your old housekeeper might have gotten it?" Rory asked.

"One of those flea markets or antique shops she was so keen on, I imagine." She paused a moment. "Does it appear valuable?" A note of interest had entered her voice.

"Perhaps," Rory said. "The artist is very talented. Whatever else your housekeeper was, she was a good judge of talent." Rory winked at me and my heart did a sort of flip/squeeze combination that made me want to massage my chest.

Mrs. Ramsbottom sniffed. "I suppose even a broken clock is right twice a day. But possession is nine tenths of the law as they say. Let me know what you discover about that piece and the others."

"Oh, I certainly will. Thank you again."

"You're welcome. By the way, I heard you've been kind enough to walk some of the local dogs."

"Yes, that's right. Do you have one you'd like me to add to the mix?"

"I do. His name is Elwood."

Rory smiled. "I'll pick Elwood up tomorrow at eleven if that works?"

"Wonderful. Good day, Ms. Castle."

Rory disconnected the call and lowered her phone. "So, if Mrs. Ramsbottom knows her family as well as she thinks she does, a Ramsbottom didn't paint that."

"Which means you're not a Ramsbottom."

"I appreciate that. I try not to be."

I shot her a wry smile. "So her twat of a housekeeper

who probably isn't a twat at all, picked it up at an antique store or flea market."

"Do you know of any in the area?"

"There are a few." I thought about it for a minute. My mom liked antiques, but she typically attended online auctions. And picking around at flea markets wasn't really the style of most of the Calliope Hills community. I rubbed my lower lip. We could simply google the closest ones, or..."You know who could tell us which ones to go to first? Haven Hale."

"Who's Haven Hale?"

"She runs a nursery at the edge of town and is married to Pelion's chief of police, Travis. And, from what I know, she frequents every flea market in a sixty-mile radius. Every time I run into her and Travis in town, they're off to another one."

Rory nodded. She tilted her head as she considered me. "Are you sure you're up for this? I mean, it's Saturday. Wouldn't you prefer an off day sailing or whatever it is you do in your leisure time, rather than hunting around in antique stores?"

"You saw the photographs, did you?" I knew the reason she'd mentioned sailing. My mother had framed photos of me from every fleet race I'd competed in while I was a member of the high school sailing team. What my mother didn't know—what no one knew—was that I'd hated fleet racing and I got seasick on the water. And yet I'd done it anyway because all the sons of Calliope's wealthiest families did it, and my parents had loved watching me win. "My sailing days are over," I said, the words clipped, and by the flicker of surprise on Rory's face, I could tell she'd caught it. I pulled in a deep breath and let it out slowly. "I didn't have any plans today, and like I said, I want to help. I'm invested in this now."

She squinted at me. "Well, okay then, if you're sure. Thank you again." She picked up her purse and turned toward me. "Ready?"

As we walked to my car after locking up Faith's bungalow, she asked, "Why are your sailing days over? For someone who lives next to a lake, I'd think you'd be out on the water all the time if you love it."

"I don't love it," I said as I opened her door and she got in. I rounded the car and got in on my side and Rory was already turned toward me.

"If you don't love it, why did you do it?"

I shrugged. "All my dad's friend's sons were on the fleet team. And I was good at it."

"From the photos, it looked like you were better than good at it."

I had been. I'd been the best. "I was on the rowing team in college too, but when I graduated, I turned my competitive spirit toward the business world."

Her gaze moved over my face, a slight dent between her brows. "I didn't know people could excel at things they didn't like," she said. "I would think that the commitment to being excellent would demand a certain level of passion."

Passion. There was that word again. "I'm good at a lot of things I don't like," I said. *Why did I say that?* Was it true? I turned a corner a little too fast, and Rory grabbed on to the handle near her head and let out a short laugh.

"Why bother putting in the time to be great at something if it brings you no joy?" she asked. "I mean, I know people have to do jobs they don't like sometimes out of necessity, but recreation?"

"It made my dad happy. Like I said, he made a lot of sacrifices. But both my parents not only worked hard to live the life they live but worked hard for a family too. They tried for many, many years to have children, and had all but given up when I came along. In fact, they had already started adoption proceedings when my mom miraculously got pregnant with me. The doctors had told her it was practically impossible and yet…there I was. My sister Lexi was placed in our home when I was only six months old which is why we're so close in age."

The consolation prize, she jokingly called herself. Meaning I, of course, was the main prize, the one they'd never expected but gotten anyway. *Their windfall. They'd have cancelled their application with the adoption agency if they'd have thought of it when Mom found out she was pregnant,* Lexi once told me. *But then they got the call that a birth mother had chosen them,* she'd gone on, *and they didn't think there was an out and so they just went ahead and took me, even though they'd already received what they really wanted in you.*

The thing was? She was probably right. And I didn't say that because my parents weren't generous, kind people who loved Lexi completely. A little old-fashioned maybe, but my father had wanted a son to follow in his footsteps, an heir who cared just as much about the company he'd poured his heart and soul into building from the ground up. He'd wanted to give the life he never had to his children, and he wanted to be assured that all the sacrifices he'd made were because he was leaving a legacy that meant the Buchanans who came after him would have the wealth and security he never did growing up.

And honestly? It was a good thing I'd come along, because Lexi had absolutely no interest whatsoever in the world of business.

Rory was watching me with that look on her face that told me her wheels were turning. "Oh, I see," she said. Yes, she probably did. I knew what she was thinking, not just because she'd said a version of it before, but because if I had been looking in from the outside, I might have thought the same thing: *that's a lot of pressure.* And…yes, okay, it *was.* And being with Rory, stepping out of the box I'd lived in all my life—even temporarily—was making me realize how much. But should I feel sorry for myself because I lived a life of luxury, complete with the guarantee that there was a multimillion-dollar company waiting for me to run? How many others would give their left arm to have that kind of "pressure"?

"I know it sounds like pressure," I said, voicing my thought. "And it is, but, God, it's also luck. I was born into this life of extreme privilege where I've wanted for nothing, my whole life. I've been showered with love." I paused, picturing that look my father got on his face when I met or exceeded what I understood to be his expectations—pride mixed with this intense gratitude like I was everything he'd always wished for and more. "If my father, who brought himself up from nothing, wants a legacy, why shouldn't he get it?"

"Because you're not a legacy, you're a human soul," she said quietly.

My hands tightened on the steering wheel, her words causing something to fill my throat that I had to work to swallow down. I also felt inexplicably defensive. "It doesn't seem like such a hardship," I said.

"Being perfect?"

I let out a bark of laughter and I could hear that it sounded as defensive as I felt. "No one's ever asked me to be perfect." I vaguely remembered saying something about not being perfect when we'd had sex, but I couldn't recall more than that. Hopefully she didn't remember my exact words either because I hadn't been in control of what I was saying, my thoughts spilling out of my mouth uninhibited, the filter between my brain and my tongue melted away by the surge of lust. But that was likely honesty, right? I'd have been hard-pressed to come up with a lie in those heated moments. And so...okay, perhaps no one had ever come right out and asked me to be perfect, but I was very aware that that's what my family expected me to reach for.

"You must just come by that naturally then," she said on a smile, obviously sensing the tension and working to dispel it.

"You barely know me, Rory," I said. Her face fell just a fraction and I felt a sharp little internal jab, knowing I'd said that to push her away because I felt attacked for some reason I couldn't identify.

"No, you're right, I don't. I'm sorry if I sounded judgmental—"

"No, I'm sorry." I gave my head a shake. "That was rude. It's just...I guess I do feel some pressure to be the so-called perfect son. But I can handle it. *Shouldn't* pressure come with privilege? I take it seriously. I want to be a good steward of all that I've been entrusted with. I would never try to play this poor little rich boy role. I'm honored to walk in my father's footsteps. I'm honored to be given the chance to carry on his legacy."

She nodded and gave me another smile that I swore held a modicum of sadness. "I understand," she said. "And I don't disagree. You're a good person, Gage."

Something about that rubbed me the wrong way too and I didn't know what. What was it about this girl that had me all twisted and confused about things I'd been certain about my whole life? I didn't like it, and yet, I didn't seem to be able to stay away from her. "It's just up the road," I said, pointing out the window and changing the subject.

We drove past the grove of aspens, the sparkle of the lake coming into view as we rounded the bend, the dock that Travis had rebuilt years ago stretching into the water where a white paddle boat was moored.

"It's beautiful here," she said as we turned onto the gravel road that led to Haven's Gate, Plant and Garden Center. The land had once belonged to Travis's father, Connor Hale, and Travis had given it to Haven to build her business on, a business that was obviously thriving.

The parking lot was mostly full on a Saturday morning, customers pulling wagons loaded with plants and flowers to their cars where they could unload into their trunks.

The number of vehicles in the parking lot wasn't the only reason I knew Haven's business was successful though. My own mother had hired her to install a French garden called a parterre that, since the spring ladies' luncheon where she'd showcased it, had become all the rage among the upper crust of Calliope. I'd heard several women complain to my mother that they hadn't been able to set an install date for many months into the future.

And now Haven was busy designing water features too.

I pulled in to a spot near the back and Rory and I stepped out of the car, the gravel crunching beneath our feet. As we started walking toward the red barn, a couple of mutts came trotting from inside and Rory stopped, bending forward and patting her hands on her knees as a grin spread across her face. I watched as the pair ran gleefully toward her and she squatted down, dogs colliding with human in a muddled blur of laughter and joyful whines and wagging tails and declarations of "what a good girl." It was honestly difficult to tell what was coming from where, Rory so easily became a part of the small pack.

After a few minutes, she stood, brushing herself off, the dogs still whining happily and head butting her legs. She looked up at me and I suddenly realized I was smiling so big I could actually feel the breeze on my teeth. "What's with you and dogs?" I asked as she let out another laugh, scratching the black and white one under her chin as the other one lay down at her feet as though staking claim.

She shrugged. "I love them. I understand them. I don't know. I just always have. We don't deserve dogs," she said on a smile. "But we get them anyway."

We stood there smiling at each other, the dog she was petting head butting my leg so that I looked down. She was staring up at me, her tongue lolling from her mouth as though she too was grinning.

"Do you like dogs?" Rory asked softly and tentatively as though my answer had the potential to cause her immense grief.

Did I like dogs? For whatever reason, I felt like I owed her a thoughtful response, neither sugar-coated nor flippant. I slowly squatted down the way she had, and looked the dog in the eye, scratching it under its chin. The dog tilted her head, studying me as though attempting to read me, somehow understanding that I wouldn't necessarily respond with as much enthusiasm as Rory had to an energetic demeanor. "I think so," I said. "I never had a dog either as a child or as an adult. My father loves animals. We run several foundations that protect wildlife and support rescue organizations, but my parents traveled a lot, and my father worked until all hours, so we never had a family pet. I haven't had a lot of interaction with them. I don't…not like dogs." They seemed like happy creatures. I knew lots of good people who were very attached to their own. I'd been told they were loyal. I scratched the mutt under her chin for a few more minutes and then stood. Both the dogs scampered off, back toward the red barn.

"Gage, is that you?"

I turned to see Haven walking toward us, peering between a large plant in her arms that appeared half dead.

"Haven," I said as she came up to us and set the plant on the ground. "Just the woman I was looking for." I smiled. "This is Rory…Castle. She's…an art appraiser who works for Faith Lorenz." God, I was a shit liar. I had to stop pausing before every falsehood.

Rory shot me a brief apologetic dipping of her brow that I thought was her acknowledging that I was officially spreading the lie and she was allowing me to. But I wasn't going to blow her cover, and she'd already presented herself as Faith's new employee, so I was kind of stuck.

"Oh," Haven smiled and wiped her hand on her jean shorts. "Welcome to town."

Rory shook her hand and smiled. "Thank you."

"I see you lost one," I said, nodding to the plant at her feet.

"Not if I can help it," Haven said as she set her hands on her hips. "I'm going to re-plant her along the fence line over there." She nodded toward a white, split-rail fence that looked newly installed. "I think she's just being a princess about the amount of sun she wants."

"Your nursery is beautiful," Rory said as she glanced around from the charming red barn to the distant orchard behind it, tall apple trees reaching into the clear blue of the sky.

"Thank you," Haven said, obvious pride filling her expression as she too glanced around at the people browsing the pots of flowers on tiers in the front of the barn. "It's been a labor of love." She looked back at Rory. "Hey, we're having a Fourth of July bonfire here if you're interested. Very simple, nothing fancy, but we'd love to have you."

"Thank you so much, Haven. That's very kind of you."

"You too, of course, Gage," Haven said. "Anyway, you said you were looking for me?"

I cleared my throat. "Yes. Rory and I are on a treasure hunt of sorts." I smiled over at her. "It's a long story, but we're trying to find some information on a piece of art that was apparently purchased at an antique store or a flea market and hoping to potentially find more pieces by the same artist. We thought you might be able to point us toward the best place to start."

"Oh! Sure, I can help with that." She gave a short laugh. "I think I've at least stopped in to every local spot. What kind of art is it? Not that I know anything very specific, but is it new or old?"

"It's probably about twenty-seven years old and likely done by a local," Rory told her.

"Okay, so not an actual antique." She chewed on the inside of her cheek for a second. "I'd start at the Pink Elephant. The owner has an eclectic mix of things, from antique furniture and paintings to more crafty pieces. She has a good eye and picks things up from local artists. After the Pink Elephant, try Ruby's Slippers. It's mostly vintage clothing, but the owner of that store also has paintings that she picks up from flea markets hung up on all the walls that are for sale."

"I knew you were the one to ask," I said. "Thanks so much, Haven."

"My pleasure," she said with a grin as she bent and picked up the plant. "Nice to meet you, Rory."

"You too, Haven."

She turned and headed for the fence where she was apparently going to attempt to meet the needs of an overly dramatic plant. Rory gave one last look around, a small smile curving her lips. She sighed as though she almost hated to leave, and then we headed for my car.

"Ready for some treasure hunting, Cakes?" I asked as I turned the ignition.

"I was born ready, Ivy League," she said with a laugh.

CHAPTER SEVENTEEN
Rory

The Pink Elephant was situated in the downtown area just down the highway from Calliope. When we entered the dim shop, the owner, who was sitting on a stool behind a counter near the back, removed her earbuds and gave us a smile. The soft noise of the overhead fan whirred above us. "Welcome! Can I help you find anything specific, or are you just digging around?"

"Hi," I said. "I hope you can help us. We're looking for watercolor paintings that were probably done by a local artist who we're attempting to identify. We have one of a portion of Pelion Lake we believe was done about twenty-seven years ago, but there may be some that exist that are more recent. The initials in the corner say M.S. Do you have anything like that?" I suddenly wished I'd taken a snapshot of it on my phone so we could show it to her, but I was also pretty certain we'd recognize one of the paintings if we saw it.

"A local artist?" the older, gray-haired woman asked. "Hmm. If I have anything fitting that description, it'd be in the back in one of the picture bins." She pointed to her left where there was a doorway that led down a couple steps into another room. "Anything I think is more valuable, I hang up on the wall," she said as she looked up and waved her arm around, "but I don't currently have a lot. Antique paintings—especially signed ones—are popular right now, and there haven't been many estate sales in the last few months. I suppose I should be glad of the fact that no one has died recently, but it's also not great for business," she said with a small laugh. "Anyway, help yourself."

"Thanks," Gage and I both said as we headed for the back room. It felt warmer back here as there was no overhead fan to stir up the air. And without the benefit of the glass front door letting in some light, it was much more dim. It smelled of potpourri and eucalyptus, scents that conjured to mind my granny's house before my mother and I had moved in and made it our own. I heard the front door open and the shop owner greet some customers, engaging in conversation.

I walked around the large shelving unit in the middle of the room that held candles and other craft items that were obviously handmade as Gage headed for the three wooden boxes sitting on the floor that were full of framed art.

He bent and started going through the first box, glancing at each painting as he leaned it against the one in front of it. I bent over too and looked over his shoulder as he worked. His movements slowed, and I became aware of how close we were, his unforgettable scent deeper and more complex than it'd been in his car. I could smell his cologne, but also his skin, and the cinnamon on his breath. A tumble of visions came back to me as I breathed him in, the memories of when I'd first experienced the smell of his skin and the taste of his tongue.

My nipples hardened, and a small buzz took up at the

apex of my thighs, the chatter and laughter of the women at the front of the store fading as blood whooshed between my ears. Gage flipped another frame and I took in a lighthouse done in oils as his breath seemed to hitch. *I should move.* The air seemed to thicken, the molecules in the space between us swelling. I felt woozy but also hyper-aware. God, I couldn't help it. Every time this man got close to me, I wanted to get naked. I was desperate to feel the slow slide of his body over mine. *In* mine. *I should definitely move away.* Only I didn't want to. And though it felt dangerous, there was also safety in the fact that we were in a public place, and so I lingered, taking what I could. All that I dared. "Rory," he said, and his voice sounded as thick as whatever was currently lodged in my own throat. His finger jerked and he flipped another frame, and I blinked as my gaze landed on a smaller-sized watercolor of a lake and a shore and—

"Holy shit," I said, reaching for it and pulling it from the stack. We both stood, my eyes meeting his when he turned. They looked slightly glazed, his lips parted before he blinked and moved around to stand next to me so we could both look down at the now-familiar art. "M.S.," I whispered. "Holy shit," I repeated. "Gage, we found one."

"Look through the other boxes," he said, bending toward the second one. I hesitated only a moment and then went to the third. My limbs still felt slightly shaky, not from discovering a picture—though my heart was now beating an excited tempo—but from my reaction to being so close to Gage… to lingering there as my blood heated and my tissue softened in response to my own yearning for him.

There was another M.S. original at the back of the crate. "Gage!" I said as I pulled it out. He turned, abandoning the box that he'd just gotten to the back of.

"Two," he breathed as he again came to stand next to me so we could both look down at the picture. This one was mostly trees, and a slip of rocky shore.

I felt like rejoicing and crying and I was *still* just a little turned on. I took a step away. "Let's go ask the owner about these," I said. We headed back toward the front where the two customers she'd been chatting with were now browsing a shelf near the front window.

"Oh my!" She brought her hands to her mouth when she saw that I was carrying two paintings. "Did you find what you were looking for?"

"Yes," I said, the excitement I felt clear in my voice. "These are by the same artist." I set them down on the mahogany counter. "Are you able to tell us where you got them?"

She frowned as she tapped a finger to her chin. "I'm sorry, but I can't recall. Most of those pieces in the back, I've had for many years. My daughter used to help me collect items for my store before she got married and moved to New Hampshire, so there's a chance she picked those up. I add to the collection now and again, but I rarely look through them."

My shoulders dropped. *Damn*. "Are you able to tell me anything at all about these paintings?" The irony that I was posing as an art appraiser and yet was asking for a professional opinion about two pieces of art didn't escape me.

"Hmm," she hummed as she leaned forward and perused the two paintings, moving her head as she looked from one to the other. "I'd say they're charming, but not masterful. The artist does seem to possess a talent for evoking emotion."

"Yes," I agreed, delighted by the fact that my instinctive

assessment matched up to this woman's more knowledgeable opinion.

Gage stepped up next to me as he removed a business card from his wallet. "If you happen to remember where you got these, or see any others like them with these initials, will you give me a call?"

The woman took the card and glanced down at it. "Certainly, Mr. Buchanan."

I moved to take my credit card from the small wallet I was carrying around my wrist, but the woman waved me away. "No charge. Consider it my contribution toward identifying your artist."

I let out a breath as I lowered my arm. "That's very kind of you."

"I can't believe it," I said as we were walking to Gage's car.

He smiled over at me. "Our treasure hunt started on a high note," he said. "But you know what I'm wondering, right?"

I looked over my shoulder at him as he opened my door. "If there's another diary entry behind these?"

"Exactly. Get in and let's find out."

He walked around the car and got behind the wheel and started to take one of the paintings off my lap, but I put a hand on his. "Let's open the backs of these once we get back to Faith's." I saw Gage nod in my peripheral vision as I ran my hand over the glass, my heart giving a thump. *My father painted these. His hand drew these lines.* I stretched my own fingers out, wondering which parts of me that obviously didn't come from my mother, came from him. Or perhaps his mother, or her mother before that. I suddenly felt part of a larger whole whereas all my life, I'd only considered myself a Mud Gulch Casteel. My father and his family felt close all of a sudden, closer than they'd ever felt, and I realized that since I'd arrived in the Pelion Lake area, I hadn't felt that *pull* that I'd experienced all my life.

Had I simply been too involved in my treasure hunt to notice it? Or had it gone away because I'd arrived just where I'd been meant to be?

I felt *energized*, not only because I'd just found two pieces of art, but because the last diary entry we'd read had mentioned the founding member flirting with my mother, reinforcing that I was on the right track. *He* was the important man she'd told me about. I was so incredibly glad I'd taken the risk and followed what I believed to be my mother's nudge.

I lay my head back on the plush leather of Gage's rental car, turning my head just enough to look at him without him being able to tell that he was being observed. My eyes wandered over his strong profile, lingering on the crease between his brows. What was he thinking so hard about? Did he realize how much he frowned when he thought no one was watching? *What are you so troubled by, Mr. Perfect?*

The more time we spent together, a better picture of Gage Buchanan emerged. I considered what we'd talked about in the car before arriving at Haven's Gate, about his continued assertion that he was honored by the pressure he felt to carry on his father's legacy. Did he even realize how tense he got when he talked about his incredible luck? His immense privilege? His duty to make his parents happy? There was no joy in the subject for Gage. Did he realize that he spoke on the subject as if it was rehearsed, like he'd been repeating it in his head all his life? I didn't think he did. Which made me suspect something about it was less than natural, like maybe he was attempting to convince himself of something that wasn't true.

So what is true, Gage? Who are you without all the trappings of being the perfect son? What would you do if you could do anything at all?

I'm not as perfect as I seem.

Thinking about the sacrifices Gage made for his father made me think of Romeo. And maybe that's why Gage's situation needled at me so much. Honestly, hearing him talk about it rubbed at me like sandpaper. Perhaps in some way, I took it personally. Because my uncle had made a sacrifice too. Romeo had been forced to give in to the pressure of family commitment despite his own dreams.

My gaze moved away from Gage to the scenery moving past the car. My heart gave an unusual squeeze as I caught glimpses of the rocky shore of the lake through the trees. Something about the view of the lake felt…familiar somehow. No, that wasn't the right word, and I couldn't exactly figure out what was. Maybe because there was no singular word. Ever since I'd first caught the glimmer of this lake, I'd felt a ball of emotion rise up in my chest. I'd felt joy, and longing, and peace and even…a strange grief for something I couldn't name. I glanced down at the watercolor in my lap. Maybe it was that I was looking at the true-life vision of what my father had looked on with his own eyes as he'd painted it. Just as I could tell there was love in the painting of my mother, I could sense that there was love for this place. Maybe the part of him that had loved Pelion Lake had somehow passed on to me.

"What are you thinking about over there?" Gage asked, breaking me from my reverie.

"My father," I said. "He loved this place," I said with certainty, lightly tapping on the glass of the painting.

Gage nodded, glancing down at the framed pieces in my lap. "I agree," he said, obviously understanding that I was making the statement based on the emotion present in the art.

Butterflies fluttered in my stomach at the thought that my father, right this very moment, might be only a few miles from me.

"There's Ruby's Slippers," Gage said. "Should we stop in while we're out and about? Maybe have three frames to open up when we get back to Faith's?"

"Sure, couldn't hurt," I said. "If you're game."

He grinned, and my heart flipped in that same way it tended to do in response to the flash of this man's white smile focused in my direction. "I told you I was in," he said.

We pulled into the lot of a small strip mall that featured a popular grocery chain at one end. Ruby's Slippers was situated in the middle and Gage parked in a spot near the front door.

The air-conditioned thrift store felt deliciously cool as we stepped inside from out of the summer heat. The space was bright with the light of the unobstructed windows along the front wall and the refrains of a nineties song about a cruel summer played loudly on the sound system as shoppers flipped through racks of clothing.

"Welcome to Ruby's Slippers," a young girl said from behind a counter as she placed an item in a bag for the customer standing in front of the register.

I smiled at her and then looked around as I took in the various pieces of framed art hung on all the walls, just like Haven had described. Gage and I started walking along the one to our left, both of us looking up as we moved. There were original paintings, some merely decent, others better—according to my tastes, anyway—but there were also reprints and posters. It didn't take us long to make our way around the entirety of the store, not having come upon even one piece that made us pause. "I have to wonder how many of my father's pieces are hanging in the homes of Pelion and Calliope residents who came upon one in a store like this and just thought it was pretty," I said.

"Yeah, I wondered the same thing," Gage said. "But you know, the fact that at least a couple of his pieces are in secondhand stores, might be a clue in and of itself."

I bit my lip. "How so?"

He put his elbow on the top of a rack next to him and crossed one foot over the other as he obviously thought about the implications. "Well, either he gave his own paintings away, or his family did. Under what circumstances, though? It's something to keep in mind, however, as we go forward."

I nodded, chewing at my lip again as I looked away. *Go forward. If* there was a forward direction to move in. And before I went back home in a few weeks.

A piece of blue fabric caught my eye and I blinked, moving toward it and pulling it from the rack. I pulled in a breath. "Oh my gosh," I said. "My mother had a dress almost just like this one." I stared at it, overcome with the feeling that I'd just been transported to the past. My gaze ran over the shimmery fabric, the blue appearing to turn different shades as I moved it back and forth and it caught the light. It had tiny spaghetti straps, was gathered at the waist, and featured a high slit up the right thigh. It was simple, yet stunning.

Gage came up next to me and took it from my hands and held it up. "The blue..." he murmured. "It's the exact shade of your eyes." He stared at it, mesmerized.

I smiled. Yes, it was close, although the dress almost didn't seem to be one singular color. My mother had kept the dress similar to this one in the back of her closet. I'd tried it on a time or two when playing dress-up. Once, she'd caught me and appeared almost angry. I'd held my breath, confused by her reaction when she'd never minded me digging through her clothes or costume jewelry before. But then she'd smiled and told me I looked beautiful and hurried away. I didn't know what happened to that dress. She must have gotten rid of it because it wasn't among her things when I finally found the strength to bag them up to donate.

"Please let me buy it for you," he said.

I let out a quiet laugh. "I have absolutely nowhere to wear something like this to," I told him. "Not here, and certainly not in Mud Gulch."

"Still, I insist," he said, turning toward the front register. "I've never seen anything that more perfectly matches your eyes."

I laughed as I followed him. He'd made it sound like he'd recently come back from a lifelong pilgrimage to find the shade of my eyes. He was being kind because I'd mentioned my mother. Perhaps he'd seen the longing in my eyes. I was going to let him gift it to me because honestly, it did feel like a small piece of my mother that I'd somehow lost. Plus, I'd seen the price tag and it was only thirty bucks.

Gage paid for the dress and then presented the bag to me as we stepped out of line. "Thank you," I told him with a smile. "And who knows. Maybe someday I'll be invited to a ball and this will come in handy."

"Perhaps you will."

Faith was in the back office eating a takeout salad when we

arrived at the gallery. "Hi, Gage," she said as she wiped her hands on a napkin and stood up to shake his hand.

"I should probably be irritated with you," he said as he took her hand. "But I guess we're pretty much on the same team now."

She smiled and I set the two paintings down on the round table in the middle of the room that held Faith's lunch and a few stacks of mail and what looked like random paperwork. Her eyes widened, and she put her hand on my arm. "Oh my God, you found two more!"

"We did," I confirmed as I turned them both over.

"And now you're going to check them for diary entries. Oh my God," she repeated. "Wait, let me get you a knife." She took the few steps over to her desk and removed a craft knife from her drawer and handed it to Gage when he reached for it.

As Gage began carefully removing the frame backing, I gave Faith the quick version of events that had transpired since that morning, including talking to Mrs. Ramsbottom, and going to the two stores Haven had recommended.

"What does it mean?" Faith asked in a whisper, as though she was worried about interrupting Gage's concentration by being too loud. "That those paintings were donated or sold?"

"We were wondering that too," I replied in an equally hushed voice. "There are so many possibilities, I suppose."

We both leaned forward, my breath catching as Gage opened the back of the first frame, exposing a folded piece of paper. I gasped softly and reached for it, my hands shaking as I put it on the table and opened it. All three of us leaned in, tears pricking my eyes as I took in my mother's handwriting.

Last night, M.S. and I had a picnic dinner on the shore of the lake and then stayed up half the night talking about everything under the sun. He's worldly and interesting. He's been so many places I've only dreamed of. But he has sadness in his eyes too. He's so different than I thought he was when I first met him. So much deeper and kinder.

He loves animals. I've never seen a man who looks so deeply into a dog's eyes. It's like he's communing with them. It makes me smile. They love him back which my mom always said means a person has a good soul.

He's smart too. He's read just about every book ever written, or at least it seems like he has. He's always referencing this quote or that quote, and I wish I could remember them later because I would write them down and think about why they mean so much to him. When I told him he must have the memory of an elephant to recall all those words, he got this troubled look on his face and said he wished he didn't.

He's a complex man, and I guess you might say I'm a simple kind of girl. But can I share a secret? I think I'm falling in love with him. Deeper and deeper by the day.

I let out another gasp, raising my head to see that Gage was already looking at me. "M.S.," I said, a dizzying spiral of joy making me want to dance. "M.S. is definitely my father." I paused, pulling in a breath as I turned and looked at Faith and then back at Gage. "I got my love of animals from him." It was a connection, a gap being filled in.

"I'm not surprised," Faith said. "The way you love dogs…it *had* to be in the blood."

I grinned.

"Let's, ah, see if there's another entry in the other one," Gage said, pulling the second painting toward him and picking up the craft knife. I watched him for a moment, sensing his discomfort. My heart dropped as it suddenly registered. He'd told me his father loved animals too. Was his father a big reader? Of course he was—weren't most highly successful people? And he'd traveled a lot as well—Gage had said so.

I focused in on Gage's hands as he worked on the second frame backing, trying my best to empty my mind of the idea that we still couldn't rule out Gage's father, despite the initials not matching his name. I swallowed down a lump.

The second frame had what looked like a bit of water damage and so the backer came off easily, Gage sliding it aside to reveal two pieces of paper with the ink bleeding on both. My heart jumped and I peeled them apart and laid them both out the same way I'd done with the first. The page on the left was only smeared a little, but the one on the right was almost completely ruined except for a paragraph at the bottom. We turned our heads in tandem to read the one that was intact.

I ran into those mean girls today. You should have seen them, all high and mighty, flouncing around like they own the town and all who reside here. You know that feeling I had that something wonderful is going to happen? That idea dimmed just a little when I figured out what snobby bitches live here, I have to admit. Anyway, I suppose things just got a tad more interesting and I always did like interesting, or at least that's what my mom says which I know is a nice way to say I tend to stir up drama. Not on purpose, I swear. Anyway, dear diary, I seem to have poked a hornet's nest—and so I suppose I should prepare to be stung.

"Mean girls?" I asked. "I wonder who she was referring to."

Faith shrugged. "There are plenty of those in Calliope, but that's probably true everywhere."

"True enough," I said. From what it sounded like, though, my mother had simply butted heads with a few local girls. Ophelia Casteel had never been one to let a sly comment or obvious slight go though, so who knew if it was anything more than that. I moved the damaged entry over and we all took a moment to read what was left of it.

I woke in the middle of the night to find him sweating and squeezing his head. I was so scared. He told me he has visions sometimes. He doesn't know if they're memories or hallucinations. They scare him too. But God, I love him. I love him, and I don't know how to bring him peace.

I looked at Gage. "Visions?" he asked. "Was he suffering from mental illness?"

"Maybe. And maybe if she didn't tell him about me, that was the reason. Do…do either of you know if any of those men struggled with a mental condition at some point?"

Again, Gage and Faith shook their heads. "No," Faith said. "But that's not exactly something most people advertise. Especially if they have the means to address it quietly."

"Maybe he went away to deal with his problems," I said. "Maybe that's why she never told him about me."

"Could be," Gage said. "Or maybe it wasn't a mental illness so much as…a bout with anxiety or depression that was related to some previous life circumstance or another."

"Did your father struggle with that at some point?" It was a personal question, but I knew Gage would answer honestly in an effort to help me find the truth. He had said he was invested, and I knew he wouldn't be running all over Maine helping me hunt down art if that wasn't true.

Gage sighed. "My father went through a rough patch when my grandpa died. I was very young. But he'd had a tough relationship with him. He never went into details, but I think there was some abuse involved."

"Oh," I said softly. "I'm sorry about that." I glanced at

Faith and then down at the diary entry, my heart feeling heavy for a man I'd never met but had obviously suffered in some manner or another. I hoped that in the years that followed, he had found the peace my mother couldn't give him, or hadn't had the chance to.

CHAPTER EIGHTEEN
Gage

I saw Blakely sitting under an umbrella on the patio at the club and headed her way, greeting a few people I knew as I moved through the bistro tables filled with members enjoying lunch. Blakely had pulled out a mirror and a tube of lipstick as I'd made my way to her and when I approached the table, she quickly deposited it into the purse sitting on the ground next to her chair.

She stood. "Gage! It's so good to see you. Thanks for meeting me."

I leaned in and kissed her cheek and we both took a seat. "Sorry it took me a few days to get back to you. Work has been crazy." A lie. Work had been slow, as my employees had started transferring ongoing projects to other managers in preparation for me leaving the country soon. I'd been thankful as it'd given me more time to skip out and leave early so I could help Rory.

Rory.

I'd been trying not to think too much about Rory since

Saturday when we'd found two paintings with her mother's diary entries behind them. The thing with the flashbacks had me concerned. I knew my father had trouble sleeping and carried emotional burdens from his childhood. It was probably another bullet point on the long list of reasons that I was so averse to disappointing him. He deserved the life he'd fought so hard for. God, this search with Rory was like a damn roller coaster. One day I had hope we weren't related…and the next provided a clue that we might be. At this point, it was just a waiting game for those results.

"Are you okay?"

"What?"

"You groaned."

"I did? Uh…" I massaged my chest. "A little bit of heartburn," I explained with an apologetic half-smile.

"I thought you must not be feeling well. It's not like you not to shave." Blakely looked around, caught the eye of a server and waved him over. "Chett, could you run to the shop in the lobby and get Gage a pack of Tums?"

"Really that's not—"

Blakely waved my protests away. "Thanks, Chett."

The man nodded and hurried off.

"That's what they're here for," she said. "Give him a big tip when he comes back. Heartburn is no fun."

No, no it wasn't.

Blakely smiled and turned her head as another server approached our table and asked if we were ready to order. "Yes, thank you," Blakely said, and ordered the same thing she always ordered—the pear and pistachio salad, hold the green onion.

I had the menu memorized at this point too and didn't require opening one to rattle off my order of a club sandwich.

Promise me you'll name a menu item after me when you open your restaurant someday. I gave my head a shake as Chef LaCourt's words came back to me, his Parisian heavy accent still as clear in my mind as though we'd spoken yesterday. Since I'd mentioned him to Rory, he'd been randomly popping into my mind and I wasn't sure I liked it. I missed him…and it'd been a long time since I'd pondered on that. *What would you think of how I turned out?* The last time I'd seen him, I'd been a kid. I was a man now.

I sighed, running my fingers over my stubbly cheek. "Do you like me like this?" I asked Blakely.

She studied me briefly, her brow dipping. "Like what?"

I rubbed my chin. "With this scruff."

She continued to frown at me for a moment as though I'd asked her a trick question. "I mean…you're good-looking no matter what you do. But you're usually more polished. I like the polished Gage."

I like the polished Gage.

Yes, everyone seemed to like the polished Gage. *I'd* always liked the polished Gage.

But recently…

"So tell me what you've been thinking," Blakely said after she'd taken a sip of water.

What have I been thinking? I've been trying not to think, honestly. Because thinking seems to lead me to all sorts of uncomfortable places. "Just…you know, about the move. There's a lot to do."

"Mmhmm. Anything else?" Blakely reached across the table and set her hand on mine, one elegant finger running lightly over my knuckle.

I used my other hand to lift my glass and take a long drink of water in order to stall. I knew what she was asking me.

I knew her touch was meant to slowly introduce a physical comfort. And it wasn't that I disliked it. In fact, it felt…nice. I was just so damn conflicted. "Listen, Blakely—"

She lifted her hand from mine and waved it around, stopping my words. "Gage, if you're not sure, don't answer yet. You said you'd give it until your party and let me know then. But listen, I already spoke with your father and he's willing to hire me to manage all the social media for the London hotel build and opening. I'd focus on the style aspect, of course, and give the designers my input. My mother put me in charge of redoing our Hamptons home last year and it was featured in several local style magazines. In addition to fashion, I'd relish the opportunity to add interior design to my online portfolio. Plus, I could bring the eyes of my two million Instagram followers to The Buchanan in London, from ground-breaking to ribbon-cutting, featuring the luxurious but au courant style so beautifully done in your hotels." Her eyes shined with excitement as I worked to arrange all the words she'd said into something that didn't feel like a fist squeezing my lungs.

Two million Instagram followers.

I already spoke with your father.

I could see Blakely now, sweeping through the London hotel, completely in her element as she talked thread count and designer wallpaper as two million young people were introduced to The Buchanan. If my father was the new Conrad Hilton, Blakely would be his Paris. She'd been born for the role. Of *course* my father was on board. Now he probably thought our union was more perfect than ever.

"Anyway," Blakely went on, "if your answer is a yes"—her smile widened—"we'll drink to new beginnings. We owe it to ourselves, and maybe even to our parents, to really live with the idea for a couple more weeks. To give it our real heartfelt consideration, don't you think?"

I took in Blakely's pretty smile and the way she picked at her cuticles when she was nervous, like she was doing now. I could tell that the idea hadn't only grown on her since we'd first spoken; she was incredibly enthusiastic about it. She was already envisioning her life—*our* life in vivid detail.

And so was my father.

I let out a slow exhale, willing the internal fist to unclench. And really? She was right. I hadn't given it even a moment of consideration—heartfelt or otherwise—even though I'd fully intended to. Why? Because of Rory and the way my mind constantly wanted to travel to her. And so I'd shut down my thoughts to the best of my ability. Because thoughts of my father spending his evenings with another woman having picnics on the lake shore and impregnating her with my gorgeous, sexy half-sister was driving me mad.

"Is the heartburn that bad?" Blakely asked, indicating I'd once again made a sound of distress without realizing it.

I gave her an apologetic look. If it was confirmed that Rory was related to me, I'd *relish* going to another country. I'd get as far away from her and the feelings of lust she stirred up in me as I possibly could.

Is it only lust that she stirs up? No, and that made the problem worse.

My gaze met Blakely's. "I'll give it some real consideration," I promised her.

She grinned and raised her glass, clinking it to mine just as our food arrived.

When we'd finished lunch, I walked Blakely outside the club where we waited while the valet brought her car around. As it pulled up to the curb, Blakely slipped her hand around my waist, leaned in close, and brought her lips to mine, darting her tongue out to lick my bottom lip before pulling away. She tilted her head and smiled shyly up at me. "I hope that was okay," she said. "And I do hope you'll think hard about…us. We could rule the world together." She gave a small, teasing laugh, and then she wiped my lips with her thumb before heading toward her car.

I watched Blakely get in her cherry red convertible and peel off, tempted to yell after her to slow the hell down, like some overbearing dad.

Or big brother.

Though she definitely hadn't kissed me like a sibling. It had been…pleasant. And only slightly weird. But not…bad.

Just not Rory.

Fuck.

I stood there for a moment feeling troubled and weighted down by things out of my control before finally turning and reentering the club in order to take the quickest route to the member's parking lot located in the back.

"Oh, hello, Gage."

I came up short. "Mrs. Bellamy," I said, taking Virginia Bellamy's hand and leaning in and kissing her on her powder-soft cheek as her perfume wafted over me. "How nice to see you."

"It's nice to see you too," she said, sniffing delicately as if to see if there was alcohol on my breath. Ah yes, the gossips had been chattering. Likely the suppositions of a drinking problem had quickly morphed into an upcoming stay at a cushy rehab center. Talk moved faster than reality—or the lack thereof in my case anyway—on the towns bordering Pelion Lake.

I'd *never* been fodder for the gossips of either town.

Part of me resented it, and part of me almost…relished the feeling of stirring up comments of anything other than how so-called *perfect* I was.

Neither charge was accurate.

"I heard about your accident," she said. "I see you're no worse for wear."

"No, just a fender bender. I looked down at my phone for just a moment and…" I shrugged and gave her my best bashful smile.

"Hmm. Yes, texting and driving is an epidemic these days. Do be more careful. Your parents would be beside themselves if you were injured."

"I will. Nice to see you—"

Virginia Bellamy pulled on my arm when I tried to turn to walk away. "I wanted to mention something to you, Gage, as I've heard you've been seen keeping company with that woman working with Faith Lorenz."

That woman.

"Her name is Aurora," I said, feeling a sudden jolt of protectiveness that had a decidedly different feel than the concern over Blakely's propensity toward speeding.

Mrs. Bellamy's shoulders came back as if she'd heard the defensiveness in my tone. "Yes," she said. "Aurora Castle. I recalled some things since she came to my home. She's the spitting image of a woman who visited Calliope many years ago from somewhere up the coast, stirring up all kinds of drama at the Metropolitan Club. From what I remember, she had those men skinny-dipping in the club pool. Can you even imagine?" She made a sound of outrage in her throat.

I resisted the cringe that threatened to take over my face. *Damn it.* She'd remembered Rory's mother. And if she made the connection, someone else might easily discover she wasn't an art appraiser. Her cover would be blown, and she'd never be welcome in another Calliope home.

Plus, whatever else Rory's mother had done while she was in Calliope, she hadn't made friends of the wives of the founding members of the Metropolitan Club. Mrs. Bellamy could be a snooty old snob, but her opinion mattered in this town if you wanted to flourish in society. Still, I couldn't help the snark that rolled off my tongue. "She *forced* them to skinny-dip? How did she manage that?"

"Lord only knows how those type of women weave their spells."

Those type of women. Good grief. "Anyway," I said. "Aurora's from New York. She's never been here before." That last part, at least, was true. "The resemblance must be a coincidence."

"I don't think so," she said with a decisive nod. "Those eyes are unmistakable. Like the Hale eyes. Once you see them, there's no denying who you're looking at." She narrowed her own. "She returned the artwork I loaned her with a nice write-up on all four pieces," she said. "But I'm not convinced there isn't something untoward going on. Edna told me she trained under a Professor Hugo Dickstoker, but I haven't found anyone by that name in New York, and some rather unsavory sites come up when I do a search."

I made a small sound that was equal parts laughter and annoyance at this pompous meddler before covering it with a cough. "I believe Aurora mentioned that she didn't study in New York. She trained overseas, but I can't remember exactly where. Sweden…or France, or maybe…Transylvania."

Mrs. Bellamy frowned, her eyes moving to the side. "Oh."

I gave her a thin smile. "Anyway, I'm sure you have

much more important issues to focus on, Mrs. Bellamy. I heard the Ladies League's golf outing was a huge success and that you have another one coming up in the fall."

She preened a little just as I'd known she would. "Oh, it was an extraordinary success. I took it over from Dottie Cavendish, you know, as she needed time to settle her," she glanced around and then lowered her voice, "*divorce*. Anyway, we outdid all prior years, and I can't imagine the board won't transfer the event to me permanently."

"Ah. Well, that's...great. It was nice seeing you." I turned, bringing my arm close to my body so she couldn't reach out and grab me again, and walked quickly toward the door.

"You too, Gage," she called. "Remember to be cautious with—"

"Virginia, hello!" I heard a female voice behind me say, and I hurried toward the door as Mrs. Bellamy began conversing with the woman who had called her name.

Well at least I knew that Mrs. Bellamy was suspicious of Rory's credentials. If she was looking into the woman she remembered from years ago, then she was also poking into Rory's background. Which meant we had to work fast.

I stepped out onto the street. Now that I'd gone out the front door, I'd have to circle all the way around the club to where the parking lot was located. I swore under my breath. I had a meeting in ten minutes.

When I got to the corner, I started to turn when I spotted a woman holding a gaggle of dogs walking along the path on the other side of the street. I stopped, a grin breaking out over my face. *Rory.* She stopped too, staring over at me, her mouth parted slightly and a look on her face I couldn't read. She looked sort of sad, or worried or...I wasn't sure.

I moved toward the edge of the sidewalk, lifting my hand in a wave. She hesitated, but then transferred the handful of leashes into her other hand and waved back.

As she did so, one of the dogs suddenly lunged, my gaze flying to the critter that had caught the dog's eye. Rory's shoulder was yanked and she tripped forward, attempting to grab the leashes with both hands. It all happened in a flash. Rory was pulled, all three dogs now riled and barking, the one in the lead—the little lunatic with the Burberry sweater—taking chase after the three raccoons that I registered as a mother and her two offspring.

The squealing, clawing mother raccoon ran into the street with the two tiny raccoons behind her, Rory barely managed to pull back on the leashes hard enough that the dogs came up short, and an approaching car, music blasting from the windows, turned the corner and hit the fleeing mother raccoon.

Brakes screeched.

Rory screamed.

Dogs continued to bark.

And somehow, without even being aware that I'd moved, I was across the street, taking the leashes from Rory as she fell to her knees next to the still racoon.

"Holy shit!" the teenage boy who'd jumped out of his car said, bringing his hands to his head as he looked down at the—most likely—dead raccoon. "I didn't even see her. She came out of nowhere."

Rory's sobs rose as she put her fingers to the raccoon's neck, obviously searching for a pulse. "The babies!" she howled, pointing to a bush where the two tiny creatures had hidden.

Oh, Jesus.

I tied the still-barking rambunctious dogs to a nearby tree. "Quiet!" I said, making my voice deeper. All three of them stopped barking and lay down, panting with the exertion of just having caused major mayhem and orphaned two baby raccoons.

I squatted down next to Rory and took in the unmoving raccoon.

"I really, ah, gotta get to work," the teen said.

I'd forgotten he was there. "Go on," I told him. "It wasn't your fault, and there's nothing to be done for this animal."

Rory's wails increased, and the teen cringed, backing away to his car, getting in, and pulling off, the loud bass of whatever song he'd been playing fading away. "The babies," she moaned, tears dripping down her chin.

The babies. I crept over to the bush where they were hiding, leaning in and easily catching them, even though they tried to flee. *My God, they were newborns.*

Rory dropped her head, her chest heaving as she sobbed. My heart constricted and I felt something akin to panic. *Do something.* "She…she…she," Rory sobbed, barely able to catch her breath.

Adrenaline flooded my system, the need to *fix this* for her a drumbeat of desperation inside me. I very suddenly understood why wars were declared and battles fought, why men donned armor and strapped on weaponry and sailed into enemy territory with a singular mission in mind: *fix this.* I clutched the two babies who were squirming in my arms and emitting high-pitched cries. "Stay here. Maybe their mother can be saved."

Rory's head rose, her tear-streaked face registering blatant hope. That spark of hope propelled me across the street and down the block, the two wriggling babies in my arms continuing to cry loudly and piercingly.

I burst through the front door of the club, members shrieking and diving aside as I ran through the lobby and then burst outside, heading toward the tennis courts where I'd seen Easton Torres, Haven's brother, earlier. One of the raccoons managed to crawl out of my hand and scramble up my chest, coming to perch on my shoulder.

"What the—"

"Oh my God!"

"Gage, are you—"

"Hi, Mom! I'm fine! Everything's fine!" I said to my mother who stood gaping at me in her tennis whites.

I rounded the corner, almost colliding with Mrs. Bellamy who let out a small screech as she jumped aside. "Excuse me," I said. "Emergency! Coming through!" All I could see in my mind's eye was Rory's devastated face. *Fix this!*

"Easton!" I yelled when I caught sight of one of the paramedics who worked at the Pelion Fire Department coming off the court, his head bent as he used the hem of his shirt to mop the sweat from his brow. The pretty brunette next to him gasped and grabbed his arm. "I need you!" I shouted.

Easton looked up, his expression registering shock and some amount of horror, as he took me in, my chest rising and falling with staggered breaths, one baby raccoon cradled between my pecs, the other one having managed to claw its way up my cheek to the top of my head where I held it steady with my other hand. "What the—"

"I have a medical emergency," I told him.

"A medical emergency?"

"Yes. There was a car accident—"

"Where?"

"Just up the street."

"Call me!" the brunette yelled after him as Easton started jogging toward the front door. I turned to follow, past the smoothie bar, around the pool and through the lobby.

"Show me where," he said as we burst out the front door back into the sunshine.

In all the mayhem, the raccoon babies had obviously tired themselves out. They'd ceased wriggling and clawing, and I was able to dislodge the one from my head and hold them both against my chest as we headed back to where Rory was on the side of the road.

As we raced toward her, she turned, her expression still distraught as she moved aside. Easton and I both came to a skidding halt. Easton stared down at the animal, clearly dumbfounded. "Easton is a paramedic," I told Rory breathlessly.

"Oh, thank God," she said with a small sob.

"It's a raccoon." Easton blinked over at me like I'd lost my marbles.

"Yes," Rory hiccupped. "Can you save her?"

"It's a raccoon," he repeated.

"Yes," I said, "we realize it's a raccoon. She was hit by a car and these babies need her. Is there something you can do?"

Easton's gaze moved from Rory, to me, to the babies now asleep in my arms, back to Rory. Something seemed to come into his expression. I didn't know him well enough to guess what it was, but I hoped to God it was understanding. "I can try," he said kindly. Rory exhaled, scooting aside as Easton leaned over the animal and started chest compressions.

My gaze hung on Rory as we watched Easton work on the animal. Rory's eyes were wide with hope, even though with each passing minute, it was becoming more and more clear that the racoon was gone. I couldn't do anything to bring the creature back to life, but I wanted to. I wanted to change the laws of nature, to strike some sort of deal with the powers that be, that would deliver to this girl the thing she was so fervently hoping for. I would have if I could have. And the power of my desire to make her happy, to manifest her every wish, to the realization that I might sell my own soul to bring back a raccoon, *for her*, scared me senseless. And yet, there it was, and it couldn't be denied. The world brightened, then dimmed and did a strange turn that tilted me upside down and then just as suddenly placed me back on my feet.

"I'm sorry," Easton said somberly after another minute, even though I could tell he'd given it far longer than was necessary to know his efforts were useless. The animal had likely died the moment it had been struck by the car. "At least we tried."

Rory nodded, another tear slipping down her cheek. "Yes," she said as she stood. "Thank you. Easton, right?"

"Yeah. Easton Torres. I'd shake your hand but..." He gave a small shrug and looked down at the deceased animal with which he'd just been delivering hands-on medical care.

"I appreciate what you did," she said. "At least we can know we tried everything." She looked over at me, taking in a long, shaky breath as she stared at the sleeping babies in my arms. "Oh," she said, the word more breath than sound, and there was so much sorrow in it, my heart squeezed again. "They have no mother now." For a moment it looked like she was going to dissolve into tears again, but she took in a deep breath, her shoulders rising and falling as she got control of her emotions.

No mother. Just like her. I imagined that this hunt for her father, and discovery of her mother's long-ago diary entries, was ripping open emotional wounds. Maybe to Rory they weren't just wild critters, or part of the animal world she loved so much—perhaps they signified a mother being torn from her young who still needed her, the way that her own mother had been torn from her.

"I have an idea," I said. "Easton, will you, uh..." I looked down at the animal. What was the protocol for roadkill?

"I'll call the appropriate authorities to take care of her," he said.

Her. I'd heard a lot of things about Easton Torres, whispered tales that suggested he was a ladies' man, but I was learning that whether or not the rumors of his exploits were accurate, what *was* true, was that he was kind. "Thanks, Easton. I mean it."

He gave me a nod. "No problem." He looked at Rory. "Are those dogs yours?" He pointed backward to where the dogs were sleeping under the tree, obviously completely unbothered by their role in recent deadly events.

"Yes," Rory said. "Well, I mean, no, but I was walking them. I've got to get them home to their owners."

"How about I drive you after the...pick-up occurs?" Easton said, glancing down at the dead raccoon. "I have a truck parked just over there," he gestured up the street.

"Is that okay with you?" I asked Rory.

"Yes, I'd like to stay until someone picks up...her body." She took in another shaky inhale of air. "What will you do with them?"

"I'll call you after I know it's a yes," I said. "Trust me?"

Her eyes met mine, the blue so crystal clear, they looked like water. "Yes. Yes I trust you."

I watched the tiny raccoons who were wedged between two bright orange kittens, as they nursed greedily on the three-legged gray cat. "You owe me, Buchanan," Travis said between clenched teeth as he watched the animals with some amount of outrage on his face.

I stared at him. I'd appreciated his willingness—begrudging though it'd been—to give this situation a try rather than allow the newborn raccoons to die, but how exactly was it putting *him* out? I glanced back down to the nursing cat. "I wouldn't even have any idea how to repay this."

"I'll think of something."

"It's the cat doing the work," I pointed out.

"*My* cat," he corrected. Then Travis scowled at me before turning and marching off. I watched him as he joined Haven by one of the apple trees where she'd been picking up discarded fruit and dropping it in a bucket. Travis wrapped one arm around her and brought the other to her barely rounded stomach before leaning down slightly and saying something to it. They giggled together, and she glanced around as if making sure none of the lingering customers were watching. I stepped back so she wouldn't catch sight of me accidentally spying, and looked back down to the animals, rolling my eyes at Travis and Haven's obvious display of affection. I hadn't noticed before because she usually wore loose-fitting clothing, but clearly she was expecting again. *Jesus.* How old was their other kid? Nine months old or something?

As if in agreement, Clawdia meowed and then leaned forward and began cleaning her two newly adopted children. I reached out and scratched her head, a burst of relief filling my lungs. "Thanks, girl," I said to the cat. Without her acceptance, I wouldn't have been able to fulfill my promise to Rory. I didn't let myself think about why in the hell it had seemed like life or death to do so.

CHAPTER NINETEEN
Rory

The sun was just setting when I stepped from my car, taking a moment to drink in the way the sky's kiss transformed the water into molten gold. I took in a deep pull of the fruit- and flower-scented air, closing my eyes as a sense of peace fell over me, despite that I was still carrying the sadness of what had happened earlier and a general frustration about the state of my search—especially considering that my time here was dwindling.

Not to mention that before the screeching of brakes and the racoon and the CPR, I'd seen Gage kissing a woman goodbye on the sidewalk in front of the tennis club. The interaction had appeared more than friendly. With a sigh, I started to walk toward the barn where Gage had told me to meet him. The last time I'd been to Haven's Gate, it'd been bustling with activity and customers, but now it was obviously closed, the only vehicle in the parking lot Gage's rental car.

"Hello?" I called when I stepped inside the interior of

the red barn. There was a counter with a cash register on the left, and tiers of what looked like potted indoor plants behind it, that stretched along the back wall as well. Muted light streamed in through the high windows, casting the room in a hazy glow.

There were potted trees in here, as well as leafy shade plants that I didn't know the names for. I stood there, looking around, and just like I'd felt the love in my father's paintings, I somehow felt the love here as well. Everything was beautifully maintained and obviously well cared for, and though I didn't know a thing about gardening, it was very clear that Haven Hale loved what she did.

What would it feel like to live a life like that? I didn't even know what my passion *was*, well, other than dogs. But loving dogs wasn't exactly a profitable business idea. Or at least, I didn't see vet school in my immediate future, not only because there was no vet school in Mud Gulch, but because I'd always been crappy at math and science.

To the right there was a doorway that looked as if it led to another small room—an office perhaps. Gage had called me here, but where was he?

"Hey, Rory."

I spun around, bringing my hand to my heart. Gage stood in the doorway behind me, a smile gracing his lips. For a moment I simply stood there, watching him, feeling somehow disconnected from the here and now. Maybe it was that I'd been daydreaming a moment before. Maybe it was the light, or the way he was smiling at me, or the way my heart had quickened when I heard him call my name. "Hey," I let my breath out and laughed. "You surprised me."

He took a few steps in and stopped, opening his mouth as though to respond to what I said, but then shutting it again. He gave his head a small shake and took another step forward. "I have something to show you that I think you'll like."

I squinted, as I walked toward him. "My uncles warned me about lines like that."

He laughed as he took my hand in his and led me from the barn. "As they should have. In this case though, you're probably safe." He winked at me and champagne bubbles fizzled between my ribs.

I shot him a grin, gripping his hand back and then practically jogging to keep up with him as he pulled me along. "Wait until you see," he said. "In here."

He brought me inside what must have been a tack room once at the back of the barn. If there had been a door that led straight from the barn at one point, it'd since been covered. Instead of animal equipment, however, there were built-in potting tables that held all manner of plants from seedlings to greenery trailing halfway to the floor. There were bags of potting soil sitting here and there, and on the back wall was a...cat tree? Gage shot me another smile as he led me to it. It looked homemade, and fit perfectly in the space, with several ledges, the first of which—interestingly—was quite close to the floor.

When he'd called and asked me to meet him here, I figured it had to do with the baby raccoons because, what else? I thought he'd found a friend with an incubator, who maybe knew what milk to feed the babies from an eyedropper. I wondered if he'd brought them here because the Hales had room in which to house a cage with orphaned babies inside. But when Gage let go of my hand and I stepped up to the cat tree and went up on my tiptoes to peer into the box on one of the higher ledges, I pulled in a shocked breath.

It was a cat, feeding her two orange kittens, and also… the tiny raccoons. "Oh my God," I breathed. The mama cat was purring loudly, obviously unfazed at having recently added two young family members of a different species. I stared, taking in the scene, tears welling in my eyes. This cat had accepted these tiny creatures because they needed her, and she could. "How did you do it?" I asked Gage as I lifted my hand and ran a finger over the cat's head.

"I didn't do anything except think of it," he said. "It was up to Clawdia, and thankfully she agreed."

"Thank you, Clawdia," I whispered, scratching her under her chin as her purrs increased in volume.

I turned to Gage. "Thank you." I hoped he saw the depth of my gratitude in my eyes. I'd been heartbroken at having been involved in leaving two innocent creatures motherless, and though there was no way to bring her back, Gage had done the next best thing and found another mother to care for them.

And he'd done it for me.

I somehow knew in my heart that even though Gage was kind and considerate, he wouldn't have necessarily gone to these lengths if I hadn't been so distraught.

"You're welcome," he said. Our eyes lingered, and I wanted to kiss him so badly it was a physical ache. I wanted him, his body and his heart. But I could have neither and so I leaned forward, wrapped my arms around him and hugged him tight.

We stayed and watched the cats and the racoons for a little bit longer, the scene bringing me both joy and peace. But after a little bit, Clawdia closed her eyes, and we left the small, blended family to sleep.

When we left the room, the sun had dipped lower, the

sky now a mixture of pale orange and twilight blue. Fireflies danced through the sweetened air, and for a moment, the world felt lovelier than it'd ever been.

"I do love a good sunset," I said. "My mom was right about this place offering beautiful ones. They're glorious."

I looked around, taking in the row of parked pull wagons that held baskets. The paths through the trees were well-worn and I could picture families strolling and collecting fruit, laughing and making family memories before going home and baking pies, or making jam, or perhaps sharing their bounty with neighbors. "Is it okay that we're here after-hours?"

"Yeah," Gage said. "Travis said we could stay as long as we wanted and just asked that I close the barn door before we leave."

I turned and squinted into the lingering line of fading orange along the horizon over the lake. "It's so tranquil here," I said. "I hope I can find this kind of peace someday."

I felt Gage's gaze hanging heavy on me for a moment and then he walked in front of me, over to a bench that was inscribed with something. Gage sat down, and I read the inscription out loud, "Dedicated to Connor Hale." I sat down next to Gage. *Hale.* That must have been Travis's father or grandfather.

"Where do you picture yourself finding this sort of peace?"

"I don't know." I considered that as a little more of the sun slipped away. "I told you about that pull I've always felt." I paused. "I haven't experienced it since I've been here. But it's like...I don't fit here either." I let out a frustrated exhale. "I don't know where I belong."

His eyes washed over my features, settling on my mouth

for a moment and then moving away. "Maybe it's not about a place, so much as...a person, or...people. Your people." He reached out and took my hand. "We'll figure out who they are, Rory." He paused. "No matter what."

No matter what.

I knew what that meant.

I nodded and looked to the side, but the warmth of his hand brought me comfort and I didn't want to pull away and so I didn't. "It makes me feel sort of guilty to even think like that. Because, I *have* people. I have two uncles who love me and have sacrificed everything for me."

Gage tilted his head, his brow furrowing. "You told me they stepped in when your mother died. How old were they?"

"Cash was twenty-six and already settled into his career. But Romeo, he was only eighteen. He was about to leave Mud Gulch right before my mother died, but...well, he canceled his plans and he stayed. Not only for me, but for the bar that my mother had run after my granny died. Uncle Cassius helped, but he's away more often than he's not." I felt a pang in my gut the way I always did when I thought about it.

Gage was silent for a moment as I used my other hand to play with the hem of my shirt. "He sacrificed for you. He's obviously a stand-up guy."

I blew out a breath. "He is. But...he obviously felt a pull too and he never answered it. He sacrificed for me—for all of us—when he was so young. He was going to see the world. Heck, he might have taken it over." And instead, he was stuck behind a bar in Mud Gulch, Maine. "Maybe he still can. If..."

"If?"

I raised my eyes to meet his. "It's not my driving motivation, but…if I have a father of means, then maybe I can give back to Romeo. Cassius too, but Cassius is happy with where he is." If I believed that my mom had a hand in leading me here, then wouldn't she also want Romeo to benefit if my father saw fit to assist me financially in helping Romeo regain those lost years?

"Ah. You want to send Romeo on that world adventure he was about to go on when instead, he ended up having to stay home and raise his niece."

"It wasn't fair," I whispered.

"For any of you. But, Rory, I highly doubt he's looking to be repaid. I don't know your uncle, but the way you talk about him, I can tell he's a great guy."

"He is. He's the best. He'd never complain."

"Maybe it's because he doesn't have any complaints."

I sighed. "He'd never voice them, but years ago, I found his drawer of travel brochures. Italy, Switzerland, Egypt…all the places he never got to see."

He was quiet for a moment as he obviously considered the picture I was painting. "If you do find your father and end up being able to send Romeo on those adventures, what will you do?"

"I'll go back to Mud Gulch and run the bar. It's been in our family for generations. It's a staple of the town. There's no way I'd let it go."

Gage looked up, staring at the stars that had just begun dotting the sky. "You're torn in two directions," he said.

I thought about that. Yes. Yes, that's exactly how I felt. I felt loyal to Mud Gulch and to my uncles, but I also felt torn to be somewhere else, even if I hadn't quite identified where that was just yet. For so long, deep inside, I'd felt like I was ignoring a call I needed to heed. That feeling had subsided here, and yet I still hadn't found what I was looking for, and so I remained just as lost.

"What about you?" I asked. "Where do you picture yourself finding peace like this? Is it a place or a…person?"

He glanced at me and then away. "I honestly don't know. I've never thought about my life in terms of peace. I've always been guided by my actions, more so than my feelings."

"Feelings? You mean dreams?"

He tilted his head, appearing momentarily confused. Then he shrugged. "Yeah, I guess. Feelings. Dreams. I've never used those terms. I have goals, and I have aspirations, of course. But dreams? What's the real difference? To me, they've always been pretty synonymous."

I thought about that for a second. "I'm not sure. All I know is that dreams are what create peace like this. You can sense it, can't you? This is Haven's dream come true, and she puts her whole heart and soul into it." I waved my arm around. "I guess if you can find a way to monetize your dreams like she obviously does, you're pretty damn lucky."

He smiled and it was sort of wistful. "I suppose you're right. And I also guess most people aren't lucky enough to be able to monetize their dreams."

"Probably not. Pesky little things like needing to buy groceries and pay rent get in the way." I gave him a small tilt of my lips and he smiled back. As our eyes lingered, I wondered if Gage Buchanan had ever in his life had to worry about "pesky things." Probably not. And if anyone had been born into a life where they had the ability to monetize their dreams, whatever Gage's might be, it was him.

Gage Buchanan required no luck. And yet he acted like that sort of life—the one where you did anything you wanted because you *could*—was an impossibility. He called himself privileged and obviously, in many ways, he was. But if he couldn't follow his own dreams, what did any of that privilege mean? Wasn't privilege without passion simply... duty?

"Walk with me?" he asked, standing and reaching out for my hand. I took it and he pulled me up, rising so fast that I met his chest with mine, laughing and slightly breathless as I gazed up at him. So close. He laughed softly too, smiling down at me, neither of us moving. God help me, I didn't want to move. I wanted to get even closer. I wanted to kiss him—

I pictured the woman whose lips had been on his earlier. The flashy beauty with the shiny car.

I stepped back and turned away, facing the trees, heavy with fruit. A slight breeze rustled the leaves and cooled my overheated skin. As I reached for a peach, Gage came up next to me. I brought it to my nose and inhaled, letting out a sigh. "Gosh, this smells good."

"I've come out here a few times and picked fruit for a cobbler," he said.

"You just whip up a cobbler every now and again, huh?"

He laughed. "You know I—"

"Enjoy cooking. Yes. You're amazing at it too." He made it sound like a hobby, but to me, it looked like more than that. The way he seemed to...sparkle, when he was commanding a kitchen, whether his own or the one at Cakes and Ale. I'd known cooks all my life. They didn't do their job with a tenth of the finesse or obvious enjoyment I saw in Gage. They didn't describe a dish as the melding of earth and sea. "Since your early days under Chef LaCourt, have you taken classes?" I asked. He'd made it sound like he'd learned from the French master when he was young, but he'd obviously honed his skills since then. I thought about the crab cakes and the pasta dish he'd made so effortlessly and how both of them almost seemed like an experience more than food. I'd never in my life eaten anything better than those two whipped-together-at-a-moment's-notice meals.

"No, I'm not professionally trained in any way."

I tilted my head. "Well, neither were Mozart or van Gogh. Some people are just naturally gifted, I suppose."

He seemed to consider that, a frown marring his handsome features as though something about the idea distressed him. "I've always had this ability to sort of... break down recipes and even scents. I'll taste something in a restaurant and know the ingredients that were combined to create it. I can tell if it'd benefit from some rosemary, or shaved truffles...if it might be better roasted or baked on a cedar plank. And then I'll go home and re-create it and I'm nearly right. A random talent that really only means I have to be diligent about gym time."

Shaved truffles. Whatever those were. "Not random. A talent that benefits chefs and recipe creators," I said. "Some people's senses are more keen than others."

He suddenly seemed very interested in a branch next to him, running his fingers along the leaves at the end. "Well, I'm obviously neither of those things. I just do it for fun." He smiled, the barest tilt of his lips. "My job is demanding and in the last few years...I honestly haven't gotten out a lot. I have to eat and so...you know..."

I'd taken a bite of the peach as he'd spoken and when I moaned at the juicy sweetness that burst across my tongue, his gaze lowered to my mouth. His eyes drooped slightly and he brought his thumb to the side of my lips, catching the peach juice that had begun to run toward my chin.

Kiss me.

No! Don't kiss me. God, this was awful. The tension between us was so thick with desire. My skin felt hot and prickly just being near him and we still hadn't gotten those damn test results back. Part of me wanted to say, *Fuck it. Who cares! We've already crossed the line. How would two times be worse than once?*

Because you'd know you were doing your brother.

I looked away. That put things into perspective.

"I saw you with that girl earlier," I blurted out.

I hadn't planned to mention the gorgeous brunette I'd seen him kiss outside the tennis club as I'd walked by with the dogs. I'd ducked partially behind a tree and then I'd watched him watch her peel away from the curb. Even from across the street, I'd seen the way his jaw tightened with protectiveness, his hand beginning to rise and his mouth opening partway as though he was going to call after her to slow down. It'd made my stomach plunge and maybe that's why I'd been distracted enough that I'd allowed the dogs to get the best of me. I took another bite of the peach to keep my mouth occupied.

"Blakely," he said. "Her name is Blakely."

"Oh." I swallowed, the small bite of peach feeling like a stone and making me wonder if I'd accidentally eaten the pit. I glanced down at it to see that I hadn't. Why did a simple name make my stomach ball up? I hadn't asked Gage if he was dating anyone, or even perhaps several someones. We'd had a one-night fling, and then we'd found out there was the possibility we were related. The circumstances had meant there had never been a question of whether we wanted to date *each other*, and so what did it matter what the details of his personal life were?

That was *still* true. It had to be true.

"You're dating her?" I asked, trying my damnedest to sound as breezy as the weather. And I thought I succeeded considering the air was utterly still.

"No." He paused, and I held my breath momentarily, sensing the *no* was a little more complicated than the one word would otherwise indicate. "She's my sister Lexi's best friend. I grew up with her." He paused and I gave the half-eaten peach a toss. The birds could have the rest of it. I couldn't swallow another bite, even though it was dinnertime and I was mildly hungry. "We joked about this pact, many years ago. We said we'd—"

"Let me guess. You'd marry each other if both of you were single at a certain age."

"That cliché, huh?"

Geez, seriously? What was *wrong* with the silver spoon crowd? I pictured the portrait of the Bellamys, the husband's hands hovering just above his wife's shoulder as though he didn't really want to touch her. Did they seek out lackluster marriages on purpose? Or was this part of Gage's expected *legacy*? "I mean, I guess it's hard when you know you want a marriage and a family to be part of your future but are worried they won't happen naturally. I assume…you both want that? A partner? Kids?"

I didn't glance at him, but I could sense his discomfort from next to me, both in the way he paused before speaking, and how his movements in my peripheral vision became less fluid. "We both want that," he said. "In the past few years, I made the conscious decision to date women with that goal in mind."

"Meaning nothing temporary or purely physical?" I stopped and turned. My balance suddenly felt off and I wished for that bench again so I could sink down onto it. I'd seen her lean in and kiss him, and the sight had distressed me, but I'd thought, well, lots of women in Calliope were probably vying for Gage Buchanan's attention. And maybe he was even dating a few of them. But I hadn't for one second thought he was considering *marriage*.

He'd broken off a leaf and he twirled it in his fingers now, staring at it as though it held the answer to that question. "I'd decided on nothing temporary or physical, yes."

"Until me."

"Until you."

My ribs felt tight and I brought my hand to the place beneath my breasts. What he was saying about what we were—a one-night fling—was something I'd already known. So why did it make me feel suddenly hollow inside?

Because you're friends now.

Were we though? Friends? Not really. Because if we were, we wouldn't care if we turned out to be brother and sister. Sexual energy still thrummed between us. And maybe that's why I felt sort of…defeated. Because Gage Buchanan *did* want something serious, he'd just never considered it with me.

Which made *sense.* We lived in two different towns. He was moving to London. And we might be related.

And yet…it *still* hurt to know he might be considering marrying this Blakely person. The beautiful woman with the beautiful car whom I'd watched from behind a tree with three dogs.

"Listen, Rory, I know things are sort of…confusing with us. The truth is, Blakely is the one who approached me with this idea." He huffed out a breath, dropped the leaf, and ran a hand through his dark hair. "I hadn't decided anything. I told her I'd think about it. But"—he let out a small laugh devoid of humor—"she's more like family to me. I don't know that I can ever see her as anything other than a sister. I don't know that I want to. However…there's also a comfort level there. And our families are close. They're involved in the charitable foundations my mother runs. Our fathers work together. There are reasons it made sense when she first brought it up."

"And she's available to go to London with you."

He paused, watching me. "Yes. She's available to go to London with me."

"I get it, Gage." And I did, even if it caused my throat to clog up and made me feel disappointed for him. It seemed like yet another arrangement he was going along with. And maybe it did make sense for him, but it also made more sense for everyone else, and Gage didn't seem to be able to do anything that didn't check that box. I also wondered if there was any chemistry between them at all and had to guess the answer was no. Because I knew very well Gage was an impassioned man when he allowed himself to be, and if he felt that way for her, I was all but certain he wouldn't be here with me.

"But Rory, I want to make it clear to you that at this point, I'm not even seeing her. I never was. I told her I'd consider the offer and then…well, you showed up here and I—"

"Found out I might be your sister."

He let out another weak laugh, followed by a grimace. "Right."

"You don't have to explain it to me. You don't owe me

that. What we had…well, it was a one-night thing and we might be related. But beyond all that, my life is in Mud Gulch. My priorities are very different." I turned and started walking even though I suddenly felt a little breathless. Gage took up beside me. "Not that, you know, you even asked about any of that."

"We make no sense," he murmured.

"No, we already decided that."

"I think I need to decide it again."

I shot him a glance. "It's hard for me to remember too."

He smiled, and it was sort of sad. It *was* somewhat heartbreaking to have such intense chemistry with someone, and to *enjoy* that person, and to still know that you just weren't right for each other for a variety of reasons, some more weighty than others.

"So…what's next?" he asked, obviously attempting to change the subject. "We could go check out a few more antique shops."

"The gallery is closed tomorrow," I said. "Faith is going to go with me to a couple shops."

"Oh."

"I figured you were working anyway."

He nodded. "I am. Working. There's a lot to do before… London."

My stomach gave a twist. But he wasn't the only one leaving soon. He was starting a new life somewhere else, and I was returning to mine. "Well, time is ticking. The fixes to my uncle's boat are going to be complete soon and then I'll have to go back."

"The brood," he murmured.

"The brood. And the bar. Real life."

"Real life," he murmured. He stopped, turning toward

me again and I came up short. "Will you call me right away if you find anything?" He offered a smile that looked sort of wobbly and maybe a little bit bashful. This confident businessman with the world at his feet was looking at me like my answer could make or break him.

"Of course I will, Gage." I smiled. "For now, we're in this together." *For now.*

CHAPTER TWENTY
Gage

I stared out the window of my office that overlooked Calliope's business district, watching the cars move along the street and people in business suits enter and exit buildings. I had plenty to do and yet...I was...*bored*. I'd never felt bored before, or rather, I'd never acknowledged my boredom, but that's exactly what it was, wasn't it? That antsy feeling inside of me was an unusual sort of boredom. *Huh.* As if I didn't have *more* than enough to occupy myself. I turned, going to my desk and sitting down, picking up my cell phone, hesitating and then replacing it on my desk.

"Damn it," I muttered, bouncing my knee. It'd been two days since I'd spoken to Rory. She hadn't called to update me on whether she'd found any art or not and so I assumed she hadn't. But what if she had, and that had led her to something else she was looking into, and I didn't know about it because I hadn't picked up the phone and called her first?

My gaze fell on the list my assistant Rebecca had put on my desk that morning regarding the personal action items

I still needed to check off in preparation for my move to London. There were printouts of the layout of my flat underneath the list and I pulled them out, my eyes moving over the one-dimensional rooms for a moment. I tried and failed to picture myself there, watching television in the living room, or standing at a window, the sight of Calliope replaced by London's skyline, or even cooking, the thing that made me feel inspired wherever I was, even in an unfamiliar bar on the docks with the equipment so old it probably dated back three Casteel generations. I pushed the pile of papers aside. "Damn it," I repeated, taking my head in my hands.

What would my parents think of Rory Casteel, whose family owned a quaint-but-in-need-of-repairs bar on the docks in a town named after mud that was likely to suck you under if you weren't careful? *They'd immediately disapprove.* They wouldn't consider her the "right" woman to stand by my side as I moved into the next chapter of my career and my life. My father loved my mother, but he'd married her because she was a society girl, like Blakely Wingate, who only enhanced his upward social mobility. He had come from a background much more humble than the one lived in Mud Gulch, Maine. His goals for me were that I take the ground he'd gained and climb even higher.

Those were some of the *airs* I'd spoken of to Rory the first night we'd met, the ones that could be so damn tiresome. But I'd embraced those airs. I'd gone all in and now they were part of my life, whether I liked it or not.

It's why I'd felt so free in Mud Gulch, standing in that kitchen with Rory cooking and just being *me.* Out from under all the pressure and expectations. My parents wouldn't even recognize that version of me.

Not that there could ever be a mention of Mud Gulch

anyway since Rory had lied to my parents and many others about who she really was.

And so had I.

"Headache?" My father's voice interrupted my thoughts. I looked up to see him strolling in the room. "Take a Tylenol, because there's no time for a headache or anything else that might distract you for the briefest moment." He gave me a smile though as he set a folder down before me and took a seat in one of the two chairs sitting in front of my desk.

Distract me? Too late. I was already helplessly distracted. "I know. I'm fine. I've got everything under control."

He gave me a considering look, likely thinking about the rumors that were surely circulating about my public shows of *distraction*. But my dad didn't give much credence to gossip. He looked at results. And despite my mind being elsewhere, my work hadn't suffered. "I have no doubt. You always do. I know things have been intense lately. There's a lot of money on the line, and a whole team of people depending on you. But, Gage, son, there's no one more capable of turning this venture into a success than you."

"Thanks, Dad." I mustered a smile that he didn't seem to notice was forced.

He gestured to the folder. "Those are the contractor schedules for the London property. Keep them handy in case you need to reference them. The schedule is tight. We can't afford to let anything slip through the cracks." My dad leaned forward. "But I have good news. The London team working under you is flying in for our Fourth of July party. You'll get the chance to meet them in a more relaxed setting. That way you'll all be familiar, and you can really hit the ground running when you arrive in Westminster."

I nodded, my eyes drifting away. *The Fourth of July*

party. The Metropolitan Club threw a big shindig every year, complete with a professionally run fireworks show. I'd thought about inviting Rory, but then I'd hesitated because Blakely and her parents were going to be there like they were every year. I'd already decided that I wasn't going to take Blakely up on her proposal. Frankly, my heart wasn't in it, and I lacked the will to try. But it'd be awkward nonetheless. Nothing was clear-cut and feelings were likely to get hurt if I didn't keep the different parts of my life separate.

And yet, it was *me* feeling like someone held my heart in a vise.

My father started to rise. "Dad? Can I ask you a question?"

He lowered himself back in the chair. "Of course."

I picked up a pen and tapped it on the edge of the desk. "Was there ever a time…years ago, that you and Mom… weren't close?"

"Weren't close?"

"You know, that you might have…drifted apart."

He stared at me for several moments. "Sure, Gage. Your mother and I have gone through rough patches as most couples do. I worked a lot when you and Lexi were young." He paused, looking momentarily troubled. "And I was working through personal issues so I wasn't always as present as I should have been. I think sometimes your mother felt lonely and overwhelmed, even though she had help."

Did you stray? Did you have an affair with a woman and then send her away when you found out she was pregnant? Or did she leave you none the wiser? But I couldn't bring myself to ask my father that. The question felt blasphemous on my tongue. Or maybe it was that I wasn't prepared to hear the answer, to have to look him in the eye after learning something like that.

To have to grapple with the layers of my despair while directly in front of him.

The test results would be in any day now anyway. I nodded. "I'm glad you two stuck it out."

His forehead creased. "Is there a reason you're asking me that, son?"

I shrugged. "I guess I'm feeling like there might be a lot I never asked about." I gave him a small smile. "I'm moving away and—"

"Gage, your mother and I are a phone call away."

"I know." I paused, more questions flowing to the tip of my tongue. *Did you ever doubt your path? Did you sometimes feel like you were on autopilot, rather than really enjoying the journey? When Mom came along, did she soothe that feeling? Or did her presence in your life create more questions?* Before I could figure out a way to ask any of that, though, my dad continued.

"Speaking of moving, though, things are going to be a whirlwind over the next week or so, so while I have you for a minute, I wanted to say something."

I gave a nod. "What is it, Dad?"

"I just wanted to convey my gratitude and my deep respect. Everything I've worked for, since I was a young man, will coalesce as you cut that opening day ribbon in London. My son, my pride and joy, at the helm as the business I built with my own blood, sweat, and tears becomes an international success." He cleared his throat, obviously holding back tears. "It's everything I dreamed of, through hungry nights, and setbacks, and scraping and scrounging. Because of you, my ultimate dream won't only be realized, it will endure through future generations."

I smiled, feeling moisture burning at the backs of my own eyes. "Thanks, Dad. Thanks for trusting me."

"Always." He smiled, obviously shaking off the emotion. "And by the way, I hope you're still giving serious consideration to taking Blakely with you to London. She has some wonderful ideas about stirring up the ultimate online excitement surrounding the hotel opening. And, Gage, the only thing that could make that ribbon-cutting moment any sweeter, is if my son is standing next to my best friend's daughter. What a powerful match that would be."

"Dad, I told you—"

"I know, it's only a possibility. The choice is yours." He winked. "But a dad can dream." He stood and glanced at his watch. "We've got that board meeting in ten minutes. Ready?"

"Uh, yeah. I've got one more thing to wrap up and then I'll be there."

My father gave me a quick nod, turned and left my office. I sat tapping my pen for a few minutes. *My pride and joy.* I felt this internal ticking that seemed to be racing the clock on the wall of my office.

It's all about timing. Too early, half-cooked, too late, tough and charred. You have a gift, but to be a master, you must master timing.

Chef LaCourt. Again, his voice in my head.

The thing was, I *had* mastered timing. In all ways. I'd taken his lessons and I'd applied them to so many things. Perhaps even more than the lessons my own father had taught me. And the guilt I felt about that...

God, I couldn't catch my breath suddenly. I stood, going to the mini bar in my office, grabbing a bottle of water from the fridge and downing half of it one swig. I needed to keep my *father's* words in my mind and instead, that soft lilting French accent kept interrupting my thoughts. I'd shut it down for a long time, but now it was back and louder than ever.

I wiped my mouth with the back of my hand, returning to my desk where I suddenly found my cell phone in my hand. I didn't let myself think before I punched in Rory's number.

"Ivy League."

"Cakes." My lungs expanded with air.

"How are you?" I could hear the smile in her voice too and energy infused my body so that it felt like I'd just come alive after days of being partially dead. This woman didn't exactly soothe me—the opposite, perhaps—but God, I craved the way she made me feel.

"I'm good. No luck in the treasure hunt you went on with Faith, I assume?"

She sighed. "No luck. I'm afraid I've exhausted every antique shop and vintage store in the area and just…nothing."

"Ah, but you still have two more attics to explore, and the contents of said attics belong to men whose initials match those of the artist."

"I know but they still haven't called Faith. She's left them several messages, but she hasn't even had a chance to tell them what she's calling about."

"Okay, we're changing tactics. If they do call her back, tell her not to mention you because I have a better idea for getting inside one of their homes."

She was silent for a beat. "Breaking and entering is illegal, in case you weren't aware."

"I'm not proposing breaking and entering. Maynard Siggins hosts a small bridge club the fourth Wednesday of every month. That's tomorrow night."

"Okay…"

"I'm pretty sure I can weasel out an invite. You'll be my date."

"And we'll what? Sneak into his attic?"

"No. I was kidding about the attic. I don't think checking out the contents of his storage areas is necessary at this point. If he's the man who painted those paintings, surely he'll have some hung up around his house. He's a bachelor, which means—"

"No wife to take over the decorating." I heard the excitement in her voice.

"Right. No wife to stuff old works of art she didn't like up in the attic or to suggest that he stop wasting time coloring pictures of lakes and grass and whatnot."

She laughed softly after I repeated Mrs. Ramsbottom's description of creating art.

"So, what do you say?" I asked.

"I don't even play bridge."

"It's easy. You'll catch on quickly."

"I guess I could...watch some YouTube videos."

"Yes, and I'll go over the rules again on the drive over. Pick you up at eight?"

She let out a thin laugh. "Well...okay. See you tomorrow."

I tried not to think about the way my heart soared at those three little words. *See you tomorrow.*

"You said you've played bridge before, Ms. Castle?" Mrs. Delia Quartermocker asked with the raise of one blond, perfectly drawn brow after Rory had fumbled her way through another round of the game. She'd tried to act cool about it, but her flushed cheeks gave away the fact that her competitive spirit was burning mad.

I pressed my lips together to stifle the laughter I could feel vibrating in my chest. Why the hell did I enjoy seeing

Rory rattled so much? Obviously she saw me attempting not to laugh because she ground down on my foot under the table.

I'd given her a quick lesson on the way over, but I'd been distracted and just so damn happy to see her that the actual rules of bridge had quickly deserted me. I'd offered the gist and hoped it was enough. The last thing I wanted was for Rory to back out. I told myself it was because the opportunity to get inside Maynard Siggins's home and look over his artwork was too good to pass up.

"Gage taught me how to play," she said sweetly. "I'm beginning to think he's not a very good teacher and that he left out half the rules."

"Oh, I imagine Gage is good at everything he does," Mrs. Quartermocker said, looking at me suggestively as she poked her tongue out and licked the corner of her mouth. *Oh dear God.* Mrs. Quartermocker was an attractive woman, but she was at least twice my age. Although her husband, a young man who looked to be in his late twenties, clearly didn't seem to mind that. Currently, he was lounging in a chair nearby drinking a martini, a beret sitting neatly on his shaggy hair, and appearing quite content with his life.

"Now, now," Maynard Siggins, who I was really hoping was Rory's father so we could put this mystery to rest, said. "Practice makes perfect. I'm just glad Gage called me this morning out of the blue and then happened to mention that he'd been learning bridge. Perfect timing as our regular partner, Curtis Nielson, was asked to work late this evening. Curtis works under you, doesn't he, Gage?"

I smiled tightly and with a fair amount of shame. I'd done a business favor for Mr. Siggins about a year ago, and I'd called him earlier under the pretense of inquiring about how the resulting deal was going. I'd asked if he was still holding bridge night and said I'd recently learned the game. Of course, he'd invited me like I'd known he would and I'd asked if Rory could come along. Clearly whatever else Maynard Siggins was, he wasn't a man able to spot one too many coincidences. "Lucky break," I muttered.

"Indeed it is," Maynard said. He looked at us both over his reading glasses. "You said Ms. Castle is new in town. How is it you two met?"

My gaze flew to Rory. We hadn't gone over a cover story regarding how we met. But Rory simply patted my hand and said, "Open mic poetry night."

"Oh!" Mrs. Quartermocker's very young husband, whose name I'd already forgotten, suddenly sat up straight. "The poetry slam at Lighthouse Lounge?"

"That's the one," Rory said, perching her chin on the backs of her laced hands and gazing at me. "Gage's piece was mesmerizing. So emotionally charged. I had to speak to him afterward. From there, it's been...a whirlwind."

"A hurricane," I amended.

Her eyes danced. "Category five."

"Utter destruction," I added with a lowered voice.

"Sounds positively violent," Mrs. Quartermocker said with a giggle before downing her drink.

"What was it about?" Mr. Siggins asked.

Rory paused as her eyes slid around the room. "Cymbals," she said. She let out a small, tinkling laugh, her lower lip trembling as though she was holding back. I wondered what object or title behind me had tipped off her answer but didn't turn around. Instead, I narrowed my eyes at her and she batted her lashes.

"That seems like an unusual topic," Mrs. Quartermocker said.

"So much of poetry employs suggestion and metaphor," her husband said. "It's why it's so powerful."

"Romantic," Maynard said dubiously, raising one brow. "I didn't take you for a poet, Gage. You must perform the piece that stole Ms. Castle's heart."

The young man who clearly considered himself some kind of modern-day beatnik, stood and placed his martini on the table. "You absolutely must." Before I knew it, he was pulling my chair out so I was forced to stand and being jostled toward the grand piano that was situated up a step on a higher portion of flooring. The young man returned to the table where cards were being played and took a seat next to his wife, four pairs of eyes staring at me expectantly, just as another older man walked in. "Timothy," Maynard greeted. "I'm so glad you made it. Did the play get out early?"

"No, it was a wicked bore and I decided to leave."

"Well, have a seat. We're just about to hear Gage Buchanan's metaphorically charged poem on…cymbals."

"Oh, are we? How exciting. I used to dabble in poetry when I was younger. It's been ages since I've heard a good poem." Timothy pulled out a chair and sat down.

Now there were five sets of eyes peering at me expectantly, one pair of bright blue ones shimmering with barely suppressed mirth.

I would kill her after this. Slowly.

Cymbals…cymbals. I cleared my throat, my mind racing. I'd spoken at hundreds of business meetings completely off the cuff. I was great at it. As smooth as honey.

I could do poetry.

Poetry was easy.

I extended my arm and tipped my chin. "Cymbals clash and cymbals bang. I like cymbals, clang…clang. Clang."

I lowered my arm and looked at the people watching me from the table. Mrs. Quartermocker coughed and then covered her mouth, the three men stared speechlessly, and Rory's face was practically purple as she obviously held her breath.

Mrs. Quartermocker's husband looked as if he was working a complex math problem in his head.

"Well, er, that was…" Maynard started.

"Unique," the man named Timothy said, drawing the word out. I recognized him from a few social events, though I couldn't recall what he did. All I knew was that he'd just saved me and presented the perfect opportunity. I stepped down from the higher area of floor. "Now that there's another player, what do you say we leave this round to the professionals and have a drink, Rory?"

She stood up so fast, her chair wobbled. "That's a marvelous idea. A drink. Yes," she said breathlessly.

"The bar is just around the corner," Mr. Siggins said. "Please, help yourself to whatever you'd like."

We exited the room and turned the corner to the wet bar, featuring a marble counter and glass bistro shelving above, stacked with every type of liquor imaginable. Rory looked over her shoulder and then pulled me as we both hurried out of that room and down a hall, Rory holding her hand over her mouth as giggles obviously threatened to burst forth.

"I should kill you," I whispered as we walk-ran.

She did laugh then, and I grabbed her hand and we turned down another hall, safely out of sight of anyone exiting the room where the bridge game was being held.

"That was the worse poem I've ever heard," she said, bending forward as though her stomach hurt from holding back laughter.

I chuckled then too, turning away and then back toward her as I recalled the looks on their faces. "Never in my life have I looked more ridiculous than that," I said.

Her mostly silent laughter dwindled, but her lips remained tipped. "I like when you're being ridiculous," she said. "You should do it more often."

My own smile faded. "You seem to bring it out in me." My heart thumped and for whatever reason, Travis's words came back to me—*Don't worry, Buchanan, someday you'll be chasing down cats too.*

Is that what I'm doing now? My own version of chasing down cats? Acting outrageously for a woman because she brings out a side of me I've never met before? A side I'm not sure if I like, even if I've never smiled more in my life?

I broke eye contact. "Check out the art," I said, waving my hand to the paintings decorating the walls. "There's a lot of it." Maynard Siggins was obviously a fan of art. I only hoped he dabbled in painting himself and had hung at least one of his own pieces.

His house was both comfortable and stylish. Not stuffy at all like all the other houses of the men who might be Rory's father.

Please let this man be Rory's father. Please let the reason he's still single be that the one true love of his life disappeared without a trace and he still holds a torch for her. Rory's mom had referenced a family needing him, but that didn't necessarily mean a wife and children. And if that was the case, wouldn't it mean he'd welcome Rory with open arms? I wanted that for her. She was good and kind and had the brightest spirit

I'd ever known. She deserved to be loved by as many people as possible. She deserved to be claimed by both sides of her family and feel that sense of belonging that I'd enjoyed all my life.

We peeked inside one room after the other, tiptoeing up a set of stairs near the back of the house and quietly exploring the second floor. There was lots of art. Unfortunately, none brought to mind the watercolors we'd come to recognize.

We were just leaving what seemed to be a guest bedroom when the click of shoes sounded on the back stairs. We reversed course, ducking back inside the room as the footsteps came closer and the sound of a woman humming met my ears. A housekeeper? Rory's eyes widened, and she pointed to the closet to her right. I nodded, and we scurried to it, pushing the door that was already open a crack and then easing it shut behind us.

It was a rather small closet and so Rory and I stood pressed together as the woman entered the room we were in. I put my fingers over my lips and then leaned to the side to peer through the slats. The housekeeper, an older woman with short gray hair, continued to hum as she put fresh bedding on the bed, snapping the sheets and fluffing the pillows.

I stood upright and met Rory's eyes, both of us staring, our lips pressed together as we hid in the dim closet, waiting for the housekeeper to leave. Her breath stalled, chest rising and falling in tandem with mine as her pulse fluttered at her throat. I wanted to place my lips there and feel that rapid pump of life just beneath her skin. My own breath stuttered, heat infusing my body, head swimming. I could smell her intoxicating scent and it wrapped around me, making me feel slightly drunk the same way it had *that* night. The night I'd been inside her. The night I'd kissed and tasted her. Christ, I wanted that again. My cock swelled, pushing against my jeans as I took in a lungful of her scent. Of *Rory*. Of the woman I wanted but couldn't have. I almost groaned out loud, but bit it back when the housekeeper moved closer to the door and then finally, gathered her things and left the room.

We waited, breath mingling, gazes clashing. The housekeeper had left the room, but it sounded like she was doing something in the hall. Dusting, maybe…waving a feather wand over all those paintings on the wall.

We couldn't leave and yet…this closeness, this tension was almost too much to bear. "I thought you said you were going to learn bridge," I whispered.

She breathed out a silent laugh. "I meant to watch some YouTube videos but…" She changed positions slightly, brushing against my erection and I clenched my teeth, trying not to alert her to the fact that I was so turned on, I was woozy. "My dog walking business has exploded," she said. *Don't say the word exploded.* "I decided to go for the fake it 'til you make it approach."

The housekeeper's footsteps moved further away, down the hall. "Which is obviously the approach of losers, because that's about all I did."

I bit my lip not to laugh and she pressed hers together. And God, despite the fact that we might be caught in a man's closet at any minute…despite the fact that my body was in a state of painful, barely controlled lust…and despite the fact that this mission was basically a failure, it was so good to be with her again. The last few days had seemed… lifeless. I'd been antsy again which had made me realize that that feeling disappeared when I was with her.

Our gazes met again, mine lowering to her lush mouth. I knew just how it tasted. I remembered the dizzying rush of pleasure when she'd wrapped her tongue around mine. She swallowed, her breath seeming to grow shallow right before she exhaled and turned her head, breaking our eye contact and making me realize that I'd been moving my face closer to hers, drawn and unable to resist the pull of her lips so close to mine. "I…I thought about the question you asked," she whispered breathlessly. "The one about the difference between goals and dreams."

My gaze moved over her lovely features, taking in the two high points of color on her cheeks. "What?" I murmured, feeling a burst of happiness at the knowledge that she'd thought about me while we'd been apart, and relishing the feeling of telling secrets in the dark.

She met my eyes again. "I think…dreams come from a place inside you untouched by outward influences." She reached up and splayed her fingers over my heart. "Dreams are things you'd do even if you didn't get paid to do them."

Something expanded in my chest, right under the place where her palm rested, and I became highly aware of the sound of my own heart, beating loudly in my ears. *I'd open my own restaurant. I wouldn't crunch numbers or broker deals. I'd* create. *I'd come up with dishes and prepare meals for others. For gatherings. For celebrations. For life's most meaningful moments.* I was overwhelmed by Rory's closeness, my defenses down, and so the vision bloomed large in my brain before I could even begin to tamp it down. That was an impossibility of course, but if I could…if I were someone different…

Not a Buchanan.

Rory's eyes widened as if she'd heard my heart singing its secret. But then she turned her head, moving her eyes to the side as she listened. "She's going down the main staircase," she said.

I felt shaken and off-balance as I turned my ear toward the slats and listened as well, confirming what Rory said. I could hear the soft clunks of the housekeeper descending the stairs at the front of the house. The vision faded, and I tucked it away, back in the place reserved for pipe dreams that had no place in the real world.

Rory stepped to the side and I turned, slowly pushing the door open so that we could tiptoe out. When I reached the door to the hall, I peeked my head around the casing. "All clear," I said, reaching for her hand. "We've been gone so long, they probably think we left," I said. "Maybe it's in our best interest to sneak out."

We turned toward the back stairs, when there was the distinct sound of two pair of footsteps climbing them, and male voices conversing. *Shit!* We pivoted, hurrying in the other direction as the voices became clearer, talking about some character in a play. We weren't going to make it to the front stairway without being seen. I yanked Rory's hand, pulling her into a dark room as the footsteps became louder, moving directly toward us.

There was no time to hide and closing the door would only alert whoever it was to our presence.

I grabbed Rory and began kissing her. At first she froze, obviously shocked by suddenly having my mouth pressed against hers. But then I felt her soften in my arms and if I'd hoped the men talking and laughing and coming toward us would move past us unaware before, I wished for it twice as much now. *Go. Keep walking. Allow me to keep kissing her. Allow me to keep pretending this is a charade.*

"Oh!" a man said from our left, obviously having stopped

in the doorway as the lights blared on. I broke from Rory's mouth, giving the man named Timothy what I hoped was a contrite smile as I let go of Rory. She stepped back, seeming to lose her balance slightly before catching herself.

Maynard Siggins who had been slightly behind the man, let go of his hand and moved around him.

"Gage? I thought you'd left," he said. "What are you doing in…our bedroom?"

"Sorry," Rory said. "That poem…it got me. Again."

I looked at Mr. Siggins and then back to the other man. "I guess we got a little carried away. Wait…I'm sorry. *Your* bedroom?" I moved my finger between both men.

Mr. Siggins stood taller, straightening his dinner jacket. "Yes. This is my longtime partner, Timothy Irwin."

Longtime partner. Damn. So Maynard Siggins was most likely not Rory's father. All this sneaking around and hiding in closets had been for nothing. I let out a long sigh. "That's unfortunate."

Mr. Siggins's face flushed, and he looked offended. *Oh, shit.* I felt my own face flush as I realized how he'd interpreted my comment. I raised my hand. "That didn't come out like I meant it. I mean, it's unfortunate for Rory. Not for you. Obviously."

Timothy narrowed his eyes slightly. "Not that it's any of your business," he said. "And this is highly improper, finding you here like—"

Rory threw herself forward, wrapping her arms around Mr. Siggins and then letting go so she could kiss the other man on the cheek. "What Gage means is, that's wonderful," she said. "For you. We're happy for you."

Both men appeared completely flummoxed, but a smile tugged at Mr. Siggins's mouth. He cleared his throat as he again adjusted his jacket. "Well, I…yes. It is wonderful. Thank you, Ms. Castle."

"It is," I agreed. "It's great." It was *good* that this man couldn't be Rory's father. We didn't need hidden artwork to prove that. Unless…"When you say longtime partner—"

"How long exactly?" Rory finished, leaning in, obviously having had the same doubt as me.

"Er, Timothy? How many years now?"

Timothy rolled his eyes. "You're lucky I love you, you old fuddy duddy, even when you forget our anniversary. It's been thirty-three years." Both men smiled lovingly at each other.

Rory sighed, drawing her shoulders up and lowering them as she exhaled. "Wonderful," she said again. "Well, we should go. Thank you for a great evening."

We turned to bolt out of there when Rory came up short, sucking in a surprised breath. "Oh my God," she said, turning toward the walk-in closet on the far wall.

"What is it, Ms. Castle?" Maynard asked.

"That painting," she said as I stepped next to her to see what she'd spotted. "Is it yours?"

I saw what she was looking at now and inhaled my own breath of surprise. It was one of his. I turned around to see Maynard and Timothy shoot each other a look of confusion. "Well, we own it," Maynard Siggins said.

"I purchased it," Timothy clarified.

"Where?" Rory asked, wonder clear in her voice as she reached out and touched the framed watercolor hanging above the built-in dresser on the rear wall of the closet.

"At Silver Horse Antiques. What is this about, Ms. Castle?"

"How long ago?" she asked. "I'm sorry. I just…my father painted this and I'm trying to find out who he was."

That seemed to take both men by surprise. Timothy approached, looking up at the painting. "I bought it a few months ago, actually. We had our closet redone and it seemed perfect. I was moved by the depth of emotion in a landscape. The combination of colors and the usage of hard and soft lines conveys so much, don't you think?"

Rory nodded, her gaze still stuck to the painting for several moments before she turned toward Timothy. "May we look behind it?"

"Behind it?"

"Yes. We've found others that contain diary entries that are very important to me." She put her hand on his arm. "I'd be grateful."

He paused only briefly before stepping forward and removing the painting from the wall. He set it on the top of the dresser and turned it over. "Maynard, hand me something sharp, will you? I believe there's a letter opener in the writing desk."

Maynard stepped out of the small room and was back in a flash, handing Timothy a small silver letter blade. Timothy used it the same way I had to pry off the back, pulling it aside to reveal a folded piece of paper. Rory let out a small sound of tearful happiness.

"Whose diary entries are they, my dear?"

"They belonged to my mother."

Timothy picked up the page and handed it to Rory. "Then this is yours. Take the painting too."

"Oh, I couldn't take the painting. You purchased it."

But Timothy smiled. "It's fate. I assume this is what you were sneaking around our home looking for."

Rory looked down but nodded. "I thought you might be my father," she said to Maynard Siggins. "I'm very sorry we were dishonest. This was my fault, not Gage's."

Maynard shot me a look but smiled kindly when he set his gaze back on Rory. "Having children wasn't in the cards for me. For us. But you seem lovely. I have no doubt your father will claim you with open arms."

Fifteen minutes later, our heads bent close together, the diary entry held under the interior light of my car, we began reading.

Lys has a secret that she won't share. I can see it's eating her up inside. When we're together, her eyes drift off and I can tell that whatever she's thinking about makes her both happy and sad. It reminds me of the way she acted before she ran away from that awful home for girls. Scared and jittery, but excited too, a look of barely-contained hope in her eyes. I was with her when she chose Pelion straight off a map of Maine. She told me it's the name of a mountain in Greek mythology and she always loved those stories of gods and mortals. Lys always did read too much, if you ask me. So that's how she ended up in the small lake town on the other side of Calliope. And I didn't dare even visit until her father died, may he rest in hell. I wonder if it's true that we're all attracted to the familiar because that husband of hers has the same mean look in his eyes that her father always did, especially when he got up to drinking. It breaks my heart to know she ran from one devil only to end up with another.

But… her husband did give her that boy of hers and God but does she love him. She looks at him like he hung the moon and all the stars. I wonder though, because it's the same way she looks at her husband's brother. What a mess. A god-awful mess.

CHAPTER TWENTY-ONE
Rory

Gage pulled up across the street from a white stone building with two massive pillars out front, a poster with a *For Sale* sign in the window. I stepped from the car, craning my neck to look up at what appeared to be an old bank, as he joined me and we crossed the street.

It had been almost a week since I'd seen Gage after we'd gotten caught snooping in Maynard and Timothy's closet, and had found another piece of my father's artwork which unfortunately spoke of someone else I didn't know. I'd spent the time since finishing the last of the fake appraisals so I could return the artwork to the families that had loaned it to me and walking my temporary brood on the lakeshore. I'd sat on a rock at the edge of the lake just the day before, the dogs lounging next to me, and was struck by the feeling of pure contentment. I'd closed my eyes and soaked in the unfamiliar sense of deep calm that was unconnected to my current circumstances. I hadn't found my father yet. I'd only managed to cross one possibility off the list and the time was drawing nearer that I would have to leave. But for a moment in time, none of that seemed to matter as I gazed out at that peaceful water, framed by trees and hills and cool, shaded shores. I felt anchored in a way I never had before. I felt…a connection that I couldn't explain.

I'd also called my uncles about the woman named Lys my mother kept mentioning in her diary entries, but they didn't remember hearing her name. Who was she? And why had she disappeared completely from my mother's life after she returned to Mud Gulch?

"This is the property your company owns?" I asked. Gage had called me out of the blue, asking if I wanted to check out the sunset from the roof of a property his company had recently purchased. It'd seemed like a semi-odd invitation, but in all honesty, and to my own great dismay, I'd been hungry to see him, just like I'd been when he'd called about the bridge night, and so I'd accepted immediately.

"Yeah. It was the old Calliope Savings and Loan. It closed many years ago and another company bought it but whatever they intended for it never materialized. Anyway, we obtained it from them." He smiled somewhat tightly. "It's a fantastic location. My father plans on demo'ing it and building here. Our other hotel location in Calliope is several miles away, so this makes sense." He stuck a key in the lock of the massive wooden door and pushed it open. "Anyway, it's in rough shape. But I thought, being the sunset-lover that you are, we might take advantage of the view while it's still here." He glanced at me. "While *we're* still here." We both stepped inside and Gage pushed the door which squeaked closed and then shut with a solid thud that echoed in the mostly empty space. He smiled, and though it was dim where we were standing, I swore I still saw something that looked like apprehension in his gaze. *Why does this old building make you nervous, Gage?*

I stepped forward, tipping my head back to gaze up at the carved ceiling and the elaborate trim. The marble counter stretched all along the right side of the space, wrought iron teller windows with numbers at the top separating the spaces where bank employees had once stood. "It's incredible," I murmured. "The things someone could do with a space like this. Your father's really planning on tearing it down?"

Gage gave a singular nod as he massaged a spot on his chest like he might have strained a muscle there. "Well, the lot is more valuable than the building. Anyway, the view… it's this way." He pointed to a rickety spiral staircase that wound up to a second floor and when I followed him over to it, I caught a glimpse of the massive vault just around the corner.

I sucked in a breath and headed in that direction instead. "Wow," I said as I entered. But then I looked back at the wide-open door, ensuring that it wasn't going to swing shut at any moment and lock us inside. The thing was about three feet thick and made of steel. If we got stuck in here, no one would ever hear us scream. I walked to the back where there was a wall of safe-deposit boxes and ran my hand along the numbers. Here was where the original crème de la crème of Calliope kept their treasures, whatever those were. "What is it about old buildings that's so fascinating?" I asked, turning to Gage. "Even when they're practically empty?"

"The stories," he said as though he'd already considered my question and come to his own conclusion. "There are stories here, ones we'll never know." He walked forward, joining me where I stood. "But maybe part of them lives on as whispers in the walls, ones you can feel, more than you can hear."

I tilted my head. "Why, Gage Buchanan, who's the romantic now?"

He laughed and pushed off the wall. "I'm full of surprises, Cakes."

I smiled. I didn't disagree, although I had a feeling he was more full of secrets than surprises, and perhaps ones he even kept from himself. *What is that intensity radiating off of you right now, Gage?*

"We'd better get upstairs if we're going to catch that sunset."

Gage and I clanged up the spiral staircase and stepped onto the second floor. Whatever had once been up here had been demolished as it was just an open space, taken down to the studs. "Careful," Gage said as he stepped over a discarded board and started climbing a second staircase situated near the back. I followed him up, and then exited through the door at the top where we walked outside into the soft summer breeze. I blinked as I looked around.

It was gorgeous.

Faith had a charming outside area set up behind her gallery. It was pretty and cozy and she told me she often hosted intimate cocktail parties there. But that space was nothing like this.

Oh, the possibilities.

And yet Gage's father couldn't see that? What a shame to demolish something with so much potential.

A stone railing enclosed the entirety of the area, black and white tiles laid out in a diamond pattern under our feet. The space was mostly barren right now, but beautiful and full of potential though it was, that wasn't what I was looking at. It was the *view*. The building that had once served as a grand bank was only three stories, but because of the massive ceilings inside, it was taller than the buildings surrounding it, and situated on a downtown street right across from the shore. As I looked out, I could see clear across Pelion Lake to Pelion itself, where quaint cottages dotted the water. The lake glittered in the glow of the tangerine sunset, the outline of the trees and the hills adding to the scenic perfection so that it looked like a painting. "My God, it's stunning," I breathed. "This place…it's pure magic."

"Beautiful, isn't it?" And I swore his voice shook slightly with…something.

I turned, considering him, and then glancing around. "The sunset…is that what you wanted to show me?"

He avoided my gaze, his eyes trained on that dazzling sky. "Of course. What else?"

He was lying. It was the place he liked. *What are you envisioning? What do you imagine this old building might become? What whispered stories do you hear? What dream are you trying to hold back?*

He looked at me, that same intensity I'd seen downstairs clear in his gaze and radiating all around him. My breath caught. It was beautiful honestly. Raw and powerful. It made him appear so vibrant and alive in a way I wasn't sure how to explain.

His gaze moved over my features, the passion still there, but also mixed with a measure of vulnerability so rare on Gage Buchanan's face. "The way your eyes look in this light," he murmured. "They're dazzling. You're dazzling."

An exhale rushed from my lungs, my heart beating so rapidly I brought my hand to it as if I could slow it down with the press of my palm. "My mother told me that someone had once described her eyes as canary blue," I said, the words breathy as I looked back out to the horizon. "She didn't say who it was, but I always believed it was my father. And now, I'm even more certain. It's the way an artist would describe something, isn't it?"

"Canary blue," he said, a note of wonder in his voice and something that almost sounded like relief. "Yes. It's perfect. Your eyes, they're canary blue, especially in this light."

I looked back at him then. I couldn't help it. Our gazes caught and everything about Gage Buchanan in that moment—the heat rolling off of him, the way he was looking at me—made me want to rush into his arms and bring my mouth to his. To drink in the intensity he was trying so hard to contain and mostly failing to—

His phone rang, jolting me from my Gage trance.

He made a small, startled movement too and then pulled the phone from his pocket and glanced down at it. His gaze shot to me. "It's the lab."

I took a tiny step back, the blood in my veins cooling at least several degrees, the emotional fogginess clearing. *The hospital. Oh my God. Our test results.* I swallowed. "Are you going to answer it?" My voice felt shaky and sounded strange, as if I had uttered the word from underwater. *Oh God. Here it is. Brace for impact.*

Gage let out a gust of air and punched at the phone. "Hello?" His voice sounded parched, as though he'd just walked ten miles under a desert sun. He listened for a minute, clenching his eyes shut. I couldn't catch my breath. "99.9% certain?" he asked in that same dehydrated voice. "That's very definitive."

I brought my hand to my midsection, wondering how my stomach had managed to tie itself into knots in the last thirty seconds.

Gage listened again, still as a statue. "Thank you. I

appreciate it. Right, yes. You too." He hung up the phone and met my eyes. "Rory Casteel," he whispered. "You are… not my sister." Then a burst of sound that was part groan and part exhale exploded from his mouth, both of us moving so fast, I didn't register what was happening until my face was between his palms and then his mouth was on mine. *Oh, thank you, thank you, thank you.*

"You had to pause, didn't you? Just to torture me?" I asked between kisses.

God, he tasted good…and when had he picked me up, and when had I encircled him with my legs? I had climbed him in the space of three heartbeats and now we were ravaging each other's mouths, moaning and thrusting and practically falling over as he walked with me, presumably moving somewhere that provided a soft place to land in the very unlikely event we toppled over.

Oh hell, I didn't need a soft place to land. I only needed a solid surface, preferably one that didn't feature protruding nails. Eh, I could work around nails. I just needed Gage naked.

"Rory, Christ, hell, fuck," he moaned as we collided with the door that led down the stairs, lucky that it didn't open easily and send us crashing to the floor below.

"Is there…somewhere we can…"

"Fuck," he moaned when I writhed against the hard bulge filling his dress pants.

"Yes, that."

He let out a sound that was part laugh and part tortured groan. "Not here. I refuse to take you anywhere other than a bed."

"I don't need a bed. Remember the pool table? We managed to have fantastic sex on a pool table. We can manage it again on the floor in a bank vault."

He pulled back slightly in order to meet my eyes. "No, Rory. You deserve a bed. And I'm taking you to mine. Because I don't want a quick fuck on the floor. I want access to your body for many, many hours in a row."

I groaned too, shivers moving down my limbs. God, I was on the verge of orgasm just from rubbing up against him. But…many, many hours? In a bed? That sounded heavenly. I slid down his body. "Okay. Take me to your place, my not-brother."

He laughed and then flung the door open behind him and we both flew down the stairs, laughing and slightly breathless. I hardly remembered the drive to his condo, other than that at every traffic light, he leaned across and kissed me until I was squirming.

He parked almost diagonally in a parking spot at his building and then tugged my arm as we ran to his condo, stumbling inside, mouths fused together.

"Bed, get me to your bed," I said as I came up for air.

"I don't know if I can make it there. I want you so bad," he groaned. I felt him reach down and undo his zipper as we teetered one way, then another and I sucked at his tongue, my hands raking through his hair.

"I want you too. So much. God, I want you in me, over me, under me. There's not a place on my body I don't want to feel you." I was tingly everywhere, my blood rushing in my veins, a drumbeat of need between my legs making me feel achy and desperate to be filled.

"Jesus, baby, you're going to make me explode against the wall in my foyer."

He'd managed to get his zipper open and now I reached down between us and lifted his heavy cock from the opening in his pants, stroking it as he stumbled backward, hitting a wall and then tilting my head so he could kiss me more deeply. He grunted animalistically as he pumped into my hand. "Need you," he said and the two stilted words made my entire body flush with heat because smooth-talking Gage Buchanan could barely form syllables and I'd done that to him.

"If you get me to your bed, I'll put you in my mouth," I said.

He practically shot off the wall, losing his grip on me temporarily so I slid down his body, but then he caught me, hoisting me up as I laughed and connected back to his mouth.

He wove and dodged and moments later, I let out a shriek that turned into another laugh as we fell back, me landing on top of him on his low bed. I slid down his body, and then removed my shirt and bra before going on my knees on the floor. He'd started to rise to a sitting position, but when I took his erection in my hand, he fell back again, groaning and gripping his hair.

I took a moment to study him, moving my thumb over the bead of precum on his tip. "Jesus, Rory. Killing me," he moaned.

"Shh," I said. The last time we'd been together, I hadn't had much of a view of him and I wasn't going to waste the opportunity even though I was desperate too. "You're perfect," I said right before I leaned up and took him in my mouth, swirling my tongue across his salty slit. And this perfect, he didn't need to try for.

He just was.

Just him.

He swore again, and the muttered sound of need made my nipples pebble, eager for his touch. I sucked him into my mouth, as I gripped the hard muscles of his legs. So strong, and yet his thighs trembled beneath my palms. God, that was sexy. I leaned up further, controlling him with my mouth as I pressed down with my hands.

"Enough," he grated, using his hand to pull himself from between my lips with a wet sound before sitting up and flipping me onto my back on the bed. My laughter was smothered by his mouth as he used his tongue to dip and tease. I wrapped my legs around his hips, our cores meeting as we both made sounds of frustration.

Gage pulled himself up, undressing in a flash and then pulling my shorts and underwear off. "This time's gonna have to be quick," he said. "We'll go slower next time."

"Condom," I said, glad I was still working with at least a few brain cells. He looked momentarily confused, then slightly panicked, before he rushed from the room, and seconds later returned, holding up a condom. I breathed out a sigh of relief as he stretched it over his impressive erection.

I watched him as he came over me, his body so incredibly drool-worthy I could hardly believe this was real. "Thank God you're not my brother."

He laughed. "Not even a distant relative."

"That's good too."

"Yes," he agreed. "That's very good. You know what else is good?"

"What?"

"This." He pressed himself forward, taking his swollen cock in his hand and circling it on my clit.

"Ohhh," I breathed, tingles tightening my belly. "Please, Gage."

"Shh," he said, teasing me the way I'd teased him. I smiled, but my smile turned into a sob of pleasure as his mouth clamped over my nipple and he took in a long suck just as he plunged into my body.

For a breathless moment, he was completely still, our heartbeats thundering together. Then he raised his head and stared into my eyes, his hazy with lust before he started to move. "Canary blue," he murmured. My eyes drifted shut as I clutched the comforter beneath my palms, shifting my hips so that he could sink in as deep as possible.

"I don't think I could have lived without experiencing you again," he said as he plunged in and then pulled out again.

"You might have had to," I said. "If things had been different. But they're not." *They're not.*

"You make me want to break all the rules, Rory." He sped up, sweat glistening on his skin, his back growing slick as I ran my fingernails up and down, delighting in the feel of his sleek muscles working beneath his flesh.

"There are no rules. We're off the hook," I said, pleasure spiraling, thoughts clouding. *Ninety-nine point nine nine nine percent. What a beautiful number.*

"There are. There are rules upon rules. Layers of rules." The final word gusted out and turned into a groan as his movements grew jerky and inelegant. His mouth returned to mine and we kissed for several more thrusts before I was hurled into the stratosphere, breaking from his mouth and pressing my head back into the pillow as bliss washed over me in waves, my muscles seizing and contracting again and again.

"Oh Rory, oh God," he groaned as he pressed into me, circling his hips as he panted against my neck.

We breathed together as the stars that had sparkled around me, and through me, faded away, leaving a deep satisfaction that made me feel somehow heavy and lighter than air. I sighed, and Gage turned his head, nuzzling his nose into my neck. "You smell like heaven," he said. He slipped out of me and rolled away, taking me with him so that we lay facing each other, our faces mere inches away. He kissed me lightly. "You taste like heaven." He smiled against my lips. "And you feel like heaven."

I smiled, feeling happy and sleepy and warm as his lips trailed down my jaw.

"Cymbals clash and cymbals bang..." he murmured. I laughed, and I felt him grin against the base of my neck. "Now you understand the metaphor, don't you?"

I breathed out another laugh. "I do. I get it now. It's brilliant."

Gage smiled again and then twisted, reaching behind him and grabbing the comforter that had ended up halfway on the floor and brought it up and over us so that we were in a two-person cocoon. We snuggled for a few minutes, hands moving lightly over skin, tracing, discovering small nooks and crannies, some of which made the other laugh, and some that elicited a sigh. "What are the layers of rules?" I whispered, my mind reliving every moment since we'd collided on that roof overlooking the sunset.

"Hmm?"

"You said there are layers upon layers of rules. What are they?"

He looked slightly confused before he let out a long exhale. "I said that, did I?" He paused, seeming a little troubled even as his eyes were soft. "You seem to find a way to remove all my barriers."

What did that mean? That he said things during sex that he didn't necessarily mean to say? "Sex can do that," I said with a tilt of my lips.

He let out a short laugh. "Not sex. *You.*" His leaned in and kissed one eyelid and then the other. "Canary blue," he murmured again. He pulled me closer so that my ear was right against his chest. I listened to the drum of his heart for a few minutes, lulled by the steady rhythm, that sleepiness taking over as my eyes drifted closed. I could feel the slow gust of his breath and the way his muscles loosened as he fell asleep.

Did he realize he held himself so tightly, even when he'd probably describe himself as relaxed? *You make me want to break the rules.*

What rules?

Ones he'd imposed on himself, or those put upon him by others? Or a combination of both? What specific rules was he so afraid to break? Did he even know? Had he allowed himself to name specifics? I had a feeling I was at least a small part of some category he'd listed as *off limits.*

But not because we were potentially related.

Listen…Rory. There's no reason we can't continue to see each other.

Under the cover of darkness? Should I wear a disguise?

The conversation with Thaddeus wove through my memory, and I recalled the way it'd made me feel so low to know that he didn't consider me good enough for him. Gage wasn't like Thaddeus. Gage was kind and considerate. Gage rescued baby animals for their sake, but also for mine. But…he'd been born into a life where expectations were high, and status meant everything. And I very well might be the product of an illicit affair my mother had with the husband of one of the elites of Calliope.

No one was going to be happy when I solved the mystery of my parentage. No one—least of all Gage's parents—were going to be overjoyed to see him with me in any context.

He had to know that.

Whereas I'd felt boneless with satisfaction fifteen minutes before, now I felt the doom of our inevitable end pressing me down. He'd never given me any indication that there was the possibility of anything long-term, but I suddenly realized, somewhere in the back of my mind, I'd allowed that hope to spark to life, and then kept the fire burning.

Small, mostly unacknowledged, but there.

Ugh, Rory. You've really gone and done it now. You've fallen in love with Gage Buchanan.

I sighed, and as if in response, Gage tightened his arms around me. "Stay," he said, as if he'd sensed my distress. "Stay the night."

The night. I would. I'd soak up the final hours that remained in his arms. I couldn't bear to leave his bed just yet, even if it was inevitable that I did leave his life soon. My heart constricted with both happiness and the pain of what I knew was inevitable: our parting.

The sun slept, and so did we, waking in the deep of night and turning toward the other. We made love, slow and leisurely as if we had all the time in the world, as though it might pause just for us. We relished each stilted breath, and every soft sigh of pleasure. I thought back to the last time we'd spent the night together, stealing hours, knowing then what I still knew now—that he and I would always end with the rising of the sun.

CHAPTER TWENTY-TWO
Gage

I'd woken and she was gone. Being that I had early meetings and was in a rush to get out the door, it was probably for the best. But still, not waking with her in my arms had been a disappointment.

Things were getting out of hand. I knew it and yet I couldn't seem to stop craving her. My head was constantly spinning and the only person I wanted to reach for was her. And yet, she both calmed my inner turmoil and also made me dizzy in a whole different way. This wasn't like me. I was inside out and upside down and nothing made sense anymore.

I both dreaded the idea of boarding a plane to London and wanted—needed—the protection of a vast ocean between us.

Protection, Buchanan? Protection from what? What does she stir up in you that you're trying so hard to ignore? I knew though, didn't I? She brought things out in me that I had long suppressed. Dreams I wanted to explore but couldn't. It *ached* because the time had long passed where my life could be anything other than what it was. Just the acknowledgment made me feel sick with guilt. What was the fucking *point*?

You said there are layers upon layers of rules, she'd said the night before after, once again, passion had demolished my well-constructed defenses. *What are they?* I hadn't had the wherewithal to respond to her question in that moment, but I knew the answer. There were rules about wearing the *right* clothes and having the *right* friends, networking with the *right* people and having the *right* social circle and the *right* business associates.

And, eventually, the *right* spouse.

Rory wouldn't check any of those boxes.

And she felt like freedom and dreams that were only mine, avenues I longed to travel but never could. And she seemed to *see* me in a way no woman ever had. Which scared the hell out of me.

So yeah, maybe I did need protection from her. And I definitely needed to get my head back on straight. *Head down. Work hard. Focus. Win.*

How many times had my father repeated those words to me in just that order?

But then another voice spoke louder, drowning out my father.

Measure with your heart. Learn the rules, then break them in a way that only you can.

I squeezed my head. That damn Frenchman. Haunting me.

I resisted calling her until five p.m. when the first employees began leaving the building. When she didn't answer, I waited until I'd gotten home to call her again. It was after nine thirty, where the hell was she? I went to my window, looking out at the dwindling light, the sun a mere slip above the water. I recalled what she'd looked like in the light of the sunset the night before, standing on the roof of the old Savings and Loan. The memory alone made my stomach tighten as a deep yearning balled in my throat and made it difficult to breathe. I pushed those feelings away, emptying my mind as again, I stared out the window and watched the water swallow the sun.

I picked up the phone again and dialed her number, realizing that I was quickly leaning into the territory of desperation. She still didn't answer.

Maybe her phone's out of battery. Maybe it's charging.

I grabbed my keys and headed for the door because I couldn't fucking help myself. Who cared? I only had limited time before there would be no choice but to leave her be. Only weeks before I'd be on another continent and she'd be back home, waiting tables in her family bar. An image flashed in my mind, the way her face looked when I ran my fingers down her inner arm. *Bliss. Contentment. Surrender.* I squeezed the steering wheel as I blew out a frustrated breath.

Maybe I could see her when I came home for visits, whenever those might be. I pulled up in front of Faith's house, but the lights were out and neither car was in the driveway. Hopelessness descended, both for the fact that they were obviously out, and for my musings about seeing Aurora here and there on brief forays home. I wanted more than that. Not just from her, but from life. I'd already decided I wanted to settle down, create a family. And not only that, I wouldn't suggest such paltry offerings. She deserved far more than some man who jetted in now and again for some pool table sex. The very thought—and even though I'd cast myself in the role of "some man"—made me want to fight someone. Probably myself.

I started pulling away from the curb when I had a thought. I braked, picking up my phone. I was pretty sure Faith used her cell number as her business contact. I pulled up her gallery website and then dialed the number she had listed there. She answered on the second ring.

"Hey Faith, it's Gage." It was loud in the background, the sounds of what I thought were country music making me raise my voice to make sure she could hear me.

"Gage! Hi. Are you looking for Rory?"

"Yeah, ah, I called her and was just sort of worried when she didn't call back."

Faith let out what sounded like an inebriated giggle. "She accidentally left her phone at home. Rory, it's Gage."

"At home? Where are you?"

"Ivy League!" I heard her call from the background. A smile tugged at my lips, my breath coming easier at even hearing the distant sound of her voice.

"We're at The Broken Spoke next to—"

"I know where it is. I'll be there in twenty minutes."

"Bring your cowboy boots!"

I didn't have any cowboy boots, and I wouldn't have taken the time to find a place to buy some even if stores were open. "See you soon," I said and then disconnected the call.

The Broken Spoke was located in a more eclectic area of town by the lake that featured several other bars and restaurants, hip clothing boutiques, and overpriced coffee shops. It was tourist heavy and provided all kinds of options as far as nightlife entertainment.

I flashed my ID at the bouncer and pushed open the saloon-style doors, the loud refrains of some country ballad filling the massive, crowded room. Despite the noise of the guy singing in a twang about a rock and a hard place—which seemed like an appropriate entry song—whoops and hollers could still be heard from the other side of the room where I knew there was a mechanical bull.

I made my way through the crowd, my neck craned, eyes peeled for a dark head of glossy hair. Where was she?

I pushed through a group of people obstructing my view of the bull ride, stopping in my tracks when I saw who was riding it. Rory. Arm raised, head thrown back, spine curled, ass jutted out as she laughed so hard she was about to fall out of the saddle, regardless of the bucking bull. Oh, Jesus. I stood there, a smile tilting my lips as I watched her throwing all caution to the wind as she so often did. So damn spirited and full of life. Willing to concoct a ridiculous plan to find her father because she'd been thrown an opportunity and she was not going to let it pass her by. I didn't know what it felt like to perpetually live with that kind of passion.

I had no idea.

But she did. We were different, we had to be. But even to witness it knocked the breath from my lungs. Over and over and over. Time slowed, the crowd faded, the noise was a buzz in the background of my mind. It was only her. And God, but she was the most wildly beautiful woman I'd ever known.

She spotted me, and the wide-eyed joy that infused her face was another swift kick to some vital organ or another, perhaps each of them in turn as the impact raced through my body in a series of blows. She let go, raising both arms to wave at me, pitching forward and then sliding to the side. I didn't even remember moving, but suddenly I was beyond the wall of people that had separated me from the platform where the bull was attached and standing next to it as Rory was flung off. I caught her, and she let out a sound that was part laughter and part "oof," clutching me and sliding down my body. She leaned her head back, her grin vibrant, canary blue eyes dancing with humor. Her gaze wandered over my face for a few moments, smile fading, and then she said, "I've got you."

I've got you. "That's my line," I murmured.

She used her thumb to run over my cheekbone. "I don't think so, Ivy League." She sighed as she slid lower and planted her feet on the floor. I became aware of the fact that the person up next on the bull was trying to get around us and took Rory's hand and led her to the edge of the platform. She almost tripped, giggling as I steadied her.

"You shouldn't ride drunk," I said with a smirk in her direction.

"I'm not drunk. Just tipsy. And I was kicking ass until you came along."

Yeah, so was I, Cakes. So was I. Only really, was that true? I suddenly didn't know anymore. That spinning took up again, my brain twisting one way and then the other. "Where's Faith?" I asked.

"She's at the bar with her boyfriend, Jarrett. Come meet him."

She tugged my hand and I wove with her through the crowd to the bar where Faith and her boyfriend had snagged some stools. I greeted the guy named Jarrett, an artist Faith had met when she featured his work in her gallery. I ordered a round of drinks and we chatted for a while before Faith gathered her purse and stood. "I have a showing tomorrow so I can't be too hung over," she said on a giggle.

"Nice to meet you, man," Jarrett said as he stood too

and they gathered their things. "I hope to see you again." I just gave a nod, though it was doubtful I'd ever see the guy again as I'd be in another country soon and if I did come to town, I wouldn't have any reason to hang out with Faith. If I'd have been drunk, those thoughts would have served to sober me, but being as I'd had one drink, they just made me feel sort of hollow.

Faith leaned over and whispered something to Rory and Rory nodded. I assumed Faith had asked if she was okay with me taking her home.

We said our goodbyes and then Rory took me by the hand. "Come on, Ivy League. I love this song." I didn't know it, but I didn't care. I was itching to get my arms around her in any way I could.

I followed her to the semi-crowded dance floor, pulling her to me as she wrapped her arms around my neck. I nuzzled the spot next to her ear, drinking in her scent, far more intoxicating than the bourbon I'd just drunk.

She sighed. "God, I want you. Why do I want you so much?" she asked.

My cock stiffened at the mere suggestion of sex with her. "I want you too, Cakes. You're like an addiction."

"You know what they say about addictions."

"Don't try to go it alone?"

She laughed. "Cold turkey is the only way."

"Mm," I hummed. She was probably right. And frankly, it was our only option. I had a feeling it wasn't only going to be cold turkey, it was going to be frigid fucking turkey. An icy blast of need that was going to rip me apart. But for now...for now, she was in my arms and I was going to enjoy her. I was going to push all that other stuff aside and just not think about it.

I swayed with her, blanking my brain, narrowing my world to the feel of her softness pressed against me and the words of the song she loved. *And I'm damned if I do and I'm damned if I don't…*

She had leaned back slightly and was looking at me again in that way that made me feel both warm and vaguely terrified. She went up on her tiptoes and kissed me, her lips running softly over mine before she pulled back. "What are you trying to silence when you stare into space like that? What are you battling, Gage Buchanan?" she whispered.

You make me want to live a different life. The thought caused a bleat of alarm, and that moment in Maynard Siggins's closet came back to me, but I pushed both the alarm and the memory away. "My desire to do incredibly dirty things to you, regardless of being in public."

She laughed softly but looked unconvinced. "I don't think so." She squinted. "But I'll accept that answer too." She stepped away and pulled my hand and I followed her.

She led me out of the bar and then laughed again as she started running. The noise of the bar dwindled as I gave chase, catching her easily around the waist and spinning her around. I grinned, feeling young and free and just a little ridiculous. Living that life I wanted to live, but only in small doses and only while I still could. "Why do I love chasing you so damn much?" I asked as she tipped her head back and smiled up at the moon.

"Because I reward you when you catch me," she said, pulling me again and leading me into a dark space between the buildings. She planted her back against the wall of one of the buildings and took my face in her hands and kissed me. Heat rushed through my limbs, making me instantly hard again. I pressed my body against hers, moaning into her mouth.

We kissed deeply, the tension between us rising and expanding and driving me half out of my mind. I wanted to fuck her right there against that wall, in a semi-public place where anyone might walk by and see us. This wasn't me. I'd never in my life done something like this. I'd even partied responsibly, never having more than two drinks in public, never…never…never. So many nevers. Those layers of rules I'd mentioned to Rory. And this woman seemed like every possibility I might have wanted but denied myself because of how others expected me to behave. But I didn't want to think about any of that. I just wanted. I let out a harsh breath, bracing my hand against the wall behind her as I attempted to catch my breath.

Rory's hand went to the button of my pants, undoing it and dragging down my zipper. "You're drunk," I breathed, a groan emerging as she took my rock-hard cock in her hand and stroked it once, twice.

"I'm not drunk, I'm tipsy," she said, stroking me again. "And I'm always tipsy with you, even if I haven't had any alcohol."

God, so was I. So was I. I leaned back in and kissed her, tugging her skirt up with both hands, some switch flipping inside me as that want turned into need, a need that felt so powerful, I shuddered.

I blearily managed to pull a condom from my wallet and slide it on right before I plunged into her. She cried out as I grunted in mutual pleasure. "Oh, Jesus," I said before I began to move, pumping into her so that her back pounded against the wall. I put my hand behind her to provide a buffer but didn't slow in my movements. Rory gripped me, panting as she raised her leg and wrapped it around my waist. "You're going to make me come, Cakes, right here in a public alley. Jesus Christ, the things you do to me."

"Yes," she said, "Oh, Gage. Right there. Please."

Her small grunts and pleas served to bring me to the very edge and I removed my hand from behind her to bring it between us and play with her clit. She gripped my shoulders and tipped her head back and rode my hand and moments later, I felt her squeeze around me and I let go too, flying into the stars that blinked overhead and then being flung between them like a pinball.

I came back to myself slowly, feeling battered and bruised the way a pinball might, but also changed in some vital way I couldn't even begin to work out in my bliss-addled brain.

Rory lowered her leg and I slid out of her. We both pulled ourselves together as best we could. Rory giggled and I looked at her in the dim light of the alley as she clamped her hand over her mouth.

"What?" I asked.

"I don't know. I just...wow." I concurred. I laughed as I hooked my arm around her neck and pulled her to me. We exited onto the street, and began walking to the parking garage at the center of it that featured most of the bars and restaurants, and she reached up and linked her hand with mine in front of her shoulder.

"I gotta say, Ivy League. You don't seem like the type to have alleyway sex and yet here we are."

I laughed and then leaned down and kissed her as we walked. "You bring out hidden depths I never knew were there," I said.

"Gage?"

I halted, and Rory tripped as we both came up short. I

looked over, my stomach sinking as I saw who it was. My parents. My arm dropped as Rory stepped away. "Mom. Dad." There was a couple behind them and they came forward too. "Hey, Shawn. Sarah. Hi." Shawn was the man who was taking over my position at the company.

Shawn and Sarah greeted me quickly. "Sorry to rush off," Shawn said, "but that's our car." He pointed out to the street, where the valet had just delivered their vehicle to the curb and was waiting with the door held open.

"Have a nice night," I said.

"Goodnight, Mr. and Mrs. Buchanan. Thank you again. It was a wonderful dinner."

My parents called goodbye and then we all stood there somewhat awkwardly for a moment before my mom stuck her hand out to Rory. "Ms. Castle, it's so nice to see you."

Ms. Castle. Shit.

And where were my manners? I'd left her standing there without any kind of introduction. I was still partially reeling from the amazing sex and coming face to face with the last people I expected—or wanted—to see.

"Hi, Mrs. Buchanan," Rory said uncomfortably, moving from one foot to the other.

"Er, sorry, ah, Dad, this is...Aurora Castle, the new art appraiser in town."

Rory whose cheeks were flushed with obvious embarrassment, greeted my dad with little more than a murmur.

My father's lips did that small twitching thing that I knew meant he was displeased. My stomach sunk farther, skin prickling.

My mother looked back and forth between us. "I didn't realize you two were...seeing each other."

"We're not," Rory said, her eyes holding on me briefly as

her cheeks flushed. Jesus. This was awkward. Was being seen with me at all blowing her cover in some way? I couldn't even think straight. We'd done so much lying and now I couldn't work out the truth. And yet, listening to her denying that we were anything to each other felt like something sharp poking at me from beneath my skin, even in the midst of my father's clear disapproval. "We were just, ah. We ran into each other and..." She looked back at the row of businesses behind her. "At the...nail salon."

"Oh," my mother said with a frown. "I..."

"Since when do you get pedicures, Gage?" my dad asked as he squinted toward the shop. "Are they even open?"

"Not now," I said quickly. "But they were. Up until a few minutes ago. Isn't that your car?"

"Yes, it is."

"It was nice running into you guys. I'll see you at work tomorrow," I said to my dad.

"Okay," he said with a frown. I knew what he probably thought. That I was "sowing some oats" before the big move. And he frowned upon it because he was hopeful I had my sights on something serious, and specifically with Blakely. I hated that he thought that about Rory, but the truth was, I *had* had my sights on something serious. So what *was* I doing? "Ms. Castle, nice to meet you."

"You too, sir. Mrs. Buchanan."

My mom gave Rory a small, confused smile, shooting me a troubled look before they both walked toward their car, my mom looking back once before getting in the passenger side.

I let out a long exhale. "What were the fucking odds of that?"

"We seem to find a way to beat the odds every time," she

said, but the frown marring her forehead told me she didn't mean it in a positive way. "I should get home. It's been a long night and the dogs are expecting me bright and early."

I turned toward her. "Hey, I'm sorry that was awkward—"

"We've been awkward from the start, Ivy League," she said. "How could we be anything but?"

I gave her a small smile and we started walking, the mood very suddenly somber where it had been full of fun and teasing just minutes before. Before real life had stepped right into our path. And fuck but that kept happening. Reminders of the limitations of *us* kept asserting themselves at every turn.

Those rules again. The ones that had been not-so-subtly listed for me since I was born.

By my parents.

The community.

I took her hand in mine and gave it a swing, peering over at her. She turned her head and looked back at me, giving me a small sweet smile. "Thanks for a fun night, Ivy League."

"No, thank you, Cakes."

CHAPTER TWENTY-THREE
Rory

"Rory! Oh, I'm so glad you made it," Haven said.

"Thank you for inviting me." I adjusted my purse on my shoulder and handed her the platter of red, white, and blue decorated cupcakes I'd picked up at a bakery on my way over.

She took them. "Ooh, thank you!" She leaned in and gave me a squeeze, taking me momentarily off guard, but in a good way that settled my nerves, before quickly stepping back. "Come with me and I'll introduce you to everyone and get you a drink. But not in that order." She laughed. "You might want a drink before meeting this group."

I smiled, letting out a sigh of relief and breathing easier at having been welcomed so warmly. I'd hemmed and hawed about coming to this gathering, even though Haven had extended the invitation. I was worried that she'd just done it to be polite and I'd feel out of place. But Faith had gone out of town with her boyfriend and Gage hadn't asked me to spend the holiday with him—in fact, I hadn't heard from him at all since last night, ever since the country bar and the amazing alley sex and the fake pedicure. And running into his parents. A list of happenings that produced a vast myriad of emotions, several of which made me want to put a pillow over my face and scream.

I told myself it didn't matter that Gage hadn't asked me to do something tonight, after all, he probably didn't have any time to party considering he was moving continents in a week and a half. *Or*, he was spending it with his parents.

His parents. Ugh. The memory of the way he'd practically shuddered under his father's obvious disapproval the night before kept flashing in my mind and I couldn't stop remembering the way I'd felt so low as I'd stood there like a dirty secret. Which, to be fair, I'd partially created by lying about who I actually was. We'd both been quiet as Gage had driven me home, both of us lost in our own thoughts. He'd kissed me gently at the curb and looked like he'd wanted to come in. But I'd been exhausted from the bull riding and the drinking and again, the amazing alley sex. And I'd been troubled by the run-in with his parents too and so I'd told him good night and then gotten out of the car before I could change my mind.

But earlier, I'd found myself sitting and sulking in Faith's guest room and decided it was in my best mental-health interest to get out and distract myself.

Haven led me around the barn to where string lights twinkled everywhere, and a bonfire danced merrily at the edge of the orchard, folding chairs placed around it, several of which were occupied. "This is our crew," she said, setting the cupcakes on a table that held snacks and drinks and waving her arm toward the two women and one man chatting at the fire. "Betty, Burt, and Cricket."

We walked toward them together. "Hi. Nice to meet you. Oh, please don't get up," I said, when the man who was clearly blind picked up a white cane and began to stand. Instead, I took the few steps over to him and reached down and shook his hand, and then shook the hand of the woman standing next to him.

"Hi, dear," the woman with the poof of blond curls said. "It's so nice to meet you. My goodness, your eyes are..." She frowned and began blinking rapidly and I brought my head back, alarmed and worried she was suddenly choking, or having a medical event.

But the other three, rather than tending to her, leaned toward me and peered into my face. "Beautiful," Haven said.

"Stunning!" the woman named Cricket with the wide smile, freckled nose and wearing overalls blurted.

"Exquisite," the man named Burt said with conviction, his blind gaze focused somewhere just beyond my shoulder.

"Yes, exquisite. Oh, your eyes are exquisite," Betty said, bringing her hands together and breathing out as if in relief.

"Er, thank you, Betty," I said. "And...everyone." *Well, that was odd.*

"It's so nice to meet you," Cricket said as she pumped my hand exuberantly. "There's plenty of hooch if you'd like some."

Hooch? "Oh, uh, okay, thank you," I said. "As long as you have enough."

Haven let out a small laugh. "There's always plenty of hooch." She leaned in conspiratorially as she led me away. "Be careful, though—it packs a punch. And I do mean that. Drink too much and you'll feel like you've gone a few rounds with a UFC champion. Ask me how I know."

"Go easy on the hooch. Noted."

"Trav," she called, and a tall, handsome man holding a baby and flanked by two young boys carrying armfuls of what looked like consumer-grade fireworks, said something to the kids—who were obviously identical twins—and then walked over to us. "This is Rory Castle," Haven said. "Rescuer of baby raccoons. Rory, this is my husband Travis Hale."

"Ah," he said, handing the baby boy to Haven and taking my hand. He squinted slightly, and I saw curiosity in his golden-brown gaze as he assessed me. "The woman who inspired Gage Buchanan to go running through the tennis club with two critters on his head." He grinned. "The whole town is talking about it. It's very nice to meet you."

I let out a breathy laugh that turned into a wince. God, I hadn't even considered what Gage had been doing, other than summoning help, as I'd been sobbing on the side of the road over the mother raccoon. I hadn't realized he'd been making a spectacle of himself in front of the whole community. For me. "Travis," I said. "It's so good to meet you. Thank you from the bottom of my heart—both of you—for what you did with the cat...and the...raccoons...It was very kind."

Haven put the baby on her hip and looped her arm through her husband's and gazed up at him as she said, "We were just happy we could help, right, Trav?" She gave him a wink and though I'd seen a small tick of his jaw, he gazed down at her with something akin to worship as he gave a nod.

"Yeah," he said. "Happy to help."

"How are they?" I asked, glancing toward the barn.

"They're great," Haven said. "They're sleeping soundly at our house temporarily. We moved them there so they wouldn't be frightened by the noise here in Calliope."

Haven unhooked her arm from her husband's. "Trav, will you bring me the baby carrier?"

"Sure thing." Travis kissed his wife quickly and gave me another smile before he left us where we stood.

Haven turned my way. "Now about that hooch..."

I spent the next hour sipping on the surprisingly delicious Solo cup of hooch while chatting with Betty, Burt, and Cricket who were an absolute riot. I gathered that Betty had suffered an injury or perhaps had an illness that made her forget words. How lovely that everyone around her raced to help her find just the right one when she got stuck. And even lovelier that it was usually Burt who suggested the term she'd obviously been searching for. I would have felt warm and fuzzy over the way they looked at each other even without the hooch.

The sun went down, stars glittering in the sky, and the fire crackling in front of us. Travis and the two boys who I learned were their nephews were busy setting up a fireworks show near the lakeshore to our right, and Haven—her baby now strapped to her chest—flitted between us and them and the handful of other employees and close friends who had shown up to celebrate.

Eventually, another couple arrived with a preschool-aged little girl and Haven led them over to me, introducing her brother-in-law, Archer, sister-in-law, Bree, and their daughter, Averie. Bree greeted me warmly and Archer smiled, reaching out his hand to shake mine and then bringing his hands up and signing to Betty, Burt, and Cricket who all signed back.

Even without the introduction, I would have known Archer and Travis were brothers. They weren't only both exceptionally good-looking, but their amber eyes were mesmerizing. I noticed the scar on Archer's throat and realized that he was mute, though he could obviously hear since he turned when the two boys who had been setting up fireworks on the beach started yelling, "Mom, Dad! Come see what we bought with Uncle Trav!"

Archer raised his hand and waved to them, then turned and signed something quickly to his wife to which she responded aloud, as her arms were full with the little girl who'd reached up to her in a request to be held. "I'll stay here with Averie and save you a seat."

He smiled back, so tenderly I was tempted to sigh with the sweetness of it. And though these people were all warm and welcoming, they also made a yearning stir up inside me for what they so obviously had—love that was the stuff of fairy tales.

And what did I have? Unrequited love. A man who was across town right now probably with his family and possibly the woman he may or may not marry and whisk off to London.

"Averie, honey, do you want a juice box?" Bree asked, breaking me from my self-pitying thoughts.

"No, thank you," the little girl said from the blanket on a portion of grass where she was now playing with a line of princess figurines that she'd removed from a pink backpack.

Bree smiled over at her daughter.

"I love her name," I said.

"Oh, thank you." Bree sat back and took a sip from the Solo cup Haven had handed her when she arrived. "Funny thing, we changed it about five times in the first week of her life." She turned to me. "There hadn't been a female Hale since 1912 and I was absolutely convinced I was having another boy. We didn't even talk about girl names." She shrugged. "So when she was born, we'd choose one and use it for a little while but none felt right until we settled on Averie Alyssa. She's named after one of my best friends back home and Archer's mother, Alyssa."

I'd been watching Averie carefully remove more toys from her backpack and arrange them on the blanket, but at the sound of the name, I turned toward Bree. "Alyssa?"

She nodded as she swallowed another drink of hooch. "Yes. That was the other reason we settled on Averie. It went well with Alyssa whereas the other names we'd temporarily chosen didn't. It was important to Archer to use his mother's name." She smiled softly. "He lost her when he was young."

Alyssa.

Lys.

Lys has had it rough here.

Archer Hale's mother.

Was that even possible? Surely not. Alyssa was a common name. There must be hundreds of them in Pelion and Calliope. *If* the Lys my mother had referenced over two decades ago still lived here. No Lys had ever sent so much as a condolence card. So, I'd always sort of assumed the Lys she had spoken of had moved away long ago.

"I'm so sorry," I murmured in response to Bree's comment that Archer had lost his mother young.

"It's been a long time," Bree said. "But…you never get over the loss of your mother." Something moved over her expression…a sort of distant sadness that made me think she must have lost her mother too and understood the pain.

I suddenly felt a sisterhood with her, the way I always did when I met a young woman who had also lived any of her young life without the solace of a mother. A wave of warmth washed through me. I was close with the other women who worked at the bar even though they were older than me, and of course, I had my uncles who were basically my best friends. But I hadn't kept in close touch with the girls I'd gone to school with, and so I had few friends my age. Perhaps I hadn't even realized how much I missed the feeling of friendship and conversation with other women I felt instantly comfortable with like Faith, and now, Bree and Haven.

Haven approached, a smile on her face as she sat down on the chair on the other side of me so that I was now between her and Bree. "Reminder about that hooch," Haven told Bree. She leaned down and moved her baby boy's hair off his forehead, breathing him in.

Bree brought the cup from her mouth and looked down into it, her brow furrowing as though she was perplexed about how it was so suddenly empty. She set it down on the ground next to her and glanced over at Cricket who was in the middle of a story, the small crowd around her practically doubled over with laughter. "That stuff is lethal," she said.

I laughed. "So I've been told."

"You're smart to stay away from it entirely," Bree said to Haven who was holding a water bottle.

"Actually..." Haven said.

Bree sucked in a breath, clamping her hand over her mouth for several seconds before dropping it. "You are? Oh my God." She jumped up and leaned over Haven's chair, hugging her and the baby as she let out a soft squeal. Haven laughed and shushed her as Bree stepped away.

Bree pressed her lips together and returned to her chair. "How far along?" she whispered.

"Three months or so."

"Travis must be over the moon."

Haven smiled, and it was filled with such open joy, it made my heart soar for her even though we'd only just met. "He is. We both are. Ryder and this baby are going to be close in age, but that's what we both want. A big family." She rested her hand on her stomach that I now could see was slightly rounded just below the strap of the baby carrier. "So, here we are."

"Congratulations," I said. "You have such a beautiful family. And this garden center is gorgeous. And peaceful and…" I sucked in a small breath, feeling suddenly overwhelmed with…something I didn't know how to define, even to myself.

I'd have called it jealousy, but that didn't seem quite right because I was *happy* for these genuinely kind people. I loved being around them and already wholeheartedly knew that they appreciated what they had.

"Thank you, Rory," Haven said, reaching out her hand and squeezing mine lightly where it sat on the edge of the chair. "Tell us about your life in New York City. That's where you're from, right? I heard someone in town mention it."

I sighed, playing with the fray of my jean shorts for a moment. I was suddenly so tired of lying. And I didn't want to tell stories to these women, who had been so welcoming and had let me in on a secret that so far, only family knew about.

And it just suddenly didn't seem important anymore. My plan was failing. Not only the one wherein I'd attempted to find out who my father was, but the one in which I didn't fall in love with the man who'd only ever been meant to be a one-night fling.

Fail. Fail. Fail.

I let out a long sigh. "I have a confession."

Both Haven and Bree leaned closer. "Go on," Haven said.

Bree simply picked up my cup of hooch and offered it to me.

I laughed and then took a small sip. "I'm not really from New York. I'm not an art appraiser. And…my last name isn't really Castle."

Bree blinked, and Haven's eyes widened.

I took the last sip of hooch, the liquid making my skin feel warm as it moved through my veins and then set it back down. I did appreciate the liquid courage at the moment, but I knew I'd reached my hooch limit. It took me about fifteen minutes to tell them everything from that darn pull, to my mom's diary, to the drawing, and to the discovery of additional pieces of art at the antique shop.

"That's why you asked me for recommendations on where to go," Haven said.

I nodded.

"My God, this is a real-life mystery," Bree said.

"Wait, where does Gage Buchanan factor into this?" Haven asked.

I fiddled with the hem of my shorts again.

They both leaned in slightly again as I told them about Gage's appearance in Mud Gulch what now seemed like a hundred years ago. I couldn't help the curve of my lips as I pictured him and his friends standing in the doorway wet and steamy and streaked in mud…to him wiping a bite of crab cake off my mouth…to that pool table…

I told them the very condensed version of all of it and when I was done, Haven leaned back in her chair, patting the baby's back when he started to fuss and wriggle. "Holy crap. No wonder he's been acting so out of character." Her eyes lit up, sparkling in the firelight. "*Finally*, someone who has managed to ruffle Gage Buchanan's perfect feathers."

Gage's own words came back to me, floating through my mind—*I'm not as perfect as I seem.*

"He does come across that way, doesn't he?"

"He's almost suspiciously perfect," Haven said, still patting the baby who'd fallen back to sleep. "You're good for him," she asserted, grabbing my hand and holding it up briefly as if in victory.

My heart did a strange little flop. "No. We're just… temporary. And anyway, he's moving to London to bring his father's company international. And he might take a woman with him…he made a pact to marry if they were unattached at a certain point. That certain point being now, apparently."

Bree gave her head a small shake. "Wait, what? He agreed to that? A marriage of…convenience?"

"Not yet, but…why shouldn't he? It'd be as perfect as he is. His father would swoon with delight. Which is Gage's main priority." I brought my fingers to my lips as I winced. "Wait, that wasn't nice. I shouldn't say that."

"But it's true, isn't it?" Haven blinked as though she'd just had an epiphany. "Ah," she said. "He's not perfect at all, is he? He's a phony and he doesn't even know it. Everything is far clearer now." She twisted toward me. "But you've brought him out of that matrix. He's glitching out because of you."

I laughed. "Glitching out?"

Bree nodded. "Totally glitching out. The raccoons. The fire hydrant. Apparently, he's been heard by more than one person muttering about applesauce."

"Applesauce?" I asked.

"No one has any idea what that's about. Oh, and then there's the *scruff*," Bree went on.

"Both towns are all abuzz about the scruff," Haven agreed.

I laughed again. Gosh, I liked these women. And I loved the scruff. Unfortunately, glitch or not, there was no future between me and Gage Buchanan.

Averie had packed up her small, pink backpack as we'd been laughing and talking and now she came to sit on her mother's lap, her thumb going in her mouth as Bree cuddled her and smoothed back her silken hair. "Listen," she said to me, "if you want to know all the details, the gossip is that Gage is either imbibing a little too much or that you have put some kind of evil spell on him."

I sucked in a breath of offense. *Evil spell?*

"What a crock," Haven said with an exaggerated eye roll. "Bad or…unusual behavior is never a *man's* fault? Never his choice? It's either alcohol or a woman's wiles that make him unpredictable? Give me a break."

"Right?" Bree asked. "By the way, why didn't you go with him to the big shindig at the Metropolitan Club?"

"The Metropolitan Club?" I asked, a sinking feeling in my stomach.

Bree looked over at me. "Crap. I'm sorry. I just figured you decided not to go."

Gage had gone to a big party at the Metropolitan Club where, potentially, my father was still a member. Hurt made my skin feel suddenly prickly. But of course he hadn't invited me. Like I had already figured, Blakely was probably going to be there, as would his parents. Sneaking around was fine, but public events? Not a great idea. "Like I said, we're just temporary. It's really no big deal. Gage has a life of his own."

I felt their eyes on my heated skin for a minute, but they didn't say anything. Down on the shore, it looked as if the guys were putting the finishing touches on their elaborate set up. Good timing because the sun had almost totally dimmed in the sky. "You don't happen to have that drawing on the napkin, do you?" Haven asked after a minute. "Maybe it'll look familiar to me."

"Oh, sure," I said, reaching for my purse, happy to move the conversation away from Gage. "I have it here." I wished I'd thought of that.

I brought the diary out and removed the napkin, handing it to Haven first who studied it for a moment, brow drawn. She bit at her lip and then held it out to Bree. "I'm not sure..." she said haltingly. "Bree, what do you think?"

Bree adjusted Averie in her lap, whose eyes had drifted closed, and took the napkin from Haven, holding it so that the firelight illuminated it. She held it for several moments as she gazed at it, and I sensed her stillness. She handed it back, and I thought there was something that looked like concern on her face, but she shook her head. "I'm not sure either," she said. "But, um, can I take a quick picture of it? If I see something similar, I'll have it on my phone to compare."

"Good idea," Haven said. I held the napkin up as Bree picked up her phone and took a quick, one-handed picture. "I'll let you know," she said.

"Thanks. I appreciate it. The more people with their eyes peeled, the more likely it is that one of us sees something if there's anything to see." And if I hadn't run out of time.

"Five minutes to fireworks!" one of the Hale twins who

had been with Travis earlier called, both he and his brother practically running in circles with excitement.

Haven stood. "I'm going to go ask Travis where he put the earplugs for the baby. Bree, do you need a pair for Averie?"

Bree nodded. "Please," she said softly. "And while you're down there, and before they start, make sure Travis took stock of all the explosives and none have gone missing."

Haven's eyes widened, before her head whipped toward the twin boys. "They wouldn't."

Then they both said together. "Yes, they would."

Haven turned on a laugh and headed toward the men on the shore.

I watched as Travis and Haven spoke for a minute and then he leaned forward and kissed her, and then yelled over her shoulder, "Hey, Burt, get down here and help us set these off."

"Coming!" the blind man shouted back.

I watched Burt tap his way down to the shore, weaving slightly, likely from both the uneven ground and the copious amounts of hooch I'd seen him throwing back from the corner of my eye.

"What do I light first?" he asked loudly and gleefully. I looked over to Bree in alarm and she just shook her head before we both burst out laughing. Moments later, my phone buzzed in my pocket as a text came through. I removed it and read the message from my uncle, letting the words settle, feeling the strangest mixture of happiness and sorrow. My uncle's boat was fixed. It was time to go home.

CHAPTER TWENTY-FOUR
Gage

God, I was spinning, faster and faster. And not because of the ear-ringing booms that had punctuated this day, culminating in blasts of sizzling color in the sky above the Metropolitan Club. I eased around a corner and came to stop at a traffic light, glancing at my phone in the center console, and then tightening my grip on the steering wheel as I released a pent-up breath.

The party had featured a full bar, a live band, and a professional fireworks show. The pool area had been decked out to the nines with red, white, and blue fresh flower arches, and an enormous flag cascading from the balcony on the second floor. The team from London that my father had flown in were a likable crew with a good sense of humor. The music was good. The food was great. The liquor—though I hadn't partaken in much—had been plentiful.

And I'd been miserable the entire time.

God, she made me dizzy from the start.

Since I'd dropped her off the night before, I'd picked up the phone a dozen times to call Rory and invite her to the club's Fourth of July party where our family celebrated every year, but something kept stopping me. Part of it was that Blakely was going to be there. I had promised to give it until my going-away party to make a decision about "us," and yet, how could I focus on Blakely when all my attention was already on another woman? Even if there was no future with that woman? How could I give Blakely a fair chance now when the feeling of another woman's skin was still driving me to distraction? Even so, it would be plain awkward to bring a date to a party I knew Blakely was attending with her parents. *What a mess I'd made.*

However, Rory hadn't contacted me either. Maybe she was having similar misgivings about spending more time together too. Maybe she'd realized that now that we'd scratched that maddening itch, we should start pulling away.

It was best for everyone.

I came to another stop and rubbed my temples as I waited for the light to turn. Since we'd been apart, the hours had passed as slow as molasses and in a yearning-filled stupor. Jesus, I'd pressed the pillow Rory had slept on to my nose so often, her lingering scent had worn off. She wasn't an itch, who was I kidding? I *ached* for her. And my emotions were all over the place. One minute, it seemed harmless just to call and check in, and then it seemed like an awful idea to let this go any further than it already had.

What was happening to me? I'd never felt this torn before. The way I felt about Rory was honestly terrifying, and the part of myself concerned with self-preservation said it would be better for everyone if I cut this off now. And yet every time I tried to stay away, I ended up folding.

Part of me wished that test had confirmed she was my sister.

Then again, I had this awful feeling that that wouldn't have changed anything, even if I didn't really want to investigate that thought in any further detail.

The flash of my young self, hiding in the stairwell that led to the kitchen and watching from a mirror on the wall while Chef LaCourt hummed and mixed and tossed and whisked, blared brightly in my mind. The way I'd tiptoe away when I heard my father arriving home.

You've let things go that you loved before, and you'll do it again.

Because there's really no other choice.

I'd told Blakely that I liked being a hero. And it was true. I derived satisfaction from making others happy and proud. But how could I be everyone's hero when everyone wanted something different from me?

I pulled to a stop, the car idling as I stared at the house I'd arrived at.

Faith's house.

I barely remembered making the conscious decision to head here. And yet, here I was so some part of my mind had obviously directed my car to this spot. To Rory.

I got out of the car and walked slowly up the path. Maybe I wouldn't even knock. This was a bad idea. She was probably sleeping anyway. I'd driven here, but that didn't mean I had to take it any further than that.

"You're lucky I'm not armed."

I whirled around to see Rory behind me, wearing jean shorts and a red sparkly tank top. My mouth went dry. *Oh.* She'd been out. Her legs were long and shiny, and I remembered the feel of them wrapped around my hips. Her hair was flowing over her shoulders and I knew just what it smelled like, even though she was currently too far away for me to catch the scent. She *was* armed. *She* was the shrapnel lodged in my skin. She was so beautiful it hurt me.

She tipped her head, watching me with those canary blue eyes I was scared would haunt me for the rest of my life. They'd follow me to work, to sleep, to any rock I tried to burrow under. To the ends of the earth. To Jupiter. London certainly wasn't safe, nowhere would be. "Are you…okay? You look ill. What are you doing here?"

I put my hands in the pockets of my khakis. "I just… ah, came to wish you happy Independence Day and ah, you know say…Let freedom ring."

She paused, looking both confused and leery and also somehow slightly amused. "You could have texted that to me. There's even this cool feature that will produce fireworks when the text is opened. I would have appreciated that. It would have been nice to hear from you."

"Yeah, I should have. Texted you. Sorry. Work was…" I squinted up at the sky as though looking for more of those fireworks that had lit up the dark earlier. Maybe they'd spell out the words I didn't seem to be able to find. But no luck. The sky remained dark, the only movement the slow blink of a star. I waited a moment, hoping it was celestial Morse code, but then remembered I didn't know how to read that anyway. I returned my eyes to her and nodded at her sparkly top. "Did you, ah, celebrate?"

She moved past me, removing a key as she walked. I turned as she stuck it in the lock, my heart thudding in my chest. "I went to Haven's."

Haven's. "Oh, that's great. That's good. I'm glad." She pushed the door open and some kind of panic sluiced in my gut and I pulled in a breath, kicking at the edging that lined Faith's walkway.

Rory turned, standing in the doorway, the porch light shining down and making light and shadow dance over her face and her body. She crossed her arms under her breasts. "What's wrong, Gage?"

I blew out a long breath, that spinning taking up again. I had this desperate need to hold onto something, but I didn't know what.

I'm in love with you. And it doesn't matter.

Oh, God, no. No. Was that true? It couldn't be. I needed to go. I needed to figure this out. There was a solution to this. A cure. Someone must have a cure. "Nothing's wrong. I just…I wanted to see you."

"Well, here I am."

I let out a breathy laugh that ended on a sigh. "Yes. There you are." *You're more than I hoped for, and nothing I expected. And you're turning me inside out and making everything far too hard when my life's always been nothing but easy.*

Or maybe it wasn't. Maybe I'd been pretending. Going through the motions.

Existing.

Living out someone else's dream.

She considered me again for a few moments. "Do you want to come in—"

"Yes." I moved toward her and she opened the door wider so we could both enter. I followed her through Faith's house. "Is Faith out?"

"Yes. She went to Kennebunkport with Jarrett for the holiday. They'll be back tomorrow."

"Oh. Okay."

I followed her down a hall, to a closed door at the end. Rory turned suddenly, taking me off guard, and causing me to step back. "Can you stay there for just a minute?"

"Uh, sure."

She gave a nod, opened the door and squeezed through a crack, and then shut it quickly. I heard her scurrying around, probably picking up clothes, and sprucing it up. When she opened the door a few minutes later, I smiled. "Rory, I don't care if your room's a mess."

She gave a small laugh as she stepped aside so I could enter. "I didn't expect company," she said. "I don't want you to think I'm a slob."

I looked around. She'd obviously put forth some effort to straighten up the room, but the bed was still half made, and I could see clothes sticking from beneath the closet door where she'd obviously haphazardly stuffed them. The tops of the nightstands were laden with water bottles and jewelry, some makeup, and a jumble of other items. But she'd propped her father's paintings up on the dresser directly across from her bed, and her mother's diary, and the napkin drawing sat neatly beneath them next to her purse as if she'd removed them both just now and set them back in their place of honor. Something about the whole scene made tenderness well up inside of me. It was just *her*. Messy and sentimental and flighty and...passionate. "I don't think you're a slob," I said, which was far too inadequate but the best I could currently do.

I moved to where she stood, stepping right up to her and inhaling. Her scent calmed me and made the confusion die down to a simmer. She gazed up at me, looking slightly wary. I didn't want her to look that way, not when she was with me. "I missed you," I admitted.

Her gaze moved over my face and I saw the questions in her eyes, the confusion, and finally, some form of resignation. Whatever thoughts and doubts had flitted through her head and crossed her mind to speak, she finally settled on, "I missed you too." It sounded like a concession, and a relief.

So many barriers between us. I wanted her, and that wasn't fair. She made me spin, and she provided calm. I reached out and slid the strap of her top off her shoulder and then kissed the small spot it'd covered.

"I can breathe when I'm with you." I sighed. Even to my ears, the statement had sounded sad. I supposed it was because I'd be without her soon and part of me understood that I'd never truly breathe again.

I ran my lips over her collarbone and then leaned up. She took my face in her hands, rubbing her thumbs over my cheekbones for a moment as she looked in my eyes. "I could bottle up some Rory air and send it with you to London."

I smiled, but that felt sad too. "I'll take it."

She set her forehead on mine and for a moment we simply breathed together, sharing that air that somehow felt vital to me, but that I'd have to manage to do without. Rory brought her lips to the corner of my mouth, kissing me sweetly, and then moving to my eyelids and my nose, and finally back to my mouth.

We undressed slowly, my blood temperature rising as every inch of her naked body was revealed to me. "You are a goddess," I said. She was. A work of art. From her dainty toes to those stunning canary blue eyes. I thought distantly about how I'd wondered why some art affected one person in a particular way and not another. *A touch of preference and a trace of magic.* Maybe attraction was like that too. This woman, this beautiful creation, struck at the very heart of me when I gazed upon her.

She led me to the bed and we lay down, exploring under the soft glow of the bedside lamp. And our lovemaking felt both beautiful and crushing in some way I could not define, and perhaps didn't want to while she was still in my arms. Maybe we'd been ill-fated from the start, but that didn't mean I wasn't going to soak in every blissful moment of her while I still could.

I'd gazed upon fireworks earlier in the night, but brighter ones sizzled and rattled now, sparks flaring as our breath came short, hands gripping the sheets as we raced toward that dizzying crescendo where exploding stars would shimmer and crackle and rain bliss through our nerve endings and straight to our toes. Light eclipsed the inner darkness, but only for a few dwindling moments before the sparkling colors slowly faded to nothing at all.

"Clang, clang. Clang," Rory whispered, her voice breathy.

I managed a quiet laugh as I fought to catch my own breath, my limbs heavy and saturated with pleasure.

"Clang, clang. Clang, indeed," I agreed, pulling out of her and rolling to the side. I wrapped my arms around her and she lay her head on my chest as we both caught our breath, our hearts slowing and the perspiration drying on our skin.

My gaze caught on her father's paintings sitting on the dresser across from us. "Do you want to go over what we have so far?" I asked her, nodding toward the pictures and the diary.

She shook her head. "It seems hopeless." She sat up, turning away from me and swinging her legs off the bed. She stood and I watched her gorgeous backside, silky black hair hanging over her shoulders as she walked to retrieve a T-shirt flung over a chair. "Plus…"

"Plus what?" I sat up, suddenly on alert.

Rory pulled the T-shirt over her head and faced me. "My uncle's boat is fixed. I'm leaving on Monday."

My brain buzzed, ice water filling my veins where sparkles of light had recently shimmered. "Monday? But… why didn't you tell me?"

"I just found out tonight. Right before I left Haven's, actually. You have your party Saturday night and then you're leaving a week after that anyway, Gage. It's not like we would have had much time together. And it's better…" She pulled in a breath. "It's better that I go, get back to life, and let you get on with yours."

I let out a breath, running a hand through my hair. This felt so wrong. And yet…there was nothing to be done about it. Plans had been made, promises…commitments. I pulled on my boxers as she stepped into a pair of shorts. How could I have just been inside her body and suddenly feel so separate from her? So…far apart. There had to be a solution to this. "Rory, you could—"

"What?" she asked. I opened my mouth to provide an answer, but nothing came. There was a roadblock at every turn. I sighed, meeting her eyes and knowing she saw the hopelessness I was feeling. "There's no answer, Gage," she said. "It's been fun. We've had a lark, as they say."

A lark? Then why did she sound so miserable? And why did that description grate on me so damn much? "We were more than a lark," I said, my jaw feeling tight. "Whatever happens in either of our lives from here, I will never think of you as a lark."

"Where did you spend tonight celebrating?" she asked suddenly.

I stared, guilt winding through me. "The Metropolitan Club throws a party," I murmured. She nodded, and I could tell she wasn't surprised. She'd known where I was. And she'd known I hadn't invited her. And yet she'd still made love to me. And that realization pricked at my heart. She'd known—believed—that's all we were. And accepted it. My actions belied any statement about us being more than a lark.

She started gathering her hair up in a twist. "Was Blakely there?"

My heart lowered even more. "Her parents are members." I released a breath as she attempted to look unaffected and failed. "Don't look like that, Rory. Jesus, I told you, that whole thing with Blakely...I've already decided not to go through with it."

She looked up. "Did you tell her tonight?"

I closed my eyes briefly. "No. It wasn't the time. My father flew the team from London in and—"

"Your father must be ecstatic. All his dreams right within his grasp."

I paused. "He is. Of course he is. He's worked hard." I knew what she was suggesting. That my father's dreams were my driving force. And okay that was probably true. Definitely true. But I'd worked hard to be where I was too. It wasn't as if my father had simply placed me in this role and I'd skated. No, I'd worked my ass off, and I'd excelled. "My father...he expects a lot of me. He has every right to."

"You keep saying that." She secured her hair and dropped her arms. "What about your dreams, Gage? Have you ever fought for something you wanted? Have you even defined what that might be? Or do you brush those aside to be the good guy? The easy one? Mr. Perfect. Never the cause of even the merest hint of trouble? God forbid you should disappoint anyone who really matters."

Resentment bubbled inside and I had no idea how we'd

arrived in this place so soon after we'd just been in each other's arms. I had the sense she was saying this because she cared about me, but even so, it served no real purpose. All it did was make me spin faster. "Jesus," I said, turning away. "Do you know how many directions I'm being torn in?"

"Maybe you owe it to yourself to be honest about what *you* want," she said softly. "You deserve to be happy too."

But I couldn't do that. I couldn't. Because that would mean disappointing everyone who loved me. It would mean halting plans already in motion. It would mean ruining lives. Didn't she understand that?

She sighed. "Duty calls."

"What about you?" I demanded. "What about your mission to do your duty by Romeo? The duty you imposed on yourself? Should I tell you to toss that aside? That it shouldn't matter? Or what about Romeo? Should he have gone after his dreams and left you to fend for yourself at eleven years old? Duty is important, Rory. It's necessary."

She winced and dropped down on the chair. "I'm sorry. I'm being unfair." She let out a sigh and my exasperation dwindled and then died. Truthfully, I wanted to fall down on my knees before her and beg her to soothe me again, to help me breathe, to stop the incessant spinning. "Anyway, like I said, my time here is up."

"But there's still one more man," I said. "One more man who could be your father."

"It doesn't matter. It wasn't meant to be."

My heart ached. Being with her, holding her and being held had lessened the torment inside for a while, but maybe it'd only prolonged the inevitable pain of letting her go. I pulled on my clothes. "Will you come to my going-away party?" I asked, wincing after the words had slipped from my lips. The invitation sounded ridiculous and desperate. The last thing I wanted right now was a fucking party and seeing her there would just add to the anguish.

She shook her head, her expression sorrowful as though she was thinking the same things I was. "No," she said. "I don't think that's a good idea."

We stared at each other, the realization that this was goodbye hanging between us. I let out a breath, looking away and Rory stood, moving quickly toward me. We wrapped our arms around each other and for several moments we simply stood there, holding tight. "I didn't come here tonight to say goodbye," I said.

When she stepped back, there were tears in her eyes. "I know. But…it's for the best. We both know that. Thank you for everything, Ivy League."

No no no. But what did I have to offer her? Zoom "dates" as my schedule and the time difference allowed? A weekend here and there? A holiday? That wasn't fair to either of us.

I gripped her beautiful face in my hands, my gaze running over her features, memorizing the details of her, both hoping they'd fade and desperately needing them to stay fresh. "If you ever need anything…some poetry on the fly or…"

She let out a soggy laugh. "And if you ever need anything…dart lessons or…"

My heart and my stomach clenched. And to prolong this one more minute was going to kill me. I let go of her face. "Goodbye," I said, turning and walking out of her room. I heard her repeat the word in a whisper as I made my way through Faith's house, and finally, out the front door, her broken voice echoing in my mind.

CHAPTER TWENTY-FIVE
Rory

The sun was shining but I still felt like I was walking through fog. The only thing keeping me grounded were the three pups strolling jauntily in front of me, pulling me along. Despite the pain emanating under my skin as I glanced at the places where I had such recent memories with Gage, I couldn't help thinking about how I loved this town, specifically here, by the park and the lake. Something about this place had started feeling like home in the last couple of weeks. The pull I'd felt all my life had been answered… here. But I didn't know if that was because of the place, or the person I'd ridiculously fallen in love with. God, I ached. I already missed him so much I was honestly considering calling him and begging him to spend the last final hours here with me.

Even though I knew it would just end up hurting all that much more if I did.

There was a restaurant with a cute patio up ahead named The Strand and I looked for Faith who'd asked me to meet her for lunch. I spotted her by the short, wrought iron gate, waving me over. "Hey," I said as I tied the dogs to the gate and took a seat next to them.

"Hi, honey. How are you doing?"

"Oh," I sighed, "okay." I'd already told Faith about how Gage and I had said goodbye, and how much it had hurt.

She reached out and patted my hand. "It'll get better."

Mrs. Bellamy's housekeeper Marta's dalmatian put her head in my lap and looked up at me with empathetic eyes. "I know," I told Faith as I pet Roxy's head, drawing as much comfort from my friend's words as from the silent support of this sweet pup. The other two, Bartholomew and Mrs. Ramsbottom's cocker spaniel Elwood, lay at my feet as though they sensed I needed the closeness as well.

"Did he even suggest you coming with him to London?" Faith asked cautiously.

I shook my head. "He knows I can't do that. Plus, honestly? I don't want to move that far away from Mud Gulch. I already miss my uncles and I'm only three hours away. I mean, can you picture it? Me knocking around London while Gage works ungodly hours, growing lonelier while he starts resenting me for whining to him about how he never spends enough time with me?"

The truth, though? If he had asked, I would have considered it. I loved him. I wanted to be with him. But as I spoke about the potential scenario, I realized what a terrible idea it would truly be. I'd be homesick. He'd be busy. Not just for a month or two, but for years on end. And it'd kill me to watch him work endlessly to please others, suppressing the spark of emotion he'd allowed to glow brightly with me because he'd clearly labeled it *temporary*.

No, he wasn't going to ask me to go with him to London.

But despite what he'd said, he seemed undecided on Blakely and the approval their union would garner. And really, maybe it was a good idea that Blakely accompany him there. She'd been his friend his whole life. She would likely be happy enough with the limited hours he had to give her. Plus, I'd looked her up on Instagram in a moment of weakness and saw that she was a stylist with two million followers. *Two million!* I had thirty-seven, and one of them was my uncle, Romeo. Blakely Wingate would thrive in London.

My shoulders slumped as depression descended. "Whatever we had together was never about London, or a future. What we had together was temporary. And now it's over."

"Things change," she murmured.

I blinked as, behind her, three familiar women approached. *Oh no.*

Mrs. Bellamy. Mrs. Ramsbottom. Mrs. Buchanan.

My heart lurched and instinctively, I leaned toward the dogs, protecting them. But that was silly. These were their masters. They didn't belong to me.

Nothing here did.

Faith's expression had morphed into confusion at what must be the sudden look of alarm on my face, and she turned as the three older women came to stand next to our table.

"Aurora Casteel," Mrs. Bellamy said, her nostrils flaring as she peered down at me with barely contained contempt. I almost groaned. *Oh God. She'd found out my real name.* Next to her the other two women looked on, Mrs. Ramsbottom's expression filled with more disdain than that of Mrs. Bellamy, while Gage's mother looked vaguely embarrassed.

Likely for me.

"We found out who you are," Mrs. Ramsbottom said.

"Ladies, is this really the place?" Faith asked as she glanced around the crowded courtyard.

Mrs. Bellamy's chin rose. "Calliope should know that there's a fraud and a liar in their midst, attempting to swindle them out of valuable artwork. Really, Faith, you should be ashamed. You must have known."

"Stop, please," I said, standing. "Faith had nothing at all to do with this. I...I lied to her too."

Roxy moaned, a mournful sound that made my heart squeeze. I reached down and put my hand on her head to calm her.

"Rory—"

"Faith," I said, my voice trembling. "I'm sorry I deceived you. I'm not really an appraiser," I asserted, because I couldn't save myself, but I could try to save her.

"Yes, I'm aware," Faith said, anger flaring in her eyes as she stared daggers at the women. "Rory has a good reason—"

"Your mother was Ophelia Casteel. I remembered the name. A troublemaker just like you. You took us all for fools. You're a disgrace."

Tears filled my eyes. I could take a lot, and perhaps I deserved this dressing down after lying to these women and taking advantage of their trust. But the mention of my mother's name brought a longing within that I could not suppress, not in that moment when I wanted her arms around me so desperately, soothing me, making it all okay. "Say whatever you want about me," I said, swiping at the tear that fell down my cheek. "But do not talk about my mother."

"We have nothing left to say about either of you," Mrs. Ramsbottom declared.

"I think that's enough," Mrs. Buchanan said quietly. "Let's go."

Mrs. Ramsbottom let out a small shriek and we all looked down to see Bartholomew with his leg lifted as he urinated on her foot. She yanked her leg back and shook it violently, letting out a series of cuss words that I wouldn't have guessed she was even familiar with.

"Oh, dear," Mrs. Bellamy said. "Bad dog." She leaned over and picked Bartholomew up off the ground and secured him under her arm. I reached for him, worried that he'd be punished for his act of defiance but let my arm drop as she turned away. Bartholomew could be a little monster, but she'd taught him to be that way. And underneath, he was a protective, naughty little sweetheart who went a little wild under a small amount of freedom and I loved him with all my heart. I sucked back a sob as I went over and untied the leashes from the gate and Mrs. Ramsbottom and Mrs. Bellamy tore the leashes out of my hands before I could even hand them over, making me gasp as another tear spilled down my cheek. I felt like Cinderella being ripped to shreds by her stepsisters, only instead of the dress I was wearing, they were ripping the dogs I'd come to love away from me. "I will return Roxy," Mrs. Bellamy said, snatching her leash as well as though retrieving stolen goods from me.

And I supposed I deserved the suspicion. They most likely thought I was a thief and a probable dog-napper too.

Mrs. Buchanan glanced back once as they walked away, toward the low gate that separated the patio from the street. A young woman who'd been sitting by the front stood and joined Mrs. Buchanan, looping her arm with hers. She didn't resemble Gage, but I remembered he'd told me his sister was adopted. Was it her? Here in town for his going-away party? How stupid I was. I'd just been talking about the potential of going with him to London when really, I hadn't even properly met his family, and now knew they all hated me.

I was a joke.

I turned quickly away. *Oh God.* I put my trembling hands over my hot face, feeling the eyes of the lunch crowd at this popular spot in Calliope. Faith stood, and from the corner of my eye, I thought I saw her drop some money on the table even though we hadn't even eaten. She ushered me out of there, turning in the opposite direction the women had gone. Behind me, I heard the buzz of conversation rise, the gossips quickly springing into action.

I hefted my suitcase as Faith walked me to the door. "Rory, please stay one more day. I don't want you driving in this state!"

I set my suitcase down. "I'm okay. I promise. I just want to get home."

Faith nodded, her expression filled with sympathy. "If Malcolm Sherrybrook calls—"

"Faith, it's over. Malcolm Sherrybrook was my last hope, and he probably already knows what the rest of Calliope knows by now—that I'm a fraud." I didn't find my father and now I was also a pariah. Oh, plus my broken heart. My plan had really gone to shit. Then again, maybe finding my father had always been a fool's errand. "I don't want them to punish you for what I did. I'm so sorry. Your gallery—"

"My gallery is fine. Like I told you, the only reason they even let me into their homes is that I regularly mingle with them at charity events and they're not likely to bar me from those. Most of them have never spent a dime in my gallery and I'm managing just fine. Better than fine, thank you very much."

Maybe she was exaggerating a bit about her lack of concern, but I really hoped she wasn't because that would mean I'd ruined not only my life, but hers too. And I'd eventually recover. If her business took a hit, I'd never forgive myself. I gave her a wan smile.

"Hey, we did this together. I was all in, remember?"

"Yeah." I let out a breath. "You're a really good friend, Faith."

"Aw, come here." She gathered me in her arms and hugged me just as my phone started ringing. I pulled back and took my phone out, frowning when I saw an unknown local number. "Hello?" I said, putting it on speaker so Faith could hear.

"Hi, Rory? It's Bree Hale."

I blinked. Bree and Haven and I had texted each other our numbers before I left the Fourth of July gathering, but I hadn't yet programmed in her name. "Hi, Bree. How are you?"

"I'm…good. Um, are you available to come over?"

I met Faith's curious gaze, giving her a small shrug. "Is something wrong?"

"No, no. I just, well, I have some information on that drawing you showed me, but I'd like to tell you in person if that's okay. Haven is here too."

My stomach rose in my throat. I was tempted to tell them to forget it, I wasn't interested in taking this any further, but my curiosity got the best of me. "I…yes, of course. I can be there in half an hour. Where do you live?"

After writing down Bree's address across the lake in Pelion and saying goodbye, I looked at Faith. "Do you want to come with me?"

"Absolutely. Let's go."

The wooden gate was open when we pulled up to the address where the GPS had led us down a winding, picturesque road flanked by pine trees that showed glimpses of the glistening lake beyond.

I leaned inside, Faith on my heels and drew in a breath before I pushed the gate open wider. "Oh, wow," I said, my nerves calming as I took in the gorgeous, peaceful property.

Muted light seeped through the feathery branches, the blue sparkle of the water shifting between the gaps in the green. I could hear the soft waves of the lake meeting the shore and smell the sharp scent of the trees. An emerald lawn rolled out in front of us, a cobblestone path just to the side that led to a cottage with a wide front porch flanked by pots of bright red flowers.

A sanctuary.

And there was something about it that felt familiar in an abstract, misty way—not as if I'd been there before, but as though I'd dreamed about it long ago and forgotten most of the details even as the feeling remained.

The front door opened, and Bree came out, raising her hand and waving us forward. "Sorry," she said as we approached. "I didn't hear your car, or I'd have met you at the gate."

"Oh, that's okay. Your property is beautiful," I said. "It feels so peaceful here. Almost like a different world."

She smiled. "Thank you. It's what I thought too, the first time I walked through that gate. Hi, Faith. Please come inside."

We both entered the house and I noted a stone fireplace flanked by floor-to-ceiling bookshelves in my peripheral vision, but my gaze landed on Archer and Travis who were standing awkwardly near an arched opening that I could see led to the kitchen.

We all greeted each other, rather stiffly. My heart had picked up speed. I didn't understand what was happening, but it was clearly serious to them.

"Please, come with me," Bree said.

"This is making me nervous," I told her.

"Please don't be nervous. I'd like to think what I'm about to show you will be, well, good news, but..." She pulled her lip under her teeth for a moment. "Just please, come with me." She reached out and took my hand in hers and her touch, the solidity of her grasp brought a measure of calm I desperately needed.

I followed her to a short hallway that had a bathroom on one side, a bedroom on the other, and then we turned into another short hall that appeared to have been added on. Haven and Faith trailed along behind us, keeping their distance. Where was Bree taking me? I stopped, sucking in a breath of shock. There were paintings mixed in with the family photographs hanging on the walls. Paintings of the lake and sky and trees. I stepped closer, my heart thundering in my ears. Each one of them had the initials M.S. in the corner. I brought my hand to my mouth and turned to Bree who was watching me closely. "How?" I asked. "Who?"

"Let's go sit in the living room and I'll explain."

I walked on legs that felt like rubber, following her the short distance back to the living room that I'd only glanced into. I sat down on the couch and from that vantage point, I could see another large painting on the wall next to the front door, obviously done by the same artist, although that one didn't seem to bear any initials at all.

The women sat down, Faith next to me and Bree and

Haven on two chairs facing us. Travis and Archer wandered closer but continued to stand.

"Archer and Travis's uncle, Nathan Hale, painted all of these," she said, waving her hand toward the larger painting and then behind me to the hallway.

I glanced at each person in turn, my gaze moving from one concerned face to another. "Nathan Hale?" I breathed. "I...but no, he wasn't a...a founding member of the Metropolitan Club."

"He wasn't," Bree said. "But he worked as a dishwasher there at the same time your mother did. I took this morning to confirm that, but after you showed me the napkin with the sketch, I...I was almost positive it was Nathan's work."

I brought my hand to the base of my throat. I could feel my heart beating rapidly in my chest as I tried to understand what they were telling me. Had I incorrectly extrapolated that my father was one of the founding members and one of the men she served when she'd been talking about her long-ago job at that fancy club? She'd said his family was important in the town and her expression had always turned slightly dreamy and slightly pained when she spoke of it...when she spoke of *them*. And then I'd found the Metropolitan Club napkin with the sketch on the other side and both assumptions had been confirmed at once. He was an artist, not one of the five men she'd told me about.

Archer stepped forward and raised his hands and when he began signing, Bree interpreted for him. "After my uncle left the army, he did all sorts of different jobs around town. Something had happened to him overseas that he never spoke about, but he came home changed. He'd been a canine handler and from what little I do know, whatever occurred also killed his dog, Duke. He said his dog's name in his sleep sometimes and woke up crying." *Oh, God.* Archer took a few steps closer to the painting and turned his head to look at it for a moment before meeting my eyes again. "I was young, so I only remember a few of the jobs he did when he returned to Pelion. He worked at a gas station for a while, and later, he did landscaping work. He must have been doing well that spring if they hired him at the Metropolitan Club."

The army—something had happened to him overseas. He must have been doing well. "He suffered from PTSD," I guessed.

Archer nodded, and Bree continued to act as his voice, his elegant hands moving fluidly through the air. "Nathan stepped in when I was a little boy. He had flashbacks, and he was paranoid. It got bad sometimes, but he was always kind, always good. He would go away for hours, or in a few cases, days, and I knew he was trying to deal with his demons, but he always came back. He always did. And I knew sometimes it would have been easier for him if he didn't."

Archer explained to me what had happened to him when he was seven years old, and the roles his father and his uncle had played. As he spoke, Travis moved closer to him and rested his hand on his brother's shoulder momentarily, offering strength. Even relaying the story was obviously difficult for him, his jaw tight and his eyes filled with sadness. I heard the emotion in Bree's voice as well as she spoke the story he was telling, the one she obviously already knew, but one that still affected her.

And I understood why. A lump had formed in my throat as he explained the horror he'd experienced as a little boy, the terrible confusion, and the resulting trauma. And yet his uncle—my *father*?—had been there, caring for him as best as he could, even if that meant they'd both been isolated.

It was all so much. Too much to take in all at once. And I

was somehow tied up in all of it. Faith reached out and took my hand and gave it a squeeze, offering her silent support.

"I know it's a lot," Haven said, she too obviously seeing that I was reeling. But I took in a big breath and blew it out slowly. Yes, it was a lot. But Archer had dealt with far more than I ever would. I was not going to fall apart in front of a man who had lived with the kind of burden he had and especially after he'd just summoned the strength and grace to tell me his story because it might factor in to mine.

"It is. Thank you," I said to Archer to which he nodded and gave me a smile.

"Do you know how the other paintings ended up in secondhand stores?" Faith asked.

Archer raised his hands, and this time Travis spoke for him. "I cleaned out the attic when I built on. There were boxes I assumed were full of old clothes of Nathan's and nothing more. I'd put the boxes there after he'd died. I didn't go through them before I gave them away. There must have been paintings underneath the clothes."

Faith nodded and glanced at me. "Could there have been more than the three small ones?"

"Maybe one more, but I doubt it. The boxes were light which is why I thought there were only clothes in them, and there were only three boxes." Which meant they were all accounted for. The full collection.

"But that does bring me to one more thing," Bree said, reaching in the drawer of a table next to the chair she was sitting in.

I gasped when I saw what she was holding. A stack of journal-sized pages.

"Oh my God," Faith murmured. "There were pages in the backs of the paintings you have too."

Bree handed them across to me and I took them with shaking hands.

"We took all the signed paintings down and found those hidden in the back, just like you described with the three you located." She looked from Travis to Archer. "We think Nathan hid them for some reason related to his paranoia. Maybe to his mind, he was protecting your mother in some way, or preserving her in the way he could. We can obviously never know for sure, but that's our best guess."

Oh, God. My vision blurred, and my hands trembled as I looked down, reading the one on top, my breath coming short as my eyes danced over my mother's shaky writing, smudges blurring the ink where her tears must have fallen.

Oh God oh God oh God. Lys is gone. Connor and Marcus are gone. Oh it's too horrible to describe. I can't stop sobbing. Nate is going to the hospital to see his nephew who is all alone now and needs someone. Nate is on such shaky ground. How will he handle being the sole caretaker for a seven-year-old in the midst of so much grief? Oh God, how will he cope when his foothold is already so tenuous? And how can I possibly add to that by not giving him the space he needs? I love him to the depths of my soul and loving him means giving him a chance to heal, and to be the source of healing for that little boy who needs him so desperately. I have Mud Gulch. I have my family and my friends. Archer only has him.

I gasped, bringing them to my chest.

"I read through some of them," Bree said. "I hope that wasn't an intrusion but I…*we* wanted to understand what happened, so that when we told you about Nathan, we could offer any additional information we might be able to."

"No, it's not an intrusion. I appreciate it." I wanted to know what happened, but I couldn't focus on the written words. I couldn't hear the story from my mother's voice without losing it completely.

Bree nodded with such kind understanding in her eyes. "There are pages missing, but we believe the gist of it was Nathan had begun backsliding and having episodes. He went into the hospital himself for a short time and because of that, she must have held off telling him about her pregnancy, and then..." She sighed a heavy sigh. "Everything happened with Archer and his mother, and Nathan's brothers. He was thrust into the position of caring for Archer, and your mother left town having never told him she was expecting his child, or it's possible she didn't yet know and decided later not to contact him." She nodded to the small pile of pages from the two-and-a-half-month period nine months before I came into the world. "There's tragedy in there, Rory, but there's also love. He'd served as a 'master sergeant' in the army and that's what she called him. Even we never knew why Nathan signed some of his paintings that way. He often did things that were inexplicable. Only, this time, it wasn't inexplicable at all. The ones signed M.S. are from the time period when he was with your mother."

"Master sergeant," I whispered. "M.S. His moniker was based on her nickname for him."

Bree nodded, her gaze moving to the paper I was holding. "It's my guess that it made him feel loved. It made him feel important and helped him remember who he was...before. Those pages are your parents' love story. I only wish it had had a happier ending."

I looked down at the pages, running my fingers over my mother's writing. No wonder she'd always seemed so sad when I asked about my father. No wonder she'd never been able to speak about him. "I just...I wish she had felt like she could tell him about me and at least bring me to visit."

"Maybe she believed he was too far gone," Haven offered. "Or that knowing about you would tear him in two. It would have made him choose between duty and love." Archer and Travis both nodded at Haven's assessment while Gage's distraught face flashed in my mind. *Duty and love. How familiar.* Even if I wasn't at all sure that Gage loved me like I did him. I pushed the image of Gage aside—I couldn't think of him now.

"One last thing," Bree said, handing me what I saw was a photograph. "This was with one of the entries."

I took it and blinked down at the photo of my beautiful, smiling mother, wearing that long-ago blue dress, and standing next to the man who was obviously Nathan Hale in his military dress clothes. "That was from the spring gala at the Metropolitan Club," Bree said softly. A tear tracked down my cheek and for a moment, I simply couldn't speak. I'd not only found the truth about my father, I had a picture of him with my mother. And from the way they were standing, the way he'd been looking down at her when the camera clicked, I could see they'd been in love. I placed the photo between the diary entries, a pile of the most precious things I owned.

"Thank you." I looked around at each of them in turn. "Thank you to all of you, for being here." I stood shakily and Faith jumped up too. "I hope you'll forgive me if I don't stay. This has all been...very overwhelming."

Bree and Haven stood too, worried frowns on both their faces. "I'll call to check in later," Bree said. "After you've processed." She shot a look at Archer, who gave her a small nod.

They walked Faith and me to the door and we exited out onto the porch. As I stepped down to the stone path, a couple of dogs came bounding out of the trees. My heart leaped and I turned, moving toward them and bending to greet the white one as she made a beeline for me. "Hi, girl. Oh hi," I said, finding instant solace in the presence of the pups. "What a pretty girl you are." The other one whined and danced around and I spent several minutes scratching their heads and then rubbing their bellies as they flopped down to the grass and grinned with happiness. My confusion lifted and my heart lightened as I found that old familiar surety that I felt interacting with dogs. The white dog came to her feet and butted my hand again and I put my hands on her head and looked her in the eye before touching her nose with my own and whispering, "Thank you."

I stood and turned to the group who were all watching me with smiles on their faces. But it was Archer who was staring at me with something akin to wonder. My smile faded and I tilted my head as he raised his hands. Bree was standing just behind him and so this time Travis interpreted for him. "He did that too," Archer signed. "He got right down to a dog's level and looked it in the eye just like you did." Travis paused for a moment in his translation. "Your father wasn't from Calliope. He was from Pelion. He bought the property you're standing on now because it brought him peace. His family owns the town." He glanced at his wife. "We thought our daughter was the first girl in generations. But we were wrong." He shook his head. "You were. If I had any doubt at all before, I don't now. Rory, you're a Hale."

CHAPTER TWENTY-SIX
Rory

I couldn't catch my breath. It'd been a day and a half since I'd found out who my father was, and I still couldn't manage to force a full inhale through my body. One minute I was jubilant, and the next I was deeply distressed. I'd solved the mystery! I knew my origin story. But it was one filled with heartache and more secrets than I'd ever imagined. I'd only barely begun to attempt to parse through it all. I hoped Archer, Travis, Bree, and Haven would help fill in some gaps if they could via text as questions arose. I had a good feeling they would. I already considered them friends—especially the women—even if I was having trouble seeing them as family just yet.

I wished for that to change, but it was going to be difficult when our lives were in two different locations. Even if we were only a few hours away. Life was busy, and they all had young children and spouses and thriving careers that naturally took up most of their time.

I sighed as a rap sounded at the guest room door of Faith's

house. I'd felt confident driving myself home the day before, despite my embarrassment at having been publicly shamed and the heartache of knowing I'd never see Gage again. But add the realizations of all that Archer and Bree had shared and I'd only been capable of collapsing on Faith's couch and letting her care for me as if I was ill.

"Come in."

Faith peeked in the door. "How are you?"

"Better," I said. Reality was settling in and the shock had begun to abate. Even if I didn't have the full picture of all that had transpired that spring before I'd been born, at least I had the most important pieces.

"Will you stay a few more days?" she asked.

I gave her the only smile I could muster. "I can't. You've been such a good friend to me Faith, and I'm more appreciative than I can express. But it's time for me to go home." I paused, glancing at the closet. "I've been considering something though, and I might need your help to get ready."

Faith sat down on the bed and took my hand. "Whatever you need, I'm in."

The Buchanan residence was lit up like an amusement park. Lanterns sparkled along the paths and within the trees. The luminous glow spilled from the windows and the balconies of the palatial estate and headlights danced as cars pulled up in front, uniformed valets hurrying to open doors.

My God, it made my head spin to think about all that had happened since the first time I'd stepped on to this property. I pictured Gage bursting into the room clad only in a towel wrapped around his hips, his expression one of shock and barely veiled excitement. *Oh, Ivy League, we've been on so many adventures together, haven't we?* Gage had helped me search to find out who I really was, and I couldn't leave without letting him know the end of the story.

I gathered my dress, lifting the hem as I ascended the steps to the front door where a butler admitted me with a bow of his head. I was almost surprised they weren't checking IDs. Apparently any old chump could walk in if they knew the address. Not that there were many chumps in Calliope Hills.

Well, except me.

I didn't plan to stay long, however. I realized I was persona non grata among the Calliope elite and I didn't want to put Gage in an awkward position. If I caught sight of any one of the three women who had confronted me yesterday, I'd hightail it in the other direction. I only wanted to tell Gage in person that I'd found my father. I had to let him know before I went home and before he left for London. He'd been instrumental in helping me. Our mission was successful after all even if Archer and Bree had been the ones to break the case.

And even if it had come at a cost to everyone involved.

It was crowded enough that I was able to use clusters of guests as shields as I moved from room to room, seeking one singular man.

When I felt a hand on my arm, my heart leaped and I pulled in a breath. *Gage.*

But when I spun toward the person who'd stopped me, I found myself staring at the man I'd met in front of the restaurant a few days before. *Gage's father.*

"Mr. Buchanan, hello."

"Ms. Casteel."

My shoulders dropped. So he knew my real name.

Of course he did. His wife must have told him after she'd confronted me. My neck felt hot and suddenly itchy.

He glanced around, the movement subtle. "May I speak with you?" he asked.

I looked around too, hoping to see Gage, hoping to be rescued. The last thing I really wanted was to speak to Gage's father without Gage present.

But what could I do? I followed him a short distance to a room off the foyer that turned out to be an office. It was an elegant room featuring a slender, French-inspired writing desk and floral wallpaper, likely Mrs. Buchanan's home office.

Gage's father shut the door, the noise of the party suddenly muffled. He turned toward me. When I'd first been introduced, I'd been struck by how different he was to his son. He was a nice-looking man, and I saw traces of Gage in his features. But he was rather short, wiry, and physically average. And here he had this Adonis of a son. Certainly this man thought of him that way. He'd created the perfect dream child to ensure all that he'd worked for didn't die. Not only was Gage everything his father was—smart, driven, successful—he was even *more.* What an incredible gift they must consider him. And he was. He was. But he was also his own person.

And maybe I was being unfair. Perhaps I'd misjudged entirely, but I had a feeling this man didn't recognize that.

"You lied to the people in that room," he said.

Shame washed over me and I felt the heat creeping up my neck. I wanted nothing but this man's respect and I'd destroyed all possibility of that. He felt only contempt for me, as did his wife and at least a few of the people out in that room. And the rest of them would in short order, once word had spread that the new "art appraiser" was a phony. "I had a reason, Mr. Buchanan," was all I could offer, and even I knew it was woefully inadequate. *Selfish.* I'd hurt people. But I'd hurt myself most of all.

"I imagine you did. But some things can't be repaired."

I nodded, a mass of emotion filling my chest, the hope I'd clutched as I'd entered this house dissipating like smoke.

"Gage is quite taken with you, it seems."

I cleared my throat and clasped my hands in front of me so he couldn't see I was shaking. *Quite taken with you.* What did that even mean? "I care for him too, Mr. Buchanan." *I love him in fact.*

"If that's true, Ms. Casteel, you'll leave this party and return home to where you belong." *Where you belong.* Not here. Not with his son.

I pushed my shoulders back. "I am returning home. I just wanted to see Gage one last time. I have something to tell him."

"I'm sure whatever you have to tell him can be emailed or texted. Give him this party, this closure with his family and friends and business associates before he sets off on his new endeavor in London. He's worked for many years toward the life that lay before him. First London, then possibly Paris, Madrid. The sky's the limit for my son. If you're here to thwart that, or hold him back in any way, then you can't really care for him at all."

A breath gusted from my mouth, heart clenching painfully.

"He won't get these opportunities back, Aurora. Many people are depending on him. He's been…highly agitated… not himself since he met you and I can't have a momentary distraction destroy his entire future. You're not the right woman for him."

I gave a slow nod. In a way, I wanted to dislike this man, but in a way he was right. He was depending on Gage to grow his empire. But also, an entire company of employees were depending on him, not just here in Calliope, but in Europe as well. His current position had already been filled, and there was no way he wasn't going to London.

I'd lied to myself. I'd donned this dress, a gift from Gage, and come here not only to tell him I knew who my father was, but with the small secret hope that there was a chance for us. That he'd have a solution. Or that maybe he'd ask me to stay. What a fool I was. Not only that, I was unfair. Mr. Buchanan was right. I was only making this more difficult.

I was not part of this community—I never was. I'd always believed I was part of two worlds, but that had never been true. I was glad I was no part of these people because most of them, at least, were awful and self-involved.

But these people mattered to Gage, personally and professionally. And I would only hurt him if I stayed. I lifted my chin. My only choice now was to leave with my dignity at least semi-intact. I would leave and they would forgive him, believing I was just a random woman who'd cast some spell on him that he wasn't responsible for.

"I appreciate you setting me straight, Mr. Buchanan. I'll leave now."

He appeared almost surprised but stepped aside as I moved to the door. "Ms. Casteel."

I stopped, my hand on the knob, but didn't turn his way.

"I'm sure you're a nice girl if my son took an interest in you. I hope you realize that sometimes things are simply not meant to be."

A platitude. What he meant was, sometimes it didn't matter what people wanted. There were too many barriers, too many mistakes...too much water under the bridge. I hesitated, but then simply gave a nod before opening the door and exiting. What did it matter what I said? Mr. Buchanan thought of me, not as an individual, but as the girl who'd gotten in the way of his son's future and caused him to act like a person other than the easy, agreeable man he'd been all his life. But more than that, it wasn't Mr. Buchanan who was going to London. It was Gage. Regardless of the circumstances, or the pressure, or anything else, *Gage* had decided to take the reins of his father's company and begin a new life overseas. And Gage was a grown man. Whatever Gage felt deep inside, whether he'd admitted it to himself or not, it was Gage who had to live his life in the way he thought best.

And Mr. Buchanan was right, if I really cared for him, and I did, *I did,* I wouldn't make that any harder.

"Thank you all so much for being here." I looked up, toward the voice coming over the microphone as the crowd grew quieter and turned toward the opposite end of the large, open room that had been cleared of furniture to make room for a dance floor and a band. Mrs. Buchanan was standing on the platform and holding a microphone in her hand, beautiful in a shimmery pale pink gown. I stopped behind an older man in a gray suit as it would be easy to spot me as the only one moving toward the door in a sea of still guests. "This party is bittersweet," Mrs. Buchanan said. "After all, we're saying goodbye to our Gage, and I know we'll all miss him terribly, but it's also a celebration of the immense success my son has achieved, and the pride we feel in him."

Another woman in her fifties wearing a silvery-blue dress stepped up on the stage and Mrs. Buchanan looked her way.

"Cheryl. Everyone, you know Cheryl Wingate. Did you want to say a few words?"

Cheryl Wingate took the microphone from Mrs. Buchanan and smiled broadly at the audience and then Blakely Wingate stepped up next to her, stunning in a strapless yellow gown that clung to her curves. She was even more beautiful in person than on her Instagram profile. "As Lana said," Mrs. Wingate began, "this is a bittersweet moment. But I hope to add to the sweetness by being the first to congratulate my daughter, Blakely, and Gage on their engagement! They'll be traveling to London and planning their wedding while abroad!"

Next to her mother, Blakely grinned and the crowd gasped and then began clapping, my heart dropping into my feet. She'd managed to convince him, despite that he'd told me he made the decision not to entertain the idea?

Did you tell her tonight?

No. It wasn't the time.

I suppose I wasn't surprised.

That's when I saw him, standing on the sweeping staircase, watching Blakely and Mrs. Wingate on the stage. A small gasp came from my throat, the vision of him alone causing my heart to ache so intensely I thought I'd fall to the floor. Oh my God, the mistake of coming here kept getting worse and worse. "Excuse me, sorry," I said as I wove between guests, almost side-swiping a woman holding a tray of champagne. "Oh I'm so—"

"Rory?" My name was called across the crowd from the staircase. I turned to see Gage, moving quickly down the staircase and heading in my direction. "Rory!" he called again.

Oh God, oh no. Why had I come here? Why?

I kept moving, heading toward the door. I needed to leave. There was nothing left here for me but pain.

CHAPTER TWENTY-SEVEN
Gage

I'd seen her from across the room, my heart leaping as I blinked, thinking I'd conjured her by the mere fact that I couldn't stop thinking about her. Aching for her.

And she was running from me *again*, even though she'd shown up here. She'd come. And she was wearing the blue dress we'd bought together. And both of those things had to mean something. Hope flared inside as I grabbed her arm, spinning her toward me.

"Rory. God, you're here."

She pulled in a breath, her expression filled with both shock and hurt. I clenched my eyes shut. The announcement. She'd heard. "I had no part in that announcement," I said. Blakely and Mrs. Wingate had taken it upon themselves to try to force my hand. It was manipulative and just plain wrong, and I was going to have some stern words with them as soon as possible. "Rory, I'm not engaged."

The breath gusted from her mouth as she stepped back.

"It's fine, Gage. It's not my business whether you're engaged or not. What we had, it was just a fling."

Hurt ratcheted through me. "A fling. It wasn't a fling. Rory, don't—"

"To me it was only a fling. A fun one but...that's all it was. I'm not right for you, and you're not right for me."

I shook my head in confusion. "You're lying. If it was just a fling, why are you here? Why did you come?" *Wearing that dress? Looking so incredibly beautiful I want to fall down on my knees before you?*

She glanced next to us, where Archer and Bree Hale were standing a few feet away, watching us with troubled expressions and wide-eyed surprise.

Rory squared her shoulders the way a prizefighter might when expecting a blow. Others were milling around now, obviously listening to our conversation. Rory looked around too but then focused back on me. "I only came to tell you our mission was successful."

Our mission. I blinked. "What? You found your father?"

"Yes," she said, glancing around again, her eyes hanging momentarily on Travis and Haven Hale who'd come to stand next to Archer and Bree. *What was going on?* "But I'm not the daughter of one of the founders of the Metropolitan Club. My father was a dishwasher there." She again glanced at the Hales. "My mother met and fell in love with him that spring."

I felt disoriented, like I'd just come awake when I didn't remember falling to sleep. *A dishwasher. At the Metropolitan Club.* It wasn't any of the five men she'd thought it was. "That's wonderful. You know who it is. You found him. Do you know his name?"

She glanced at the Hales again and I saw Archer Hale give a small nod. "Yes. My father was Nathan Hale."

My gaze swung toward the Hales. No wonder they'd drawn near. How had this all come to be? "That's..." I couldn't remember much about Nathan Hale other than what I'd heard around town. He was kind of kooky. When people talked about the older generation of Hale brothers, he was often referred to as "the crazy one." "Rory, that's great."

She was watching me closely, and I got the impression she'd seen something on my face that spoke of what I'd just been thinking. But the truth was, all I knew of Nathan Hale were whispered rumors. When her eyes moved to the right, I followed her gaze to see Blakely come up beside me. She grasped my arm and gave Rory a decidedly hostile look followed by a fake smile. "Gage, can we talk?"

"Not now, Blakely—"

"Cakes!" my friend Trent said, suddenly appearing out of nowhere, his timing as excellent as always as he put his arm around Rory. "I didn't expect to see you here!" He looked around at the people who'd obviously come closer to hear what was going on. "We met this girl in a bar on the docks! She bamboozled us out of a lot of money!" he told everyone. Rory closed her eyes for a second and Trent blinked as I clenched my jaw so hard I bit my tongue. "What? Was I not supposed to say that? It was the first time we ever heard Gage call dibs on a woman. It was just...a funny story from that night we met her. Right? She's his *applesauce.* I mean, it doesn't matter now that you're engaged, but..."

Bree and Haven both stepped forward at once as though coming to Rory's rescue.

"Gage," Blakely said again, pulling on my arm as though she owned me. "We should—" I shook her off and stepped toward Rory.

Rory looked behind me, her face paling and when I glanced to where she was looking, saw that my father had come to see what was going on. I looked back at Rory. "Let's step outside. I want to hear more. I want to hear how—"

"Blakely obviously needs to talk to you," she said with a smile that I could tell was forced. "And there are so many people here to celebrate you. It's your night, Gage. I'm sorry I ruined it."

"You didn't ruin it. I'm glad you're here."

My father came to stand next to us and the Hales moved closer too. I looked around at everyone, filled with confusion. What was this strange standoff that was happening? I felt hot and cold, dread descending where there'd only been joy at seeing Rory here minutes before and the perhaps irrational hope that we could figure *something* out.

"We had a good...experience," Rory said, her voice both breathy and choked. "I used to think...well. But. Experiences can be good. I hope you'll remember me as a good experience. And...London will be lucky to have you," she said haltingly as if grasping for words.

The murmurs of the crowd had dwindled as we'd first began speaking, but now they grew louder, word obviously moving through the room that Nathan Hale had had a secret love child, or at least, that's what I gathered from the few loud murmurs that made it to where we were standing.

Even over the rising buzz, a series of gasps could be heard as the crowd parted behind Rory and every person in the vicinity swung to see who had entered.

It was the pirate.

And next to him stood...well, Rory had described him well because I knew immediately who the man who looked like a cross between Elvis and Prince Charming was—Romeo Casteel. In the flesh. As tall as the pirate, but not nearly as hulking.

"Rory," the pirate said, planting his feet wide. *Cassius. His name is Cassius.*

"Cassius. Romeo," Rory said and the absolute, utter relief in her voice almost killed me. She sounded *saved*, as though we were all hyenas coming in for the kill and she was a deer. Her uncles had shown up to rescue her from the circling horde of predators.

For several stilted moments we stood across from each other, the Casteels and the Hales standing against…the rest of us.

Rory turned away from me and I reached for her, my fingers grasping only air as she practically flung herself at her uncles. "You sounded awful on the phone, darlin'," I heard Cassius tell her.

"We were really worried," Romeo said. She replied with a nod as she took their hands in hers.

My heart knocked hollowly, my fingers curling. *Rejected. Shut out.*

And the worst part was, I knew she felt the same way.

Cassius looked around, letting out a low growl that made the circle around the three Casteels widen. He set his stony glare on me. "We'll be takin' our leave now," he said.

Blakely pulled at me again, my father stepped up next to me on my left, and my mother and Lexi appeared to my right. Rory met my eyes for only a moment before she turned her head and leaned behind Cassius.

To me it was only a fling. A fun one but…that's all it was. I'm not right for you, and you're not right for me.

Was she lying? Maybe. She was undermining what we'd had. But the fact remained that she was going home. She seemed to need it. My gaze found that of one of my coworkers, peering at me with confusion. I was going to London, after all.

Cassius put his solid arm around Rory and though every cell in my body called out to her, she was being protected, and she was walking away from me by choice.

She'd made a decision. She had looked me in the eye and ask that I stand by it.

She'd solved the mystery of who her father was. And now she was leaving. That had always been the plan.

CHAPTER TWENTY-EIGHT
Rory

I wiped the table listlessly as the strains of an old Patsy Cline song played from the jukebox, which, to be perfectly honest, wasn't doing a damn thing to boost my mood. Who'd chosen that song anyway? Probably someone who made a career of wallowing.

I picked up the tray of empties, tossing the towel over my shoulder as I turned with a sigh. "You look like the poster child for this song," Romeo observed as he set clean glasses he'd brought out from the dishwasher on the shelf behind the bar.

I managed a lackluster eye roll as Patsy wailed about falling to pieces.

"Stop wallowing and pull up a chair,"Romeo commanded and though there wasn't actually a chair to pull up, but rather barstools bolted to the floor, I slid into one. "You're a real mess, you know that?"

"Gee, thanks. I feel better already." I put my elbows on the bar and propped up my chin. "Remember when you told me to stop looking for my happiness in Claremont Landing? I wish I'd extended that advice anywhere past the town limits."

"I don't think that was your mistake."

"Then what was it, wise one?"

Romeo leaned forward, looking me in the eye. "It seems to me, you didn't make the wrong choice in locations, you made the wrong choice by coming back."

I grunted. "I had to come back. My life is here in Mud Gulch. And…Gage's life is in London."

"You could have asked him to stay."

I sat back and shook my head. "No. No I couldn't do that. So many plans had already been made. So many people are depending on him. I couldn't tear him in yet another direction. I couldn't add another layer of pressure, Romeo. And if I did ask, and by some miracle he *did* stay, I couldn't live with wondering whose choice it really was. Gage is naturally inclined to want to please people he cares about. And I love…I…respect that about him. But he's done enough of that. I refuse to be another person making demands of him. God, look what I did to you. Look what happened to your dreams because of me. Even if the situation is different, I can't derail someone else's life."

He stared at me for a moment, understanding coming into his eyes. "Ah. I see." He turned and set another glass on the shelf. "That's what you think? That everyone is forced to give up the life they're meant for because of you? That you're a dream-killer?"

Dream-killer. I couldn't help cringing. He'd hit the nail on the head.

I didn't want Gage to give up on his dreams. In fact, I was hoping he'd strive for his own over attempting to constantly fulfill the desires of others. But being with me would mean sacrificing the respect of his family, and that of his community as well. I couldn't ask that of anyone, not when I had another option. I'd already done that once.

Romeo braced his hands on the bar. "That's it, isn't it? Loving you always involves some amount of sacrifice. Of losing."

"It did for you," I whispered, the terrible truth puffing from my lips like poison vapor.

"Mm," he hummed, giving me a nod of concession that made my stomach tighten in misery. "I could be so many things other than a"—he made a face of disgust—"bartender."

I bobbed my head in agreement. "You could be so much more." My shoulders slumped, the weight of the sacrifice he'd made for me weighing me down. But it was good that we talk about it, wasn't it? Even if I hadn't exactly come back an heiress capable of sending him on that long-awaited trip around the world. "Look at you, Romeo. You could be anyone anywhere. So many doors would open for you if you stepped out of Mud Gulch."

"What doors? Fame? Fortune?"

I shrugged. "For starters." And maybe he still could. Maybe I could still find a way. A Plan B. An alternate route out of here for him. I just had to set this misery aside, so I could *think*.

"Jesus, you're full of it." Romeo laughed, surprising me as my gaze flew to his. "Rory, look at some of the people who already have all that. You've gotten an up close and personal view recently of the joy riches and clout bring. Do those people seem happier to you? Do they seem more joyful? Or even satisfied?"

"I…what? I mean, some of—"

"Regardless, I never wanted any of that."

I stared at him in confusion. How could he not want that? It had been his plan. His dream. "But you were leaving," I reminded him. "You had one foot out the door." *Before me.* Before I made him cancel all his plans.

"Yeah and I probably would have been back in a week. I would have missed this place and these people because it's home and I love it here."

"You're lying to make me feel better. And I appreciate the kindness, but, Romeo, you and I well know your face could have been your ticket in to anywhere."

He leaned forward, giving me an up-close view of that beautiful, legendary face of his that had once caused a woman tourist to walk right off the dock into the water. "I don't want to be loved for my face, Rory. I want to be loved for my heart and my work ethic. I want to be loved for me, same as you and everyone else on this wide green earth. And someday I'll find that woman, whether she's already here, or whether she's passing through town and the mud pulls at her feet and asks her to stay." His lips tipped. "I'll find her and I'll marry her and have a few kids who'll either be pulled to stay, or pulled to leave." He leaned forward. "And someday, this mug of mine will be dust in the ground, but the love I shared will never die because love is more than skin and bones."

I shook my head, trying to readjust my worldview after Romeo had just given it a good shake-up.

"You thought people like your snobby ex-boyfriend Thaddeus's opinion of this place counted for more. You accepted his take on Mud Gulch over mine. Not everyone has to aspire to some so-called fancy life, Rory. I like it here. I don't want a life *on* the sea, but I love being by the water. I love waking up to the sound of the waves hitting the rocks.

I love the way the lighthouse beacon cuts through the mist and directs those we love back to shore. I love the salt air and the salty women." He grinned. "I love the foggy mornings. I love the way the mud pulls at my feet when I step outside on a rainy morning. Claiming me. Anchoring me to the earth and the generations who lived here before me. In my heart and soul, I belong here, Rory. This place brings me peace. I love this bar and the people in it. Maybe it's not grand to you, Rory, but I never asked for that. And so you don't get to tell me I only settled for the life I'm living when I never felt that way, not one single day."

Romeo reached behind him and placed another glass on the shelf as I let out a harsh exhale. My God. I had put Thaddeus's opinion of Mud Gulch and of me over the people who lived and loved in this dockside town. *I* was the actual snob I called everyone else. *Me.* "God, I'm really a screwup," I said.

"No, you're not a screwup. You just made some bad assumptions based on wanting the best for people you love. But people get to decide for themselves what's best for them. And I'm sorry, but you think too much of me if you believe that anything, even an eleven-year-old orphan, would have kept me here if I wanted to go."

"Liar," I muttered.

"Maybe." He grinned. "But maybe not."

"So if you don't want to leave Mud Gulch, what will you do? Run this bar for the rest of your life?" All my life, I'd kept this vision in my mind of Romeo, waving to us as he boarded a plane. It'd been my goal. My atonement, truth be told. And all along, it hadn't even been necessary. No one had placed any blame on my shoulders—false or not—except for me.

"Hell yeah, I will," he said. "And I'll have a great time doing it."

I started to smile, but then remembered why I could prove what he was saying was BS, whether he was delivering it with seeming candor or not. "Wait, though," I said. "All those travel brochures in the desk drawer, for places far away—"

"All those brochures were for you, kid. You've always seemed so restless, searching for something that wasn't here. I wanted to help you find what Mud Gulch could never provide. I was saving up to let you choose where to start."

I groaned. *Oh, God.* I was really batting zero lately. *That* was why he'd put off the roof and all the other repairs this place could use. For me. Only this time, his sacrifice had been unnecessary. He'd watched as I'd constantly tried to figure out where I belonged when all along, I belonged to the people of Mud Gulch, and if that hadn't ever been enough, it was only because of my flawed vision. Romeo was wrong on one count—I hadn't made the wrong decision by coming back.

I glanced out the window, ashamed of the fact that I hadn't hidden my dissatisfaction when they'd so selflessly worked hard to give me a good life here in Mud Gulch.

And yet…even now, when my gaze hit the sea, I felt that pull. It was back, even though I'd found out who my father was. Nathan Hale. He had died without ever knowing who I was or even that I existed at all. I had no reason any longer to search for answers, or for belonging. It was here, right where I'd started.

I looked back at my uncle, grabbing his hand and squeezing it. I'd misjudged a lot. But the fact remained that my place was here. My people were in Mud Gulch. "Call a roofer," I said. "Get someone here in the morning."

"Rory, there are a couple of people here to see you."

I looked up at Romeo from where I was sitting at the desk in the office. "A couple?" I frowned. "Who is it?"

"I think you should come see for yourself."

The chair scraped over the floor as I stood, following Romeo from the office out onto the mostly empty floor of the bar. It was four thirty and so only a few regulars took up their normal spots. The place would be buzzing by five thirty or six when happy hour began. I stopped short as I turned the corner and saw Archer and Bree standing near the bar next to Cassius.

Archer and Bree both gave me tentative smiles as I approached. "Archer. Bree. Hi. This is a surprise." I looked at Cassius. "And you're home early."

"Yup," Cassius said, wasting no extra words as usual. For a moment, I looked between all of them in confusion. "Sorry," I said, giving my head a small shake. "Where are my manners? Archer and Bree Hale, these are my uncles, Cassius and Romeo Casteel."

"We've all already met," Romeo said. "Which is good, being that we're family now." He slung his arm over Archer's shoulder and Archer gave him a somewhat wary glance.

"Yes, we are," Bree agreed, looking back at me with a smile that appeared sort of nervous.

We've all already met. Why did it sound like he didn't just mean a few minutes before when they'd walked in the door? Why did they already seem more familiar than that? I was on sudden alert. Romeo sat down on a barstool, his expression telling me he was enjoying himself.

Bree took in a deep breath and let it out. "First of all," she said, picking up a canvas bag at her feet and handing it to me. "Your father's paintings are in there. He painted them while he was falling in love with your mother, and I think he'd want you to have them."

"Oh," I said, taking the bag from her. "But…I couldn't take these from you. You were close to your uncle—"

Archer raised his hands and Bree interpreted. "I was. Because I had him with me. I have years of memories." He nodded to the bag filled with his art. "You have those. I wish it was more."

I felt strangely choked up as I nodded, accepting the one tangible thing—other than that faded photograph—of my father's that I'd ever own. "Thank you," I said. I had traveled to Calliope in search of my father, and though I hadn't found him in the sense that I'd hoped, his art was a part of him, it was the expression of his heart, and to me, they were treasure. "I'll cherish them."

Bree glanced at Archer and I saw the small flash of understanding pass between them, there and gone, as though they didn't need more than the breath of a moment to read each other. "We're also in town because thanks to your mother's diary entries, we know more than we did about Archer's mother, Alyssa. She grew up in a girl's home here in Mud Gulch."

Archer raised his hands and Bree spoke. "I never knew anything about my mother's past, Rory," he said. "All my life. I had no idea where she came from, or what her childhood was like, and now I have a place to start because of you. Now, I can begin building my mother's past so that her family has the full picture of who she was. We're meeting with a woman who worked at that girl's home after we leave here."

"Oh," I breathed, a burn rising under my breastbone. "That's…that's wonderful. I know better than anyone what it feels like to have missing pieces surrounding your past—so if I had a part in helping you discover a few of those pieces, then I couldn't be happier."

"I want to do the same for you," Archer signed, glancing at his wife. "Which brings us to the final reason we're here."

Bree brought a folded piece of paper from her purse and put it on the table in front of me. I opened it, staring down at a legal document. "A plot of land came up for sale," she said. "It's right down the road from Haven's Gate. It's on Pelion Lake, but right on the border of Calliope."

"What? I don't understand," I said. My brain had begun buzzing and I was suddenly having trouble thinking straight.

"If Nathan had known about you," Archer signed, "he'd have taken care of you too, in whatever way he was able. That's what he did. He stepped up when no one else did. He showed up despite all the reasons he had to bury his head in the sand and stay hidden. He was damaged, Rory, but he loved me, and honestly, without that love, there's no way I'd be where I am today. So, with that in mind, I purchased that land and I'm giving it to you, along with the sum of all Nathan's army payouts, with interest of course." He glanced back at my uncles who were pretending not to watch us from the bar. "The one small caveat is that you use it to open up a business focused on dogs. A dog park, a training school, whatever feels right. And if you would, please name it after your father because he spoke their language too and he passed that on to you and," his hands faltered, and Bree took a small breath as Archer seemed to gather himself quickly before finishing, "he'd be so incredibly happy if he knew that."

My mouth had dropped open as Archer's hands flew through the air and Bree voiced his thoughts. I looked over

Archer's shoulder to see Romeo at the bar, wiping out a glass, a small smile on his face and Cash "reading" the bar menu that he certainly had memorized.

My gaze moved back to Archer. "A business where I work with dogs all day?"

He nodded.

"We heard that might be something you'd be interested in," Bree said, the corners of her lips trembling slightly.

Again, I glanced at my uncles and saw that Cash was fighting back a smile. I caught Romeo's eye and he winked. *Oh*.

"Nathan's Legacy," I breathed, naming the business I hadn't even agreed to yet as I met Archer's golden-brown eyes.

He grinned and signed, "I like it. He'd like it too."

"Please accept," Bree said, reaching across and taking my hand in hers and squeezing. I lifted my other hand to hold hers in mine for a moment before letting go.

"I…but…" I mostly held back a grimace. "I can't move to Calliope, or even Pelion. I'm not welcome in either of those towns." The stories about my dishonest exploits were probably growing and spreading as we spoke. Blakely might have put me on blast to her two-million-strong Instagram audience for all I knew. Even my thirty-seven followers had probably deserted me. Well, except one, but he was family. "I'm a social leper." *And I brought it on myself.*

"You are no such thing," Bree said. She smiled at her husband. "Plus, we're not afraid of a little gossip. We'll ignore the people we don't care about and set the others straight. Please don't let that be the reason you say no, Rory. I promise you, there are good, sincere people in Pelion and Calliope who are eager to extend second chances. I know

Travis isn't here right now, but next time you see him, I'm sure he'll be happy to add on to that with some personal experience on the matter."

I released a breath, hope rising within me like the tide after a storm, all the stronger for what came before it. "Hold on," I said. I stood, walking the short distance to the bar. "You did this," I said to Romeo and Cassius.

"No," Romeo said. "They did this. They wanted to give you the legacy you deserve. I only offered up the idea about the dogs."

"But…I can't. The bar—"

"Rory, go answer that call," Cassius said, his voice gruff. "The Hale family—half your bloodline—has been living in that town since the town came into existence. Your father's been beckoning you."

Your father's been beckoning you. I'd thought the same thing, hadn't I? And yet, the poetic words, coming from my gruff uncle's mouth, surprised me. "Do you really believe that?"

"The dude swears he saw a mermaid once," Romeo offered.

Cassius shot him a look, but then shrugged. "We come from a place with magical mud. Why not? Anyway, it's not about what I believe, darlin'. It's about what you believe."

What I believe. I glanced back at Archer and Bree. Did I believe I belonged in Pelion, the land my father's fathers had lived on? I thought about the peace I'd felt there. I thought about the man I'd fallen in love with there. But I took in a deep pull of air and put thoughts of Gage Buchanan aside for now. This choice would not be about him. This choice had to be about following my own heart, regardless of anything else. I closed my eyes and pictured that glistening lake and swore I could feel the gentle breeze on my skin and hear the soft swish of pine trees swaying. I opened my eyes, tears making it difficult to see. Yes, I felt called there, to Pelion, to that peaceful lakeside town my father had loved with all his heart and soul. The place that had brought him the strength necessary to take care of a little boy who had no one else but him. Still, I loved the people here. How would I leave? "The bar..." I croaked, attempting one final argument.

Romeo smiled gently, but there was a twinkle in his eye. "Rory, I know you're vulnerable right now, and I don't want to add insult to injury, but I suggest you accept because you're kind of a shit waitress and your baking is a crime against humanity."

I laughed, a soggy sound full of tears and joy. I looked back at Archer and Bree who stood and approached as Romeo came from behind the bar and Cassius stood. Then I hugged them all in turn, laughing and crying, meeting Bree's eyes and nodding to accept their offer because at the moment, words failed me.

CHAPTER TWENTY-NINE
Gage

"Get up," I heard yelled over the pounding of my head. I moaned, bringing the pillow to my face to shut out the grating sound of whoever was talking now, a running dialogue of how disgusting my condo was.

"I said, get up!"

I yelped, springing off the bed as ice water hit the naked skin of my chest.

"What the hell?" I yelled as Lexi came into focus, holding a now-empty ice bucket, the contents of which had melted and were now soaking into my couch. "Did you seriously just pour freezing water on me?"

"Yes, I did. You need to snap out of it." She started pressing buttons on my built-in espresso machine. "How does this thing work?" she muttered.

I rolled my eyes, which, thanks to the two bottles of wine I'd drunk the night before, hurt like hell. "I need to snap out of what?" I demanded.

"A lot of things, actually, but let's start with the fact

that"—she leaned toward me and sniffed—"you obviously haven't showered in…too long. Aha!" she said as coffee started dripping from the machine and she slid a mug under it.

"These are the first few days in a row I've had off in years. Can't I enjoy them?"

"If this"—she swept her arm in my general direction—"is your idea of enjoyment, then no." She put her hands on her hips and glanced around the condo. "For someone leaving in a couple days, you don't look very packed."

I scrubbed a hand down my face. "All I need to do is put together a couple of bags," I told her. "I'm keeping this place for when I come home for holidays."

"Ah."

I looked at her, sensing more behind that short, singular word. "Ah, what?"

"A half-formed contingency plan," she said. Before I could respond, she turned and started pushing me. "It's a start. Go on. Take a shower while I make you some breakfast and then we're going to chat."

"You don't cook," I reminded her, but acquiesced as far as the shower and started heading to the bathroom. It had been a couple of days since the disaster known as Gage Buchanan's Bon Voyage Party and I wasn't expected in the office as I was supposed to be preparing my apartment for my departure. Instead, I'd been doing some moderate drinking and some heavy wallowing. Maybe a hot shower would help clear some of the fog from my head. I started walking more slowly. I didn't want to clear the fog from my head. Underneath the fog was…her.

"Go!" Lexi scolded, obviously having heard my feet begin to drag. I sighed, and continued on but halted again when she called, "Do you cook eggs with or without the shell? Kidding!"

I closed the door to the bathroom and went about the business of cleaning my body on autopilot. But when I got out, I stared at myself forlornly in the mirror as I ran a hand over my scruff.

The misery I'd been trying my best to hold at bay came washing over me like a tsunami and I put my palms on the counter to brace as it did its worst, battering and drenching.

I'd never suffered. Not like this.

I'd never hurt and yearned and felt a desperate need for something I couldn't have. And I didn't know what to do with it.

I'd done everything "right" and yet everything was wrong.

Everything.

My head fell forward, and I simply let myself feel it. For the moment, it was all I could do.

A sharp rap on the bathroom door jolted me from my pain stupor and I lifted my head. "What?"

"Just making sure you didn't drown in there."

I *was* drowning. Emotionally, anyway. "I'll be out in a minute."

I opened the medicine cabinet and removed my razor, but then stood there looking in the mirror again. The scruff felt like all I had left of her and so I put the razor back, unwilling to let this very small piece of her go in the dwindling hours before my responsibilities could no longer be ignored.

I dressed quickly and went back out to the kitchen, where Lexi was just sliding a plate of bacon and eggs onto the counter. I sat down and studied the food warily. It appeared edible and I couldn't remember the last time I'd eaten, so

I picked up a fork and took a bite, chewing for a moment before admitting, "This is decent."

"Well, thank you," she said. "I'll take that as a high compliment from you, Mr. Foodie. I'm more capable than you might think."

"I never said you weren't capable." I picked up the coffee she'd placed next to the plate and took a sip.

"No, but you think it. I can tell. That's okay. I have nothing to prove to anyone, unlike you."

I looked at her over the rim of my mug. "What's that supposed to mean?"

"Listen, I'm not going to beat around the bush with you, Gage. I've taken the last two days to investigate exactly what went on since the last time I was here. I talked to Mom and Blakely and Faith Lorenz too, and I drove over to Pelion and visited the Hales as well because I wanted the full scoop from everyone involved. The only place I didn't go was Mud Gulch because while I obviously don't mind overstepping, I thought that'd be a step too far." She put her hand up when I opened my mouth to interject and demand that she not to make this more difficult on Rory. "However, I don't think that's necessary anyway because I figured out the gist based on"—she waved her hand around in the air—"the club and the critters and the scruff and the fire hydrant in the park." She exhaled and then pulled in another breath and went on. "It's obvious you've landed yourself in a big ol' mess of your own making, brother of mine. I'm not surprised, and I'm actually not disappointed because I think it might be exactly what you need."

What the actual hell was my sister going on about? "Lexi, whatever you're trying to say, just spit it out."

She raised her hands and then dropped them. "An

engagement to Blakely, Gage? Really? A woman you've never treated as anything other than a sister because it's obvious that's the only way you see her? In an effort to move on from her heartbreak, she came up with this? And then she pushed you into it because she knows your weak spots. Not to mention that low-down move at your party." She set her hands on her hips. "It might have actually worked under different circumstances," she murmured. "Jesus, I'm annoyed with the both of you."

"I made it clear that I never agreed to an engagement." I'd spoken to Blakely and her mom who had both apologized for attempting to force the issue with that false announcement. "But, initially, she didn't push me into thinking about it...and it wasn't the worst idea," I muttered, because my sister was looking at me like I was something she'd found on the bottom of her shoe and I felt the need to defend myself. "Marriages have been built on less."

She slammed her hand down on the counter, making me startle and slosh coffee onto my half-eaten eggs. "Is that what you think you deserve, you imbecile? A marriage of convenience that will never be anything more? I can't believe you even considered the proposal for a hot minute. Of *course* you'd come to care for Blakely—you already do. But you were willing to accept a life lacking in passion?" She shook her head, looking heavenward. "God, why am I even asking? You've already accepted that." She paused, watching me for a moment. "Who *are* you, Gage? What sets your soul on fire? I'd really like to know. And I'm sorry Dad never asked you that question, never encouraged you to find yourself. He tried to create a clone of himself, and he succeeded, not because he's a bad person, but because he clawed and fought for everything he had all his life, and he turned that ambition on you too. And you, so eager to please, so kind and generous and good at everything you do, you went along with it out of love and out of duty. But Gage…the world needs *you*. The people who love you want *you,* whether or not they know it yet. Fight for yourself first, and then fight for the life you want. Fight for the people you want in it. I'm pretty damn sure there's one in particular."

I let out a loud whoosh of breath, overcome by the ball of emotion that had made its way up my throat at her words. God, Rory had said something similar to me but she'd said it with understanding because she felt duty-bound too.

Lexi was right. Maybe I didn't fight for the things I wanted because I was still able to have a small portion of them. I'd made due with scraps, giving most of myself to others and suppressing my strongest desires. But I couldn't do that with Rory. I wanted *all* of her, every imperfect bit. But I knew that I owed it to her to give all of myself as well. And if I was going to do that, it meant acknowledging my dreams and trying my best to live them.

"If I do, it'll kill Dad," I said on an exhale, the words streaming together.

Lexi watched me for a second and I saw the empathy in her eyes. "You underestimate him. Dad pulled himself out of squalor with nothing more than a library card and the grit of a thousand men. He forged his own path and he can handle you choosing your own for once as well. He can adjust his sails. If given time, I know he can. And even if he can't, you get to be more than Dad's legacy, Gage. Your happiness matters too."

I leaned back in the stool and clasped my hands behind my neck as I considered my sister. Perhaps I'd underestimated my father, but I'd definitely underestimated her. I'd thought of her as flighty, someone to write off because she was doing something I considered whimsical and unnecessary. But who was I to say whose dream was irrelevant? She was out living her life in the way she wanted to live it while I was accepting an existence where, most of the time, I felt cooped up in a Gage-shaped mold of other people's construction. I didn't fit in it, and I didn't want to. Not anymore. "Most of my life, I've done things for other people," I said, the words gritty, scraping past my throat because even now, I was afraid to say them. "I was never scared to lose because I wasn't attached to the outcome—it wasn't mine. But now," I released another pent-up breath, "I want her for me. I'm all in. Every piece of my heart and soul, and I don't know how to lose because I've never experienced it before. I'm so scared," I admitted to my sister.

She reached out and grasped my hand in both of hers, holding tight. "Good," she said. "It's about damn time."

My father stood as I entered the room, his smile slipping when he took in my expression.

"Hi, Dad," I said, my voice cracking slightly. Jesus, my heart was knocking so hard in my chest I felt breathless.

"Gage? Are you okay?" He glanced at his watch. "I would have thought you'd be on the way to the airport by now. Your flight leaves in a couple of hours."

I sat down in the chair in front of his desk and he lowered himself back into his, his expression growing more concerned.

I took in a shaky breath and let it out slowly, running my palms over my thighs. "Dad, this is the hardest thing

I've ever done. And I hope to God you'll understand, because the last thing on earth I ever wanted to do was disappoint you."

My dad sat back slowly, his stricken gaze latched on my face. "What is it, son? Tell me what's going on."

CHAPTER THIRTY
Rory

I grabbed an apple from the basket Haven had brought over the day before, tossing it in the air before taking a big bite of the crisp, sweet fruit. The door to the trailer squeaked as I opened it, halting when I saw the Rolls Royce pulling to a stop on the cleared portion of land that would soon be a parking lot.

I stepped down onto the patchy grass, using the back of my hand to wipe the apple juice from my lip as I finished chewing, and waited for the person to get out of the shiny luxury car.

My dog Waffle trotted from the trees, making his way to me as the car door opened and...Gage's father got out. "Oh no," I breathed as the passenger door and the back door opened, Gage's mother, and the woman I'd seen in the restaurant that day, and then again at his party, who I thought was likely Gage's sister got out as well.

Waffle bumped against my leg, barking as the three Buchanans began walking toward me, Gage's sister slipping on a pair of sunglasses as the rest of the brood appeared from different parts of the property where they'd been out exploring or romping or sleeping, but generally loving life on the larger plot of land.

Jinx and Keanu started barking too, but I shushed them with a wave of my hand as they came to stand sentry next to me, their wide grins and wagging tails belying the impression of any real danger.

Mrs. Buchanan smiled as they approached. "Aurora," she said. "It's nice to see you."

"Mrs. Buchanan," I said warily, half preparing to be accosted in some way again.

"Please, call me Lana." She glanced at Mr. Buchanan who had come up next to her. "And you've met my husband, Jonathan, who I believe owes you an apology, as do I."

I stilled, my gaze moving between the two elder Buchanans. I released a breath as Gage's sister stepped forward, extending her hand. "I'm Lexi," she said with a smile. "The only Buchanan who doesn't owe you an apology." I clasped her hand and let out a small, breathy laugh, surprise at this unexpected visit throwing me into an emotional tailspin. They'd barely said anything and yet, already, I had no idea how to respond.

"Hi, Lexi. It's nice to meet you." The dogs whined, butts wiggling as they resisted greeting these people in front of us.

"Who are these sweet pups?" Lexi asked, putting her hands on her knees and bending forward. With her obviously welcoming stance, I nodded toward Lexi and said softly, "go ahead," letting the dogs know they were free to say hi. They rushed her, wiggling and licking and bumping her hands with their noses, and Lexi laughed and allowed them to love her somewhat frantically for a minute before standing straight. When she met my eyes, I realized I'd been smiling as I watched the interaction that let me know without a doubt that she was a good person that I already liked.

"May we sit down?" Mrs. Buchanan asked, gesturing with one hand toward the picnic table I'd placed under a massive, elegant willow tree the week before and scratching Jinx under her chin.

"Um, sure," I said, snapping my fingers at the dogs and pointing back toward the trailer. "Go lie down." They all turned and went to lie in the shade as the four of us walked to the outdoor eating area where I'd been enjoying my meals al fresco for the past week.

I tossed my apple into the trees for the birds, my stomach in too many knots at the moment to eat.

"This is a beautiful plot of land," Mr. Buchanan said as he looked around, his gaze moving from the willow tree we were sitting under, to the roof of Haven's Gate's red barn that could barely be seen beyond the copse of trees, to the slip of shimmering lake, and finally resting on the temporary trailer I was living in.

"Thanks. I'm…um, in the midst of getting construction bids." I cleared my throat. "Eventually, next summer if everything goes according to plan, this will be a dog park and a boarding facility…and um, I'll offer walking services and maybe grooming facilities. Later. If I build on. I'll need a few licenses and some employees and, well, it's going to take a lot of work, but, I'm excited about it. So…" God, my heart was beating so fast I feared it might explode from my chest. Mrs. Buchanan had mentioned an apology, but I owed them one too. And I didn't necessarily want to, but I cared so deeply what these people thought. I hadn't wanted to consider that at all because I'd believed they hated me and that I'd have to prove myself to them—to the town at large—but now they were here, and hope was building, but I was afraid of that too. Afraid to feel gutted when they rejected me again, even as a member of the community.

But the three of them were watching me with small smiles on their faces and so I released a deep breath and tried my best to relax my shoulders. "It appears you have a sound business plan," Mr. Buchanan said. "And you've done a lot in only a couple of weeks." He glanced at his wife who gave him a barely perceptible nod. "Like my wife said, I owe you an apology, Ms. Casteel."

"Aurora, or Rory. Please," I managed. "And I owe you an apology too. I lied—"

"Rory. We talked to our son, who explained everything to us." His smile widened as heat infused my face. "It was clever, honestly, and I admire clever. Someday I'll tell you stories about the ways in which I got my foot in a few closed doors."

"Oh," I breathed. *We talked to our son. Gage…Gage.* At the mention of him, my heart constricted, birds flapping between my ribs. I pictured him standing at an office window, looking out over London and missed him so badly I felt like weeping. My heart ached at the vision that blossomed in my mind constantly, but since I'd moved to Calliope, and even though it'd been such a short time, that ache had been mixed with the deep peace I felt as I'd gotten to know my father's family and begun learning my history…and walked the same lakeshore that he'd loved so deeply. "I appreciate that," I said. I felt a breath away from tears. "Your forgiveness. More than you know. And I'd love to hear those stories someday. I know the town hates me now but I'm hoping to gain back—"

"The town doesn't hate you," Mr. Buchanan said. "Rory, we were concerned for our son and only wanted the best for him. Our intentions were good, but our actions were misguided. The way we spoke to you, and the judgments we made without fully knowing the truth, were wrong. We've talked to our friends, and they understand that the way in which they treat you will be the way in which they treat us."

Tears did prick my eyes then. "Thank you," I said, my voice choked. "Gage is lucky to have you." I meant it, though part of me crumbled inside because I understood why Gage loved these people so much and why he wanted nothing more than to please them and make them proud.

Why he was so willing to set his dreams aside to make theirs come true. Even if that knowledge crushed my heart for all the things he had to offer that would never be experienced by him or others.

"I think you currently know our son better than we do, although we're looking forward to getting to know him better." He took his wife's hand on the tabletop and gave her a smile that she returned. "There's so much...we never asked about. So much we recognized but didn't encourage."

I looked back and forth between them. "Oh...well, that's wonderful," I said. Gage's parents had all the money in the world to make frequent trips to London and to get to know the parts of Gage that he'd held back over the years. His dream...the joy cooking brought him...his sense of humor and ability to have fun and be silly just because he could. He'd moved and was beginning a new life in a different country, but I hoped that if he took anything with him from our time together, he took that and built upon it.

"Okay," Lexi said as she stood up. "Good talk. But I have a plane to catch tonight and so we've gotta move this along."

She looked at me. "Rory, are the dogs okay here while we take you somewhere?"

"Uh…I mean, yes, they're fine for a couple of hours, but—"

"Good." She reached out and took my hand and I stood, a myriad of emotions battling inside me. Joy. Confusion. Sadness. Longing. Peace.

"Where are we going?" I asked as I started walking toward the car with the three Buchanans.

Lexi linked her arm with mine. "You'll have to trust us. I know we didn't earn it yet, but hopefully you can find it in you to extend some anyway."

"Well, I'm pretty untrustworthy at the moment too," I said on a laugh. "So maybe we can all take a leap of faith."

Lexi laughed as Gage's parents both smiled over at us. "I was hoping you'd say that."

The Rolls Royce pulled up in front of the old Calliope Savings and Loan, the one where Gage had taken me what seemed like a lifetime ago, the place we'd discovered we no longer had to attempt to ignore the sizzling chemistry between us. I gazed out at it, the memories mixing with my confusion. "Why are we here?" I asked, and even I could hear the tremble of hope in my voice, the ideas that were forming that I was too afraid to acknowledge in case I was way off base.

"You're on your own from here," Lexi said, patting my knee. "Go on." She inclined her head toward the building, a small, secretive smile on her face. "There's someone waiting for you." I glanced at Mr. and Mrs. Buchanan in the front seat, both of them wearing similar smiles.

I took in a deep, fortifying breath and then I opened the car door and stepped out. I only looked back once when I made it to the front door of the old bank and saw the black car pulling away. Whomever was waiting inside, I'd been left in their charge. The door was unlocked and let out the same long squeak as it had the first time I'd entered this building. My heart pounded in my chest, hope leaping in my veins and making my blood rush faster. I felt lightheaded and so scared I hardly felt my legs as they somehow carried me into the dim space where treasures and stories had once been left here for safekeeping. And now one more was unfolding too—mine. And God I hoped against hope it had a happy ending.

The footsteps sounded first, and I brought my hands to my mouth, holding back the sobs that threatened to burst forth. I knew those footsteps. I knew how the body moved that created just that cadence of sound. And he was coming toward me.

He rounded the corner and for a moment we simply stood there, staring at each other. "I didn't go," he said after a moment.

I dropped my hands but wrapped my arms around myself to attempt to calm the shaking. "I see that," I said breathlessly.

He nodded, his lips tipping ever so slightly as he moved closer. "Rory—"

"What about all the plans? London—"

"London's fine. There are very capable people who are going to make sure the project in London goes off without a hitch, including Blakely who's there doing…something or other with my father's social media."

"Oh," I breathed. "Okay. But…why didn't you go?"

"Because I don't want a life without you, Rory. I don't

want to exist without the passion you bring into every moment of every day. I don't want to live without passion anymore at all." He paused, a frown marring his face. "I only really know two things in this moment. One, I want to turn this into a restaurant."

I nodded, letting out a soggy laugh as a tear spilled over and tracked down my cheek. "I know," I said. "I know you do. I knew it the first time you brought me here."

His smile was soft. "You did, didn't you? You knew so much about me, right from the start, things I've kept locked down for so long, dreams I've been afraid to acknowledge because there was no way they'd ever come true. You shook me up. You exposed me to my own dreams. You asked the question I really needed to answer—what I was trying to silence when I stared into space. I've been thinking about that over these last couple weeks. It was a voice, Rory. My own. And zoning out helped me ignore it." He glanced around, craning his neck as he looked up at the vaulted ceilings. "I've got the whole menu in the back of my head. I have for years."

"Oh, Gage," I breathed. How hard it must have been to carry his dream around like a secret. One that he nourished and grew anyway, despite the belief that it would never see the sunlight.

"I bought this building from my father," he went on. "He offered to be an investor, but I declined and took out a loan. I wanted this venture to be mine and mine alone." He brushed a piece of hair off my cheek. My God. *Both* of us had been busy taking those first steps toward fulfilling our dreams. I could hardly believe this was happening. "So I stepped down in my role at my father's company, and I won't be taking over when he retires. I've decided to go a different route, one that most likely won't make me a mogul, but one that I'm so eager to begin I can barely sit still."

I let out a sniffly breath of laughter. I could see that. He was radiating with happiness and anticipation. It was starting over though, mostly from scratch. And I understood the bravery it had taken.

"So, that's one," he said. "And the only other thing I know for sure is that I love you so much. I want to go on adventures with you, both big and small for the rest of my life. I want to cheer on your business because I'm so damn proud of you and I can't wait to watch you living your dream too. I want to continue to live in this beautiful town that I love with all my heart. I want to learn how to live with all the emotion you do. I want to laugh, and I want to be ridiculous sometimes too."

He breathed out a small laugh and I did too, though it was more of a sob than anything. I couldn't hold myself back anymore and I launched myself into his arms, crying and laughing and gripping him so tightly.

"I love you too," I said, so overcome with elation I needed him to hold me up. "All those things I said at your party—"

"Rory, I know. I heard about how you were confronted. I'm so sorry about that. And also, you're a terrible liar. Once I allowed myself to take a step back, I realized everything you said was out of self-preservation. I understand. I do. But please, say it again anyway."

I knew the part he wanted to hear repeated. "I love you. I love you so much, Gage Buchanan."

"No one—not a single person—will ever speak to you with disrespect in this town, Rory. Ever."

I nodded. I believed him. He'd sent his entire family

to reassure me of that first and then to deliver me to him because he knew how much family meant to me. It was the very reason I'd arrived here in the first place. To complete my own.

He released a breath and closed his eyes, bringing our foreheads together where we simply existed for a few joy-filled moments where the biggest obstacle of all had been overcome. Everything else would fall into place. His body was so warm, his arms so solid. My heartbeat slowed, breath coming easier.

"Those two things you know for sure," I told him, "they're enough. For now, they're all we need." *Dreams and love.*

He leaned back and used his thumbs to wipe the tears streaming down my cheeks and tipped his chin slightly. "It's a little messy and a lot risky. It's less than perfect," he told me.

"Far less," I agreed with a grin, bringing my lips to his and kissing him before drawing back and looking him in the eye. "And I wouldn't have it any other way."

EPILOGUE
Gage

One Year Later

It was Saturday night and a packed house. Just like every Saturday in the last three months since Canary Blue had opened…and Fridays and Sundays, and even most weeknights. Reservations were booked months in advance and several national food critics had already visited and subsequently left glowing reviews that I now had proudly hung on the wall.

While I'd originally prepared the menu and created all the recipes while the remodeling of the old building was being done, I had since hired a full culinary staff and now only worked four chef shifts a week, this being one of them. The rest of my time was spent creating recipe specials, refining the menu, and sourcing products from local vendors.

I poured a splash of bourbon into the skillet and watched as the fire leaped and the liquor sizzled as I constructed Rory's favorite desert—bread pudding with caramel bourbon sauce.

Rory. The warmth that infused my chest had nothing to do with the fact that I was standing in front of an industrial stove.

She always came by for dessert and to keep me company as I closed for my final shift of the week, but tonight she was also at the restaurant celebrating Bree's birthday with the rest of the Hale crew. It blew my mind to think of how much had changed since the evening the year before when I'd run into their family celebrating the same occasion.

I'd opened Canary Blue and I'd also assisted Romeo Casteel in coming up with a new menu for Cakes and Ale featuring some of those crab cake recipes Rory and I had made together the first night we met. The night I'd first begun falling head over heels in love with her, even if I hadn't realized it at the time. I knew what the country club in Claremont Landing served and I also knew that now, Cakes and Ale's menu far surpassed theirs. The Casteel family business had already begun expanding and Rory and I traveled there often to visit and help fine-tune their kitchen operations.

But I'd also been by Rory's side as she'd built and opened her own business, Nathan's Legacy. She'd turned the land the Hale family had given her into a retreat built around dogs. There was a beautiful, shaded, fenced-in dog park where dogs romped and played, and dog-lovers met and bonded. She'd had a doggy daycare built and also offered training and dog walking services. She was already overbooked and while she'd hired five employees initially, she was currently looking to hire two more.

We certainly had our hands full. Only...it didn't even really feel that way because all of it brought joy and purpose and a satisfaction I'd never even knew existed. And Rory, she brought more passion and love to my life than I'd ever dreamed of. I woke every morning wondering how in the world I'd managed to begin living a life that so thoroughly and perfectly filled my mind, heart and soul.

And I knew that it was all because of her.

Samantha, one of the servers, breezed through the door just as I set the final dessert for table twelve on the counter and began placing them on her tray. "Ready?" she asked as she stuck a candle in the slice of raspberry cheesecake.

I blew out a breath, running my hands down my hips as I came from around the counter. "Yeah, I'm ready."

She winked as she picked up the tray. "Deep breath. You've got this."

I gave her a smile as she turned and hoisted the tray onto her shoulder. The thing was? I wasn't nervous. I was excited and my heart beat with anticipation of baring my heart in a room full of people. But the surety I felt inside soothed my nerves and propelled me forward, through the swinging doors and out into the main dining room.

"Gage," Mrs. Ramsbottom greeted as I moved past their table. "Dinner was absolutely splendid. I haven't had such incredible coq au vin since we dined in the south of France. Yours might beat it, truth be told. Everything was perfect."

I shook her hand. "Thank you, Mrs. Ramsbottom." I greeted Mr. Ramsbottom and then moved on to another table, stopped by one after the other, my gaze wandering briefly toward Rory who sat watching me with a small smile on her lips, her eyes filled with pride.

I moved between tables, over the black and white tiles and past a marble pillar, the chandeliers and crystal wall sconces bouncing light around the room and highlighting the molding that had been revitalized. It had been important to me that we preserve as much of the original building as possible, from the formal main dining room to the more casual rooftop seating where Haven had helped me plant a rooftop garden near the back where I sourced all my herbs and several other items.

The conversation Rory and I had once had about stories whispered back to me and my heart filled the way it always did to know that more stories were being told in this space… celebrations that marked life's sweetest occasions…

Finally, I headed toward the table near the vault where the Hales were gathered, including Haven's brother, Easton. Rory laughed at something Haven said, Bree joining in. *Those three.* They always had their heads together, laughter ringing out, as close as sisters who'd always known each other, sharing secrets, giving advice, and handing babies back and forth. And one day soon—very soon, I hoped—ours would be one of them.

Samantha set the last of the desserts at their table and then lit the candle on Bree's cake. Rory stood and laced her fingers with mine as she gave me a quick kiss on the cheek, the soft brush of her lips even on that small patch of skin, causing a flare of heat to ignite in my belly. Travis Hale started signing *Happy Birthday*, the rest of the family joining in, Archer beaming at his wife as she turned toward him, her hand running over his cheek as she kissed him and whispered something against his lips that only he could hear before turning and blowing out the candle. Applause erupted, not only from their table, but from the fellow diners as well. I caught Bree's eye and she gave me a wink as Rory turned to see her uncles come through the door, followed by my parents. She let out a small sound of surprise and they all stopped, obviously barely holding back smiles as their eyes turned toward me.

And then I went down on one knee.

A collective gasp was heard and several sighs as I reached in the pocket of my chef's coat and removed the ring.

Rory followed their gazes, bringing her hands over her mouth as she too let out a muffled cry that I could hear was mostly joy. My heart slowed, eyes meeting hers, everything and everyone fading so that it was only us.

"I thought long and hard about how to do this and finally decided that this was the perfect place." I smiled softly. "You knew, that first day I brought you here, that I was opening my heart and showing you my secret dream. I don't even think I fully allowed myself to acknowledge it at the time. But you've done that from the start. You've seen me, you've exposed the parts of myself I didn't even know existed, and you've brought me more joy and fulfillment than I knew life offered." I glanced around at the people then, the world expanding, so many expressions of pure love beaming at us. "And I wanted our families and the community to be here because I intend to spend the rest of my days talking about how much I cherish you—they should get used to it now, because it's going to be excessive."

A small murmur of chuckling was heard, and Rory let out a tearful laugh.

I removed the ring from the box and took her hand, sliding the diamond Haven and Bree had helped me pick out onto her finger. "Aurora Casteel, I love you with all of my heart. I want to live the rest of my life with you. I want to create a family with you. I want to wade through a sea of dogs to get to you on the other side of our bed." She let out a tearful laugh. "I want to go on adventures with you. I want to break rules and create new ones. I want to find perfect in unexpected places, and I want to embrace messy and risky sometimes too. I want to love you all the days of my life. Will you do me the great honor of becoming my wife?"

She went down on her knees then, too, taking my face in her hands and bringing her tear-streaked face to mine. "Yes," she whispered against my lips. "Yes, yes, yes."

The room erupted in applause again and we both stood, continuing to kiss and smile against each other's lips. "I don't want a long engagement," she said. "I hope you feel the same way. A month…maybe two."

I laughed. "Anything you want, Cakes. Anything."

She grinned. "I love you, Ivy League."

The barrage of love could be held back no longer and our families pushed forward, enveloping us with unrestrained joy, all talking over each other, hugging us and one another, and as always, making room for more. Mud Gulch mixed with Pelion and Calliope and Bree's hometown of Cincinnati and also California where Haven and Easton had arrived from to create this beautiful melding of clans.

Yes, there were stories here. And our moment would sink into the bones of this building, to whisper through time. I had a feeling that Ophelia Casteel and Nathan Hale were looking down on this celebration and I made them a secret promise to always take care of their daughter, mind, body, and soul.

And I promised myself that I'd strive to create a healthy balance between pleasing other people and living with all the intensity I had to offer the world. Rory had taught me that part of my legacy was to live my life to the fullest. To meet it head on and then to open my arms wide and fall, knowing—trusting—that she'd always be there to catch me.

WANT MORE MIA SHERIDAN?
CHECK OUT HER
STANDALONE ROMANCE

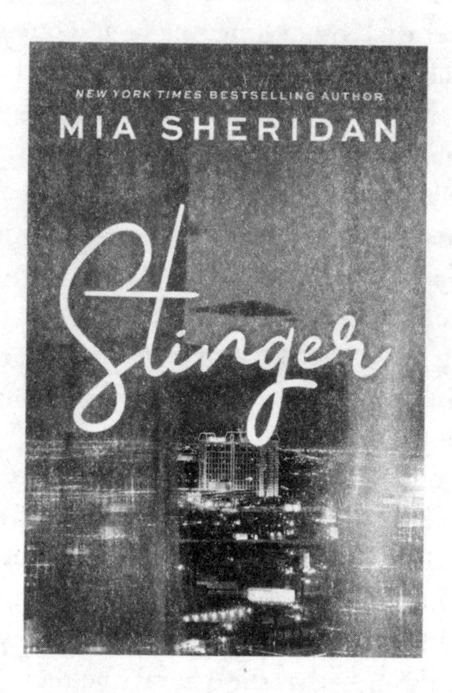

CHAPTER ONE
Grace

Las Vegas, Nevada

As I walked into the luxurious Bellagio Resort and Casino, tired and rumpled from my flight, I saw two signs directing guests to the conferences being held that weekend. There was the one I was in town to attend, the International Law Students Association Conference, and then there was another one, the Adult Entertainment Expo. Well. *I guess that's Vegas for you*, I thought. *Where you can see everything from law students and tourists, to porn stars, and perhaps even aliens from distant planets. It hadn't taken me long to realize—just walking through the airport actually*—that when it came to the City of Sin, shock value was practically nonexistent.

If I didn't figure that out from the pantless man the cops were chasing through the airport upon my arrival, then I definitely got it from the G-stringed Elvis impersonator who flew by me on roller skates as I stepped from my shuttle in front of the hotel. "You're not in Kansas anymore, honey," the driver had said, laughing as my head swiveled to watch the rolling, half-dressed Elvis glide away.

Apparently not.

As I walked farther into the lobby, my mouth dropped open and I halted as my head fell back. The ceiling was filled with the most stunning glass blossoms—hundreds of them in every color imaginable. I moved in a circle, my breath halted, unable to look away from the gorgeous, overhead art. *Wow.*

When I finally tore my eyes away from the ceiling, I realized there was beauty everywhere. I was so completely awestruck by the stone pillars and gallery of fresh flowers and floating hot-air balloons behind the check-in that I almost didn't hear the woman desk clerk call out to me. I wheeled my small suitcase up to the counter and smiled brightly at her. "Grace Hamilton. I have a reservation."

The desk clerk smiled back. "Okay, let me just look you up… Okay, here we go. You're here for the law student conference starting tomorrow?"

"Yes."

"What school do you go to?" she asked as she took my credit card and swiped it quickly.

"Georgetown," I said, returning the card to my wallet.

"Great school! Well, have a good time. You're on the twenty-sixth floor, checked in until Monday. Checkout time is noon. Here's a folder for those attending the law student conference. You'll find a schedule, a name tag, and some other information you might find handy for this weekend."

"Thanks," I said, taking the folder and then grabbing my suitcase handle before turning to walk toward the elevators. As I rounded the corner, I ran smack-dab into a hard, male chest. "Oh, gosh! I'm so sorry!" I exclaimed.

"No, I'm sorry—" he started to say at the same time.

Our eyes met and we both fell silent, me blinking as he steadied me with both hands on my upper arms.

He was about my age, twenty-three or so, with sandy-colored hair that was just a little too long and curling up at the ends, and one of those handsome faces that manages to be both manly and boyish at the same time. Simultaneously rugged and pretty. *Double wow.* His hazel eyes were fringed with thick, dark lashes, and his full lips were curved into a half-smile.

I cleared my throat, pulling myself together as I managed to quickly take in his frame. He was lean but muscled, clad in dark jeans and a conservative, button-down, white shirt, sleeves rolled up.

He stared at me for a couple beats and something in his expression seemed to soften as my eyes moved back to his and his smile grew bigger, revealing a small dimple to the left of his bottom lip. He bent to pick up the key card I had dropped when we collided.

As I watched him scoop up my card, the strangest feeling washed over me, almost like déjà vu, like we had met before. I frowned, confused by the odd sensation, wondering if he was a law student that I had seen in passing at school, here for the same conference. Yes, that had to be it.

He straightened, holding the key card out to me, and I caught sight of the name tag clipped to his shirt. "Oh, you *are* here for the conference," I exclaimed. "I thought I might—" And that's when I read it: *Carson Stinger, Straight Male Performer, Adult Entertainment Expo*.

I stared at the words for a couple beats, re-arranging them, *digesting* them, and then meeting his eyes once more. He was smirking now and his eyes no longer held that softness I had seen just a minute before.

I pulled my shoulders back. "Well, then, I'm sorry again for the…uh, not watching where I was…" I let out a small, uncomfortable laugh, beginning again. "Well, have a good time…er, a nice time, um, enjoy"—I gestured toward his name tag—"the show. Or rather, not the show, but the… well, enjoy the weekend."

What the hell was wrong with me? I was never flustered like this! I was going into law because I was good at finding the right words under pressure. And here a good-looking, *straight-male,* porn star rattled me so much, I could barely form a coherent sentence?

And that's when he burst out laughing, deepening that tiny dimple by his mouth. "I will, buttercup. And you enjoy your weekend too. Let me make a wild guess, law student conference?"

I had started to walk around him but stopped when I heard the clearly condescending nickname and the amusement in his voice. "Yes, actually. Is there something wrong with that?"

"No, not at all. Looks like we're both here to hone our skills when it comes to *getting people off.*"

My brows snapped down. *Ah, a double entendre. How clever.* "Well that's…that's a disgusting way to put it."

He moved closer to me until I was forced to step back. "Why? Getting people off is such a rush, buttercup. Don't be ashamed of wanting to do it well."

I coughed and narrowed my eyes. *Eww.*

I tapped his nametag with my index finger. "I do a lot of things well, *Carson*, none of which I'm ashamed of," I said, leaning into him so that he knew I wasn't going to be intimidated by his blatant, juvenile, sexual innuendos.

Acknowledgments

Unending appreciation to my editing team at Bloom Books who put forth so much time, effort, and wisdom in helping me bring this story to the next level. Thank you for asking more of me and teaching me so much. I am lucky to work with you.

Thank you to my agent, Kimberly Brower, my personal superwoman.

To my beloved readers (some of whom have been with me since I first created the world surrounding Pelion Lake), words cannot express how grateful I am for each and every one of you. Thank you for your love, your kindness, and for showing up again and again.

To all the book bloggers and influencers, we authors owe you an entire world of gratitude. Thank you for helping us spread the word about our books by creating beautiful posts, photos, and videos. I am so often awed by your creative hearts and your enthusiasm for the stories that move you.

To my husband, my partner in all things—thank you for always boosting me higher and always catching me when I fall.

About the Author

Mia Sheridan is a *New York Times*, *USA Today*, and *Wall Street Journal* bestselling author. Her passion is weaving true love stories about people destined to be together. Mia lives in Cincinnati, Ohio, with her husband. They have four children here on earth and one in heaven.

Mia can be found online at:

MiaSheridan.com

Instagram: @MiaSheridanAuthor

Facebook: MiaSheridanAuthor